The Crawlspace Conspiracy

The Crawlspace Conspiracy

A Novel

by

Thomas Keech

BASKERVILLE
PUBLISHERS, INC.
DALLAS • NEW YORK • DUBLIN

Copyright © 1995 by Thomas Keech

This book is a work of fiction. Names, characters, places and incidents are either the product of the author's imagination or are used fictitiously. Any resemblance to actual events or locales of persons, living or dead, is entirely coincidental.

BASKERVILLE Publishers, Inc.
7616 LBJ Freeway, Suite 220, Dallas, TX 75251-1008

Library of Congress Cataloging-in Publication Data

Keech, Thomas, 1946.
    The crawlspace conspiracy : a novel / by Thomas Keech.
       p.   cm.
    ISBN No. 1-880909-34-0
    I. Title.
    PS3561.E334C7 1995
    813'.54--dc20   94-48935
                                                   CIP

Manufactured in the United States of America
First Printing, 1995

For M.

PROLOGUE

The eighteen-room Georgian mansion that "Bob" Fiore purchased on Baltimore's Greenway confirmed the suspicions of many citizens about his appointment as Secretary of the Maryland Department of Public Welfare. Tourists, and even native Baltimoreans, couldn't help but gawk at the huge brick edifice nestled so comfortably in the shadows of the great white oaks, surrounded so geometrically by its tennis courts, its covered outdoor pool and its secluded gardens. Anyone on the sidewalk eyeing that mansion through the bars of the wrought-iron fence would have thought that Fiore had always been wealthy, and that his generous campaign contributions had purchased his high position in the governor's cabinet.

There had been, in fact, a curious parallel over the years between the profits of Fiore's contracting company and the political fortunes of his lifelong friend, Governor George Mallard. But Fiore had not purchased his cabinet position. He did not believe in using his private wealth to buy a government job. He believed in using his government job to amass private wealth. This philosophy had enabled him to live the last five years of his life without a financial worry, and to die a wealthy man. If he ever realized that his schemes would some day come back to haunt the Department of Public Welfare, and its new Secretary, he might not have arranged for his son-in-law, Brendan Gotterdung, to inherit the job.

Then again, he might have done so anyway.

1 STATEMENT OF THE CASE

Each combatant in the war that suddenly broke out over Charles Gage and the house that he inherited on 442 Jasper Street was dead certain of his own plan, and of his own power. The mayor wanted to be governor and was confident that his archenemy from the state senate could no longer pose a threat to him. The state senator believed that he could deceive a friend without cost to himself. A welfare official was certain that he could cover up an ancient illegal act. And Charles's own attorney assured himself that he alone could bring justice to thousands.

No one was prepared for Aunt May's act of faith from beyond the grave. When Charles first received the letter about Aunt May's house, he read no further than the first paragraph that mentioned her name. Stricken by sudden guilt, he folded the letter and jammed it in his pocket. The usual thing for him would have been to avoid thinking about the letter until he lost it and could forget about it entirely. But there was no safe place to put such an important document in the rooming house where he lived, so he carried the letter around for weeks. It was still with him when he finally broke through all the obstacles and made contact with a lawyer at the Legal Assistance Society.

The pain in his side came more often now. The old back-

3

country remedies he had learned from his mother decades ago did not work. He had been sent home from his last assignment from the day labor agency when they found him leaning motionless on a box he was supposed to be lifting, his face frozen in an ugly grimace. That same night, his housemate Jimmy had another seizure. Charles was gradually taking over the care of his much younger friend, but his own spasm kept him from ministering to Jimmy on the floor that night. When the clenching in his stomach eased up, and after Jimmy's thrashing stopped, Charles collapsed onto the ancient overstuffed chair that had been left out in the hallway, letting his sweat drip into the stale fabric. He then waited for Miss Agatha to come by; it was a habit. But the letter in his pocket poked him uncomfortably, as if Aunt May were egging him on to admit to himself that waiting was wrong, that Miss Agatha's hot tea would not be enough any more.

Weeks later, he still had the letter about Aunt May in his pocket when he walked down the steps into the lobby of the Legal Assistance Society's building in Baltimore. As he reached the basement landing and looked through the clear glass door into the reception room, he fingered the letter like an amulet.

Fifty feet away, attorney Sport Norris carefully arranged on the desk in his office the piles of papers that constituted the lawsuit that he and Angela were filing that day. His hands moved quickly, arranging the stacks into expanding cardboard folders in the exact order in which he would have to hand them to the clerk in federal court. Everything was timed precisely.

Angela had been pushing him for months to get this class action filed. In the last two years, he had taught her everything she knew about litigation. Now, suddenly, she was acting as if he were too timid a lawyer. He quickly threw on his suitcoat, pulled a thick cardboard folder under each arm and turned to go.

Through the glass door, Charles saw Linda, the receptionist, and her little eighteen-month-old son, M.C., waiting for him. He pushed open that door and took a long, tremulous step forward, now holding the letter about Aunt May in front of him like a shield.

The first time Charles had tried to contact the Legal Assistance Society, Linda put him on hold so long that his hand went numb in the phone booth. He dropped the receiver, and it banged his knee so hard he forgot why he was trying to call. The second time, he screwed up the courage to come down to the building in person, but little M.C. then bit him on the finger as he was waiting in the reception room. Refusing to cry out in front of the triumphant toddler and his mother, Charles scrambled out of the room and up the stairs and retreated across the street to the Sacred Heart emergency room. There, he got into an argument with the triage nurse and ultimately could not convince anyone that he had not bitten himself.

His demeanor this time showed that he would not take no for an answer. He advanced toward the receptionist slowly, like a bullfighter entering the ring. M.C. spotted him and let out a trumphant coo of recognition. Charles stared at the child, but did not flinch. Then he resumed his march toward Linda.

Charles was sixty-one years old. His face was a wrinkled but smooth brown, like the soft pocket of an old baseball glove. His grey hair was short and springy. Charles was afraid of Linda, and even M.C. But he was more afraid of what was happening to himself. He knew that he needed a doctor. If he could not handle a shovel, or unload a truck, or even direct traffic for eight hours at a time, he would not be of any use to an employer. His single little stick of pride would be gone, and there would

5

be nothing to keep him from being turned out on the street.

The only thing that Charles had inherited from his parents was a stubborn streak so strong that it probably accounted for his family's ability to survive over the last two hundred years—and so blind that it probably also accounted for the fact that he had never in his life held a job for more than a month, or an apartment for more than a year, or a woman for more than an hour. The letter about Aunt May reminded him of a time long since gone, when he had had more faith in himself. He did not want to be reminded of that time any more. But the letter steadied his hand now.

"I said, I want to see a lawyer!" This was a demand.

Sport Norris had to get the case of *Throckmorton* v. *Gotterdung* filed before the federal court closed in twenty minutes. Forty-two thousand people would lose their medical care if he didn't make it on time. Eighteen months of his and Angela's work would have gone for nothing. Sport had to walk the papers to court himself. The Legal Assistance Society was located outside of the prime legal and financial district. It was eight blocks to the federal courthouse. This far out, you couldn't even call a cab to come to Calvert Street.

Without making eye contact, Linda pivoted on her swivel chair, slowly wadded up a phone message in her hand and dropped the paper into a grey metal trash can behind her. Just at the point where her head was facing directly away from Charles, she muttered her response.

"Have a seat."

"Woman, there ain't nobody else waiting."

Linda hoisted herself from the chair, her blank eyes focusing through Charles at the dark blue enamel on the wall. Then she turned her back on him, leaned over and began rearranging the blankets in little M.C.'s playpen.

6

M.C. ignored her and growled ominously at Charles through the bars. Charles glared back but also retreated until he bumped into a metal rack of army surplus in-and out-boxes lining one wall of the reception room. A few telephone messages fluttered out like drowsy butterflies. Charles dropped the letter. He had told himself for weeks that the letter was not important, but he now found himself scrambling after it desperately on the floor.

The letter was from the law firm of Peck, Peck and Peck. It explained that Charles had just inherited from his Great Aunt May her tiny brick row house at 442 Jasper Street. Charles had not been to that house in over forty years. He didn't even know how to find it. Because this house had been given to him, he assumed that it was worth nothing. Charles had no way of knowing that 442 Jasper Street was the last unpurchased parcel in the plot of land soon to be known to the public as the site of the Mayor Crosley T. Pettibone Waterside Towers Luxury Condominium Development. Charles didn't even want this house. He wished that this whole new problem would go away, but he did not have the nerve to throw the letter out.

Sport swung into a fast walking motion as he left his office and hurried along the dim back corridor, striding across the cracked brown asphalt tiles. Angela, as junior attorney, would normally be given the task of actually filing the papers in court, but Sport wanted to do it himself. There was even more at stake than Angela realized. The bulging cardboard folders felt uncomfortable under his arms. He tried to adjust his hold on them even as he picked up speed.

Charles scraped up the letter from the floor and gripped it tightly. Then he stood up. Linda was still ignoring him, leaning over into M.C.'s playpen, giving Charles a view only of her enormous rear end.

There were long green arrows painted on the crackly beige floor tiles, pointing away from the reception room. Charles decided to follow them. He had taken the first timid step in that direction when Linda's voice battered him from behind.

"Get back here!"

Charles faltered, and almost fell, but he stuck his letter hand out ahead of himself for balance and bounded forward on shaky giant steps down the hall.

In one of the offices off that hallway, Angela checked her watch just as the shadow of Charles slid past her doorway. She worried that Sport was taking too long to get the lawsuit filed, and she decided to go back to his office to see for herself.

Charles picked up speed, following the green arrows carefully. But then the floor tiles suddenly changed color and the arrows turned a corner into the dim back hallway. Confused, Charles whirled around, staring at the floor with one eye and trying to keep the other eye out for Linda. He didn't see Sport Norris coming the other way with the papers for Throckmorton v. Gotterdung under his arms. He did, however, because of his twirling motion, manage to undercut Sport's gripand knock all the papers and files up into the air. Then his wild, twisting momentum tangled their legs together and they both crashed to the floor in the midst of a shower of papers and pleadings.

The letter from Peck, Peck and Peck brushed the wall and came to rest directly under, and not six inches away from, Sport Norris's startled eyes.

Charles pushed himself away until his lanky body was stretched out against the wall of the corridor. The short guy he had run into was sprawled on the tiles, not three feet away.

"Are you okay?" The voice came out of the pile. Charles

peered ahead in the gloom. He saw the wide face of the man smiling at him through a forest of folders and files. Short wisps of blond hair drooped down across his forehead. Charles tried to remember his purpose in coming.

"Need a lawyer."

"Okay, okay! I'm a lawyer! Sport Norris." Sport Norris stretched an arm across the gritty beige tiles and shook his hand enthusiastically. "You've gotten a letter from some private attorneys?"

"No. No." Charles did not want to talk about Aunt May. He took another envelope from his shirt pocket and handed it to the lawyer, but Sport Norris just put it underneath the letter from Peck, Peck and Peck. He took that letter out and scanned the whole thing quickly.

"Your Great Aunt May was very generous to you."

"A good lady," Charles mumbled into the tiles.

"You must have been very close to her."

Charles raised himself to his hands and knees and snatched both letters out of Sport Norris's hands. This was not the kind of lawyer he wanted. He did not want to talk about Aunt May. He did not want to be reminded of that old lady and her righteous ways.

"I just guessed you were close to her," Sport apologized. "Because she left her house to you. It's none of my business. I see that you're having some trouble about that house. I'll help you if you want me to."

It was the soft friendliness of Sport's voice, and the engaging grin on his broad face, that began to soften the edges of Charles's stubbornness. It seemed like Aunt May had a way of not letting him forget her. Even this young white lawyer wanted to talk about Aunt May. And the green arrows, Charles noticed, were now pointing directly at Sport. He handed the letters back.

Sport spoke slowly and distinctly. "I'm leaving right now to file a case in federal court that has to be filed today. But I will help you when I get back. Or, you can walk with me, and we can talk along the way."

"Talk on the way."

A tall young woman came out of a doorway off the hall. She had brown glasses perched in her dark hair.

"Oh no! That's not *Throckmorton*!" She leaned over them. She was wearing a black skirt and a pressed white pleated blouse.

"Angela, I think I have it under control. My new client here is Charles ...."

"Oh! Are you hurt, sir?"

Charles reached up a hand to her. There was an instant's hesitation before she reached down and helped him to his feet.

"Sir," she spoke politely. "We have a very important case that must be filed this afternoon. If you'll just go back and wait in the reception room ...."

"No! This man's *my* lawyer. He's working on *my* case."

"Angela, he's my client. We're gonna walk ...."

"Sport, I know that you care about all of your clients. But please put this whole thing in perspective..."

But she knew he had. For over a year they had known that forty-two thousand people were being screwed, and who was doing it. They had negotiated for months, waited to find the perfect client, then negotiated again. With Mrs. Throckmorton, the perfect plaintiff, they could file the suit.

"If we don't file it by five we'll have to start all over again."

"I know that, Angela."

"You won't let me file the papers." She crouched down, assembled the papers into piles, straightened them by banging each sheaf separately on the floor, very slowly. She lowered her head and darted out of the hallway with the papers. They heard the brisk rap of the stapler on her desk. She reappeared with the lawsuit in order once again, stuffed the sets of papers into Sport's brown cardboard folder, wrapped the attached elastic band around the folder and put it in his arms. "And if you don't get the case filed today, then I'll know—I hate to say this, Sport— why so many of our colleagues think that we are so ... ineffectual."

Sport grabbed Charles by the arm and guided him quickly up the stairs and out of the building. Buffeted by a blast of hot, humid air, they had to squint against the brightness reflected off the sidewalk. Sport seemed stunned. He walked down the crowded street like a mechanical man wound up too tight. Charles had a little arthritis in his ankles that he hadn't admitted to yet, and he soon fell behind.

"Hey!"

Sport turned around. He was already fifty feet down the sidewalk and moving away fast.

"Can't stop."

Charles stopped completely and stared after him. The flow of pedestrians on the sidewalk parted around him. Charles pushed his way to the curb and settled onto it. He began to make slow chewing motions, with his lips closed, as if chewing on a particularly bitter wad of gum. He stared straight ahead. No one bothered him. He didn't have his papers anymore.

Charles was used to things not working out. He had adjusted to the kind of life where he expected nothing and was rarely disappointed. Recently, the pain in his stomach, and Jimmy's problems, and the letter about Aunt May, had combined to convince him that things might be different if he made a little plan, showed a little courage. Now, he stared at the traffic going by, chewed on his imaginary wad of gum, and wondered if he had been wrong.

"Mr. Gage?" Sport's face appeared in front of his. Sport was crouching in the street.

"Go on! Go on!"

"I have to, but I'll be back to talk to you, Mr. Gage." Charles looked away.

"You have to have faith in me, Mr. Gage."

Sport weaved through the crowd on the sidewalk in the 101-degree heat. He crossed the cobblestone side streets near the Society's building, veered through thicker crowds in the commercial center, crossed St. Paul Street against the light while highstepping his way across the gummy tar of all six lanes. He slowed only when a group of young office girls in short summer skirts crossed in front of him, their colorful, fitted new clothing magnetizing his solitary gaze. He checked his watch: eleven minutes left.

Throckmorton would be the most important case that the Legal Assistance Society had filed in more than a decade. Angela had been right to scold him. She had been right about the case all along.

Angela had been the first to notice a suspicious pattern in their Medical Assistance cases. One of the functions of their office was to represent clients whose applications for Medical Assistance had been turned down. As a staff attorney, Angela handled their appeals routinely. In her first six months on the job, she won eight of these appeals in a row.

"This is good work, Angela." Sport was doing his duty as a supervisor, reviewing all of the new attorney's cases.

"Don't you think there's something happening, Sport?" He had only recently gotten her to stop calling him "Mr. Norris." "These cases are all the same. The Department of Public Welfare tells our clients that they have too much money to be eligible for Medical Assistance. Either that,

12

or they say that the people have too many assets. I file an appeal. I use the same numbers they use. We go to the hearing, we do the math at the hearing, and my client is found eligible. It's hard to believe that the department is making so many simple math errors."

"It's probably the same eligibility worker. That department has some really bad employees, especially down ...."

"No, it's not that. It's coming from all over the city, and the county. Even one from Havre de Grace."

"An epidemic of bad math?"

"It's hard to believe, Sport."

Beginning the next day, they demanded to see the financial worksheets for every client who had been turned down for Medical Assistance. At some point in every calculation, a mysterious figure, either an unexplained $2,500 asset or a sudden decrease in rent, was introduced. On most of the sheets, there was no explanation at all. But Angela found an old one where "basement—$2,500" was added to assets, and Sport found a scribbled reference to "nonessential rental of storage space (basement)—$125," on another.

"That makes twelve out of twelve. They're doing this to everybody."

"We can't be sure." Five years of legal experience had made Sport more cautious than Angela. "I'm going to call Jody Hechtmuller again and see what he says now."

"He's the department's lawyer, Sport. Won't that just give him a chance to cover their tracks?"

"We have to give the department the benefit of the doubt. Maybe there's an explanation."

There were several explanations. But Angela kept bringing up new clients with the same problem.

"Mrs. Jackson lives on the third story of a three-story rowhouse. She's being told that $125 of her rent goes for renting storage space in the basement. Sport, she's never even seen the basement. She's afraid to go down there."

"They did it again."

"They're doing it to everybody."

"Have you checked the regulations? Is there something that says they can do this?"

"No regulations. No policies. No instructions. Nothing in writing. Sport, can't we just file a class action with Mrs. Jackson as the named plaintiff? Once the judge certifies the class, we can see all the worksheets, take depositions of the workers, everything."

"Just file a class action?"

"Why not?"

The little note of exasperation in her voice signaled the beginning of the end of her apprenticeship. From that point on, she tried to hide her growing disillusionment with him, but he had always known that it would show some day.

"The fact that they did this to twelve people doesn't mean that they are doing it to forty-two thousand."

"You know it's happening, Sport."

"Let me try one more thing."

He sent a Freedom of Information request to Brendan Gotterdung, the Secretary of the department, asking how many applicants for Medical Assistance had been assigned basements. Three weeks later, Angela dropped the reply letter on Sport's desk.

Dear Mr. Norris:

As attorney for the Department of Public Welfare, I have been assigned to respond to your inquiry. The information which you requested is not a category of information which is currently compiled by this agency. It could be compiled from records on hand, but only by our own employees, due to the confidential nature of welfare records. A reasonable charge for the preparation and analysis of these records will be imposed. In this case, these costs will total $15,016.75. Upon prepayment of this fee, this analysis and compilation will begin.

On another matter, please rest assured that we have looked carefully into the application of your client Mrs. Jackson and have discovered that she was indeed being inappropriately charged with renting space in a basement. We have recalculated her income accordingly, and have determined that she is indeed eligible for Medical Assistance benefits. We have made her eligibility retroactive. I trust that she no longer has any quarrel with this agency.

Very sincerely yours,

Jody P. Hechtmuller
Counsel to the Department
of Public Welfare

"They're stonewalling us," Sport interpreted. "They're not going to tell us anything voluntarily."

"And we can't sue them now. Now that Mrs. Jackson has been given a Medical Assistance card, we can't use her as a plaintiff."

"You were right, Angela. They're doing this to everybody. And we can't stop them until we get another client who has been given a fictitious basement. My fault."

It was two long months later before Sport finally burst into Angela's office, waving a new case file. "We've got it! Mrs. Virginia Throckmorton. Charged with a basement, but she lives in a second-floor apartment on West Ostend Street."

"We can go ahead?"

"Start writing the complaint for court. This could be a nasty and complicated lawsuit; I'll have to tell the Director about it in advance. He won't stop us. He's not afraid of suing anybody, except maybe Mayor Pettibone. I'll go and get this cleared with Doxie right now."

Doxie, the Director of the Legal Assistance Society, had to be approached carefully. It was always best if Doxie believed that *he* was the one who had decided to sue. After two hours of rambling conversation, interrupted by many phone calls, Sport convinced him to let them go ahead.

The rush of tasks to be done in order to get the suit filed united them again. In their meetings Angela glowed with a passion to right this wrong. Sport once again found himself distracted by the swing of her dark hair, the crossing of her long legs, and the movements of her pressed white pleated blouse.

Working with Angela had been fun again. But, less than an hour ago, she had appeared in the doorway to his office, her hands down at her sides, palms open, shaking her head in disbelief.

"You gave them Mrs. Throckmorton's name?"

"As a professional courtesy. Just five minutes ago, when I called Jody Hechtmuller to tell him we were filing suit. Don't worry. There's no way he can get her a Medical Assistance card this afternoon."

"But they can get her one tomorrow. Then we won't have a live plaintiff."

"It's today or never, but I can make it on time."

"*Please* hurry."

For two blocks, Sport walked next to the plywood perimeter of a huge construction site. Plastered all over the site were bright orange signs: "GOING UP! THANKS TO MAYOR CROSLEY T. PETTIBONE AND HIS VISION OF THE CITY OF BALTIMORE!" The mayor was not known for being shy, and much of his gigantic ego was invested in his construction projects. Sport glanced away and stepped off the sidewalk. By the time the generic, concrete-slab building that housed the federal court came into view, he had been walking in the street against traffic for three blocks. He was an experienced lawyer and had the whole trip timed down almost to the second.

He reached the clerk's office on the seventh floor at five minutes before five. But there was someone ahead of him. A short man with a protuberant stomach was sifting through stacks of paper at the counter. Only one employee, the chief operating clerk, Mrs. Brazelton, was on duty, and this man seemed to be engaging all of her attention. But she looked up expectantly at Sport.

"Hello, Mr. Norris."

The man turned and squinted at Sport. His round face, receding hairline and short goatee broke Sport's eye contact with Mrs. Brazelton.

"Mr. Mallory, if you will just slide these papers down the counter a little ...."

"Excuse me, Ma'am. I have a right to your assistance in viewing and copying all of the papers in each of my lawsuits."

Mrs. Brazelton's eyes were tired. Sport guessed that this man was one of a type seen in every court clerk's office on America—the full-time amateur litigator. This man showed all the signs: the high piles of papers, the belligerent attitude toward the clerk, the inane requests for copies of documents which he had probably filed himself.

It was time to interrupt. "I have a lawsuit here, *Throckmorton* v. *Gotterdung,* that must be filed today!"

Sport's ploy seemed to work. Mrs. Brazelton appeared happy to turn away from the goateed man and spend the last few minutes of her day on a more rational project. But the man had rattled her, and her look up at Sport

17

was perplexed. "This is an *in forma pauperis* suit," Sport coached. "The judge needs to be given the motion on top for his signature, before it can be filed."

Mrs. Brazelton pored over the documents with an excruciating slowness as the clock hand swept past four minutes to five. Screaming at her, or even acting nervous, would only make things worse. Feigning unconcern as he watched her out of the corner of his eye, Sport saw her twice get almost to the point of stamping the complaint in with the all-important time-and-date stamp. Then, each time, she stopped with a slight frown on her face, read something very slowly on the front page of the complaint that she apparently hadn't noticed before, put the complaint down, unstamped, and moved to another pile of his documents with an even more puzzled look on her face.

Mr. Mallory, the man whose copying requests had been pushed aside, seemed to have momentarily forgotten his belligerence. He now looked curiously back and forth between Sport and Mrs. Brazelton. Sport nervously gripped the edge of the counter. He had to keep her attention on this case, keep this Mr. Mallory out of the way until Mrs. Brazelton finally reached the series of logical conclusions he was waiting for. (1) She could not log the case in until it was filed. (2) A case could not be filed until the filing fee was paid. (3) In the case of poor plaintiffs, the case could be filed without a fee, but only after a judge signed an order allowing them to proceed in forma pauperis. (4) The judge couldn't sign the order unless she took the papers to him.

Sport twisted his legs around each other in anticipation. Mrs. Brazelton finally convinced herself of this course of action, picked up a few of his papers with a motion that seemed glacial, looked him warmly in the eyes and said: "You know, I'll have to take this to the judge."

"Okay." At last she picked up the *in forma pauperis* motion and the proposed order and walked away with them toward the judge's chambers.

Sport sighed, buried his head on the counter. The lawsuit would be filed on time, the case would be certified as a class action, and the Department of Public Welfare would be placed in the untenable position of trying to prove that a crawlspace was a basement. He shuddered with relief.

"Counselor?" Sport's head snapped up at hearing Mr. Mallory's voice again.

"Yes?"

The man glanced significantly at Mrs. Brazelton's desk top on the other side of the counter.

"Wha...?" Then Sport saw it. The affidavit of Mrs. Throckmorton was supposed to be attached to the Motion to Proceed In Forma Pauperis, but the affidavit was still lying on Mrs. Brazelton's desk, right in front of his eyes. Sport scrutinized the area behind the counter in the hope of catching the eye of another employee, but the whole area was empty.

He didn't even have time to search for the hidden latch that would swing the counter open. He quickly heaved his body onto the counter and swung himself down gracefully on the other side. He grabbed the Throckmorton affidavit and turned toward the corridor that Mrs. Brazelton had taken. As he moved, the two pages of the document separated in his hand. He glanced at the second page, then stopped cold.

There was no signature on the Throckmorton affidavit.

The content, the format, the caption of the affidavit were fine. The document even had the imprint of the notary seal of Linda, the receptionist, certifying that the

19

(missing) signature was authentic, and that it had been signed in Linda's presence that day. Sport had insisted that Linda become a notary just so that she could notarize documents like this. Linda had been reluctant and had never taken any interest in what she was doing. She really didn't understand it. But it was his fault, his responsibility to see that all of these details were correct.

He had blown it. The department had the Throckmorton name. He could not use it tomorrow. It was two minutes to five.

He turned and laid the document on Mrs. Brazelton's desk. He took a quick breath, pulled out a pen and, in a large, tremulous hand, wrote "Virginia Throckmorton" on the signature line of the affidavit.

Mr. Mallory looked on with apparent interest.

Sport bolted from the desk and down the corridor after Mrs. Brazelton. She turned at the sound of his footsteps. Without a word, he took the original motion from her hands, placed the affidavit under it, put both documents back in her hands, and walked away.

He avoided the eyes of the goateed man. He found the latch, lifted the counter panel, crossed through the outer office and stepped quickly toward the hall.

"Counselor?" Mr. Mallory turned to follow him.

Sport reached the hallway, turned without looking back, then ran toward the elevators. *The suit is filed in time. Thousands of people will be saved.* When he saw the elevator door standing open for him, he took it as a sign that he had done the right thing. Then he saw Mr. Mallory come around the corner after him. Sport clicked the elevator's "DOOR CLOSE" button frantically, praying for those panels to slide shut. Mr. Mallory reached the doorway to the elevator and held up his hand. But, just as Mallory was about to break the beam of light to hold the elevator open, the doors finally began to snap shut.

Mallory jerked his arm back.

Sport heard his puzzled voice even as he avoided Mallory's eyes.

"Counselor? Counselor Throckmorton?"

Charles sat on the bench at the bus stop where Sport had led him. Bold orange letters on the bench declared: "TAKE A LOAD OFF, THANKS TO MAYOR CROSLEY T. PETTIBONE!" Charles wasn't surprised now that Sport was interested in Aunt May's house. There was something about that letter that would not be ignored. He hadn't been to that house since he was fifteen years old, but he could see now that he would have to go again. Aunt May would have no less.

But Charles had actually come to the Legal Assistance Society for medical help. Jimmy had been having seizures two or three times a day now without his medication, and the pain in Charles's stomach had kept him from working. But neither Charles nor Jimmy had the money to pay a doctor. They had both been denied Medical Assistance cards—and both for a mysterious reason that neither of them could figure out. When Charles asked the welfare lady to tell him why, she had mumbled something about a basement.

21

2 DEFENSE OF THE STATE

L eonard Tynan, Assistant Secretary of the Department of Public Welfare, clasped his hands in front of himself on the table. Each of his starched white shirt cuffs protruded exactly an inch and a half from the sleeve of his dark blue pin-striped suit, contrasting pleasingly with the brown skin of his hands. He sat with the relaxed, graceful posture of someone who was used to assuming control. Tynan was the person who actually ran the Department of Public Welfare. Secretary Gotterdung was a figurehead. Even now, when Gotterdung was sued in his capacity as head of the department, it was Tynan who was responsible for coming up with a defense. He met with the department's lawyer, Jody Hechtmuller, the day after the suit was filed.

"I understand Legal Assistance's allegations," Tynan continued. "We've talked about this basement issue in the past."

"Well, now they've sued, just like they said they were going to." Hechtmuller sounded peevish. Tynan ignored the tone of the lawyer's response.

"What do you think they can prove?"

"I don't know, Leonard. What *is* there to prove?"

"Come on, Jody. The department needs to know what

evidence you think Legal Assistance has against us."

"Leonard, *I* need to know what evidence *exists.*"

The Assistant Secretary stared at his lawyer, then sighed. Leonard Tynan realized that it was no longer advantageous to keep Jody Hechtmuller in the dark. It was time to move on to a new phase of the lawyer-client relationship. Hechtmuller would have no less.

"Leonard, it's true what they say about crawlspaces, isn't it?"

Eighteen months earlier, when Jody Hechtmuller had first heard these allegations about irregularities in the Medical Assistance program, he had visited Leonard Tynan's office, ready to share a laugh.

"Listen to the crazy stuff Sport Norris is telling me about crawlspaces!" he had exclaimed to the Assistant Secretary. "He thinks the agency is creating fictitious basements. *I* think those people over at Legal Assistance are really getting paranoid!"

Leonard Tynan had looked up at him and said nothing, signalling Jody instantly that the worst was possible. But Jody knew how to do his job. So he immediately shifted gears. The minimum response that he needed that day was a statement which would enable him to brush off Sport's accusations without clearly lying. So he persisted: "This can't be *completely* true, can it?"

"Of course not," Tynan had lied. "There is no such policy," he edged closer to the truth. "I can show you the manual," he finished strongly, speaking by now almost with a sense of indignation.

Then Tynan added, almost as if it were an afterthought, "If you've seen a weird case or two where someone was given a basement in an inappropriate situation, give it to me and I'll have it checked over carefully." Three days later, Sport's first crawlspace client had her case reconsidered by the department. It was discovered that she did not have a basement after all, and she was declared eligible for Medical Assistance benefits.

Jody had been satisfied for that day, but over the next few months Angela and Sport kept pushing him. They showed him more clients who had been assigned basements; they pressed him as to why there wasn't a policy *against* assigning basements. He returned to Tynan's office.

"Well, these are done on a case-by-case basis," Tynan lectured. "Remember, a lot of these people *do* have basements. A lot of them might consider them crawlspaces, but our eligibility people might consider them to be basements."

"What about the people who live in apartments? Sport Norris gave me two cases where apartment dwellers were assigned basements."

"Some of them do have access to those basements. They really do. But maybe the eligibility technicians in some of our local offices are getting a little too strict. If you'll let me have those two cases, I'll have them double-checked."

It was thus that Sport and Angela's second group of clients were paid off.

After these early conversations with his own lawyer, Tynan quietly met with the agency's forms czar, Kenneth Molson. Soon thereafter, revised forms were issued for all applications for Medical Assistance. Question No. 17 was added:

Does your home contain, or do you have access to a crawlspace/basement? Yes___ No___

Unwritten instructions were issued. Eligibility workers were to check "yes" in every case in which an applicant could not document that he did not own, and did not have access to, either a crawlspace or a basement. As a result of these unwritten instructions, virtually everyone was still assigned a basement.

Jody Hechtmuller was not informed about this change. Tynan had sensed that this knowledge would complicate Jody's task of holding off those snoopy and dangerous lawyers from the Legal Assistance Society. And Jody had held them off for a year.

Jody knew that he and Tynan had been playing peek-a-boo games with the truth. He didn't mind that; he was a lawyer. But when the crawlspace lawsuit was finally filed, Jody had resolved that he would not litigate it blindly.

"It's true, isn't it?"

Tynan met Jody's eyes.

"It's true."

"Why are we doing this?"

"Thirty-five million dollars. Possible federal investigation. Theoretically, decertification of our whole Medical Assistance program, cutting off medical care for every poor person in the state. At the minimum, recalculating everyone's grant—six months' work, during which everything else will have to stop.

"We didn't start it," Tynan was half explaining, half complaining. "It's been going on for years and years."

"Why can't we just stop it?"

"We don't have the money. To take away those basements just for the current fiscal year, we'd have to cut out *all* major discretionary programs—emergency dental, dialysis, preventive high blood pressure, eyeglasses for kids—you want to do that?"

Jody met Tynan's eyes. "We could ask for more money from the legislature."

"Yeah, theoretically that's an option." Tynan didn't

25

have to say more. Begging for more money was an expected thing from any department, but asking for millions to make up for the tricks of past bureaucrats was career suicide. No one who wanted to keep his job would recommend this solution.

"Leonard, I know you would never have started anything so stupid as this basement business yourself."

"That doesn't help us now, does it?"

"But who did start it?"

"I honestly don't know. Nobody seems to recall."

"Knowing how it got started might help me defend it in court."

"I understand. But these basements have been around for so long that people in this agency think they are written into the law. I don't want to stir up the employees by asking questions now. It will make us look like we don't know what we're doing."

Jody sighed and stared at the wall.

"I can argue this in court, if it's not an official policy to assign everyone a basement, whether they have one or not."

"Oh, it's not a policy."

"... and the eligibility technicians complete the forms in good faith."

"They will."

"And that will mean that you will be able to give me cases, every once in a while, which would prove to a judge that some of our workers, sometime, somewhere, decide that some of the applicants do *not* have basements."

"That's what that will mean," Tynan said, giving Jody a look that said that he understood completely.

"Okay. Then, the first order of business is to get this Mrs. Throckmorton a Medical Assistance card. This will eliminate her as a named plaintiff and make it a little harder for Sport Norris to get this lawsuit certified as a class action."

"I've already given orders to locate her and get her a card."

"You're one step ahead of me, then."

"Jody, the really damaging evidence, if it exists, is in the old clients' individual casefiles—the ones that were set up before we changed the forms. Can you keep these files out of Legal Assistance's hands?"

"Possibly."

"Then we might have a chance."

As the focus of the discussion shifted from a moral to a legal viewpoint, Jody's enthusiasm seemed to pick up. He walked out of the office a few minutes later with an energized and self-satisfied look on his face that Tynan now recognized. It was the government lawyer's smile, reserved for times when his client had just been sued. The lawyer's smile meant that the agency officials would have to be careful from now on. They would have to pay attention to the legality of their actions. They would have to listen to him.

Tynan's office was on the sixth and top floor of a lesser state office building on Eutaw Street. The building was in the shape of an overturned cardboard box, and its outside walls consisted of alternating panels of glass and turquoise-colored steel. From his sixth-floor corner window, other state office buildings (also boxes) could be seen, as well as parking lots, a granite armory and a Gothic church. The steeples and domes of other churches, and a synagogue, cold be seen above the greenery of the oaks growing on Eutaw Place.

Bobbi Jo, Tynan's secretary, slid a carefully folded newspaper across the top of Tynan's vinyl veneer meeting table.

"What is this? There was nothing in the *State* this morning."

27

"Page F 1 of the *Free American*. Joe Keane."
Tynan read no further than the headline on Keane's column:

HOME IMPROVEMENTS FOR THE POOR
-Bureaucrats add basements-

He took a deep breath and let it out slowly. Despite the differences in their backgrounds and ages, he had found himself confiding in Bobbi Jo lately. She was not a gossip. She was faithful to the department. And she was thinking about retiring soon anyway.

"Do you know what my instructions were, when Gotterdung took over this department four years ago? I'll give it to you word for word. 'Do whatever you want, as long as we look good in the press.'"

"Leonard, I wouldn't worry. The worse things get, the more he needs you."

"I don't want to go into this case blind. I'm going to find out who thought up this harebrained basement scheme in the first place. Maybe it's the feds' fault, or someone else's. Maybe we should get somebody to go back through all the history of this to see how this crawlspace business started."

"Maybe we shouldn't."

"What?"

"Maybe we shouldn't."

"You know something? Would it help our case?"

Bobbi Jo shook her head.

"I still want to know why."

"Leonard, are you sure?" He was being given a chance to remain safely ignorant. But Tynan nodded vehemently.

"Well, Leonard, old Secretary Fiore—you know how he operated."

"I thought I did."

28

Tynan had actually run the department himself for long periods of time during former Secretary Fiore's tenure. On those frequent occasions when Fiore was away on business, or pleasure, someone had to keep things going, and Tynan had taken the initiative. He had been doing so when Fiore died of a heart attack at the age of fifty-eight at Pimlico Racetrack one Thursday afternoon. Fiore's pals from the Northwest Baltimore Political Club had dutifully left Pimlico in the middle of the eighth race, followed the body to the emergency room, informed his wife and children, and generously made all the funeral arrangements—but hadn't thought of calling the governor, anyone in the department, or Tynan. The result was that, on the next day, Fiore signed and promulgated several executive orders, apparently from the grave.

The press didn't notice, but Governor Mallard did. He had not been eager for the public to discover what a minimal difference there was between a live cabinet member and a dead cabinet member. So he mentioned it officially to no one. But once, finding himself alone with Tynan at a memorial service for Fiore in the City Council Chambers at City Hall, he let his curiosity get the better of him.

"He was a good man."

"Yes he was, Governor." They both looked ahead intently at the memorial service speaker so as to avoid each other's eyes.

"Mr. Tynan, if you hadn't read in the newspaper on Monday evening that Bob Fiore had passed away, how much longer do you think he would have been signing those executive orders?"

"It's hard to say, Governor," Tynan kept his eyes straight ahead. "But, speaking as an Assistant Secretary, in the future it might be good if somebody made a point of no-

29

tifying a department whenever its leader has died."

"You're thinking that you did it yourself, by accident," Bobbi Jo interrupted Tynan's reverie. "You didn't. He thought up those basements all by himself."
"How do you know?"
"I saw it."
The order creating the fictitious basements had been a very deliberate act on Fiore's part, and it had been issued a whole year before he died.

It had all started with that terrible scandal over the construction of the second, parallel Bay Bridge over the Chesapeake Bay, connecting all of Central Maryland with the Eastern Shore. There was, of course, no interest in connecting anything with the Eastern Shore itself. The Eastern Shore was thought of by other Marylanders as just one flat, boring six-pack of a stretch on the drive between their homes and their vacation destinations in Ocean City. The idea behind building a parallel bridge was that a second Bay Bridge would make possible a huge superhighway that could get people across the Eastern Shore as quickly as possible, in order to reach Ocean City in the minimum amount of time—and with the maximum amount of money left in their pockets. The construction process itself was designed to leave a maximum amount of money in other pockets also. For this reason, the bill to build a second bridge passed the legislature easily, despite strong evidence that the people did not want it.

The legislative decision to build the bridge was taken to a referendum and was soundly defeated by a 2-1 popular vote; but the Maryland Court of Appeals, citing a previous ruling made back when Maryland was a slave state, ruled that construction of the bridge was a matter immune from the referendum process. And construction proceeded.

30

A number of nationally known engineering, architecture and construction firms had been employed in this monumental project. Their bills ran tens of millions of dollars over their estimates—a fact which they successfully blamed on the state's ever-changing specifications for the bridge. But what the public never found out about were the special cost overruns which never made it into the official budget. These were all due to special engineering and consulting contracts with firms that: (1) had no previous engineering or consulting experience, (2) did no work on the project, and (3) were controlled and directed by friends and relatives of Bob Fiore, whose close personal friendship with the governor went all the way back to the days when, as kids, they would go together to the polling booths on primary days to see if any Republicans showed up.

Governor Mallard had been really incensed at the stupidity of the scheme. He had refused to appropriate any more money to cover these particular cost overruns. Since the money was already paid and gone, the governor simply called Fiore one afternoon and told him to cut $2.7 million out of his department's budget, beginning the next day—and to keep it quiet, on pain of having the auditor's secret report released to the public.

What happened next was perhaps a case study of government by default. A new computer system for budget projections had just been installed in the Secretary's office. While Fiore paced the reception room in circles around Bobbi Jo's desk—"I can't think! I can't think!"—he had noticed the satisfied gleam in the eyes of a budget analyst working in one of the side offices. Fiore walked in and found the young man practically chortling with glee as he busily typed on a computer keyboard. As the analyst watched with happily glazed eyes, long columns of numbers flashed across the screen, disappeared, returned.

"What's this?" Fiore said distractedly.

The analyst had been waiting for someone to ask. "It's our new computerized budget! It's on this computer software called a spreadsheet."

"It's really amazing!" the analyst continued without being asked. He was still staring at the numbers on the screen, oblivious to Fiore's high position, and the deep furrows on Fiore's brow.

"For example, I can put in any number here, and the program adjusts all the others. See, if the federal government changes the eligibility level $500, that will add—(a one-second pause)—162,642 people to our rolls, costing an additional (pause) $19,172,642.81. You can do crazy things. You can work backwards. Here. If you add $5 million to the program, you could lower the single person's eligibility limit to ... $285 a month."

"Tell me something quick you could do," Fiore blurted out, "to cut $2.7 million off."

"Oh. Ha ha. That's easy. A million ways. Just watch."

One way, the spreadsheet showed, was to add to every person's countable income. As the whole population of applicants grew theoretically richer, a certain number of them spilled over into that category of people who were too wealthy for Medical Assistance. Another way was to add to the assets of each member of the group. This would cause people to spill over the asset limit and also become ineligible. Fiore stared at the columns on the computer screen for a long time, seemingly transfixed by this new form of magic. He asked the analyst how many applicants were renters, and how many owned their own homes.

He picked up the phone and called Jody Hechtmuller's office.

"This is Fiore. Is a roof an asset?"

"Um, yes, I guess it could be."

"A side porch. Is that an asset?"

"Yes, but it all depends on the context. What are you getting at, Mr. Secretary?"

"How about if you get your basement clubbed? Is that an asset?"

Fiore himself had once been in the home improvement business, before you had to have a license. The lawyer on the other end of the phone tried to explain some of the complications of the law, but Fiore hung up and resumed staring at the screen over the analyst's shoulder.

A few minutes later, Fiore emerged from his private office to give the order. Secretly, without notifying any of his Assistant Secretaries, he called the Program Policy Director and told him to change the eligibility forms. From that moment on, everyone who applied for Medical Assistance was automatically assigned a basement.

Over the years, the department gradually papered over the basement issue with more and more sophisticated disguises. At first, the department's Forms Office had simply added in small print: "basement—$2,500" to every homeowner's application for benefits, and "non-countable rental of storage space—$125" to each renter's income and expense worksheet. After a year or two, these forms disappeared, but the policy manual then told every worker to enter these figures on each and every application. Then, this written instruction was taken out of the official policy manual, but every office supervisor was told that every worker must still add a basement in every case. Tynan's final change to the form had been designed to make it appear that the applicants themselves were declaring that these basements existed.

As the years wore on and the memory of Secretary Fiore faded, it became not easier but actually harder to remove the basements. With inflation, the budgetary savings from these basements had now swollen to $5.2 million a year, and there was always the nightmarish danger that some day, some court would order the department to pay retroactive medical payments totaling tens of millions of dollars. Changing the system now would bankrupt the agency and throw it into chaos. Everyone in the Department of Public Welfare now had a vital interest in covering up the dead hand of Fiore in the state cookie jar.

Tynan sat back and stared at Bobbi Jo intently. "I had no idea. It's all Fiore's fault. A dead man did this to us. Gotterdung will go crazy—Fiore was his father-in-law, you know.

"This lawsuit is going to take a major effort all around. I've got to ride herd on the Statistical Unit. Call the head of that unit and get him in here right away. I want to make sure he knows what we want—or what we *don't* want from his statistical unit. Cancel all the rest of my appointments for the next two weeks."

"But what about Mallory?"

She showed him his calendar, which had the word "Mallory" printed in thick black ink over most of the remaining days of the month.

"You're right. How could I forget about Mallory? God, I wish that man would just go away."

"But he won't," Bobbi Jo lectured, "unless you make him, Leonard. All the workers here are counting on you."

"Trust me, Bobbi Jo." Tynan smiled broadly. "I can handle this lawsuit and Mallory at the same time. I'm used to being weighed down by that human ball and chain."

3 MALLORY'S FUNCTION

Mallory showed up for work every day promptly at 8:30. He always returned from lunch on time. He did not take excessively long breaks. He was well versed in the exact extent of the duties a state employee owed his supervisor, and the exact duties a supervisor owed a state employee. In fact, he wrote numerous articulate memos on these subjects. He had years of experience in state government when he was first transferred to Tynan's office. But he had not yet done any work.

Mallory was considered to be one of the most intractable personnel problems in the Department of Public Welfare. Six successive supervisors had failed to get any assignments, or any rational explanations, or even any reaction out of him—other than his vitriolic memos attacking the supervisor's intelligence or integrity, and his contemptuous little smile. Day after day he sulked in his cubicle, wedged upright between his chair and his spotlessly clean and organized desk, his pants tightly belted around his hard, protruding belly, his hooded grey eyes silently smirking from their refuge in his round, pink face, steadfastly determined to be of absolutely no help to anyone.

Over his sixteen-year career in state government,

Mallory had been transferred to six offices. Each office, after the normal orientation period, during which Mallory and his supervisors accustomed themselves to each other's styles of working, simply learned to route all of its business around him. After that fundamental management decision was made, each supervisor in turn had plotted ways of transferring Mallory out.

Mallory was a Procurement Administrator II, responsible for supplies, purchase agreements, contracts, forms approval, payment procedures, and the design of supply delivery systems. He had been single-handedly responsible for the reorganization of three separate offices. That is, each of these offices had reorganized itself after he came. Once Mallory had arrived, each supervisor had been able to submit to his superior a detailed justification for the proposed reorganization. Each of these reports had described in compelling and businesslike language why the work assignments of that particular office had qualitatively changed, and how the reorganization was the only rational way to adapt to meet the changing challenges of the workplace.

Although he was an experienced administrator, Mallory was not involved in the preparation of any of these reports. That was because each of them had as its only real purpose the elimination of the position that Mallory was occupying at the time.

Mallory had been rated as a satisfactory employee for sixteen years in a row. In twelve of those years, his supervisor had not actually submitted any evaluation at all. By regulation, anyone who was not rated in writing at all was officially marked "satisfactory." This method not only spared Mallory's feelings, but it also salvaged his supervisors' sense of personal integrity. The supervisor could always claim that *he* never *said* that Mallory was satisfactory.

Because of this process, and because he moved through six divisions in his long career in state government, Mallory started an institutional trend. The supervisors began to notice how much easier it was just to give everyone one of these "regulatory satisfactory" ratings. The hurt feelings of the employees, the grudges, the recriminations, the grievances, the appeals—all the pain of the evaluation process—could be wiped away with the simple magic words that almost all supervisors in the department now employed: "I don't do evaluations."

When Mallory was first transferred to the Statistical Unit under Tynan, he failed to order pens, pencils, paper, computer ribbons, or any other office supplies for months. When Tynan first mentioned this to him, Mallory acted irritated.

"They're a non-audit item. You can get them from any office up and down the hall." Mallory turned his attention back toward his blotter.

For six months, Bobbi Jo borrowed pencils and paper from the other offices. Then she went on strike.

"Leonard, I am tired of looking like a fool," she said. "Everyone in the other offices is laughing at us. You never should have put him on such an important job."

For three more months, Tynan asked, then implored, and finally ordered Mallory to obtain office supplies. There was always some reason it couldn't be done. Tynan pointed out that all of the other offices had office supplies.

"Then we can get ours from them," Mallory replied.

When they had been out of supplies for a ten-month period, Tynan decided to act. He gave Mallory an unsatisfactory rating. He knew that Mallory would file a grievance with the Employee Relations Department, and he knew that he, the Assistant Secretary himself, would have to defend the rating he gave to Mallory at a hearing. But he thought that he had an airtight case against him.

"But isn't it true, Mr. Tynan," Mallory's lawyer had intoned at the grievance hearing, "that this involves a lot more than just ordering pens and pencils? Wasn't there a *forms* problem, Mr. Tynan?"

"I don't know what you mean."

"Isn't there a certain *form* for ordering office supplies?"

"Yes."

"Form DPW 6043/886 REV 6/84?"

"Yes, I guess so."

"And what does 'REV 6/84' mean?"

"I guess it means that it was last revised in June of 1984."

"What color is this form, Mr. Tynan?"

"Pink."

"Pink? Why would it be pink?"

"I guess ... because it's pink."

"Very clever, Mr. Tynan. But isn't it true that all other internal departmental forms are yellow?"

"Oh. I see what you're getting at."

Tynan admitted that the form which the office had previously used to order new stationery was outdated, and that a new form should have been developed. But Tynan did not see how this could help Mallory. The old forms could still be used. Many other offices still used them. And Mallory was also in charge of forms development anyway. If a new, yellow form had not been developed, it was Mallory's fault.

But Mallory and his lawyer complained that he had not been adequately *trained* to revise the stationery request forms. In fact, it was proven that the state gave a Forms Revision Workshop every two years—and it was further revealed that Tynan himself had turned down Mallory's request to attend that very same seminar less than three months before.

This action of Tynan's turned out to have been in sharp contrast to the actions of Mallory's six previous supervisors. It was shown at the grievance hearing that the previous supervisors had approved, in response to Mallory's numerous requests, an average of seventeen such workshops per year. The truth was that Mallory had done little else at work but file requests to be sent to these workshops, and his supervisors had been only too happy to get him out of the office for a day. Tynan had put a stop to this as soon as he saw that Mallory wasn't doing any of his regular work. But the evidence looked bad, and the Employee Relations Department issued a decision which found as a fact that Tynan's office was without paper and pencils for one whole year solely because of Tynan's "arbitrary refusal to send the appropriate employee to the Forms Revision Workshop, despite that employee's repeated requests for such appropriate and necessary training." The evaluation was changed to satisfactory, and there was a gratuitous recommendation made that Tynan be sent to a Supervisors' Refresher Workshop.

Although he had average-sized arms and legs, and an average-sized chest, Mallory was a portly man, with an egg-shaped, apparently solid bulge just in the front, from his groin area to just below his heart. In sixteen years, this bulge had gotten no smaller and no larger. Mallory did not follow the accepted Baltimore dressing pattern of continuing to wear the pants that fit you when you were thin, with the beltline slung so low that your belly protruded glutinously over the top like soft ice cream over a cone. Nor did he buy a pair of those enormous overscaled tent pants designed with the idea that stomachs of all sizes deserve pants that fit. Instead, Mallory belted his old pants tight exactly where his old waist used to be. He always wore dark pants and a white shirt, unashamed of the physique thus starkly revealed. In fact, he was more than unashamed. He carried his little egg of tissue and fat proudly before him like a protective shield. He had short, thin, reddish-blond hair, lately gathered together in the front to compensate for the receding hairline, and a round face set off with a sandy goatee whose demonic connotations had not escaped him.

Prior to becoming a public servant, Mallory had held numerous jobs in the private sector. In each of these jobs, he had demonstrated a sixth sense as to when the boss was about to fire him. Then, each time, he had suddenly quit in a rage.

This pattern had served Mallory well in the past, gratifying his need to be noticed and criticized, giving him a change of scene every few months, and giving him something to fight about between jobs. But the pattern had been broken when he came to work for the state. He no longer could engineer this cyclical pattern of indifference, aggravation and conflict. He lost that queer feeling of satisfaction he got when his boss actually yelled at him, called him obscene names, pounded on his desk. He missed the big fights at the end. As Mallory sat, year after year, at his desk in the Department of Public Welfare, with no one ever screaming, no desks pounded, with twelve straight years of "regulatory satisfactory" ratings given, no matter how little he did, he grew more and more deeply embittered. Co-workers often asked him why he didn't leave the department if he hated it so much. In reply, he always named his present supervisor and said that he wasn't going to give him the satisfaction. In reality, he couldn't leave, because he had not yet gotten what he had come for.

Tynan had not given up. He had even gone to the Supervisors Refresher Workshop. Following the recommendations he was given at the Workshop, Tynan had given

40

Mallory precisely 68 assignments in the following year. Each one was logged in, each had a completion date assigned. Mallory had completed three. He had claimed that 21 were beneath his position and that he should not have to do them at all. For 24 of the assignments, he claimed that he needed specialized training. The other 20 were either delayed due to the fault of someone with whom Mallory had to work to complete the project, could not be done because the information needed had not been handed to Mallory in the precise format which he wanted—that is, in such a complete state that all Mallory would have to do was put his name on the bottom—or could not be done pending Tynan's own "clarification," which Mallory often requested in his multi-page memoranda in response to being given a task.

Tynan then confidently took his case to discharge Mallory before the Employee Relations Department. He lost. The Employee Relations Department, noting that no one else in Tynan's office had tasks logged in, or had been given written due dates on assignments, recommended that Tynan attend that department's Non-Discrimination for Supervisors Workshop, to be given sometime during the following year.

Tynan skipped this Workshop, but he did not give up. After two more years of preparation, Mallory's discharge hearing was about to begin.

An hour after she had brought him the complete file on Mallory, Bobbi Jo walked into Tynan's office. The records on Mallory filled two cardboard boxes, each crammed with manila file folders two to three inches thick. Tynan had the newest folder open on the desk before him. He was turning the pages quickly, his eyes quickly darting from top to bottom of each. Still, he appeared unruffled, more like a model for *Gentlemen's Quarterly* than a frantic bureaucrat. He looked up.

"The thought going around here," he began, making it sound as if deep philosophical discussions had been held, but referring really only to the insides of his own head, "is that we're going to need a lot of statistical help from the Statistical Unit when this Legal Assistance Society lawsuit really hits. I wonder if we can afford to have *everybody* preoccupied with Mallory's discharge hearing for the next several weeks."

"This might not be the time for wondering, Leonard."

Tynan drew back from the accusatory twang in Bobbi Jo's voice. She never argued with him, but she found ways to communicate her opinion.

Bobbi Jo did not notice that Tynan was black. To her, he was almost inhuman, a remarkable kind of administrating machine. She had seen him look at a page filled with columns of budgetary numbers and instantly figure out the hidden agenda of the person who had prepared it. She had seen him argue the most flippant and recalcitrant colleague into babbling incoherence in seconds. She had seen him make people forget everything but what he wanted them to remember.

Tynan inspired a confidence in those above him that he would have their exact orders carried out; but he also inspired just a little fear, because every supervisor he ever worked for knew that Leonard Tynan was fifteen times smarter than he was, and that Leonard Tynan had his own agenda, an agenda whose number one item was Leonard Tynan's career.

He was just over medium height, with medium-brown skin, long, elegant limbs and a naturally graceful posture. He dressed meticulously, always in starched, fashionable shirts sometimes adorned with delicate silver cuff links. He had a great flash of a smile, and a genuine sense of humor. When his fellow administrators talked with him, they felt that he understood their problems.

"What's the case about?" The head of the Statistical Unit was known for getting to the point quickly.

"Eligibility rules. Basements and crawlspaces."

"Oh God! There's always been something funny about that. You know, I've never checked, but it almost seems that we have more basements than we have people."

"Don't check."

"Yeah, but—it's okay, isn't it? I mean, haven't the lawyers given us the okay all along?"

Tynan didn't answer the question. Instead, he said, "You don't actually keep total gross figures like that, do you? I mean, like the total number of basements?"

"No. But I guess if we had to ...."

"We have no reason to think that the numbers would be incriminating," Tynan cut him off. "Whether there is a basement is a decision made by each worker in each individual case. I assume it would be very hard to get accurate statistics on all of this?"

What he really meant was that he *hoped* that it would be hard to get accurate statistics. As soon as his subordinate demonstrated that he had gotten the message, Tynan dismissed him.

Bobbi Jo came in and found something to do at the end of the table. He looked at her.

"There isn't going to be any statistical smoking gun for Legal Assistance to stumble onto during the legal discovery process. This thing is under control. I think I can settle it."

Bobbi Jo nodded and walked out of the room. He could hear her keyboard clicking a moment later. He looked down at the thick file still on his desk.

The file showed that Mallory's behavior was getting even worse. For months, he had planted himself defiantly

43

at his empty desk, hour after hour, with a small sarcastic grin on his face, making sardonic comments about Tynan to whomever would listen. He now spent all of his time filling out applications to take courses, or applications for transfers, or composing grievances, or, mostly, drafting memos criticizing Tynan.

These memos all followed a certain pattern. Each began with a lurid description of Tynan's two unsuccessful attempts to get rid of him. Each claimed that the grievance process had exposed Tynan's malevolent, twisted and discriminatory personality. The memos always repeated a list of problems that Mallory had experienced on the job, ranging from the size of his chair through his unsuccessful attempts to be promoted. Mallory usually charged in these memos that Tynan was too weak a voice in the department to get his division all of the staff and equipment it needed, and that he, Mallory, was being made the scapegoat for that. At the same time, the memos often accused Tynan and Secretary Gotterdung of plotting together against him. These attacks were often accompanied by psychological opinions about the root cause of Tynan's discriminatory treatment of him (a dedicated employee who had been rated satisfactory for twelve years in a row). Each memo ended with a long litany of reasons why Tynan's order to do the task at hand was legally questionable, thoroughly unfair and (always) "unprofessional in the extreme."

These memos always demanded an immediate written response from Tynan. This response, the memos always demanded, must respond to "each and every circumstance mentioned above," and also must take into account the other allegations made in numerous previous memos which Mallory had written to him.

Mallory didn't bother to actually attach these previous memos, or to dig them out of his desk and refer to them more specifically, by date, or by title, or by any other means. This was just as well, since Bobbi Jo, who was the lead office secretary, had taken it upon herself almost six months earlier to nip this memo mania in the bud. First, she had stopped delivering any of these memos to the multitude of people Mallory ordered copies sent to. She sent only the original, and she sent it only to the person it was actually addressed to. She wasn't surprised when no one seemed to notice or care about that. Then, she decided to take it one step further. She kept Mallory's last memo on her computer, and when the next one came in she typed only the first and last pages and just spliced in the middle from the last memo. When this also passed unnoticed, she began paring down Mallory's original work until, finally, no matter how furiously and assiduously Mallory sweated over the language of his latest multi-page recrimination, she was allowing him only one paragraph at the beginning and one paragraph at the end.

Tynan called her back into the office. Bobbi Jo was twenty years older than Tynan and was thinking about retiring. She was a thin, sinewy, tanned, tastelessly dressed woman with fast-greying hair and few doubts about what was right or wrong. She had been taught by her mother fifty-eight years ago not to let a day go by without something to show for it. Since she had never listened to anything else that her mother had told her, it was unclear whether she had miraculously accepted this one piece of advice or, since she was basically playing with the same deck of gene cards, she had just arrived at the same conclusion herself; but there was no doubt that she attacked every day as a chance to make her own individual little mark on the world. If she did retire, she told everyone, she was going to work in her husband's snack store in Pasadena, or else start up a competing one across the street.

"These memos of Mallory's," Tynan began exploring delicately. "These memos seem to be all very similar. I wonder: do you think he's finally really lost it?"

Bobbi Jo looked very significantly at Tynan over the reading glasses that she had bought at her husband's snack store. "I don't think there ever was much content to them, Leonard," she opened with. The tension between them did not seem to be caused by fear. Rather, she seemed to be searching carefully for the right words. They both knew that he would soon be grilled by Mallory's lawyers.

"Tell the truth, it's kind of a relief, them being all so similar," she went on, boldfaced, "what with the computer being able to spit one of them out in about half a minute."

Tynan tried not to smile. Every day, this tough lady found herself caught in the state's bureaucratic web, and every day she cut her way out with her own common sense, always making sure to squish a few useless bugs along the way. He had to smile. But then his smile broadened, and overcame him, because he realized that Bobbi Jo never did anything at work just for her own convenience.

"I can't seem to remember," he said, looking out the window. He stared at the vague orange disk in the sky trying to fight its way through the milky blue haze that had been suffocating the city for weeks. He smiled down at the table. He knew he should have guessed. She really was a great secretary. "Have I ... um ... *responded* to any of these memos of Mallory's?"

"Every damn one of 'em."

"Were my responses ...?"

"All very short. All very similar." There was not even a glint of a smile on her face. Tynan had an image of Mallory as a very fat little pink beetle with a goatee, careening in circles, just out of squishing range of Bobbi Jo's sequined high heeled shoes. He did ask her for a copy. It said simply: "With respect to your memo of————, I suggest that you devote your energies to the task at hand." Tynan stared at it for a long time in silent appreciation. He knew that he couldn't have said it better himself.

Tynan also knew that, if Mallory's attorney found this out, it would blow his carefully crafted discharge proceedings out of the water.

4 EXTENT OF THE ESTATE

Charles followed Sport back through the heavy glass door to the reception room.

"You're with me, so you won't have to worry about Linda this time."

"I'm not scared of her any more."

They made three right turns into the deepening paneled gloom. The back hallway, where they had first run into one another, was particularly dim. Some of the brown asphalt floor tiles were missing. They were following the green arrows again for most of the way.

They suddenly turned left into a tiny office. It was painted bright white. One wall was cement, one was plaster, one was wallboard and one was dark, wood-look paneling. Posters of nature scenery and of beautiful women, all fully dressed, were attached to the walls in various ways. The color of the asphalt floor tiles changed to a kind of dark green.

"Have a seat."

Sport stood until Charles was settled in one of the curved plastic chairs, his knees almost touching Sport's oversized metal desk. Sport maneuvered himself into his own green vinyl chair behind the desk. Bookshelves made from cinderblocks leaned against one wall, and a table lamp obviously brought from somebody's club basement sat on the top shelf, providing accessory lighting. A tiny casement window up at the ceiling level gave an occasional view of passing feet on the sidewalk outside.

Sport handed Charles back all of his papers, except for the letter from Peck, Peck and Peck.

"No," Charles began. "I need to see you about ...."

"Take these other papers back for now," Sport interrupted. "I can see what your problem is. Let me see if I can explain it to you."

"I tried to sign up for Medical Assistance..." But Charles didn't finish the sentence. Sport was not even looking at him.

It was these other papers which were important to Charles and his housemate, Jimmy. He didn't want to talk about the letter from Peck, Peck and Peck. But he was happy that he had gotten his foot in the door at last. He had a lawyer. His life was taking an unexpected turn. He thought that maybe it would do him good to listen to someone for a change. As Sport talked, Charles sat back in the chair, and he relaxed.

"You want to talk about the letter from Pecker or whatever, go ahead."

"This is quite unusual," Sport said, frowning. "Is there anything special about your aunt's house? Is it worth a lot of money?"

To Charles, money was something that you got at the last minute from your boss or from the welfare and handed over to your landlord. You took it to the food store. You lost it betting on the numbers. It had nothing to do with houses or property. Some people just owned houses and some didn't. When asked to compare a house to a sum of money, Charles drew a complete blank.

Sport immediately understood. "What they're saying here is that they already have a buyer ready to take it off your hands—buy it from you—for ten thousand dollars. The residual legatee has enclosed papers here by which you can renounce all of your interest in the estate in return for the ten thousand. They're trying to buy the house before you even have it."

"Ten thousand dollars?"

Sport had finally succeeded in getting Charles's interest.

"Yes, but it's highly unusual that this letter is coming from Peck, Peck and Peck. Something like this usually comes from someone who's contesting the will, not from the executor." Sport had to say these words because he thought this way—in legal terms, deliberately, with his lips moving—when he was first figuring out a problem; but he realized that these words meant nothing to Charles.

"This could be a good offer," he translated, speaking slowly and loud. "Or it could be a trick."

"Could be a trick," Charles echoed. He looked at Sport blankly.

At the repetition of the word "trick," Sport suddenly stood up, stepped onto the seat of his chair, reached up and pulled open the little casement window. He jumped back down, wiped off the seat with his hand and sat down again.

"Maybe we should just go and look at the house."

"Look at it?"

"How can we know how much it's worth if we haven't even seen it?"

"It's . . . a long time."

"I don't know if there's really anything I can do for you, Mr. Gage. It would help me to look at the house."

"To see if ...?"

"Just for me. To get away from this other case that's driving me crazy. To get away from the phone. To see a real house, that you own."

Charles searched in another envelope and came up with the key. The house was only a mile away, but that day it was one long, confused hour's drive in rush hour. The evening sun was turning orange by the time they got to the block where Aunt May's house stood. A small square of the asphalt was torn up and blocked off just in front of the house next door. An orange sign advised: "CROSLEY T. PETTIBONE, JUST CHECKING FOR LEAKS!" Sport pulled his car to the curb at 442.

Sport saw a mean, wide concrete sidewalk littered with papers and little pieces of broken glass. There was a bar across the street, and a soup kitchen at the end of the block. Lining the sidewalk were the flat facades of the dark brick houses without porches. Only the marble steps and mantels, and the fancy cornices, distinguished their exteriors from those of the awful flat blocks of row houses built in the outlying districts of the city after the war.

Sport was renovating his own row house in the city, and he often bragged to his friends about the features he loved: the tiny stone porch with its massive wooden columns, the ten-foot ceilings, the three-sided bay on the second floor. But everything that made his own neighborhood so appealing seemed to be missing from this block.

Charles saw Aunt May's street and house. He remembered for the hundredth time the day she had made him sit outside on the stoop in his Sunday clothes, but for the first time he recalled the incident from an adult perspective. His own father had always been sick when he was growing up in North Carolina. Drinking, his mother always said, but it wasn't just that; and Charles hated his mother for saying that. The only clear memory he had of his father was the day he died, the beautiful coffin, the layers of sweet flowers, and thinking that this was the better life they all said was in store for everyone in the hereafter. His mother moved in with a sister, and Charles was dragged along. Twice she put him on the train to Baltimore to see her Aunt May. He stayed with her for over a week each time. This was perhaps why, when he left home at seventeen and began his zigzag path through half the towns between the Appalachians and the sea, he always knew that in the end he would probably find a place in Baltimore.

But in forty-five years of living in and out of town, he had never called her. After his mother got a phone, and when she could track him down and get him on the line, she would say, why don't you call Aunt May? But throughout his life he had been convinced that his Aunt May didn't really want to see him. He never really thought about why, but there was always a picture in his mind of the Sunday clothes he wore there the day she made dinner for him on her good china plates, clothes that he had borrowed for the visit. She had said that she understood his country ways, but that they wouldn't pass muster in the city. She wanted him to talk to the neighborhood kids. He could be loud with them, she had said encouragingly, but he didn't want to be loud. He had just wanted to be home. But when he went home, he didn't want to be there either, and when he grew up he realized that there was nothing for him to do in the country. So he followed little dribs and drabs of jobs up and down and across five states, and he relied for a long time on a new friend that came in a bottle and helped him forget the pointlessness of it all.

He pulled his long, thin frame out of Sport's car, stared at the stoop, then walked over and rested his foot on the bottom step. Somehow, all the alcohol and all the jobs and all the confusion of his life had just put things on hold. He felt no more at home in this city now than he had nearly fifty years ago when he had sat here for the first time. He could suddenly feel the pain of all the wasted time in between. He sat on the top step and demanded that Sport sit with him. He liked this crazy short white man. For once in his life, Charles had dropped one of his own ideas and let someone else talk him into something, based just on enthusiasm and blind faith. Sport had taken him on a surprise pilgrimage that Charles now recognized was necessary, and long overdue. A lot of time had passed, and Aunt May was dead, but Sport made him feel that he had a friend now, and that it wasn't too late.

They went inside the house. Sport was surprised to find a little vestibule with a marble-tiled floor and dark-stained wooden walls. The interior door had a large clear glass pane and a scratched and wobbly crystal doorknob. Inside, the walls were an old-gold print almost faded into a background of cream. The closed house smelled of heated wood and dust. Sport lifted the edge of an old, cheap rug, brown with age, and saw the original hardwood parquet floor, scratched deep by decades of dogs. But the whole house was crammed with furniture that Sport envied. A dark mahogany buffet with intricately curved legs stood next to a delicately carved bowfront china closet whose interior was all glass. The bed upstairs must have been made from a ton of dark hardwood, though the mattress was made of cheap, shredding foam.

Aunt May had never been in a furniture store in her life, but she had been working in other people's homes for fifty-some years. She had the sense to keep the best of what she had inherited from her employers. While fashions had changed to tacky and back again, these furniture pieces, which would become priceless antiques twenty years later, had been left out in the alley for the maid.

But the structure itself was in bad shape. The two basic front rooms were as solid as stone, but the one story addition on the back that housed the primitive kitchen was warped and wobbly. Patches of sheet steel nailed on the floor covered small holes. The linoleum was clean, but it was also so old that the pattern was hardly discernible. Upstairs, in the back room, there was evidence of serious water damage to the ceiling and walls. A wooden back bay had been added to the back bedroom a half-century ago, and fifty years of its own weight had pulled the framing an inch away from the brick. The heavy iron grates on all the back windows were thickly coated with rust.

They creaked back downstairs. They sat on the hardwood steps that ascended from Aunt May's tiny hallway between the living and dining room. Each man was lost in his own thoughts.

"Do you think you can keep a house up? Can you do anything—carpentry or anything?"

"No. No. I seen it all done, but I never tried."

Charles was beginning to like this house. He was touched that his Aunt May remembered him, after all the time that had passed. He had always thought that he was remembered in this house as a scraggly, stupid country boy, a joke. Sitting now inside the house she had given him, he saw what she had seen: a shy, skinny boy without a father, a beloved nephew whose quiet country dignity reminded her of her own brothers, a lonely boy worthy of her care. Even after her death, she had reached back and touched him, tapping him on the shoulder, as it were, to say that she still believed in him. All of his life he had thought that his sins and his excesses and his failures since then had put him in a different category from Aunt May, and from that innocent boy in South Carolina staring at the flowers at his father's funeral. He had never felt righteous enough to call her. He hadn't called her. But now she had called him.

"I have no idea what it's worth," Sport said, staring at the wall, lost in his own thoughts.

"It was my Aunt May's house."

"I know."

"She worked hard to keep this place straight. Wasn't no dust like this in here before she got sick. I can tell you that. She musta been sick or gone blind .... "

"You don't know?"

Charles looked away. Orange evening skylight filtered in through the tall dusty front windows of Aunt May's tiny living room. He began his ruminative chewing motions. No, he didn't know. There was no point in lying to Sport, or to himself, about that. He wished that he could have grown up in the dignified way she had seen him capable of. But he knew now that he should have just called her anyway, that his life had been off the mark, but maybe not that far off. That he could have helped her.

Charles suddenly got up and stood with his back against the wall, across from the steps, facing Sport. To his right, Aunt May's furniture stood mutely in the middle of the living room. There was something both forlorn and dignified about the way the old wood stood there, as if awaiting someone's return. Charles then peered to his left, into the expectant shadows of the dining room. For the first time that day, a broad smile broke out across his face.

"I think," he shook his head, surprised at himself. "I think I'm gonna keep this house."

5 COMMON INTERESTS

Secretary Brendan Gotterdung had not been able to interest himself in the affairs of the Department of Public Welfare. He had been appointed to the position upon the sudden death of his predecessor and father-in-law, Bob Fiore. Upon assuming the office, he had been forced by circumstances to allow a core group of Assistant Secretaries who were familiar with the department to stay on, but these people were together the biggest bunch of godawful know-it-alls and can't-do men he had ever met. Every idea he had, it seemed, one or another of the Assistant Secretaries claimed to have had years ago and to have found out that it was against federal regulations, would cost too much, was going against the thrust of the governor's initiatives on poverty, or just plain wouldn't work. Brendan Gotterdung had to resist the temptation to shout out at these meetings: "Well, what do you need me for, then?" because he was afraid that the room would then be stilled by an embarrassing silence.

Gotterdung had never wanted to be the head of the Department of Public Welfare. It catered to no powerful constituent groups. It did hand out enormous amounts of money; but those who got the lion's share of it, the doctors and the hospitals, acted as if he should get down on his knees and thank them for taking it. Even the landlords blamed him if the welfare checks didn't go out on time. The politicians never had a good thing to say about the department, and the do-gooders acted as if you were taking money away from the poor people instead of giving it out, free. The employees were never happy, and the poor people themselves just had more and more babies, none of whom would ever grow up to have the sense to cast a vote of gratitude for their benefactor.

Worst of all, the department didn't deal with any issues that would fire the hearts and minds of the business leaders who were now so openly flirting with Gotterdung's former political ally, Mayor Crosley T. Pettibone of the City of Baltimore.

As Secretary, Gotterdung was in charge of the entire Department of Public Welfare, and a member of the Governor's cabinet. But he had considered it a dead end job until the day that, with one master political stroke, and without any rationale except crude political gain, he secretly prised his department into a crucial decision-making role in the plans for the Mayor Crosley T. Pettibone Waterside Towers Luxury Condominium Development.

The history of the legislation producing this political coup had been so devious that Gotterdung, exultant, had hardly been able to control himself when the governor called to see if he should sign the trick bill into law. He knew that his unrestrained excitement would be inappropriate for a bill that was supposed to be so minor. So he had forced his Assistant Secretary, Leonard Tynan, to take the call.

Gotterdung had inherited Tynan from his father-in-law. He was completely content to let Tynan run the department on a day-to-day basis, and to handle those irritating and complicated legal matters that the Legal

Assistance Society always seemed to be complaining about. Gotterdung had learned that the best thing to do in these cases was exactly what Tynan told him to do. He would never, however, trust Tynan with the kind of back-room political intrigue that he himself indulged in. Gotterdung considered these political maneuvers behind the scenes to be the really important part of his job. No one at the Assistant Secretary level would normally be trusted with these matters anyway. And Tynan was a stranger to him; he had no connection whatsoever with Gotterdung's family or to any political machine. Moreover, Tynan was black.

The morning the governor called about the trick bill, Gotterdung, sitting right next to Tynan, hurriedly wrote out instructions for him on back of a carryout lunch menu on his desk: "SOUND BORED!" He then scribbled out, word for word, the precise answer Tynan should mouth into the receiver: "Yes, we have seen the bill. We could conduct the study it requires without any increase in staff. It's a minor hassle, but no big problem."

Tynan made every effort to sound confident and professional, but he could read only as fast as Gotterdung could write.

"Are you all right?" The governor didn't know Tynan well. He hadn't spoken to him since the day of Fiore's funeral. He thought that Tynan sounded slow, almost as if he were retarded. Tynan could sense this, and he became quietly furious. But he recovered beautifully.

"Yes, I'm fine, Your Honor. You did catch me off guard. I was speaking extemporaneously and looking for the file at the same time. Oh, here it is." Tynan was taking a big chance with this new lie, since the governor might ask him to interpret one of the bill's provisions, and Tynan didn't have the faintest idea what the bill was about or where it was. But he was willing to bet his career that the governor had no interest in the specifics. "Okay, here it is, at the bottom of the 'minor bills' pile. Sir, the department has no problem with the bill. In fact, I did discuss this bill briefly with Secretary Gotterdung just this morning," Tynan embellished his tale, "and he indicated that it was fine with him."

At this point, Gotterdung began waving his arms and silently mouthing the word "NO" to Tynan. Tynan stopped, calculating whether he could pull off a retraction of the statement he had just made without sounding even more stupid. He reacted instinctively. No. The governor wouldn't buy it right after the retarded stunt. Gotterdung was just going to have to live with that ad lib.

"Sorry," he said after the governor clicked off.

"Is he going to sign it?" Gotterdung was more animated than Tynan had ever seen him.

It was always a mistake to let Leonard Tynan find out that you were covering up something.

"He said he would."

Gotterdung then quickly changed the subject and didn't bring it up for the rest of the morning.

Tynan made an extra copy of the bill. That afternoon, he walked one door down the hall to Gotterdung's office with the bill in his hand.

"I've been looking at the new bill that the governor called about this morning. It says we're supposed to do a study."

"Yeah, well," Gotterdung put his large hand up in the air and held it out, his thick fingers spread, as if he were pushing someone away. "There's nothing immediate there."

"I think we should make arrangements to do a study. We don't want to be accused of slowing down urban development."

"Don't ..." Gotterdung took a quick breath. "Don't worry about it."

"It's my job to worry about these things—so you won't have to."

"Um ... It's nothing." Gotterdung was a huge, barrel-shaped man with a large, square, fleshy face. Tynan had never seen it red before, except in anger.

"It's ... just a little study. No requirements. We can do it quickly when we have to." Intending to make a meaningful gesture with body language, Gotterdung turned his head and made a show of closely examining something on his desk. Tynan noticed that it was the sports page.

"I agree that it does look simple. Let me take care of it and it'll get done right a...."

"No!"

"Don't do the study?"

"Don't do it."

Back in his office, Tynan drummed his fingers softly on his desk. He couldn't understand why Gotterdung would want to stop any development, much less one of Mayor Pettibone's development projects in the city. Gotterdung and Pettibone had come out of the same Northwest Baltimore Political Club, run by the Fiore-Cohen machine. They were not known to be enemies. And Gotterdung didn't have the courage to pick a fight with Pettibone anyway. Pettibone was much more powerful, and incredibly vindictive. No, Tynan decided, Gotterdung would never be so stupid as to challenge the mayor.

Tynan, of course, had no way of knowing that Slip Slidell was in on the deal.

State Senator Samuel "Slip" Slidell definitely had the courage to challenge Mayor Pettibone, and he had found his perfect co-conspirator in Brendan Gotterdung. Slidell did not know Gotterdung well on a personal basis, but he saw that Gotterdung had all of the qualifications necessary. First, Gotterdung hated Pettibone. Second, no one knew that Gotterdung hated Pettibone. Third, Gotterdung was in a position that didn't appear to have anything to do with Pettibone's development plans. Fourth, no one would suspect that he'd have the nerve to do it.

It had been said that Slidell was too professional a politician to hold a grudge, but the truth was that he was too professional a politician to *reveal* that he was holding a grudge. He had hated Crosley Pettibone ever since the day eight years before when Pettibone had skillfully quashed his political hopes and had begun his own self-glorifying tenure as mayor. And in the process of glorifying himself, Pettibone had made Slidell look small-time and old-hat.

But it hadn't always been so clear that Pettibone would be the dominant politician. From his power base among the working people of Southeast and East Baltimore, Slidell had extended his control over South Baltimore, and for decades his ward captains had delivered a huge chunk, maybe 25 percent of the votes, in every citywide election. Slidell and Pettibone had uneasily shared power over the city government for several years. This arrangement had seemed to promise a lifetime rotation of mayoralties between Pettibone's Northwest Baltimore Fiore-Cohen machine and Slidell's Deep Devotion Democratic Club. But Pettibone found this deal too constrictive, and he fought his way out.

Crosley T. Pettibone's philosophy of government merged conveniently with his career plans. After years of serving the interests of the Cohen and Fiore department stores, insurance agencies and paving contractors—being in the pocket of these small businesses—Pettibone wanted to be in the pocket of big businesses. Within a period of a few short years, he achieved this goal, and the chairmen of the boards of the public utility companies, the large, established banks, the brokerages and financial firms, and numerous other blue chip Baltimore businesses, including the nationwide Bold Tip Development Company, became Pettibone's daily dinner companions. Under the influence of his businessmen friends, Pettibone became the city's prophet of economic development.

Slidell kept his head above water politically by representing the groups that Pettibone left behind. The unions. The neighborhood groups. The lodges and sportsmen's groups and religious bodies. He knew that people cared about things besides economic development. He understood ethnic tradition, homeowner's pride, racial bigotry, religious devotion, love of family, Oriole fever, fear of drugs, contempt for the bureaucracy. Slidell dealt with such passions cunningly and well—but felt none of them in his own heart. Part of his ability to manipulate his constituency, to make some constructive use of reactions jolting out of the mean streets of his neighborhoods, came directly from the fact that he wasn't really involved. He could always cut the best deal because his vision was never clouded with passion. The only passion he felt in all his dealings was the need to be the dealer. He wanted to be the governor, the Big Dealer; and if he'd have been the type of person who thought about why he wanted this, he'd never have gotten as far as he did.

But he didn't think that he deserved to be called Slip, and it was Pettibone's discovery of his childhood nickname—a name invented by his ten-year-old classmates years ago, after an ice-skating party—that torpedoed his hopes to be mayor. That nickname was deviously released to the press by Pettibone's aides on a particularly slow news day, and it was repeated so often off the record thereafter that reporters soon felt free to describe it as a commonly used nickname. The nickname struck a chord in the public mind. Voters were so accustomed to reading of complex deals Slidell had pulled off that they were ready to believe that there was no purpose behind any of them except to line Slidell's pockets.

Pettibone's PR people expertly picked up on this weakness and strummed the Slip chord until the whole town resonated with it. Eventually, the press, when reporting anything that Slidell did or said, began to print a little explanatory passage which might as well have said that this man was known as Slip and that nothing he said was likely to be completely true. Meanwhile, Pettibone made a number of appearances with bankers and corporate executives of such overstarched patrician rectitude that it didn't even need to be said that these people would not even speak to anyone named Slip, much less commit large amounts of investment money into his hands.

After the Slip moniker stuck, the mayoralty race was all but over. The irony was that, while it was often alleged (but never quite proven) that Slidell engineered political acts that put money in his own pockets, Pettibone, once he became mayor, openly gave away huge amounts of the city's property. Money, land, buildings, development rights, loan guarantees, bond proceeds, letters of credit, rights of way, sewer hookups, environmental waivers, and other valuable city properties and rights were given away wholesale to potential investors. These businessmen were given free use of the mayor's vehicles, free use of his office and car phones, free haircuts from the City Council barber, shoeshines, gum, calendars, combs, pens, pins, stickers, Oriole schedules, play money, little flags, keychains—all of the items necessary to give away to the wealthiest corporations in America in order to convince them that Baltimore was a tightly run ship and a businesslike place to do business. And Pettibone was praised for this.

While Slip had his name on nothing but the letterhead of the Deep Devotion Democratic Club, Pettibone plastered his name and his title everywhere in the city. Thus, the Unisys Company's new skyscraper was officially named The Crosley T. Pettibone Computer Science Building, the new bay cruise liner was named The Mayor Crosley T. Pettibone, the number 8 bus became The Mayor's Number 8 Bus Service, and so on. Like the rest of the inhabitants of the city, Slidell was used to Pettibone's name being added to everything; and he thought that he understood the size of Pettibone's ego. But even Slidell was unprepared for the grandiosity of Pettibone's Waterside Towers plan.

"Two hundred and fifty million dollars," Slidell's informant told him flatly. "I heard it from a CPA friend of mine in Chicago. He does some work for the Bold Tip Development Company there.

"So I says 'oh yeah,' like I know what he's talking about. Really, I just want to get him off the phone. I'm payin' for the call. He says 'no, it's impressive, a two-hundred-and-fifty-million-dollar development right on the waterfront at Fells Point.' I say I haven't heard of anything like that, and suddenly I can tell he's real sorry he mentioned it. So I try to check with my cousin who lives on Jasper Street, and guess what? He's moved. Track him down, somebody came to his door and bought it for twice what it's worth."

"I hadn't heard."

Slidell quietly asked around and found out that the story was true. It was a terrible political insult to Slidell that this project was being planned right in his district without any notice to him. Worse, it was a threat to Slidell's career. This was the kind of dramatic, flamboyant project that would get nationwide publicity for

Pettibone; it would make him appear to be the obvious choice to succeed Governor Mallard. Through this project, Crosley Pettibone might, once again, and again by devious means, block Slidell's path to power.

Fells Point was densely populated, and ringed by clean, tight ethnic neighborhoods—Italian, Lithuanian, Greek, Polish—all of which had pulled back a little from the rusty seaminess of the remaining maritime trade of Fells Point itself. A broad shopping boulevard lined with everything from cheap furniture stores to gun shops ran all the way to the water's edge. Foreign sailors and grizzled neighborhood veterans eyed each other uneasily in the tiny wharfside bars. The people of Durham and Regester and Fleet and Jasper streets had kept up their houses and somehow hung on for fifty years as the economic power base of the city had slipped out from under them.

The developers' vision of Fells Point was of something like an urban Miami Beach with mammoth condominiums strung all along the waterfront. Each building would try to evoke, in its own way, as its special cachet, the ancient, nautical atmosphere of the salty old waterfront with its rat-infested wharfs, its rusty tugboats, its ship chandlers' warehouses, its tiny waterfront bars—all of which would be bulldozed months before the first precast concrete wall unit would be lowered into place under the guidance of the laser beams. But this was the type of authentic local color that the yuppies from out of town demanded.

Pettibone's secret Waterside Towers project would dwarf the proposals and plans of the ordinary private developers and monopolize the best property on the waterfront. There were many obvious reasons for the mayor to keep it secret. If the current property owners got wind of the scheme too soon, land values would skyrocket, and the project could become financially impossible. The city usually got around this problem by condemning some parcels of property while purchasing others. But Pettibone had been severely criticized in recent years for practically giving the land away, then guaranteeing the developer against losses. His power to condemn property had been curtailed by the state legislature. Pettibone's reaction had been to engage in this even more massive, even more secret plan. And secrecy, Slidell knew, was a sign of weakness.

Slidell soon discovered that Pettibone had an additional reason for this secrecy. The Bold Tip Development company was a nonunion developer. All of the construction unions were going to be cut out of this lucrative action. If they had known this, they would have made such a fuss so early that the project might have been stalled. In bypassing them so deliberately, Mayor Pettibone would infuriate organized labor and flaunt his independent political strength, in the process making a bold statement about the direction in which he wanted the state to go.

For months, Slidell gathered information and bided his time. Then, one frigid Sunday afternoon during the legislative session in the preceding January, he saw his opening. While his fellow legislators were gawking at the female lobbyists or guffawing at bars and receptions all over Annapolis, Slip sat in his hotel room, read bills, made a few phone calls. From over a decade's experience in reading bills, Slidell could tell what lobbyist or special interest was behind each bill. He could tell which legislator really cared about which bill. He knew that there were many legislators who would blithely put in a bill for anybody who asked—then just as casually let it die.

He laughed out loud when he first read the bill about relocation assistance in the Fells Point redevelopment area. Its sponsor, Reverend Bain, was known to be a man of integrity and compassion, completely incorruptible and legislatively inept. Slidell admired Bain's quiet, dignified manner, but he had never worked with him on a bill. Nor, to his knowledge, had anyone else.

"Who in the world ...?" Slidell questioned the walls of his hotel room.

The bill required developers, together with the city, to jointly plan for, and finance, and account for, the relocation of each and every resident displaced by any large commercial development. Reverend Bain would put in any bill for anyone who asked; but no one Slidell knew, not even the Legal Assistance Society, was so naive as to ask for this.

The bill was such a dead duck that Slidell couldn't think of any way that he could make use of it. He flicked it across the table and onto the floor. The bill didn't fit into any category. It was useless, he thought again, but he kept glancing at it where it lay on the rug at the foot of the plate glass, overlooking the frigid skeletons of the sailing ships in Annapolis Harbor. It was late afternoon, and the brave winter colors of the recreational harbor were already tinted with the red-orange of early sunset. The edges of the glass doors were rounded with fog fast turning to frost. Slidell felt a tinge of sadness that another day was drawing to an end. Since his divorce two years before, he stayed down in Annapolis even over the winter weekends, when everything was pretty much dead.

A dead duck. There was hardly any duck so crippled it couldn't at least flap its wings and scare a few timid creatures. And if it couldn't even do that, it still could make great bait. But a bill was useful for neither of these things if no one, absolutely no one, took it seriously. As Slidell stared out across the frozen harbor, he suddenly saw a lonely flight of geese, just about five or six of them in a ragged V, totally out of place over the city on the western side of the bay. Totally out of place, and halfway out of season, Slidell mused. They would probably make it all the way down to Florida unmolested by hunters. They just wouldn't be expected. Slidell glanced down at the bill again. It was wedged in a crevice, faintly flapping in the draft from the heating vents. A broad smile slowly crept across his face. He suddenly had a terrific idea.

He met with Brendan Gotterdung at lunch in Baltimore the next day.

"Governor Mallard's term is up soon," Slidell began. "I wonder how big a job Pettibone is going to find for you if he becomes the next governor?"

"Pettibone. He doesn't even return my phone calls."

"You don't have much feeling for the boys of the old Fiore-Cohen machine?"

"They don't give a shit about me."

Slidell waited for the obvious question, but it didn't come, so he went on.

"How would you like to run for Lieutenant Governor on the Deep Devotion ticket?"

"How would .... Yeah! Yeah, I would do that."

Slidell waited patiently for Gotterdung to catch on.

"What do I gotta do?" Gotterdung finally asked.

Slidell smiled.

"All you have to do is keep your old friend Pettibone from building in Fells Point."

"How am I gonna do that?"

"For now, just keep your mouth shut, and wait for my magic to work."

6 THE LAST FANNER

Charles couldn't rest. He creaked down the hall to Miss Agatha's room to watch TV. He could hear it from his room anyway.

Ten minutes later they heard a terrific banging, loud enough to overcome the voices from the TV, at the front of the house. Agatha glanced sideways at him.

"Everybody's paid for the week," Charles said. "So it ain't the landlord. And he got a key anyway."

Charles rented a room in a deteriorating three-story brick row house in West Baltimore. It had once been a large single-family house. There were four other roomers. They all had use of the bathroom and the kitchen. Charles had a hot plate in his room where he sometimes heated things. But on days when he felt rich, he and Jimmy would go out and get chicken, or even a pizza, making sure to get back before dark when the sidewalk grew thick with junkies, drunks and ignorant young toughs. Charles could still work, and he showed up most days at six o'clock outside the day-labor pool office downtown. They knew him there, and on most days there was work for him; but he had had to stop work in the middle of the afternoon one day the week before because of the pain, and they told him they didn't want him back on that

69

particular job.

Jimmy arrived home just as Dean Johnson was giving up on anyone answering the front door. When Jimmy opened it with his key, Johnson walked in behind him. He climbed the stairs behind Jimmy and walked right into Miss Agatha's room.

All Jimmy understood was that this was some kind of man in a suit who wanted to see Charles. Miss Agatha glanced over just long enough to see that the man was looking for Charles, then went back to watching *Wheel of Fortune*. Johnson was middle-aged, black, and wore black-framed glasses, a white shirt, a dark suit that looked a little lived-in. He carried a lot of pens in his pockets, and a black zippered leather portfolio. He was not a big man, but he had the air of someone who was carrying important news.

Johnson's real estate company dealt with houses in neighborhoods which the big real estate agents wouldn't even drive through, much less do business in. He was used to dealing with people essentially like Charles, but who had had a little better luck. He could find mortgages for people who had never been inside a bank, and he could finance repairs through his own finance company, a legal operation that charged 33 1/3 percent interest and which had no credit standards whatsoever.

"Charles Gage?" Johnson's voice boomed.

"Me."

"Dean Johnson, Johnson Realty. Do you even understand what 'realty' means?" Charles said nothing, and Johnson was forced to continue. "I have a very significant offer for you, one that may be worth a lot of money."

At this point, the faces of both Miss Agatha and Jimmy turned, and they looked at Dean Johnson. But just when he felt that he was gaining control of the situation, their eyes wandered back to the blond woman in the silver sequined gown turning over the letters on the TV screen. Experience told them that, no matter what Mr. Johnson promised, their chances were better that the blond woman would walk out into the room and fill it with dollars. Charles said nothing, but began making chewing motions with his lips.

"Do you mind if I sit down?" Johnson boomed again. When no one said anything, he sat down on the edge of Miss Agatha's bed with an air of gratitude. He had closed a lot of deals in crowded rooms above the blare of televisions, and he didn't expect Miss Agatha to offer him iced tea and cookies. He was happy that Charles was at least looking at him, though he worried that Charles might soon have to expectorate the thing in his mouth. Some day, he thought, I will close deals over polished oaken tables.

Johnson then shouted out his proposition to Charles.

"I am representing several clients who are looking for houses in the Fells Point area. These people are in a big hurry—you understand? They don't want to wait. I know you got that old falling-down house on Jasper Street. Some people like to fix up these old wrecks. They want to offer you $20,000 for that house. You look like a man who knows a good deal when he sees one.

"I know you don't have title to that house yet, but let me show you how easy I can make this. I can give you cash right now to convey any property you might inherit—you get the money right now, you sign over the papers whenever you get them. Or a straight contract to sell the house in the future. Or I can give you a thousand dollars for an option to buy."

The specific meaning of the words used by Johnson passed right over Charles's head. He had no exposure whatsoever to business terminology. Even if he had heard these words before, the incessant background noise of

71

TV, or radios, or of people screaming in the next room or in the next alley, or the glazy, interfering hum of the alcohol that had seeped deeply into the crevices of his brain, had formed during his entire life an impermeable barrier to understanding the kind of terms that Johnson used. But tonight he realized that it was only the words that he didn't understand.

Charles had been wondering all evening if he could be the kind of person that Aunt May thought he was. It was hard to be dignified, going through life not even understanding the words that other people were using. But Aunt May had no education herself, and that hadn't stopped her. Charles stared at Johnson's face and said nothing. Johnson, suddenly worried, started talking a little faster.

"If you don't want to sell, I will give you $500, today, just for giving my realty company the right of first refusal if you do decide to sell later. Are you interested now, sir? Five hundred today, and you still own the house. Am I going too fast? Take your time. And look at this."

At the end of this speech, Johnson fanned out on Miss Agatha's bed a sheaf of papers, each representing one of Charles's legal options. To make things simpler for Charles, he said, he then laid on each set of papers a $100 bill, and wrote with a felt marker on each paper the number of $100 bills which he would turn over to Charles *right now* for his signature. One of the papers had the number 200 on it. (Jimmy's and Miss Agatha's eyes tarried a little longer this time.)

Charles said nothing. All of his life, whenever he had earned any money, there had always been someone there fanning out the options in front of him. From the pimps in Detroit to the moonshiners in West Virginia to the card sharks and Bible sharps everywhere, there had always been someone to tell him what he wanted. And whatever he chose, he had always been told that it was a wise choice, that he was a smart man, a real gamer. There had been no one to tell him differently. He had always been proud of being a hard worker. He had been proud to be in the system at all, to have his money count, to see the choices fanned, see the fanners wait for him to choose. These bold and sometimes dangerous people had accepted him, and he had admired their wares without reservation. But none of these fanners, he now realized, were people that Aunt May would have even let sit on her front steps.

Charles's chewing motions stopped somewhere in the middle of Johnson's high-volume spiel, when he studied the man and came to the conclusion that he was desperate to get his hands on Aunt May's house. And he thought that it would be a sacrilege to sell her own house to a fanner. He decided that he would not tell this seedy real estate broker which pile of bills to turn over. The piles were all the same. None of them would do him any more good than the letters turned over by the sequined blond on the TV screen. They were all just selling their winks and their hellos, and he was ashamed of all the times he had let them suck the life out of him in the past. Aunt May's house, and its new owner, he decided, were not going that cheap.

On the way out the door, Johnson suddenly turned bitter. "They're going to take it from you anyway, stupid old coot! The white man's going to take it. They're going to contest the will. They'll reassess and tax you to death. Or they'll condemn it cheap. You'll have code violation notices that look like the telephone book. They'll squeeze it out of you and you won't have so much as a nickel to show for it. I was going to cash you out and take the heat. But you won't let a brother in on the action, and now there's going to be nothing left when they get finished with you."

Charles closed and bolted the door. He worked his way

back up the steps to his room. He lay down on his bed without taking his clothes off. Two windows, each propped up by a short, expandable screen, let in the noise from the street. Scores of people outside were partying on their steps, hanging on the corners or playing radios in the sultry air. Charles worried that maybe Johnson was right. It did seem that a lot of people besides himself wanted the property. He didn't know if this was normal or not. He was surprised how hard you had to fight just to keep what was yours.

He felt a new shot of pain in his stomach that curled him up on the bed. He could taste bile in the back of his throat. He could have used Johnson's money to go see a doctor. But he didn't want to sell Aunt May's house. The spasm lasted for three or four minutes. Then he got up, took his clothes off and lay under the sheet in the stagnant air with the light still on. He lay awake for a long time. The pain reminded him that he had failed in his mission to get a lawyer so he and Jimmy could get their Medical Assistance cards.

He reached out for his pants on the floor and pulled his Medical Assistance rejection letter from the back pocket. The letter itself gave no information as to how his income and assets had been calculated. His eyes wandered across the page in search of clues. He noticed the red and black letterhead of the Department of Public Welfare, and the pretentious printed signature: "Brendan Gotterdung, Secretary." He thought that he might try to go and see this Mr. Gotterdung, if there really was such a person.

He liked his new lawyer. He hadn't been able to get a Medical Assistance card, but he had received something more important, a message that had been waiting fifty years for him. Charles had been an eager worker all of his life, but he had always been thrashing around blindly, uncertain if he was meant to be anything of significance. What he felt now was an utter certainty that Aunt May's house was meant for him, and that he must keep it at any cost.

7 TRICKS

So subtle was Slidell's legislative scheme that it was not until months after it took effect that anyone knew that he had had anything to do with the bill, and it was even longer before anyone had any idea why. So unlikely was the alliance he had forged that not one of the score of newspaper reporters, or the hundreds of his colleagues, who had seen him conferring at the back of the committee room with the plainly dressed young woman with the beautiful dark eyes, had guessed for a moment that she was an essential part of the conspiracy. She was, everyone soon realized, Sister Elena, a nun from Baltimore. You had to talk to nuns, and you had to do it politely, and Slip was the best in the business at this.

Slip was on a first-name basis with all of the religious powers in his district. Although he had done most of them a favor now and then in his many years in office, he had generally adopted a strict view of the necessity of the separation of religion from government. He had therefore not let scruples of any kind interfere with his manipulation of the legislative process. Nor did any scruples prevent Slidell from manipulating religious personages themselves, in cases where it served his own purposes. In the case of his plot for revenge against Crosley Pettibone, Slidell

76

hadn't hesitated to make expedient use of Sister Elena.

Just before the beginning of the legislative session in Annapolis, Sister Elena had asked Reverend Bain, a delegate, to put in a bill for her. The purpose of the bill was to slow down the displacement of poor people by the massive real-estate development and speculation afoot in Fells Point. Sister Elena, who wore a dark blue dress instead of a habit, ran a soup kitchen on Jasper Street in Fells Point. As soon as she asked, Reverend Bain had agreed graciously and without hesitation to help her. It was his policy to put in any and all bills that the decent people in his community wanted. For this reason, his bills were secretly regarded with scorn, sloughed off to the bottom of the committee's calendar, then politely listened to and killed.

When this particular bill met such a different fate, the entire legislative community was shocked. Everyone knew that the bill's notorious success had nothing to do with Bain. Many believed that it was entirely due to the mysterious powers of that remarkable young nun.

When thirteen-year-old Elena had explained to her father that she wanted to become a nun, he held back his opinion. To his wife, he confided that he didn't think that a vocation as a nun would provide her with enough people to boss around.

Elena came from a long line of strong-minded women. She felt that God had called her to be a nun, but she decided that He was leaving all of the details up to her. She knew that she wanted to help people *directly*. She saw how others who wanted to help change the world often got their own egos tangled up in their projects, and spent most of their energy wrestling with other people's egos. She was determined that her life would be simpler.

She had hardly become an official nun before she left

the order. She had visited some friends who worked in a soup kitchen in Canton, in Southeast Baltimore. There she saw, in the wrinkled, blank face and emaciated alcoholic stare of her very first customer that day, the face of all those who hunger and thirst, not for justice—they did not ask for justice, which was something she could not promise anyway—but just for bread. And bread was something that she *could* give. Elena believed she had found her vocation.

She stayed. Within two years she had set up her own soup kitchen on the fringe of the bar district of Fells Point. It was an area preferred by alcoholics, as there were plenty of empty buildings the speculators hadn't bothered to board up tightly enough, plenty of bar customers to bum a dollar from at night.

She dunned the Polish and Italian Catholic churches in the area, and the archdiocese itself, for money. When making these financial raids, she always found herself dealing with men—pastors, archdiocesan charity officials—who were pretty well satisfied with their own organizations and the limits of what they could do. She managed to convince them, almost to a man, to help her in her mission. Some said it was the justice of her cause that inspired them, and some said it was her audacious spirit; but one young priest said very quietly one day that it was the fire in her eyes. She went back to her mission that day deeply bewildered, and she wondered if she should put her habit back on; but she decided, no, it would get in the way in the kitchen.

Elena had a special love for her alcoholic customers. She had never seen a poison that could ravage a face so thoroughly, yet still leave the person standing after fifty years. She had no experience in her own life with alcoholism, and she saw her customers as victims of a special curse, a strange suffering of the spirit that only Jesus

Christ could comprehend or cure. But as the country's bills for the excesses of the 80s came due in the 90s, the line of derelicts on the sidewalk outside her mission was infiltrated by larger and larger numbers of sober people: unemployed men, employed but abandoned mothers who couldn't afford to pay rent, families who couldn't afford security deposits or who had just been evicted.

It was not that she didn't try to help this new type of client. In fact, she redoubled her efforts to get money out of the local Catholic institutional pockets. A vocation, she was willing to admit, might have to change due to circumstances. She realized that the exact course of things was not always going to be entirely in her control. But with this whole cross-section of society marching through her kitchen every morning, she felt as though she were losing her special mission and was now becoming sort of a government agency, filling the gaps left by some comprehensive plan of deviant social engineering.

Speculators began to tighten their hold on the properties, and developers quickly marked off big sections of the neighborhood for themselves. Sister Elena was shocked that the local religious officials did nothing about this new trend. They seemed to be hoping, right along with the developers, that the low-income population would be pushed far enough away to become someone else's problem. Sister Elena saw that no one was speaking for the people of the neighborhood. She felt that she had to do it herself.

To enter the political battleground over Fells Point, she had to break her own rule about plans and schemes and egos. She meditated on her lifelong admiration of St. Francis of Assisi, who simply fed the poor until, by his example, simple human charity became an accepted doctrine in the entire western world. Now she was taking a different road, one not as simple, not as pure. But Sister

Elena had made up her mind on this, and when Sister Elena had made up her mind, there was *nobody* who could persuade her differently.

She approached Reverend Bain with the idea of slowing down this development in Fells Point. He agreed with her immediately. She was surprised that Bain did not even question her closely about the content of the bill she proposed. When he said that he would put in anything that she wanted, she thought that she had found a secret window into the realm of real power, and she pressed her point too far. Working with the rough copy of the bill returned from Legislative Drafting, she boldly crafted it into a comprehensive treatment of the issue, a law which said everything she really thought it should say. In doing so, she accomplished two things. First, she experienced a powerful thrill by writing a law that set out the way things really ought to be. Second, she doomed the bill to failure before it was even filed. For any bill that truly sets out into law one person's complete view of life and society has already found its maximum audience.

The stated purpose of the bill was to plan and finance in an orderly way the relocation of anyone forced to move because of any large redevelopment project in the city. The bill would have eliminated entirely the concept of the tough break for anyone unlucky enough to be in the path of any intended development. In fact, as one lobbyist later pointed out, it made so many promises to anyone in the intended development area that it would entice people to move *into* the path of any intended construction. It would have tripled the cost of acquiring properties, and it would have immediately paralyzed all large construction projects in the Baltimore metropolitan area.

The bill reflected Sister Elena's priorities. All she saw was the suffering her poor clients were undergoing as they were pushed out of their neighborhoods by the grandiose plans of others. She did not see any way in which massive redevelopment was benefiting the ordinary people who actually lived in the area at all. So the bill basically did away with it.

The day after Slidell first realized the potential of the bill for advancing his own career, he called Bain.

"I know very little about that bill, Senator Slidell. That bill is sister Elena's bill. Perhaps you'd like to meet with her."

"I believe I would, Delegate Bain."

Sister Elena's bill was politely, courteously and respectfully left off of the hearing calendars for the first six weeks of the session. This factor in itself cut down the bill's chance of passage to about zero. Maryland had only a three-month legislative session, and getting on the hearing calendar was just the first step in a long and tortuous legislative process. Even a bill completely without controversy (or effect) would have difficulty if heard so late in the session. And Elena's bill was calculated to offend just about every business group and profession that had anything to do with land, buildings, real estate, construction, conveyancing, financing, road repair, architecture, zoning, code enforcement, renewal projects, historical trusts or government contracts. As Sister Elena talked to the first few delegates about her bill, she noticed their eyes first pop, then politely glaze over with meaningless sincerity. She realized that she might have gone too far.

The bill prohibited any governmental approval of any project in Baltimore City which was of a value of over ten million dollars unless the relocation plan was implemented. Although this seemed like a reasonable plan to Elena, the idea that private developers should have responsibility for those less powerful, whose lives were in the way of their plans, was revolutionary. And, in truth, this bill did more than assign a modicum of responsibility to those developers; it actually placed *all* of the responsibility there. The line of lobbyists champing at the bit to testify against the bill would have stretched all the way out of the committee room and down the streets of Annapolis to the doors of the Maryland House Bar—thus providing an opportunity for the lobbyists to persuade an equal number of committee members at each end. But there would be no need for this onslaught of purchased persuasion if the bill didn't even get on the hearing calendar before the first of March.

"You're saying that the only way I can get my bill on the hearing calendar is to make it meaningless. If that's true, then I'm powerless here, and I might as well go home."

The young woman with the dark eyes spoke with such vehemence that Slidell was momentarily thrown off-balance. Most people with bills to push were obsequious in their courtesy to the powerful legislative chairman. Sister Elena had quickly accepted Slidell's dinner invitation, but she was not acting impressed with Slidell's power, or with his plans. As soon as she heard that he wanted to amend the bill, taking out all of its important provisions, she got up to leave.

Slidell suddenly reached across and put his fingertips on her wrist. "Please stay."

The gentleness of the gesture from the world-weary politician caught her off-guard. She looked at his hand. Slidell, who had twisted a thousand arms and slapped a million backs in his long and checkered political career, was suddenly embarrassed. He pulled back his hand, sat back in his chair and took a sip of ice water.

This was the first year that Slidell had ever lived in Annapolis full-time during the legislative session. He was not enjoying himself since his wife had left him. In the past year, his sons had both gone, one to college and one to the Navy. The *Baltimore State* had published a column speculating that his political influence had peaked. He had been thinking too much, entertaining middle-aged doubts about the value of his life in general. As Elena sat down again at his request, he stared at her with curiosity and admiration. He wondered how much different his life might have been if he had had a daughter. He had to force himself to concentrate on his plan.

"All these things are the simple truth," he insisted quietly. "The bill just won't pass. It's not on the calendar yet. It probably won't even get a hearing. Even if it does get a hearing, it won't come to a vote—nobody wants to vote against a nun. The official sponsor, Reverend Bain, won't even make a fuss when it's killed in the back room. All this stuff—surveys, relocation grants, social work, escrow funds, bonding—it's not going anywhere. But what do you really want? Just to slow down this high-rise mania in Fells Point a little, so people have time to get out of the way?"

"I want the city to take some responsibility for the families that are pouring through the doors of my soup kitchen with no place else to go. I don't want another thousand families wandering around homeless. These people can't afford rent in new places. Fells Point might look a lot fancier when it's completely redeveloped, but I can tell you that these people will be out on the street."

"Maybe ..." he said, looking at her closely. His plan seemed to be working. "... we could get something passed that is not quite so far-reaching and radical, but which will still slow down development. Isn't it more reasonable to accept half a solution than to insist on everything and get nothing?"

"What do you mean, half a solution?"

"I can't tell you," he said enigmatically. Slidell was capable of looking extremely enigmatic, with his thick shock of pomaded white hair, his icy green eyes, his chiseled but well-worn Irish face, his thin-cut grey mustache.

"But I need a couple of promises from you," he continued. He listed the things she must do. She must not question any amendments put on the bill. She must support it all the way through the process, no matter how it was amended. She must never mention his name in connection with it.

"So I'm supposed to just have faith?" she huffed.

"I'm just saying, Sister Elena .... Who is Saint Elena anyway? I never heard of her."

"There is none. That's my real name. You can just call me Elena, Senator."

"Call me Samuel."

"That's your real ...?"

"Yeah," he said, "there's no Saint Slip." Elena thought she saw a trace of bitterness around his mouth.

"All I'm saying, Elena," he continued, "is, when somebody's trying to help you, don't let your ego get in the way. A lot of the time down here bills get lost because people would rather go down in glorious flames than take away a little piece of what they came for."

"I didn't come here to play ego games. I'm very wary of that happening."

"Then you might have some success."

"But I can't go along with your plan," she said flatly, getting up quickly from the table. Elena did not suffer for long the company of those whom she could not manipulate for her own purposes. She had already begun to blank him out of her mind. But Slidell glanced up at her as she passed his chair, and she was arrested for a second by his penetrating eyes. He looked sad and resigned, so earnestly clean-cut in his old-fashioned way. She put her hand on the shoulder of his tailored suit jacket. She felt that she had to explain.

"How do I know if it's just my ego? How can I tell if what I'm being offered is good enough unless I try for a little more by myself? It's my first time doing this. Do you understand why I have to try for more?"

After she left, he ordered a drink and sat staring into it. He was hurt more than he should have been by Sister Elena's implication that he wasn't good enough. He knew that it might have something to do with his having been told basically the same thing by his own wife two years earlier. Probably, he thought, Elena *should* try things out for herself. All the really important things had to be learned by experience. But he still felt hurt, and unnecessarily slighted, like the home-town boy whose girl rejects him for no better reason than to try out a few more men.

The next day, a bill providing $50,000 in grants for Sister Elena's soup kitchen was introduced by Slidell. Under a suspension of the rules it was read on the Senate floor and assigned to the Health and Welfare Committee that first day. Normally, such a bill would have almost no chance of passage. Under a longstanding Maryland constitutional provision, the governor had to submit to the legislature a balanced budget early in the legislative session. The job of the legislature was basically to pass it as submitted. Technically speaking, there were ways for the legislators to add expenditures on their own. They could create a new tax, or they could cut out a specific part of the governor's budget and reassign it to their own pet project. But each of these methods constituted virtual political suicide. Neither was ever successfully employed. As a result, the legislature had almost no say in the programs and finances of the machinery of state government—a fact which the citizens of the state instinctively acknowledged by ignoring their elected state legislators completely.

A common way of avoiding this problem was to pretend that a new program had no cost. The legislator would simply assert that the existing bureaucracy could squeeze his proposal in under its present budget. If the legislator wasn't particularly popular around Annapolis, the answer would simply be: no, it will cost millions of dollars. If there was a strong push behind the bill, a war of nerves would begin among the legislature, the bureaucracy involved, and the governor's office, during which the estimated cost of the program might range from five million to zero and back again. All of this was accepted as normal. What was really unusual was for a bill to provide for a direct grant of a specific amount of dollars. Something like this couldn't be disguised. It was going to cost money. The money had to come from somewhere.

Slidell's bill was given an almost immediate hearing in the Health and Welfare Committee, and Slidell showed up to speak for it—the first test of how seriously a legislator took his own bill. He was later seen in an animated, whispered conversation at the back of the room with a dark-eyed woman. "She's a nun," was the word passed around the U-shaped convocation of desks at which the committee members sat during the hearings. Their eyes were distracted past the next speaker toward the intense, whispered conversation taking place at the back of the room; but their puzzled looks changed to knowing smiles as the word reached each of them. It was a soup kitchen nun, one of Slidell's constituents, a beneficiary of the bill.

"What are you doing?" Sister Elena fairly hissed at Slidell.

"Sister..."

"Don't give me this sister crap! My bill doesn't even have a hearing date. Do you think you can buy me off for $50,000? That wouldn't pay for one month's rent for all the people who will be kicked out of their homes in Fells Point."

Slidell nodded, like a fighter ducking to avoid the full force of a blow. He put his face full up to hers, unrepentant, and whispered. "Do you oppose this idea of giving money to soup kitchens? Is the idea too small for you?"

"I can't stand the way you play God," she hissed, "sitting there so competent and composed and relaxed, telling me what we can get, and what we can't."

"A little bit of money is better than a big, useless fight with everybody in Annapolis." His eyes were a bit weary, his face looked as if it had been battered from within, but he stared unblinkingly, vulnerable but unapologetic, at the wide seething eyes of the young nun. He'd never seen anger in so pure a form.

Elena was not like Slidell. She batted things down that got in her way. She only played games that she could win with her energy and her smile alone, games where there were only as many people involved as she could keep confused or charmed at the same time. To her, Slidell was a representative of a colder, more complicated, less worthy world. She would have felt better about the $50,000 grant if he had tried to convince her that this was all that he could do. But they both knew he could do more.

The man distracted her. He kept her dissatisfied with her own performance on her newly chosen political battleground. Slidell was too smart and self-aware to be dismissed as just another political buffoon. Vulnerable as his resigned green eyes made him seem sometimes, she knew by the complacency in them now that there were obstacles she could not move, hearts she could not touch. Her wrath boiled around him like water around a boulder in a mountain stream.

"I don't know what coming down here has done to me." She was not whispering anymore, but intoning in a deep exhausted voice, her eyes looking off to the side as if she were talking to herself. She didn't want to catch Slidell's eyes. They were too honest. They knew the limits of everything. Maybe they had her number. She was infuriated that the world could be so complex, and so cold, and that she couldn't find a secret opening to get to the heart of the matter. One reason she liked her soup kitchen was that she liked the directness of it. She liked actually handing a plate of food to a hungry person. And she liked campaigning for its support and *demanding* its rightful share from the local churches and organizations. But she was foundering here in Annapolis. She knew that this slightly sad, green-eyed man was using her, but she didn't know if this was good or bad; she only knew that she was not in control, and that she did not like that feeling at all.

She heard her name called. Governor Mallard's lobbyist had just finished testifying, listing in tedious detail all of the governor's efforts to help the poor this fiscal year, stating that there was simply no money in the budget for this bill, subtly challenging the legislators to come up with a new tax to pay for it, then taking the heat off by saying that the governor would veto any new tax anyway. Then he joked with the committee members about something that was in the press last week about the vice chairman. His attitude was that of a slightly superior buddy of the committee members who was really enjoying talking with them, but who had more important things to do. As soon as he finished, he strode out of the room quickly.

Elena had hoped to have more time to think about what she was going to say. About what she was going to do. But there really was no choice. As she stepped up to the little wooden lectern facing the committee, the weight of her responsibility to her clients fell on her spirit and helped her tolerate feeling like a dog groveling after a bone that Slidell might throw her. It was a bone that her poor people needed, so she went up to the podium and performed her tricks for it. She said she wanted the money, could use it; she gave a few examples of how much it was needed.

"But you just heard the governor's man say that there isn't any money for it. Where would the money come from?" the committee chairman asked.

Elena's dark hair briefly shimmered as she shook her head. "I haven't the faintest idea." Her voice dropped low, her syllables sounded almost hoarse. "But Senator Slidell was kind enough to introduce this bill on his own initiative, and I'm sure he wouldn't have done so unless he had in mind some way of paying for it."

Sister Elena was correct. As he had for the last ten years the Comptroller had underestimated the amount of tax revenues for the coming fiscal year. As had often happened in the past, his analysts were able to come up with a more precise (and higher) figure at just about the time that the governor noticed that his pet bills seemed to be stalled in several key committees, among them Slidell's Employment Matters Committee. When the new, corrected mathematics were done, it turned out that there was, after all, enough revenue to fund just a few especially meritorious bills. Within a few days of the hearing, the governor submitted a supplemental budget bill to fund the entire amount sought for Slidell's soup-kitchen.

With the money problems out of the way, the bill fairly flew out of the Senate. The only question raised in the House was whether it was fair to fund a bill that would benefit only one particular soup kitchen. So many delegates needed Slidell's help in one way or another that he could have called in his favors and bulldozed this idea through; but it didn't seem right to him to give money away to the homeless and to be criticized for it at the same time. So a compromise was reached, and the bill redrawn in such a way that the money would be shared with two other soup kitchens, one in West Baltimore and one in Prince George's County. In the Baltimore *Free American,* Joe Keane mentioned Slidell's apparently spontaneous generosity in a short column which was deftly worded in such a way that you could almost hear Joe's eyebrow raised. Voting for the bill was a small price for anyone to pay for staying on Slidell's good side. After the House Committee approved it, the bill made it right to the top of the very next voting calendar in the House, and it passed unanimously.

Only Slidell knew that the state had just paid $50,000 for a decoy.

Mayor Crosley T. Pettibone's biggest political weakness was his inability to figure out who would be antagonized by any course of action he was planning to take. He expected to have some enemies, but they always seemed to arise from nowhere and come after him personally. Part of the problem was that his own staff was too terrified to tell him that there were bound to be people who disliked his plans. His staff was also afraid to tell him any bad news. When something bad happened as result of one of his plans, his staff would insist an enemy had foiled it. When these new enemies popped up from nowhere, Pettibone smashed them. But there always seemed to be more.

When Slip Slidell secretly took over the shepherding of Sister Elena's original bill into law, he knew that Crosley Pettibone would soon, once again, be surprised at a new coalition of enemies. And since Slip was the only one involved with the bill whom Pettibone already did classify as an enemy, he made sure that his name would never be mentioned in connection with the bill until it was too late.

The red herring soup-kitchen bill had passed easily, but Sister Elena's original bill would not have such smooth sailing. Pressed and pressed again by Elena, the committee chairman grudgingly agreed to put the bill on the hearing calendar.

"Sister, there isn't enough time in a year to hear all the people who will sign up to testify against this bill," Chairman Ruffage said, flirting as closely to sarcasm as you could when talking to a nun. "But I think I saved the committee some time. I've personally promised eleven different groups that this bill will not get out of this committee, and so they don't even have to testify. So I'm gonna put it on the calendar right away. Take your shot."

Technically speaking, Chairman Ruffage did not keep his promise to the many groups lined up against the bill. The bill did come out of committee with a favorable recommendation, though it was amended so heavily that it posed a threat to absolutely no one by the time it reached the House floor. It also was totally meaningless. It became known as "The Nun's Bill," and its provisions were watered down until they accurately reflected the legislature's total fear of anything that would slow down any kind of development. The amended bill provided, after twenty-three pages of crossed-out original text, that it was the sense of the legislature that an outside group should be formed to study the effects of massive development on the homeless. Even this was a little off the mark, as the problem was not those who were homeless already, but those who were going to be made homeless.

When the nun's bill passed the House in this form, Sister Elena decided that she would be better off spending her time putting food directly on plates in Baltimore. After she abandoned Annapolis, however, the bill was amended in the Senate to request that the State Housing

Department conduct the study. This meaningless provision conflicted with the equally meaningless House provision. The bill was sent back to the House, along with over a hundred others, on the last night of the session. To the extent that it crossed anybody's mind, the House members were willing to go along with the Senate's version; but Chairman Ruffage, who had just returned to the House floor after a brief conversation with Slidell in the lounge, acted confused about the Senate's wording. The bill was therefore sent back to the Senate as disapproved. A conference committee consisting of two members of the House and two members of the Senate was appointed at 11:45 p.m. to see if the two houses of the legislature could agree on a compromise and have it voted on by midnight.

Although 21 different conference committees were appointed to compromise 21 different bills in those last fifteen minutes of the session, this particular conference committee was the only one to reach agreement in time for a midnight vote. Of the four members of this conference committee, only three felt that this bill was worth spending time on in the last night of the session. One of the three had an attack of diarrhea and missed the conference completely. The other two met as a subcommittee of the conference. The subcommittee member from the House said he didn't care what the bill said as long as "all the crap about business and titles and banks and zoning" stayed out.

The remaining member of the committee was a sixty-year-old freshman senator from Baltimore. Ely Schatzenhauser was from southeastern precincts of the city and was a lifelong member of the Deep Devotion Democratic Club. He pulled an old-fashioned fountain pen out of his pocket. The conference committee member from the House smiled, thinking that the old man was taking this too seriously.

"Well, let's just write something noncontroversial about a study." Schatzenhauser appeared nonchalant, but he quickly started writing on the bill.

Within minutes, the conference committee of two had agreed to adopt Schatzenhauser's language. Three minutes later, the conference committee compromise was brought back to the Senate, where it mysteriously jumped over a number of bills ahead of it on the calendar and was passed without being read by the clerk. Five minutes later, a similar process took place in the House, and the new bill was enacted with two minutes to spare.

If any legislators had actually had the chance to see the bill, they would have noticed a slight change of emphasis from the bills that originally passed each house. The bill still provided that a study of the effects of development must take place. It still provided that the results of the study would not be binding on anyone, or have any official effect. But the bill now stated that no massive development could take place in the city of Baltimore until the study was *completed*. And it now required that the study be conducted by the State Department of Public Welfare.

"What you have to do now..." Slidell had found that he had to explain everything very carefully to Gotterdung, "is to get the governor to sign the bill into law. Pettibone will be trapped. He can't go ahead with Waterside Towers until your department does the study. Your department won't do the study until he meets our terms."

Three weeks later, Gotterdung called Slidell back, reaching Slidell at his unofficial office at the back of Eddie's Restaurant in Fells Point.

"He did it! He signed the bill!" Gotterdung was exultant, but Slidell noticed that the voice on the phone was muted, as if Gotterdung was afraid that someone would hear through the walls of his office. "We'll be running the state by next January!"

"We'll have a shot."

"We've got Pettibone by the balls," Gotterdung gloated. "Nothing can go wrong."

8 RHYME, BUT NO REASON

Mayor Crosley T. Pettibone's black-windowed limousine hissed to a stop in front of the Department of Public Welfare building, sliding in to the curb between a hot dog stand and a chrome lunch wagon. Pettibone jumped out quickly and strode across the small courtyard. His chief aide and his bodyguard followed frantically behind. Pettibone knew that something was wrong. This meeting with Secretary Gotterdung should not have been necessary at all.

Not a lowdown bureaucrat, but a slowdown bureaucrat. Pettibone had known Gotterdung for years as a fellow member of the Northwest Political Club. But, mysteriously, Gotterdung was not cooperating with him now. It could not be that Gotterdung had had a sudden attack of obstinacy, or courage. It had to be that the pressure hadn't been correctly applied.

Pettibone held a staff meeting every week, and he made it clear there that he did not like to hear about problems. At these meetings, only solutions could be discussed. This made life much simpler for Pettibone, and he left his office feeling good about all that he had accomplished. He was proud of his top executive staff; anyone with difficult opinions had long ago been weeded out. Pettibone

95

enjoyed his job. He thought that these meetings were fun. The same could not be said of his executive staff. Each week, each staff member had to report one solid accomplishment, and one plan for next week's agenda. Those who pussyfooted around and tried to pass off intangible items as progress were told that they needed two accomplishments the next week—if they were lucky enough to get a next week. City Hall quickly learned that when Pettibone spoke of concrete accomplishments, he meant that almost literally. Anything concerning building, construction or repair could be safely reported. Anything else, Pettibone suspected, was fake. His idea of effective government was to have the city maintenance chief get up in the middle of the night and pay six men overtime to repair a pothole the mayor had noticed on the way home that evening.

Because it served his ends so well in other ways, Pettibone couldn't see how inefficient his method of governing really was. Since all his bureau chiefs were competing like excited children for the chance to carry out his every command, his every command became their only real agenda. Performance of the normal, routine, and repetitive functions of a city government department was considered boring by Pettibone; thus, his departmental heads adopted the same attitude. They concerned themselves only with the things that Pettibone was likely to ask about. Consequently, if an ordinary resident of the city had a problem and wanted anything actually done, there was little chance of a quick response from the department that was supposed to be handling that problem. Instead the resident would have to come to Pettibone personally and ask it as a favor. Then, if Pettibone agreed, the favor would be granted and accomplished with lightning speed. Pettibone thus took on more of the attributes of a king than an executive. This made him feel good.

This system of government also kept out of positions of power any employees who weren't willing to grovel before him. Those staff members who wanted to survive in this atmosphere had to be willing to do *anything* the mayor wanted, and to do it *when* the mayor wanted it done. To save their own sense of self-respect, these surviving employees had to convince themselves that the mayor was some kind of political genius, a veritable prophet of a new kind of city government, a man who was magically almost always right. Mayor Pettibone's staff spoke to the press, to other government officials, and even among themselves, as if the mayor were God himself. This made Pettibone feel even better.

Although the next election for governor was almost six months away, Pettibone's chief of staff, Fosback, and a lot of Pettibone's other top aides, were already acting as if they were state officials themselves. Fosback himself planned to have Gotterdung's job in the coming Pettibone gubernatorial administration. Fosback treated Gotterdung, and the rest of Governor Mallard's staff, as lame ducks whose only remaining function was to line up and beg for a spot on Pettibone's second string.

But Fosback was worried now. The fact that this matter even had to be brought to Pettibone's personal attention was a black spot on Foster's career.

"You're screwing up the mayor's development plans for Fells Point."

Fosback had began his first phone conversation with Gotterdung bluntly. After two weeks of trying unsuccessfully to get Gotterdung on the phone, he had been impatient, and worried.

Fosback had been surprised that Gotterdung had not returned his call. Gotterdung should have been only too happy to do a favor for the mayor. Was Gotterdung just too simpleminded a buffoon to return a call from the

97

mayor's office promptly? Pettibone's ego was so large, and the force of his temper so strong, that instant compliance with his wishes was the normal course of events. Gotterdung's failure to return his calls should have been a warning signal to Fosback.

In that first phone call Fosback spoke to Gotterdung in general terms about the mayor's "redevelopment plans in the Fells Point area." He did not use the official title, because the project was still a secret. A confidential memo about the official title had already been passed around. No one in the Pettibone administration was ever to refer to the project, either at City Hall or in public, by any other title than its full legal name: the Mayor Crosley T. Pettibone Waterside Towers Luxury Condominium Development.

"You have to do a study," Fosback shouted into the receiver. "It's a new law. Some lawyer for the bank just found it. We have several important projects ready to go. The financing packages are in place, and all the papers are all ready to be signed. But the banks won't release the funds until your department completes this relocation study."

There was a pause on the other end of the line.

"Did I go too fast? Do you get it? There's some kind of meaningless study your department has to do. It has no effect on anything, but it has to be done. The mayor can provide any technical help that you need. What he wants is your commitment that it will be done by Monday afternoon. Do you understand?"

"You're talking about the Pettibone Waterside Towers project." Gotterdung's voice was cold. "Your timetable for my department completing the relocation study is not feasible at all."

Fosback took a very deep, disturbed puff on his cigarette and blew the smoke into the receiver.

"This study is really a very minor thing, Mr. Secretary. I'd hate to have to go to the mayor personally on this. He's awfully busy, so frustrated, really ... all the delays already."

"I can understand why he's concerned." Gotterdung's voice sent a chill through him.

"I hope you are not saying that *you* are not concerned."

"Of course I'm concerned."

In the Pettibone administration, there was only one acceptable answer for not having accomplished what the mayor wanted done. Pettibone did not want to hear of faithful but fruitless effort, or of the time necessary to overcome political and legal obstacles, or—especially—of the differing opinions of others about the matter. The only acceptable reason for something not getting done was that an enemy of Pettibone's was deliberately confounding his plans. Fosback had failed. But he knew how to locate an enemy.

Fosback was always the first to jump up at staff meetings to volunteer to satisfy every whim and wish of the mayor. Pettibone required that everything—from fixing potholes to publicizing a new program to putting curtains on the windows of city-owned houses—be done immediately, and personally, by his highest staff members. Fosback eagerly volunteered to carry out even the most ridiculous and degrading of these chores; and he attacked them with relish. He loved to use the mayor's name to throw a quiver of fear into someone who had never heard the name Fosback. Because of this eagerness, Fosback was very popular among the rest of Pettibone's executive staff. They treasured the secret little hoard of personal dignity that they managed to maintain by letting Fosback do the worst of these errands.

But Fosback had now let Gotterdung string him along for two weeks without giving him an answer. Gotterdung did not seem intimidated at all. Fosback was now in danger of being considered by the mayor as a man who could not apply the necessary pressure. And a man who could not apply the necessary pressure, he knew, need not apply for a high position in the Pettibone administration.

"No man worse than a slow man / Better a po' man than a slow man."

The bodyguard opened the thick glass doors, and Pettibone and Fosback stepped into the spacious, terrazzo-tiled entrance lobby of the Department of Public Welfare building. The Mayor sneered at the sparsely decorated walls. The room was not designed for opulent effect, but for changes in the unemployment rate of a fraction of a percent that would flood the building with unemployment claimants. Pettibone smirked at the spartan emptiness of the lobby anyway. *"A cheapskate gets nothing done / The people with the money want to have some fun."*

Pettibone rolled his eyes dramatically when the elevator doors clattered open and the elevator itself stopped about four inches below floor level. It was already crammed with sullen-looking people, many of whom had some type of snack balanced in their hands. Pettibone, of course, had no way of knowing that this was their third attempt to get out of the basement, and that this was the highest they'd gotten yet. Fosback and the bodyguard immediately moved as if to protect the mayor from mixing with this crowd. They tried to steer him to another elevator. But Pettibone's every instinct was attuned to the necessity of showing these men constantly who was the boss. He sensed their suppressed horror at having to come into close physical contact with this group of shirtsleeved men and flat-heeled women. Pettibone stepped down into the elevator and quickly turned around to enjoy watching his henchmen scramble. They gulped down their hesitations and followed, lurching into the elevator, forcing the crowd inside to shuffle reluctantly even more toward the back.

The elevator doors didn't snap shut on their heels after all. The mayor and his aides waited at the opening, silent, watching the doors for signs of movement. They stood, breathing hard, for another forty-five seconds, while nothing at all happened. Pettibone was confused. He stared out of the doors and across the wide, empty lobby. The expressionless face of the receptionist there behind her massive wooden counter gave him no clue. Didn't anybody notice that nothing was happening? *"Dead in the water / dead on the land / dead in the elevator / dead in the sand."*

At last, the worn rubber gaskets that protruded from the edges of each elevator door wobbled toward each other, and the doors rattled closed. The elevator slowly rose in a defeated, exhausted way to the second floor, where it rested for a minute before it got up the energy to open its doors. Pettibone was astute enough to recognize the hypnotizing effect this had on the riders, who oozed out of the door like zombies, obviously having adjusted their pace over the years to this wheezy central engine of their workplace. By the time he got to the sixth floor, the elevator itself had confirmed Pettibone's suspicion that Gotterdung was just the type of lazy, careless, indifferent government official that he hated so much—the type of official who was unafraid because he was too lazy to be afraid.

Pettibone liked his officials afraid. Paradoxically, he admired no one so much as bold, decisive men who weren't afraid to break all the rules, thumb their noses at the public, contribute to his campaign and then tell him to keep the city the hell out of their business. He liked men who could make him squirm inside. *Squirm, squirm, the worm turns.* The real bottom line was that Pettibone didn't mind whether he himself was the squirmer or the squirmee. He saw that squirming was the essential force of government, and he felt a deep, almost physical satisfaction when playing either role, as if he found himself at those times taking his God-given place in the psycho-political food chain.

What Pettibone could not stand was someone who was totally indifferent to him, and this whole building smelled of indifference the way a state typing pool smelled of Wite-out and Avon product samples.

Just as Pettibone was stepping out of the elevator on the sixth floor, Brendan Gotterdung was in his office at the end of the hall, finishing a tense phone conversation with Slip Slidell.

"Everything's in place. Tell him what we want. Tell him about the unions now," Slidell instructed.

"Yeah, okay ... okay ..."

Gotterdung's hesitancy worried Slidell.

"Are you sure you can handle this? Do you want me to be there?"

"No, no. Tell him what we want. I can do it."

"Don't let him scare you." Slidell felt that his co-conspirator needed pumping up. "We hold all the cards. There's nothing he can do. Don't let him push you around. We've got the power. We're in charge."

"I know, I know. He's gotta do what we say."

"You gotta know," Gotterdung took the offensive immediately, "that I take this study seriously. The legislature takes the problems of the homeless very seriously. This department is going to do a serious study, in accordance with the will of the legislature. We will complete it in good faith—no matter how long that takes."

These words could not have been calculated more precisely to enrage Crosley T. Pettibone. Gotterdung could see their effect immediately, and he had to repress a triumphant smile. He had gotten an advantage over the mayor and his aides from the start of the meeting. His small office was arranged with his own massive vinyl chair behind a massive veneer desk, facing an extra-low three-seat sofa backed against the other wall. Once Pettibone, Fosback and the bodyguard sat down, they were immediately at a disadvantage. The sofa was so low that they couldn't even see out the windows, and they were lined up like schoolboys before the principal's desk. Only after the mayor and his aides were thus uncomfortably seated did Gotterdung call in Tynan and introduce him. Tynan carried in his own chair and set it well to the side before he sat down.

At Gotterdung's opening remarks, Pettibone's skin flushed red all the way from his white shirt collar to the topmost edges of his grey widow's peak. His aides on either side of him visibly cringed. Pettibone clenched his hands. Everyone could hear the sound of him grinding his teeth. Then his mouth opened slackly, and he began to mumble something under his breath. *You'll pay, you'll pay, you'll kiss my feet someday.* No one had the nerve to ask what he was chanting. Even Tynan, who was rarely at a loss for words, was awestruck. He wondered if the mayor was having a seizure. Fosback nervously lit up a cigarette.

Among Maryland politicians, talking about concepts like "the will of the legislature" was reserved for public occasions and court arguments. No one spoke about "the will of the legislature" *in private,* unless they were trying to hide their real purpose. Gotterdung's use of this phrase had been the giveaway. He was not only willing to stall, he was now challenging the mighty Pettibone, holding back the study on purpose. And he wouldn't even tell Pettibone what he wanted in return for completing the study.

The plan, as originally designed by Slip Slidell, involved much more than simple revenge on his archrival. But it was basically pretty straightforward. Mayor Pettibone's pet project would be stopped cold by this new legal obstacle, the requirement of the study, just at the point when the financing commitments were being made. The banks' lawyers would advise their clients to refuse any final commitments until this matter of the legally required study could be cleared up. To get this study business cleared up, Pettibone would have to come to Gotterdung.

And Pettibone would have to come to Gotterdung *in secret*. He could not afford to announce the Waterside Towers project publicly, since all of the properties in the tract had not yet been acquired. Revealing the project to the public now would also invite a lot of public comment and arouse some controversy. The mayor hated it when newspapers and radio talk show callers criticized his plans. And any type of controversy would make the banks think twice about their commitments. But the main reason that Pettibone would have to come in secret was not a political or economic reason at all. Slidell and Gotterdung had staked their careers on a hunch about Crosley Pettibone's psychological state. They were betting that Crosley Pettibone simply would not be able to admit in public that he'd been bamboozled.

When Pettibone came in secret to ask for Gotterdung's help, he was supposed to be told the price. The price was eighty million dollars for Slidell's new friends, the unionized workers of the state, and their representatives.

The unions still had a strong political foothold in Slidell's part of the city, and their cause still evoked some sympathy throughout the Baltimore and Washington metropolitan areas. Crosley Pettibone was supposed to be told that the study would not be released until the Bold Tip Development Company, the prime contractor on the Waterside Towers project, agreed to use union subcontractors. About one third of the $250 million project cost would be paid out in wages. Under Slip Slidell's plan, those wages would be union wages. The union leaders would be ecstatic, and a decent percentage of that huge payroll would inevitably find its way into the treasury of the Deep Devotion Democratic Club, and from there into the Slidell for Governor Campaign Committee. Slidell would be a hero to this massive and strongly organized interest group, and he would have a campaign treasury rivaling Pettibone's. He would be able to compete with Pettibone on even terms for the governorship of Maryland. For doing his part in not completing the study, Gotterdung would be rewarded with a spot on Slidell's ticket. Meanwhile, Pettibone's big-business backers would be deeply disappointed in him. They would wonder if Pettibone really was the kind of politician who could deliver the goods.

Slidell knew that Pettibone would rather eat dirt than voluntarily give over any part of the Waterside Towers project to organized labor. Pettibone had been openly quarreling with organized labor for years. The municipal workers' unions regarded Pettibone with loathing, and the feeling was mutual. Two basic unspoken tenets of the municipal union's credo, that workers were hired only to perform specific tasks, and that workers were always on the clock, were anathema to Pettibone, whose main enjoyment in life was the exaction of instant and precise obedience from his subordinates.

And Pettibone had lately come to alienate much more powerful labor interests when he hadn't bothered to conceal his scorn for the flagrant featherbedding enforced by the longshoremen and dock workers in the port. So the municipal workers and the longshoremen were now two sizeable groups willing to line up solidly together against Pettibone. The problem had been that there was no one to line up *with,* since no politician had been willing to take Pettibone on.

When Pettibone asked his business friends for advice, the idea of using union labor on any of his development projects was not one that spontaneously popped into their minds. In fact, it was well known that the Bold Tip Development Company, in its worldwide operations, avoided those projects in which there would be strong union involvement. T. Oscar Fundertow, now president of Bold Tip, had guaranteed his own future on the private enterprise lecture circuit when, as an Assistant Secretary of Labor in the first Reagan administration, he had made a widely publicized speech calling unions "a cancer on American competitiveness." Although his statement was disavowed and disapproved all the way up the governmental chain of command, his career underwent a transformation for the better from that moment on, and his meteoric rise carried him into the Cabinet within a few years.

It was only six months later that Bold Tip lured him away with promises of a salary and stock options so lucrative that a true believer in the positive power of greed could not refuse. Two years later Fundertow had gained Pettibone's personal assurance that Bold Tip could build Waterside Towers with a minimum of union involvement.

Of course, Susumee Development, the local enterprise, was cut in on the deal. Susumee, or a company owned by Susumee, was always in on the deal. It might as well have been written on the forms that any bid on any major construction project in Baltimore had to guarantee the participation of a local subcontractor connected to the Fiore-Cohen machine. Susumee itself could make a lot of money going either way, union or nonunion, but the word from Pettibone had been that the Waterside Towers project was to be strictly non-union.

With characteristic secrecy, Pettibone had kept this and every other aspect of the project out of the public eye for as long as he could. The construction unions, and the whole AFL-CIO, would have risen in opposition at an early stage, when it would have made a difference, had they known that there was a plan to exclude all union contractors and subcontractors. Had the unions known this, for example, Sister Elena's original bill would have had scores of supporters in the legislature, and their professed concern for the poor and displaced would have been a major topic of conversation during the session. But only one legislator had known all this back then, and Senator Slidell was now on the verge of channeling all that concern, all that fear of Pettibone and his arbitrary ways, all that anguish over losing $80 million worth of bread from the tables of union households—all of it into his well-timed and orchestrated campaign for governor. And he would be heralded, in this workingman's town, as the man who stood up to Pettibone and the big-money men on behalf of the working man.

"His Honor the Mayor doesn't seem to know what to say."

Gotterdung glanced at Tynan when he said this, as if Tynan were in on the joke. Tynan had not even been told what this meeting was about. He guessed that this was supposed to be some sort of lesson to him, given in Gotterdung's patented, patronizing way, about big-time, old-boy politics. He didn't understand why Gotterdung was antagonizing the mayor. He was glad that he hadn't

107

just gone ahead and completed the study, as he had been tempted to do.

Pettibone's face stayed red, and he started mumbling again. Fosback pretended that it was his own turn to speak. He used a threatening, arrogant tone that a subordinate can use only if he is absolutely sure that he has the boss's backing.

"Mr. Secretary Gotterdung, I know that the mayor is concerned in *many* respects about the efficiency of your department, since it affects so many of the poorer citizens of the city." Fosback stopped, to let his insult hang in the air. Whenever he traveled with the mayor, he carried with him a battery-powered ashtray that sucked the offending smoke out of his boss's eyes. He deliberately placed his cigarette on the chrome grill of the whirring little device.

"We don't want our study to be caught in some kind of bureaucratic slowdown...."

"*Not a lowdown bureaucrat / a slowdown bureaucrat!*" The mayor's words cut off Fosback.

Fosback waited respectfully for four beats, but nothing more was forthcoming from the mayor. Pettibone's eyes were open, but he gazed down at the floor, unfocused.

"I understand that your figures don't exactly add up on that crawlspace case. The mayor was considering lending the Municipal Auditing Department to the federal court, to help Legal Assistance make a really thorough study of your budget and caseload—get to the real cause of the problem, if you know what I mean."

Pettibone slowly raised his head and stared across the room at Gotterdung. His icy blue eyes were emphasized by the long face, the two spots of bald skin rising upwards from his brow, and the widow's peak pointing downward. Tynan had never seen such a look of pure hatred. Fosback's words alone had already caused drops of sweat to run down from Tynan's armpits.

Tynan's face showed no emotion, but his mind was racing. A true, thorough audit of the Medical Assistance records would be a disaster. He calculated what he would say if he were in Gotterdung's position. What was needed was some kind of threat that, if the crawlspace suit went badly, the city would be pulled down just as fast and just as far as the department. But Gotterdung couldn't counterattack like this, because he didn't know anything about his own department, or how it operated.

"Oh, that lawsuit's nearly over," Gotterdung replied blandly, with a wave of his meaty hand. "We've just about reached settlement with Legal Assistance on that," he continued, teaching Tynan by example that a bold and outright lie is sometimes just as effective as a subtle and sly one.

But Tynan could tell that, for all of Gotterdung's self-assurance, something was wrong. A meeting, even a meeting of enemies, was supposed to have a purpose. Gotterdung was enjoying himself too much, and Pettibone was too angry, for any deal to be cut. Gotterdung had not even revealed what he wanted, and he was flying too high now to stoop to explain.

"What is it that you want, you bastard?" Fosback blurted out.

"Your Honor, I don't think you need concern yourself with the study." Gotterdung smirked, ignoring Fosback entirely and staring back at Pettibone as if he had wanted this sort of power over the mayor for a long time. "We will proceed with all deliberate speed in completing that study, so you can build your little project when we're finished. Providing that we don't run into any special glitches in the crawlspace lawsuit, we'll be able to start work on the study in, say, two or three months."

Pettibone stood without a word and headed for the door, limping as if his foot had fallen asleep. Fosback quickly picked up his ashtray. He and the bodyguard almost stumbled over each other in their haste to follow. Gotterdung didn't seem concerned at all. He looked over at Tynan as they were leaving, with a smile of altogether too much enjoyment on his face.

"Leonard," he commanded, "make sure this study is assigned to Mallory."

9 TRIALS AND ERRORS

The voice on the other end of Sport's telephone was confident and businesslike.

"Sport Norris? Ken Kiger of Susumee Development. You have a client, Charles Gage? He gave me your name. We're buying some property in the Fells Point area. One of our real-estate people has a contract with Charles. He assigned his rights in 442 Jasper Street to us ...."

Sport's heart sank. He realized that he had to accept, for the hundredth time in his career, the fact that one of his clients had done the worst possible thing for himself. He had thought that Charles was different, and would show some mettle in this matter. But Sport's lawyerly duty was to swallow his own disappointment and salvage for Charles what he could.

He remembered seeing Kiger on television. Fortyish, lean and handsome, with thick greying hair, Kiger had looked uncomfortable wearing a suit. He looked like he had built all of his developments with his bare hands.

"What was the consideration for this contract?" His tone, suddenly more businesslike and calculating, put Kiger on the defensive.

"I can't discuss price," Kiger was very smooth. "I need to know if there's going to be any contest over this will.

111

Is it going to go through as is?"

"You're telling me you don't really have a signed document. You want to know how much to offer."

"Mr. Norris, I don't do business that way. We do have a signed contract. It's for $25,000. I've even seen the will, and it looks okay. If you want to get this over with and get your client his money, you could give us an idea of whether we can expect any obstacles."

This news wasn't all bad. At least Charles had gotten a decent price for the house—more than double the offer from Peck, Peck and Peck, in fact.

Sport had discovered that the state legislature, appalled at the extent of Pettibone's generosity towards some of Baltimore's wealthiest and most uncouth citizens, had stripped the city of some of its condemnation powers. Land for development could not be easily taken by the city. It would now have to be bought from the owners, at whatever price the market would bear. If 442 Jasper Street was in the way of a big development project, the bidding for the property might become frantic. Sport wondered if $25,000 was enough. He decided that the best thing to do right now was to stall.

"You may not have a legally binding contract. I haven't seen it."

Although there was no logical connection whatsoever between these two sentences, this was the kind of thing that lawyers said all the time. The implication, of course, was that the document didn't exist until the lawyer had seen and approved it. If lawyers were philosophers, they would have no difficulty dealing with the famous conundrum about a tree falling in the forest.

"I'll have to talk with my client. He had last indicated to me that he was not interested in selling the house. I can tell you that, even if everything goes smoothly, he won't have the power to convey the property for at least

... several months."

"But I was told that he's already living there!"

"Oh my God! I'd better check with him fast."

But after Sport hung up, he realized that he couldn't. In thirty minutes, he had to argue the crawlspace suit in federal court. The argument was on his motion to certify the class so that the case could go forward as a class action. The important point in this argument would be the "numerosity" issue. The federal court was not supposed to issue broad, sweeping orders unless it could be shown that there were so many people affected that it would be impractical for each one to file his own lawsuit. In other words, if there weren't a lot of people in the class, there couldn't be a class action. And there was another problem.

"We need a new named plaintiff to represent the class," he told Angela. "As we expected, the Department of Public Welfare reevaluated Mrs. Throckmorton's case. She got her Medical Assistance card the day after we filed suit."

"Don't worry about that point," Angela was professionally reassuring. "I've researched all the precedents on Rule 23. The only requirement is that the named plaintiff be really suffering the alleged wrong at the moment her suit was filed. We have that situation here, since Mrs. Throckmorton wasn't paid off until the next day. The statistical evidence is solid. There's no doubt that there are thousands of crawlspace people."

"I know you're right, Angela, legally. But I don't think it's all so simple."

A class action against a state government exposed any federal judge to criticism, not only from state officials but also from the higher federal courts themselves. Intervening in anything that was traditionally a matter of state business was generally frowned upon. The federal courts were so leery of interfering that they had invented a whole body of esoteric doctrines, all of which basically had the purpose of keeping the federal courts' profile low whenever they wished to avoid issuing orders to a state government.

"We've done all we can, legally. Angela, your brief could not have been better. But Judge Barnett has to *want* to do it. He has to care."

"I think you can make him."

"I hope so. Then we have to worry about the meeting with our own Director."

Following the court argument there would be a meeting with Doxie Clearwater about the lawsuit. The rumor was that the city and the state, who together kicked in a small percentage of the Legal Assistance Society's operating budget, were putting pressure on Doxie to drop the suit. From the point of view of the City of Baltimore and the State of Maryland, the Legal Assistance Society was just a grant recipient. They didn't like being sued by their own grantees. Sport had never seen Doxie tested before; but he suspected, from seeing Doxie's smooth, smiling, oily, glad-handing ways, that he hadn't gotten where he was by being willing to offend people with power over his program.

Charles was not alone in his new house. When he moved into Jasper Street, he took his friend Jimmy with him. There were two bedrooms, and he saw was no reason why he couldn't share his inheritance. Charles had emphasized to Jimmy that he would have to act differently now, because Charles was a homeowner, and he would not tolerate Aunt May's house being filled with trash. Jimmy had nodded, and Charles was satisfied with that response. But Charles had never noticed that Jimmy always nodded, and that Jimmy could barely remember his own address.

The part that Jimmy caught was that they had to act differently and take on some new responsibilities. Taking his cue from Charles, Jimmy tried to be accommodating to all of their new neighbors. Whenever someone came to the door of Charles's new house, Jimmy treated them with the gravest respect. If they asked to come in, he graciously invited them in. If they wanted to talk, he sat there, politely nodding. If they wanted him to sign a contract to sell the house, he scribbled his signature as well as he could. He sold the house three times in the first two days, once to a local speculator and twice to different agents working for Susumee Development. He also signed up for monthly deliveries of frozen meat, a subscription to the Catholic Review, and a diaper service. He joined the neighborhood Crimewatch Club and was assigned the special identification number EDO 26. There was a little badge that went with it. But after two or three days, all of these duties wore him down. He complained to Charles, but he couldn't put into words exactly what was wrong. He just didn't like being a homeowner.

"I like the other house better. Watch somebody's TV. Lights in the rooms. Water come out of the sink."

Charles was so intent on straightening out the house that he hardly noticed what Jimmy was doing. He wasn't sure if he'd inherited Aunt May's furniture, but he dusted it off and straightened it out anyway. The water and electricity were bigger problems. He had originally brought Jimmy over, one sweltering Sunday afternoon, just to see the house. The trip took them two hours on three buses. As soon as he saw the house again, Charles was overcome by the feeling that he belonged in this place. He knew that he wanted to stay in these rooms and let the remnants of Aunt May's life sink deeper into him. He thought that maybe his new smart lawyer would help him with whatever he had to do next.

Most of the houses on their side of the street were empty, so they had almost the whole block to themselves. There was a bar almost directly across the street where he could get water in buckets to pour into his toilet tanks. You could even buy sandwiches there. Everything had to be passed through a little revolving turret of bulletproof plastic. There were many people still living on the other side of the street.

Charles came in beaming one day. He had been talking with one of his neighbors outside of the liquor store.

"Jimmy. Know what they called Aunt May here when she was alive?"

"What?" Jimmy didn't even try to guess.

"All the folks on the block called her 'Aunt May.' That's something funny!"

"Yeah? So that's her name, right?"

Charles decided not to explain.

Even Jimmy noticed that Charles had a sickness that sometimes doubled him over with pain. "Why don't you go to a doctor, man?" Jimmy asked him every day. The immediate reason that Charles didn't go was that his Medical Assistance card had been taken away when he and Jimmy had both been assigned fictitious basements by the Department of Public Welfare. But even before then, he had not taken the tests that his old Medical Assistance doctor recommended years ago. He hadn't taken the tests, because he had been afraid of the results. Now, he wished that he had. Every day the pain came, and it insisted that he acknowledge it; but he didn't want to think about what it might be. On the third day, very early in the morning, when the house was momentarily quiet, and the pain had gone away, he allowed himself to think about it. But even then he kept it very simple. "If it's my time," he resolved, "I'll just have to go."

It rained hard the fourth day. In the back bedroom, where Jimmy was sleeping, water started dripping slowly down the walls. Charles was furious when he found out that Jimmy was ignoring it. But the explanation for Jimmy's silence was simple. Jimmy, like Charles, had spent a good part of his life in rooms that leaked when it rained, and he had learned that it didn't do much good to complain. He had never thought of doing anything about a problem like this himself. He hadn't had the ability. Charles hadn't either. Rain just came in sometimes. If it got bad enough, you moved.

But now, Charles organized an expedition to move Aunt May's furniture out of the back bedroom. Her beautiful mahogany furniture, he noticed, didn't have any signs of water damage, so he figured out that this leak must be something recent. Aunt May had lived there for almost fifty years, and she wouldn't have tolerated this kind of slow death for her house. Charles suddenly realized why. Unlike her nephew, Aunt May did not shrug her shoulders, or move away, or open up a bottle of wine. She took care of her things.

"She was a grownup!"

Charles stared into Jimmy's uncomprehending eyes.

He remembered how uncomfortable and sullen he had been as a boy when Aunt May had given him choices. Did he want gravy on his potatoes? Did he want beans or did he want rice? Did he want to go to the park, or go downtown window shopping? He had never quite understood what she was saying. At his mother's house, you got what you got, and you weren't expected to comment on it, ever. Later, when he began working, he never trusted any employer who offered him anything other than plain, hard labor. He had always skipped all of the preliminaries and raced for the back of the line. His resignation to this fate had for a while made it even more delicious when, as a young man with an occasional pocketful of money, he had chosen greedily from the wares of the fanners. But it had never occurred to him until now that this choosing was something he was entitled to do every day, and that most of it was free.

The choice he made this day was to take Jimmy and retreat back to their rooms in West Baltimore. He realized now that he didn't just want the house. He wanted the whole deal: lights, electricity, water, a way to fix the roof. He wanted to become the kind of person who could see a house problem coming up and would have a chance at doing something to head it off. And he recognized that he couldn't pull this off by himself.

Sport and Angela were encouraged by the sophistication of the hearing before the federal court on the crawlspace suit. Judge Barnett appeared to be completely aware of all the ramifications of class-action rulings. He had read both briefs, and he appeared familiar with the cases they were citing. The questions he asked were right on point, the very same ones that she and Sport had been preparing for all week. It was comforting to know that they didn't have to start from scratch, educating the judge on the basics of the law involved.

But Jody Hechtmuller, representing the Department of Public Welfare, put on a performance that stopped the case in its tracks. All the lawyers involved knew that Judge Barnett was not too sympathetic to this kind of class action brought by the Legal Assistance Society. But he was a good judge, and he would follow the law. Jody couldn't really beat them on the law. At the hearing, he suddenly assumed an entirely different persona. He wasn't the worldly lawyer whom Sport and Angela had been negotiating with for eighteen months. He pretended to be taken aback and disoriented by the whole idea of the lawsuit,

The Crawlspace Conspiracy

as if he'd just been dragged from his sleep into an overly bright room.

"Your Honor," he began, "the plaintiffs in this case, if we assume there are any plaintiffs—I haven't seen that yet, are represented by two really brilliant lawyers." He turned halfway toward Angela and Sport. They had enough experience not to be flattered, or to even dignify that comment with a smile.

"What they have ... *constructed* here," he continued, making the word "constructed" sound devious and evil, "is a masterful piece of legal maneuvering. This case does do a lot of what they say it does. It does just barely fall within this court's federal question jurisdiction, though there are a lot of state law issues involved. The pendant state claims are really the heart of what the plaintiffs are after, but they may have a valid federal claim. So maybe the case does pass muster on that issue. They've also constructed this case"—that dirty word again—"so that it weaves its way just around the doctrine of exhaustion of administrative remedies, and they've constructed an excellent argument as to why the doctrine of comity does not apply. I ..." he pretended stammering, "really have to admit that there might be a way that you can look at this case so that this court does have jurisdiction to issue the kind of massive order they're calling for.

"But I don't see a single real person, Your Honor, whom that order would effect. This case is a legal masterpiece, but the harm done is a phantasm. Of course, there have been a few people whose eligibility was calculated wrong. Why didn't they just appeal, through the ordinary state administrative procedures? Each and every time Mr. Norris or Ms. ... er, Watkins here brought one of these cases to our attention, we have expeditiously straightened it out. Our procedures and forms are very complex, and there have been system-wide problems with them in

119

the past, but they have now been pretty much all straightened out. Mr. Norris and Ms. Watkins believe that there is a problem, but they are apparently the only ones who believe it. If there really are 42,000 people being harmed, isn't it likely that we would have heard of it before this? Isn't it unlikely that only these two sophisticated lawyers would know it?"

"Your Honor," Angela rose in rebuttal "the Department has been keeping these fictitious basements a *secret* for years. The process, and forms, are so complicated, it's no wonder the department successfully pulled the wool over the eyes of most welfare recipients. The department tricked the whole recipient population into thinking that this was the right way to do things. Furthermore, the statistical evidence shows that, of the 45,000 people originally cut off Medical Assistance, 93 percent are still being denied. These people have been trickling into our office for two years. Every time, the department acts as if it is just a clerical mistake, but 93 percent of the eligible people will never get the medical help they need unless they now get their day in court."

"You make a good point, Ms. Watkins," Judge Barnett began. It was usually a bad sign when the judge began by saying that you had made a good point. This time was no exception. "While there is no doubt in the court's mind," he continued, referring to himself, "that you have produced pretty reliable statistical evidence that something unusual is going on, there still seems to me to be a chance, though I admit it's an off-chance, that the massive policy of deception complained of here is no more than a figment—or I should say, suspicion—in someone's mind. This is not to say that suspicion isn't warranted, given the past practices of this department." This was said with a look over the top of his reading glasses at Jody Hechtmuller. "And I do note that present counsel also represented the department at that time, the time when that admittedly deceptive application form was in use." Jody stood up to respond, but the judge was only giving him a knock because of his overly sanctimonious air today. He gestured for Jody to sit back down.

"Even with these doubts, I do think that the plaintiffs have shown that they do exist in such numbers so as to make impractical the joinder of all of them," the judge continued, paraphrasing the requirements of Rule 23. At the counsel table, Angela spontaneously put her hand on top of Sport's and squeezed hard with joy. It was all downhill from here on. The dominoes were all in place and falling. The department would inevitably be placed in a position that everyone knew was untenable, the position of having to prove that a crawlspace was a basement. She looked to see if Sport was as excited as she was, but Sport was still looking at the judge. Judge Barnett, she suddenly realized, was about to say something more.

"But I'm going to withhold entering that ruling, until such time as the attorneys for the plaintiffs locate at least one more current live plaintiff and file an Amended Complaint naming that additional class member. At that time, the order certifying the class will issue automatically. This is just for my own peace of mind, you understand?" he added, looking directly at Sport.

Sport nodded back. "Thank you, Your Honor," he said almost graciously.

"Why did you let him do that!" Angela turned to Sport in the elevator. There was a trace of exasperation in her voice. "He has no right to do that. Once he decides that those people do exist, he *has* to issue the order."

"He didn't want to. We had to make him *want* to."

"We have to appeal this."

"Angela, don't you see what fools that will make us

look like? Saying there are 42,000 people in this predicament, but then claiming that Judge Barnett was wrong to make us come up with one more of them."

"So that's your excuse for going along with the judge who just screwed 42,000 of your clients?"

"I didn't make the ruling."

The subdued rumble of the elevator machinery echoed in the silence. Sport tried to keep his eyes from lingering on Angela's ripe figure. Sport always prided himself on being a friend to all, but Angela had a way of letting him know that she was not interested in his easy warmth.

It was yet another kind of embarrassment and humiliation planned for him, Mayor Crosley Pettibone felt certain. *Man with a gun / ain't no fun.* He knew that he would eventually find out exactly what Gotterdung wanted in return for releasing the study and allowing the Waterside Towers project to go ahead. He didn't understand why Gotterdung wouldn't say what it was.

What Pettibone's aides feared now was a public explosion by their boss. If Pettibone blasted Gotterdung in public, Gotterdung could then turn around and issue a report saying that Pettibone's project would screw the poor and working class to make way for the rich. That, of course, was exactly what Pettibone was doing. But he had justifications for trying to increase the tax base, and he was committed to his businessmen friends. On the way back in the limousine Fosback advised Pettibone to wait a few days and see what Gotterdung was up to. But Pettibone was not the type of person to sit and stew. *Sit and stew, sit and stew, sit and stew and turn into glue.* He decided to blast Gotterdung that night.

When he reached the office, Pettibone was given another reason for acting now. Fosback knocked gently on the frame of his open door and asked if he had a minute.

When Pettibone nodded yes, Fosback tiptoed in. Then, with a great show of secrecy, two men whom Pettibone had never seen before wheeled into his office a huge bulletin board covered with a sheet. The sheet was pulled off and "Susumee Development" appeared at the top in bold red letters. At the bottom the caption read "Tract B." Tract B was evidently divided into thirty or forty little pieces of property. Each one had a neat red "S" imprinted on it, except for the one that stood for 442 Jasper Street, which had a blue plastic thumbtack on it.

"We wanted you to see this," one of the men said without introduction. He then reached down ceremoniously and pulled the blue thumbtack from 442 Jasper Street. With a special pen, he printed a red "S" on that property. "It's done," he said. "We're ready to roll."

Pettibone surprised them by not smiling. "I'll make the announcement this afternoon."

Sport and Angela walked silently back to the Legal Assistance Society against the flow of the sidewalk traffic. Sport was confident that they had made no errors in their legal argument. Angela, he knew, was too inexperienced to accept that these things just happened sometimes. He wanted to tell her that an individual judge's whims had to be dealt with in every case, but he was afraid that he would sound patronizing if he said so now. He was waiting for her to break the ice. Her first words, however, shot a dose of adrenaline through his body.

"Sport, you need to talk to Linda about her screwing up this case."

They walked another half block while Sport tried to figure out how much she knew.

"Why?"

He tried to sound calm. He turned his head to look at

her, but she kept walking as she talked, as if this were a routine conversation. Sport dared to hope that she had not noticed the irregularities with the Throckmorton signature. None of the photocopies of the Throckmorton affidavit were even signed, but no one else had been diligent enough to notice it. Sport had an explanation prepared that might be good enough to save his license to practice law if he were caught, but he knew that it would not fool Angela.

"Because we'll never find another plaintiff if she keeps chasing everyone out of the reception room. She and M.C."

"I know," he said, trying to hide his relief.

"None of my clients can call me, she puts them on hold so long. Now I can't even make a call out. This morning I had to run across the street to that bar to call Judge Barnett's clerk."

"She wasn't so bad before she brought M.C. in." Sport was glad to confess. "I should have said something that first day."

"He's eighteen months old. How did this get started?"

"She just did it the first day. I thought she was just showing the kid around."

"What does she say about it?"

"Linda's a hard person to talk to."

"We need another plaintiff, Sport! I can't stand this any more. I'm going to talk to her about how she's screwing up this case."

"No, Angela, I'm the Acting Chief Attorney. It's my duty, and I'll do it."

"No," she said thoughtfully. "We'll do it together."

Angela was not one to put things off. They had a meeting scheduled with Doxie in fifteen minutes, to talk about the case, but the moment they reached the Legal Assistance reception area, she told Linda that they had to meet right away. Linda ignored her, but she did glance sideways at Sport. "Yes, you have to come," he said.

The unoccupied office was so large that it was commonly referred to as "the gym." The room was a flat, gloomy rectangle of indeterminate color, with three casement windows on the outer wall protruding down eighteen inches from the ceiling, giving a view of the feet and ankles of the occasional pedestrian outside. The walls were stained from leakage from these windows. The ceiling was blotted with marks from leaky pipes. A silver bell-shaped object protruded from a network of radiators in the back of the room. In the winter, it emitted a constant halo of steam, causing this part of the room to be known as "the showers."

Sport entered first and sat behind the empty metal desk, the desk that was being reserved for the Chief Attorney who had yet to be appointed. Linda came next, carrying M.C. on her hip. Angela came next, shoving M.C.'s rattling and screeching playpen in front of her. She pushed it in front of the Chief Attorney's desk and tried to set it up. She couldn't see the mechanism, which was hidden under a pile of M.C.'s little blankets, but she made a rough square out of the sides of it and pushed the bottom approximately flat.

"Is that good enough?"

Her face contorted with unspoken disgust, Linda barely bothered to glance at her. She put M.C. down on the floor and reached in and connected the playpen mechanism. She began to walk around to lock the sides in place, but M.C. grabbed her by the ankle. When she reached down to pick him up, he twisted his fingers in her hair and screamed. She gathered him up and did something to him they couldn't quite see which quieted him instantly, then dumped him onto the floor of the crib.

"Linda, have a seat."

Linda rolled her eyes, then squeezed herself into a chair. "This is about that case, ain't it? My little stamp."

"No, no, nothing about that."

"Well, it is about the case," Angela interjected.

Linda looked from one to the other.

"It's about M.C."

"You can't continue to bring him in every day. The office is falling apart." Angela was still being helpful.

"He's no trouble."

"He's chasing away some of our clients. And when you're taking care of him, you don't answer the phone."

"Linda, I'll try to help you find day care, make some calls for you."

From the floor of the playpen M.C. began to utter a low wailing sound, as if he knew that these two lawyer-fiends were trying to separate him from his mother. But his mother said nothing.

"Linda, the bottom line is, I will give you a couple of extra days off with pay to find day care. But he's got to be out of here within two weeks. You've never listened to anything else I've said before about this, so I hope you'll listen now. If he's not out of here within two weeks, you'll be fired."

M.C.'s low wail evolved into a high-pitched scream. Angela put her hands to her ears. The boy stood up, grasping the bars of the playpen like a condemned prisoner. Linda leaned forward to get up but found herself stuck between the arms of her chair. Sport rushed to help pull her out. Angela was no more willing to deal with M.C. than Sport was, so she also turned gingerly toward the woman stuck in the chair. M.C. took advantage of this opportunity to ingest the contents of a bottle of Wite-out that he found near the edge of the Chief Attorney's desk.

10 MEET THE ENEMY

Slidell hung up the receiver and walked back to his table, shaking his head, furious. He was in Eddie's restaurant in Fells Point. It was really just a large, square room whose door opened directly out onto the sidewalk. There was a counter with stools down the left side. Slip always asked for a table near the back because the phone was there, hanging on the back wall. It would have never occurred to Slip to ask for a private room, or to use an office. In fact, there was no back room or office. The light was spotty, and the solid wooden tables sat on worn golf-course-green indoor/outdoor carpet. Slip felt comfortable here, as he did in any of a dozen tiny restaurants in the city. Despite his legendary power, he never had any desire to be given special privileges. Part of his success came from the fact that he really was in many ways the ordinary person that so many politicians pretended to be. Eddie sensed it, and the customers sensed it. They never hesitated to pull up a chair and talk to him, whether they had anything to say or not.

Slip had heard that the Mayor was going to make an announcement about Fells Point that afternoon. He called Gotterdung from the back wall phone, puzzled. He knew that Gotterdung had met with Pettibone to explain the

127

deal. So he couldn't understand why the mayor was making a statement. Pettibone was supposed to be slinking, licking his wounds. He was supposed to be explaining quietly to the Bold Tip Construction Company why he had to go back on his word and arrange for hiring union workers after all. Gotterdung was then supposed to get the study done quickly, and in an efficient-appearing manner, while Slip was supposed to announce later the real victory they had achieved for the working man, the constituency that Pettibone had neglected in his fascination with business glamour and glitz.

"What's he going to say?" Slidell pumped Gotterdung over the phone.

"I don't know. He sure hates me now, the skinny twerp."

Slip let his exasperation show. "Well, what did he say when you told him?"

There was a long pause. Then: "Oh. I didn't tell him. Why, I mean. Maybe that's why he was so mad. His face turned almost purple. You should've seen it! I thought he was going to take a swing at me! I was *hoping* he would take a swing at me!" Gotterdung chuckled stupidly.

Slidell made a mental note not to let Gotterdung do anything at all as Lieutenant Governor. But before Gotterdung finished his story, Eddie beckoned to him. The mayor's image appeared on the little nine-inch TV which was propped right on the edge of his table. Slip dropped the receiver on its hook as the mayor's face loomed larger and larger on the screen.

Even on the little black and white TV, Pettibone's face seemed flushed. He had the petulant look of a little boy whose mother had too often given him exactly what he wanted. Standing behind him as he spoke were the men whose companies stood to make fortunes if the Mayor's Waterside Towers Luxury Condominium Development succeeded. Ken Kiger of Susumee Development, Richard Ostramund of the Builders National Bank, and T. Oswald Fundertow, former U.S. Secretary of Commerce and now president of the mammoth Bold Tip Development Company, stood in a semicircle behind Pettibone, just inside the range of the cameras. With the exception of Ken Kiger, who had made a career out of keeping his name and picture out of the paper, all of the corporate men on the speaker's platform were used to having their pictures taken with great fanfare whenever one of their companies embarked on another profit-making mission. But today, something in the camera angle, or perhaps something in Slip's keen sixth sense about people and their feelings, made it appear to him that each of these men had drawn back about a quarter of a step from where he was expected to stand. Before the mayor said a word, Slip knew that Pettibone was somehow jumping the gun.

"We have good news," the mayor said. Then he waited, his hands on the lectern, for an amount of time that would have been considered impolite for anyone except the mayor, "... and we have bad news.

"The good news is the announcement we are making today, the official unveiling of the plans for the Mayor Crosley T. Pettibone Waterside Towers Luxury Condominium Development.

"These people behind me," Pettibone turned and gestured toward the men in grey suits and red ties behind him, "These are smart, smart men. These are the kind of people we need helping us if the city is going to save itself. They've come up with an idea that's going to bring new business—and new taxpayers—into the City of Baltimore." He looked over the gathering of reporters and officials

"You know me. I'm just an ordinary guy, got an I.Q. of 98 on a hot day. I couldn't figure out all this financing and acquisition and construction, all the legal technicalities. But these men have the expertise, they have the experience. They have arranged the financing, with the help of the city's Corporate Acquisitions Department. We have some great planning people in the city, worked together with these smart, smart men behind me—and what did they come up with? Nothing less than a plan to redevelop the whole Fells Point waterfront. Shops, offices, condominiums, a marina. A $250,000,000 development. Two hundred and fifty million, all taxable. Luxury apartments for 1,000 people. Slips for 150 boats. Sixty-two shops, employing over 400 people on a permanent basis. It's a grand plan, and a great step forward in the development of Baltimore City. In a minute I'm going to let these smart men tell you all the details."

Instead of turning the microphone over to the smart men, however, Pettibone stood silently. The reporters were supposed to tell by the look on his face that all was not well. It was a little game that Pettibone played. The reporters recognized that the future of the city was more tied to Pettibone's secret moods and pet peeves than all of the official city planning reports put together. So a game had developed between Pettibone and the press which, if it had a name, would be called "guess what the mayor is thinking." Pettibone liked the way his every smile, grimace and pout was scrutinized and speculated upon. Even in this moment of real anger, he paused for an extra moment with his arms extended to the lectern, and his eyes downcast, so that the reporters and the TV cameras could study his face as if it were an oracle.

"But we have people, we have *state officials,*" Pettibone began almost in a mumble, but the scowl on his visage couldn't have been more clear. He knew that his words would be given more importance if his listeners had to strain for them. "...we have *bureaucrats.* I've gotten rid

130

of most of them in the city, but there are still a lot left around the state. Not lowdown bureaucrats but *slowdown* bureaucrats. We have people who are trying to slow down redevelopment, slow down jobs, slow down the city. This grand project is ready to go, these smart men behind me are all waiting to help us—they won't wait forever, they have other fish to fry—but one man is holding this whole thing up, because he hates the city. And he scorns its people. And if you have any doubt about that, remember that this is the same man who has taken the Medical Assistance cards away from thousands of poor people. We're trying to help Legal Assistance and the federal court get those people the medical care they deserve. But this development—there's not a penny of state money in this project—it's private money, private money and city help, local government and business working together. But it's not state money, and here you have a *state bureaucrat* holding it up!"

Pettibone dramatically turned away from the microphone and quickly walked out of the room. Ken Kiger and Richard Ostramund took the podium and tried to explain the details of the massive project, but no one was listening. Most of the reporters buzzed around the room, their journalistic juices surging at high tide, trying to find out who the "slowdown bureaucrat" was.

All of the businessmen hated to be paraded on stage right then. This implied that they had taken Pettibone's side in this newly declared political war. But Pettibone had been good to them in the past, and they were now forced to accept the fact that they were trapped. They were on Pettibone's side. Pettibone was known to have this way of extracting a little more out of you than you originally planned to put into the deal.

Pettibone hadn't had time to tell the businessmen about the new legal requirement of the study, or about

Gotterdung's refusal to complete the study. He hadn't had time because he had scheduled the press conference precipitously. He believed that this was a political matter, and that he should take care of it personally, before he was made to look like a fool. Also, Fundertow and Kiger and Ostramund needed this special instruction in the way that things were going to be. The lesson was that there was a price to be paid for his favors, and that the exact price was not always going to be announced in advance.

Even as Oswald Fundertow was concluding his presentation with the unveiling of an architectural model of the development, Pettibone's press aides circulated around the room, spreading the word that it was Brendan Gotterdung who was the "slowdown bureaucrat" who was putting this great project in jeopardy. They also accused Brendan Gotterdung of illegally denying Medical Assistance cards to thousands of poor city residents. It was one of the most savage attacks on another public official launched by a mayor of Baltimore since the city was under the control of the Know-Nothing party in the middle of the nineteenth century. It was pure Pettibone— petty, personal and vindictive. His speech writers hadn't had a chance to smooth it out very much, and so it caught the attention of the press in a way that no slickly written press release possibly could.

Slip Slidell bent his head and brought his hands to his face. Gotterdung was supposed to have to put a gentle, subtle but implacable pressure on Pettibone, expertly timed to take advantage of the mayor when he was the most vulnerable. Pettibone was supposed to have ignominiously but privately given in. Word was supposed to leak out very slowly about the surprise accomplishment of Slidell and Gotterdung, the two new working class heroes.

Common political sense dictated that there was no advantage to be gained by openly attacking another incumbent politician. But Pettibone was dangerous precisely because he was not a common politician. His true inner feelings sometimes surged to the surface, as they had just now, in spite of the best efforts of his political aides. The result was that a spark of honest feeling was revealed. This spark woke people up and entertained them, and Pettibone would for a moment seem as real in the eyes of the voters as the soap opera characters whose lives they followed so closely every day on TV. Pettibone had escalated this battle into another dimension entirely. But there was no turning back for Slidell. He would never abandon his ally, Gotterdung, just because the fight got messy. He tilted back in his chair now, twirling the remains of the ice and tea in his glass, thinking hard.

He was reaching for the phone on the wall to punch in Gotterdung's private office number when he saw Sister Elena burst through the door of the restaurant. She stood boldly in the doorway for a moment, waiting for her eyes to adjust from the bright sunlight outside. He hadn't seen her since she had departed from the legislature so dispiritedly at the end of March. Her soup kitchen was just a few blocks down the street, but he hadn't felt that he would be welcome. It would have been better if he had simply deserted her in Annapolis. The red-herring soup-kitchen bill had been a necessary part of Slidell's legislative strategy. But he knew that it had made her feel as if she were being bought. He had made her humble herself and beg for the little bit of money being offered for her soup kitchen clients. And he had done all this to her just to distract attention from his grander scheme.

The men at the counter pulled back a little on their stools to get a better look at this breathless young woman standing in the open doorway. Slip found himself looking at her, again regretting that he had never had a daughter as he watched the passion light up her face.

The fiasco between Gotterdung and Pettibone could eventually be repaired. Any political situation could be repaired, patched up, made the best of. That was the nature of political efforts. Very often, the best you could say of any project was that it was salvageable. But Slip had always held back one thing from this slippery process in which everything was patchable, all positions negotiable. He had always held inviolate the central core of his own personal life. He had believed that his married life with Audrey was immune from the haggling, the bargaining and the compromising of this process. Their life had been based, he believed, upon an unstated but absolute trust. But the process of going through his divorce had taught him that there was no inviolable territory.

What he learned after Audrey had finally gone was that he, Slip Slidell, expert politician, had all of the time secretly been prey to some of the same hopeless hopes and irreconcilable desires that drove and deluded every citizen he had ever met. Now, he was suddenly attacked by that same fragmented despair that had driven so many of these men and women to come to see him in his office over the years. And he wondered how he had ever been able to comfort them.

Sister Elena walked a few steps into the restaurant and let the door swing shut behind her. Her eyes quietly searched the room, drawing even more of the men's silent attention to her presence. Slip saw her eyes fix on him. He had to make an effort not to flinch. She walked right past the counter and up to him, her dark eyes so large and open so wide they caught and flashed back the points of light in the room. Slip sat up straight as she pulled up a chair next to him. Then she sat down, took his hand in both of hers and pressed her face into it.

"Sister," he said, embarrassed. She lifted her face up,

but she kept her firm grasp on his hand. She looked directly into his face, studying it. There was color in her cheeks as she tried to control her emotions. Her dark brown hair, pulled back on each side into a barrette, shined in the lights. Her study of him was hesitant, not bold. She sat back a little, as modest as a woman could be who was at the same time gripping his hand so tightly.

"I just saw the mayor's statement on television." She studied his eyes. "You did it, just like you said you would. You stopped the whole Waterside Towers project right in its tracks. You are a genius, Samuel." She leaned forward and embraced him. "You're a good man, Samuel. I was such a jerk." She sat back quickly, her face flushed, the beginnings of tears suspended in her long lashes. "You don't realize how many people you've helped."

Slip devoutly wished that it was even a little bit true. But helping the neighborhood residents by stopping the development was the last thing on his mind. The people Slip and Gotterdung intended to help were people who could help them in return.

"I understand what you did now. You made my dead-duck development bill work anyway. You said you would help, but I wouldn't listen.

"I can't explain to you," she continued breathlessly, "how humble this makes me feel. I wouldn't listen to you or work on the bill with you. So much pride. I talked so much about doing good and accomplished nothing. But you ... you're the one that had the competence, and the courage, in the end."

Slip looked at her ruefully. Although she was smart enough to have figured out most of the mechanics of the plot, she was just too *good,* and she had too much faith, to understand why he had done it. To be honest with her, he'd have to tell her the truth, right now. He was horribly uneasy. Nothing was working out right. He hadn't come to this restaurant to make a confession to a nun.

Sister Elena released his hand and relaxed against the curved hardwood back of the nautically styled chair.

"I want to tell you about some plans I have for fixing up the neighborhood. Well, they aren't really my plans. I've been going to a lot of neighborhood meetings since March. These are really all other people's ideas."

She did not know what to make of this complex, powerful, mysterious man. She stared at that old-fashioned grey pompadour, those used green eyes, the slick layers of trickery so finely disguised in the moldings of his enigmatic countenance.

"You've done more for the poor in a few months than a hundred holy persons could have done for them in a hundred years."

But Elena was impressed most of all with the fact that she had been unable to use him. He was immune to her little girl/big girl charm. He had done it because he wanted to do it. She sat, fascinated by his quietly troubled face, and began to think that it might even be called distinguished, or handsome. She was also impressed by the fact that it had no resemblance whatsoever to her father's face.

Slip knew that misunderstandings were the stuff of which human disasters were made. He knew that there was a real big one here between himself and Sister Elena, and he knew that a politician had to follow up quickly on his first reaction, expose the problem ever so gently, and convince everyone that everything was okay anyway. He had to tell Elena that she had overestimated him. But he could not do it.

And, to justify not telling her, he lied to himself. He was used to facing reality head on, but he just let Elena's soothing words slide over him, and he dreamed that what she thought about him was true. This kind of wishful thinking wasn't really any good for long-term understanding. She would find out soon enough that the neighborhoods of Fells Point were to be sacrificed anyway, and that the only difference between his political trickery and Pettibone's was that a different politician would benefit. But Slip suddenly found himself among that more desperate mass of humans who go through every day not being able to think of the long term, because they need more desperately to get through the present day, or hour, or minute, struggling to keep alive, or to keep someone from leaving, or to keep their hopes from evaporating away.

Slidell could see his future withering away just as surely as he saw his body beginning its slow decline into old age. He had always assumed that, when his ship finally came in, Audrey would be there to enjoy it with him. But he had assumed too much. He got nothing from her any more except what was negotiated through her lawyers. Until this moment, he hadn't realized that he wanted so much more. He needed that spark of non-negotiable passion that they had shared. It had been the fuel that he had burned while he played his amusing political games. But now, suddenly, he didn't even want to play.

"A cup of coffee?" he said in a tiny, hoarse whisper. "I just want you to know," he said after she had stirred a little cream into it, "that I've thought about you ever since we met down in Annapolis last winter. This is a year for me ... when I've been wondering what's the point of it all. Working against you was more fun than working with anybody else down there."

"You weren't working against me ...." she began.

He stopped her with a look, his hand raised slightly off the table as if to say: don't ask. This was as close as he could come to the truth today. He needed her belief in him, today. He kept her there for half an hour, asking her about her soup kitchen, about her daily life, about her family. He kept the conversation away from Fells Point. He wanted to know her in some other context than the battle over Fells Point. He promised himself that, by the time she found out the truth about Fells Point, he really would be at least half the man she thought he was today.

Doxie Clearwater was brimming with pleasure as he descended the steps all the way from his third-floor office to the basement. His portly, sausage-shaped body was unaccustomed to such fast motion. Doxie was fifty-eight and did not believe in exercise, but his administrative lawyers were late for their meeting. As much as he enjoyed playing the father figure, philosophically reclined in the soft chair in his own office, he couldn't sit still today. He was too excited about the phone call from the mayor. Mayor Pettibone, furious at Gotterdung, had offered help in the crawlspace suit.

"Anything to screw that bastard to the wall."

"Thank you, Your Honor."

He didn't really understand Angela or Sport, or any of the young white people in that unit. But Doxie was a good enough leader to take advantage of the strengths of people he did not understand. He enjoyed unleashing his rabid young lawyers on the enemies of the poor in the state. When Doxie had actually practiced law, he had done it in a more dignified and courtly way than Sport and Angela did it now. Some might have called it a timid way. But he was becoming a convert to the all-out-attack method of practicing law.

Doxie, of course, did not change his old outward habits. The former Democratic block captain still went to every bull roast and crab feast; his face was always there at every political affair, grasping the proffered hands warmly in each reception line. A whole generation of lawyers on the bench, and in the bar association, and in the big firms, and in the legislature, considered him as a buddy from the old days, a buddy slightly more idealistic than themselves. Because of Doxie's moral stance, and his political connections everywhere, there was hardly anyone in power anywhere in the state who would feel quite right about putting the squeeze on the Legal Assistance Society.

Doxie was in a hurry. He knew that the Society's new-found favor with the mayor was an evanescent thing. There were ways of taking advantage of it, and Doxie wanted to make sure that his lawyers understood the smooth, graceful way this had to be done. As he approached the basement landing by way of the back stairs, he wondered again why they had missed their appointment in his office. Sport and Angela should have long since been back from their court hearing. It was not like any of his lawyers to miss an opportunity to strut and fret their hour in front of the Director.

He reached for the iron railing as he descended the last few steps into the dimly lit area at the bottom of the stairs. Halfway by sight, halfway from memory, he navigated his way around the corners, following the green arrows until they turned off toward the men's room, then groping through an even darker back hallway. He always heard a lot of complaints about the working conditions—the dark, crumbling tile, the absence of janitorial service, the sickening state of the restrooms, the difficulty in getting a phone call in or out, and, especially, the difficulties of getting a client by the twin guards of Linda and M.C.—but he shrugged off these details, proud that his lawyers stuck with their jobs of helping the poor in spite of all these obstacles. Besides, none of these problems affected him. His private phone line was never backed up; his personal secretary/receptionist was efficient and eager to please. His own office was spotless, and furnished just

cheaply enough to impress his legal and political con-
temporaries with his self-sacrifice. He cherished his reputation for running an efficient, lean, professional
organization. He was quite surprised at the scene he observed when he suddenly turned from a dark hallway into
the brightly lit doorway of the Chief Attorney's Office.

M.C.'s scream was deafening. He had one hand twisted
in Linda's hair and one in Angela's. They were trying to
pull him out, but his ankles were entangled in the playpen rails. Sport was grabbing at things on the top of the
desk, trying to keep them from being knocked into the
playpen.

"Am I interrupting something?" As he opened the door,
Doxie could feel other employees at his back, peeking in
to see what was being done to M.C.

Doxie walked in as Linda and Angela finally extricated
M.C.'s hands from their hair. As soon as he was entirely
in Linda's control, M.C. stopped crying. She put him down
in the playpen again.

"You don't have to explain this," Doxie offered.

"No, Doxie, I think we do." Sport's tone was aggra-
vated, almost insolent.

"I don't think it has anything to do with Society policy."

"It has everything to do with Society policy."

Doxie turned to the employees standing in the hallway,
still peeking through the door. He waved them in.

"This is something that is more important than the
Throckmorton case?" Doxie's raised eyebrow expressed
doubt.

"Maybe so. Remember when Linda first became preg-
nant? I asked you what our maternity leave policy was?"
This was a bold move, cross-examining the director. Doxie
would not be intimidated. He pulled up a chair and sat
down, facing Sport. Curious employees pulled up chairs
around him or stood behind him in the cavernous office,

which was soon packed all the way back to the showers.

"I recall that conversation."

"But we never did come down to making a decision."

"Yes, we did, as I recall."

"Yes, *after* Linda's water broke in the reception room and I had to call you from the hospital."

Doxie smiled. "When I was a young man, men weren't even supposed to know things like that."

"That was a long time ago."

Doxie drew back. His very nickname, inspired by an older brother's comparison of him to a dachshund, was secretly a sensitive issue. He could not tolerate mockery.

"How is any of this relevant?"

"M.C. is eighteen months old now. I just told Linda that she can't bring him to work any more. I know I'm just the Acting Chief Attorney, but something had to be done."

On hearing M.C.'s name, Doxie reached into the playpen and pulled the boy toward him, grinning. He didn't actually know M.C., and he didn't actually like babies or toddlers very much, but this was the kind of thing a father figure was supposed to do, and he thought that it would get him immediate sympathy of most of the people in the room. M.C. was strangely compliant. He allowed himself to be pulled over to the side of the playpen, and he stood there, smiling complacently, holding onto Doxie's gently circling arm.

When the staff absolutely insisted that Doxie involve himself in a dispute, he customarily heard all the parties' views until they had exhausted themselves; then he delivered a low-keyed pep talk, exhorting his workers to get along with one another and to go out and work for their clients, followed by a vague homily about the benefits of working for others. Making a decision always seemed to offend somebody, and he tried to avoid doing that.

"We're supposed to be—we *are* a compassionate agency." He began to give his judgment on the case, feeling very much at ease in his role as the wise father figure. "We are also supposed to be a professional organization, and we have to operate our reception room so as to get the respect of the bar, and the bench, if we are going to do any good for our clients in the long run. But what Linda, and little M.C. here need," he smiled down on the child, "is just time. Everyone thinks that the disadvantaged have nothing but time, but I know that time is more precious, and presses down more *exigently,* on those who have no resources, like Linda. Can't we give her six more months?"

"It's so dim in that reception room, Doxie. Have you thought about how it might affect him developmentally to be raised in there? He may never attain normal vision." Sport was pulling out all the stops.

"Well, I guess we can get lights ...."

"Doxie," Sport surprised everyone by his firm tone of voice. "I'm willing to put up with a lot, because I know we accomplish a lot of good here. But if you're telling me that I have to spend the rest of my career running across the street to Clyde's Bar and Grill whenever I have to make an urgent phone call ...."

"I'm not talking about *the length of your career,* Sport." Doxie smiled to himself over the impatience of the young. "We're only talking about six, or maybe only three ...."

At this point in the discussion, M.C. effected a further decrease in his longevity there by biting down hard on the soft skin between the forefinger and thumb of Doxie's right hand. Doxie screamed and slid off the chair and onto his knees, with his right arm draped over the railing of the playpen, the skin of his hand still tightly clenched in M.C.'s bulldog grip. He reached frantically inside the playpen with his other hand and tried to pry the child's mouth off, but the playpen began to collapse.

It took all his strength of character to keep himself from pounding that little child's head against the playpen rails. Sport and Angela reached in and tried to help, but the playpen collapsed even further, pinching the skin under Doxie's arm in the process. He screamed again. M.C.'s teeth sunk in even deeper, and it seemed as if the pain were never going to stop. Eight lawyers, five paralegals and four clerical people stood up and exclaimed, but no one seemed capable of doing anything.

Linda deliberately crossed the room, squatted down in front of the collapsed playpen, reached her hand in between the bars, and with two fingers held M.C.'s nose closed. In one second he had let go of Doxie's hand and Doxie was pulled out.

Doxie held out his hand. Each of M.C.'s three front teeth had drawn blood with its own distinctive mark. More alarming was the thick white substance that seemed to surround the wound. Linda, who had said nothing since Doxie arrived, spoke to her boy during that moment of stunned silence that followed the showing of Doxie's injured hand. Everyone in the room heard her shout.

"Boy, what's wrong with your mouth? You look like you got the rabies!"

Quickly and quietly, the rest of the staff sifted out of the room. Sport walked Doxie down the street to the Sacred Heart emergency room, where his wound was cleaned, disinfected and bandaged, and he was given a tetanus shot. On the way back an executive decision was made: this had been M.C.'s last day at the office.

11 LOTS THROWN IN

"Even my dog," Keane always started his phone calls unceremoniously, "knows the difference between a basement and a crawlspace. Don't you?"

"What are you getting at?" Tynan's voice revealed the strain of the past few weeks.

"He knows where he can poop and where he can't. Don't you?"

"Are you looking for some kind of colorful quote?" Tynan didn't try to hide his antagonism toward the columnist.

Keane seemed to realize that he wasn't going to scare anything interesting out of Tynan this way, but he persisted. "Do you really think people rent out their crawlspaces and have income from them?"

"Who have you been talking to?" Tynan was going to give nothing, no information, no quote, to this man who had already made up his mind that the department was run by a bunch of ignorant and callous dopes. He would force Keane to write his daily diatribe without government help.

"I'm just giving you one last chance to correct my information, if it's wrong," Keane retorted. "Let's see. Forty-five thousand people had basements added to their applications without their say-so."

"Nothing was added to assets without their say-so."

"But it was added right on the form, before they even said anything at all."

"They could take it off."

"And how many did that?"

"I don't know," Tynan lied.

"None did, did they?"

Keane was correct. The department had desperately gone over every one of the old applications in the weeks since the suit had been filed, hoping that some poor applicant had been smart enough and brave enough and tenacious enough to force the eligibility technician to cross out the automatic basement added to the form. But it had never happened, not even once. *Everyone* had been given a basement. But how did Keane know this? Even Legal Assistance had not been able to get this information through its first set of interrogatories, since Jody Hechtmuller had successfully argued in court that going through all the applications was too burdensome on the department.

"I don't know."

"Then you don't deny that, do you?"

"I don't know if it's true or not."

"That's not a denial."

"He was relentless," Tynan confided to Bobbi Jo later that morning. "He knew everything. Not just what we released to Legal Assistance. He's threatening us with 'source' stories worse than anything that's ever really happened at all. Things that make it look like *we* started this whole mess."

"Don't worry about that newspaper nitwit, Leonard. You and I know that you didn't start that crawlspace business."

"But I have to cover it up anyway."

145

"And you done good things too."
"Right now I can't think of any."
"You forgot about Mallory?"

Tynan had pulled out all the stops in the effort to get rid of Mallory. Mallory had been served with charges for his removal and was just now completing the second week of his trial before the Employee Relations Department. Jody Hechtmuller himself was prosecuting the case for the department, even though this meant that he had to divide his time between that and the crawlspace suit. They had already been to court twice on Temporary Restraining Orders filed by Mallory's attorney in attempts to delay the proceedings. They had responded to his EEO Complaint, his Human Rights Commission Complaint, his personnel grievance, his complaints to the state Wage and Hour Board and the National Labor Relations Board. Taking advantage of an obscure provision of Maryland law, Mallory had petitioned the governor himself for the removal of Tynan, on the grounds of corruption and inefficiency. He had caused several letters to be sent from local politicians to Secretary Gotterdung, questioning why Mallory, a dedicated public servant with sixteen years of satisfactory service, was being treated so severely.

In short, Mallory had unleashed the standard arsenal of legal counterattacks that any state employee was expected to use when it became clear that he was about to be fired. These same counterattacks were always used because: (1) they were free; (2) they didn't require the hiring of an attorney; (3) the state would be tied up for months answering investigators' questions; (4) the employee didn't even have to participate in the investigation until the trial, and (5) there never was a trial. But Mallory had gone even a step further. Mallory had actually *paid money* to a lawyer to file some of these suits and counterattacks. Only two types of employees did that: people with legitimate cases, and nuts. In either case, the act of hiring a lawyer put Mallory into a different category of antagonist, a category which would get a lot of attention.

Although it would serve him well in delaying, prolonging and complicating his departure from state employment, having a lawyer was probably a disadvantage to Mallory in the long run. As soon as Mallory hired an attorney, the Attorney General's Office was required to take a real interest in the case. Every letter to Mallory, every reprimand, every response to every investigating agency was pored over by a lawyer in Jody Hechtmuller's office before it was ever mailed or delivered. In this way, no accusations too broad, no tones too harsh, no criticisms unsupported by the record ever found their way into Mallory's file.

Equally as important, there was not the slightest hint in any communication to Mallory that he had ever done a good job, tried to mend his ways, or shown any improvement. Any document showing any of these things would have been a tremendous setback to the case against him, due to an unofficial policy of the Employee Relations Department. Under that policy, any statement of praise for an employee virtually canceled out any previous warnings, reprimands or negative evaluations of that employee. Mallory had, over the past few years, made one or two attempts to do a small fraction of his work. He hadn't accomplished anything definite. Tynan had been wisely advised not to acknowledge in any way these sporadic, halfhearted efforts on Mallory's part. The case against Mallory was therefore clean. There was nothing positive whatsoever in his personnel record. Mallory's hiring of a lawyer had practically insured that the case against him would proceed relentlessly forward.

Tynan had been attending the Mallory hearing for a week and a half, making sure that Jody Hechtmuller had every shred of documentation that he needed for the case. In a series of repetitious and overlapping requests, Mallory subpoenaed every conceivable document from the employer's files. A few of these requests, which asked for the detailed personnel files of all the other workers in the office, had gone too far, and Jody Hechtmuller had refused to produce them. This had occasioned another battle in court. Such a setback might have sidetracked the dismissal case against an ordinary employee, but Tynan and Hechtmuller made sure that Mallory's case plowed on.

One of Mallory's demands was for the production of all the memos that *he* had written. When he heard of this request, Tynan remembered all those identical memos that Bobbi Jo's computer had spit out. He sent the documents to Mallory's attorney without mentioning their contents to anyone. He was betting, like Bobbi Jo, that no one could bear to read them. But Tynan hadn't realized that this huge stack of papers would be sitting on the counsel table, right in front of everyone, all day, during each day of the hearing.

A full inquiry into these identical memos would make Mallory look like the victim of a diabolical persecution. These papers could sink the whole case if anyone looked at them. Tynan was on edge throughout the hearing, and returned to his office late every afternoon to count down the days he would have to watch that pile of memos loom over his career.

Inevitably, given the great amount of the state's resources that were devoted to that end, and given the fact that Mallory really hadn't done any work for the past sixteen years, the case against him at last began to grind toward a successful conclusion. Mallory testified for two days in his own defense and was unable to utter a sentence short enough for anybody to understand. His defense seemed to veer unpredictably between technicalities and personal attacks on Tynan's emotional state. The hearing officer kept interrupting Mallory to say "I don't follow you," and he was clearly not the only one who didn't.

"This is the part," Jody told Tynan after a hearing in the second week, "where Mallory's lawyer starts to feel real bad. He realizes that he's almost used up his retainer, and he's afraid he will never get another nickel out of this case. He also realizes that he should have negotiated a dignified resignation for his client early on, and that he didn't pay enough attention to the case when it could have really helped."

"The Mallory case," Bobbi Jo now repeated. "That's something you're doing well, and it's going okay."

"You're right. I guess it is."

There was a sudden hubbub in the hallway just outside their office. Bobbi Jo leaned sideways and squinted to see the crowd outside the door.

"Don't talk to them!" Tynan lunged past her and pushed the door shut.

"Who are those people?"

"News people. Here. Sit down. Gotterdung's about to make a statement from his office."

"You aren't out there with him?"

Tynan didn't answer directly. "Gotterdung's planning on responding to Mayor Pettibone's attack," he said.

"What's he going to say?"

"I don't know."

"If you don't know about it, Leonard, it must really be big time."

Tynan ignored her. He adjusted the television set and sat back in his swivel chair to watch.

149

"I'm afraid Gotterdung is jeopardizing this department by holding back this study and antagonizing the mayor." Tynan looked straight at the screen. He appreciated having a secretary who understood.

"Leonard, I don't think it makes a dime's worth of difference what that buffoon says."

Gotterdung's face looked flushed on the TV screen. He was smiling. His office looked cheap and tacky in the bright lights, and it was hard to believe that this oversized, large-egoed man worked in this chintzy office. He looked as uncomfortable and out of place there as he had always felt. He started to read a prepared speech, but threw it away after a few sentences. "You guys want to ask me any questions?" he challenged.

He hadn't been able to reach Slip for instructions, so he decided that he would just take a shot at the mayor. This was his idea of a successful start to the plan he was executing with Slidell. Thanks to all of the publicity, he was already being treated as an equal to the mayor.

"Did you see the Mayor's speech?" was the first, obvious question.

"What we've seen today," he said, "was a display of temper inappropriate for a high public official. I don't know why Crosley Pettibone thinks that he is above the law, and that he can bend it to suit his purposes. The legislature passed the law, and it remains the law, that this department must complete a study before he can go ahead with his Waterside Towers project. And as for the Legal Assistance lawsuit, everybody knows we are giving Medical Assistance cards to everybody who deserves them. This idea that we have illegally cut off thousands of people is b.... poppycock." This last word was so out of character for him that the reporters roared with laughter.

In the next room, Tynan raised an eyebrow in appreciation of Gotterdung's unexpected eloquence. It was basically the material that they had rehearsed together, but it was stated in Gotterdung's style—crude, forceful, and to the point. Gotterdung, who had run government agencies for years from positions obtained through family connections, was for the first time in his life stepping in front of the public and trying to explain his actions. He clearly wasn't used to it. But he wasn't that bad at it.

Gotterdung's public persona was actually not much different from Pettibone's—assertive, demanding, and petulant. But unlike Pettibone, he didn't have the necessary grasp of the issues to go with his aggressive style. Fortunately for him, this was not anything that anyone could tell by watching a 30-second clip on the television news, and that's all that most people would see.

Since Gotterdung didn't act defensive, his blunt statement blaming the mayor would get equal airplay with the mayor's accusations. There would be no followup unless one of the two started the feud up again. The net result of all this would be a public relations draw: Pettibone 1, Gotterdung 1. And Gotterdung, who was only aiming for the lieutenant governorship anyway, would be quite satisfied to end up with a tie for the first round.

There was, however, one drawback to this plan. Gotterdung knew very little about what was going on in his department. This was a real weakness for a politician who was facing open questioning before live TV cameras. This weakness was compounded by his arrogant belief that the public should know only what he wanted it to know. The net result of both of these weaknesses was that he thought that he could lie and get away with it.

"It is completely untrue," he huffed in disgust, "that this study is being purposely delayed." Then, to Tynan's

151

utter horror, he began to elaborate. "We have assigned this project to Mr. Kevin Mallory, an experienced administrator and analyst, an exemplary employee with many years of service. I can't and won't say that it will be done tomorrow, or even next week. But I can guarantee you that Mr. Mallory will have all the resources at his disposal that he needs, and I know that he will get it done as soon as humanly possible, as he has always done before."

Bobbi Jo slumped down in her chair and put her face in her hands.

"I quit."

"No, no, no. Okay. Our boss is a jerk," he offered. Bobbi Jo looked paralyzed. Tynan gently grabbed her elbow and pulled on it. "Let's get out of here. I'll take you wherever you want to go. We can talk about this. It's not all over."

He pushed her through the outer office and through the group of reporters lingering in the hallway. They ran down the fire stairs at the end of the building, bursting through a heavy door at ground level onto the simmering, tar-scented parking lot. Tynan's BMW was parked under a shelter in a reserved parking spot.

"Get in. We're going to lunch," he commanded. "You show me where."

The cafeteria in the state office building was out of the question, since it had been recently closed down by the city health department. Tynan drove down Eutaw Street, past the ring of eateries and carryouts that catered to the state workers' desire for quick and cheap meals. He drove down narrow, shaded Read Street, where more substantial lunch places were interspersed among antique furniture stores, antique clothing stores, specialty bakeries and low-rent boutiques.

"Here?"

"No."

They crossed Cathedral, named after the huge Romanesque basilica a few blocks south, and came to a stop at the light at Charles. Here, just a few blocks north of Mount Vernon Square, genuine restaurants served Szechuan food, vegetarian food, ribs, or eclectic food to those with a little more money and a little more time. When he had the time to take lunch, Tynan often came here to avoid the tuna salad and pizza that culturally predominated near the state office buildings. Charles Street was in decay a few blocks north, but here it had retained just a trace of its old elegance—though at night the whole area turned into a homosexual party town.

"Here?"

"No."

Bobbi Jo made him turn right onto St. Paul and cruise downhill toward the commercial center of the city.

"Burke's? The Old Harbor? You've really got me guessing now."

"You won't be disappointed. Quick. Turn left."

They took a narrow alley down a steep hill and into the concrete gulch spanned by the Orleans Street bridge. They came to an area of brick row houses converted to business use that seemed to be squeezed between a high-rise parking lot and the Pettibone Jones Falls Downtown Access Ramp, one of Pettibone's massive road projects.

"Park. No, not in the high-rise. That costs money."

Every third or fourth rowhouse had been torn down, and the empty lots now served as parking lots. Each of these was filled with cars jammed in randomly and overflowing onto the sidewalk.

"We can find a free space under the Pettibone Ramp, or a cheap meter somewhere behind the restaurant. Here! Here, pull in!"

Bobbi Jo absolutely insisted that Tynan pull his BMW up over a small curb and onto a patch of damp red dirt, next to a collection of old cars and pickup trucks.

"We're parking right under the ramp. It's still under construction!" Tynan protested.

"Right. See these cars? Construction workers' cars. Don't worry. I do it all the time. They even recognize me now."

Tynan wondered if a black man's BMW would get the same consideration from the construction workers as Bobbi Jo's old Chevy Bel Air, but he didn't think it would be right, just now, to show distrust in her judgment. Walking toward the restaurant, they detoured around construction sites, passed fenced-off parking lots, crossed a wide cobblestone street with railroad tracks running down the middle of it, cut through another cobblestone alley and crossed through one of the narrow parking lots to reach Calvert Street. Edging sideways through the crowded cars, Tynan couldn't avoid getting dust marks on his navy suit. As they reached the street, Bobbi Jo called back encouragingly.

"It's only two doors down."

The sidewalk on Calvert Street was already, at one o'clock in the afternoon, in the shadow of the massive office building across the street. At least, Tynan observed, the sidewalk was relatively clean. In the alley, they'd had to step around piles of manure left by the horses of the mounted police.

"Why does our department have to do a study anyway? We got nothing to do with land or development."

Tynan shrugged as he opened the door of the restaurant for her.

Getting a table was not a small accomplishment. Forty feet long and twelve feet wide, the building had served well as a row house at the turn of the century, but only a desperate immigrant had been able to picture it as a restaurant. Tynan and Bobbi Jo had to fight their way through the carryout line near the front door, then through another line of people milling around the cash register.

One concept that the owner had not brought with him from Greece was the concept of the division of labor. A carryout order might be interrupted in mid-transaction while the waitress responded to the bell ringing for her back in the kitchen, only to be sidetracked on the way there by a chorus of requests for napkins, more water, the check, a menu, a dishrag, some silver, etc. The three lunch waitresses were bumping into each other and handing each other food and money and silverware and napkins and pointing to this customer and that table and holding up carryouts to the crowd almost as if asking for the highest bid—all of this done on the honor system and in a dedicated, eternally confused but nonplused way that made it clear that either these women had nerves of steel or they didn't have any neurological systems at all.

They wedged their way past the cash register and into the dining area. Bobbi Jo expertly picked a formica table which didn't wobble, then shoved the extra chairs away in the direction of another table. She grabbed some napkins from another table and wiped off the soapy water that Nate, the busboy, had left when he'd finished clearing the table. Nate was small and very dark. His head was covered by a thin cap of grey fuzz. He looked like he was about 101 years old, and he was extremely difficult to communicate with. It was rumored that he had once been a slave, but the current opinion among the customers was that he was now a slave. John, the owner, and all of the waitresses, snapped at him continually, but it was hard to tell if Nate understood. He worked constantly, though in slow motion, and the customers understood that they were expected to help out. After Bobbi Jo dried the table, Nate dropped a pile of clean dishes and silverware on the table for her to sort out. By the time Tynan

155

looked up in surprise, Nate was already soaping down another table halfway across the room. Throughout their meal, he bumped around the room, delivering clean silverware, plates, cups and napkins at random.

"I'll tell you what I do know about the study," Tynan responded as soon as they had divided up the utensils. "It's obviously some type of gimmick. I know Gotterdung got Governor Mallard to sign it with the idea that it was meaningless. I know he wants to hold up the Waterside Towers project, but I don't know why. He wants to take on Pettibone, one on one, but I don't know why he's doing that either."

"He shouldn't have screwed up the Mallory case."

"Maybe we can minimize the damage."

"Leonard, you and I know that Mallory and Gotterdung are just two little parts of everything that's been wrong with this department for years."

"Then," Tynan met her eyes and shocked her with a startling coolness, "we just might have to cut those parts out." He picked up the menu by its edges and made a show of trying to read through the scratched plastic cover.

Tynan's meal was astonishing: roast veal, mashed potatoes and peas, all for the price of a sandwich anywhere else in town. Bobbi Jo ordered a hot roast beef sandwich which she swore was delicious. But the gravy was a bright lemon yellow. They never did get their drinks, until they asked for their check. While they waited for their check, tablesful of potential diners lurched and stumbled around them, rearranging the seating plan as they pleased.

"Gotterdung's going off the deep end, Bobbi Jo. You and I are the top sane levels of government left. You have to stick with me."

"Will you *promise* me, Leonard, that Mallory will go?"

Just then, a group of men in sports jackets and ties came in and grabbed the last open table. All three of them looked as if they had been dining on John's full-course lunches a little too regularly. To get room to sit down, they had to push their table right up against Tynan's and Bobbi Jo's. As a result, the intruder with the largest belly and the loudest tie was pushed sideways against Tynan, practically sitting at their table. His arm actually was on their table. As he started to talk with his friends, he even began to absent-mindedly finger the sugar pourer that was set between Tynan and Bobbi Jo. The man had a square, thickly fleshed red face and old fashioned, black-framed glasses with extremely thick lenses. His hair was blond and was cut in a flattop that had not been fashionable since Johnny Unitas's heyday. He had a strong build, but had allowed himself to get pudgy. He began tilting the sugar pourer this way and that with his short, thick fingers.

Tynan was perturbed. This was the last straw. "The food may be good and cheap, but I can't stand this place." He got up to leave.

Bobbi Jo's eyes grew suddenly very large. She waved Tynan back down into his seat. She took out one of her cheap state ball point pens, scribbled something on a napkin and passed it to Tynan. It had an arrow on it pointing to the man whose arm was on their table. And one word: "KEANE!"

Tynan froze. Keane's tie did not match either his shirt or his sport coat. He was already talking, already dominating the conversation with his loud nasal opinions. Tynan pulled himself away and sat at a corner of the table sipping his lukewarm cup of coffee, listening. It was a delicious feeling to be able to eavesdrop on the press, especially since Keane himself had become his antagonist just that morning.

One of the other men at Keane's table was saying that "it" might really be just an honest difference of opinion.

157

Keane guffawed loudly and smacked his palm down in front of Tynan's plate.

"No, no, no. It's Slip Slidell. His bill. Can't anybody think? Did that study bill just come out of thin air?"

"It was Bain's bill," one of the other men objected.

"Ha! It did start that way, but it got amended about a hundred times. Even the conference committee amended it the last night of the session. And the only one who cared about the original bill, that nun, had long since gone home. I just found out this morning that the conference committee member who actually wrote the language that night was Ely Schatzenhauser. Schatzenhauser owes his entire political career to the Deep Devotion Democratic Club. Schatzenhauser doesn't take a shit unless Slidell tells him to. Slidell did it, all right. I think he was just throwing a bone to that nun. Now Gotterdung's got the bone, and he's worrying Pettibone to death with it."

They edged through the parking lot once again. In the alley out back, Nate was picking up clods of horse manure and throwing them into a public trash can with his bare hands. A black and yellow steel medallion on the trash can informed everyone: "CROSLEY T. PETTIBONE, AWAITING YOUR INPUT." Tynan stopped and brushed the dust from the car fenders off his pants. He vowed that he would never come to this place again for lunch, no matter how good the food. He started worrying about his car being parked on that construction site.

Before they had gone another half block, a more serious concern arose. A man crossing the street immediately in front of them suddenly groaned, clutched his chest and crumpled to the street. Tynan instinctively grabbed him and pulled him to safety on the sidewalk. He was a fairly tall, thin black man wearing clean but completely mismatched clothes. He curled up on the sidewalk now, still clutching his chest or his stomach. He was in too much pain to speak.

As soon as the man was safe from being hit by traffic, Bobbi Jo looked at Tynan significantly.

"He's a wino. He'll be all right."

The man was on all fours now, breathing deeply, but hanging his head. He said nothing. His hair was medium length and half grey. It looked like it had been cut at home with scissors. Tynan was trying to remember the signs of a heart attack. Up close, the man didn't look, or smell, like a boozer.

"He needs to be seen in the emergency room," he said.

Bobbi Jo began to edge away. Her reaction would have been completely different if the man had been wearing a suit. A strong prejudice told her that people who dressed like this were often in trouble, and that it was usually trouble of their own making. But Tynan kept leaning over the man, asking him if he could stand.

"Not yet, not yet. This happened before. I'll be all right," the man whispered.

"Do you know what it is?" Tynan asked.

The man shook his head no.

"Where does it hurt?"

The man put a hand on his stomach, right under his ribs. Tynan told him that he was going to call an ambulance. The man stopped talking, turned his head to the gutter and threw up. Tynan watched the vomit start to roll down the gutter.

"Call an ambulance," he ordered. Bobbi Jo, looking around for a place to make a phone call, saw the large plastic sign of the emergency entrance of Sacred Heart Hospital shining down on them from less than fifty feet away. The man resisted going with Tynan, but Bobbi Jo grabbed his other arm. They put their arms under his shoulders and forced him down the sidewalk.

"I already feel a little better," he insisted.

"You need help, sir."

In the emergency room, the man was treated with a little more deference than the others because he was brought in by someone wearing a suit. The emergency-room personnel were not surprised, since they were only three blocks away from the Legal Assistance Society, and the lawyers would occasionally bring their clients in. But big problems arose: the man had no insurance, no Medical Assistance card, no doctor. The lady behind the counter pointedly asked Tynan if he was going to be financially responsible for the bill. That stopped him cold. He looked at Bobbi Jo, then down at the ground. Then he sighed.

"If your people here tell me it is an emergency, I'll be responsible," he said finally.

"If it was an emergency, we'd admit him anyway."

The man didn't say anything, though his breathing did seem to be more regular and relaxed now. The woman turned aside from them and mumbled something to a nurse, who in turned wandered across the room and mumbled something to a young resident. He motioned for them to come into a little area separated from the others by a sheet partition. They talked to Tynan about the symptoms as if the man were deaf and mute. The resident took the man's blood pressure and listened to his heart. The man told them he had been having stomach problems for months, but he didn't have a doctor now. He said he had thrown up only once or twice before. Certain foods made it worse. The doctor and nurse were listening very intently, but nothing was being written down.

"I don't think this is a heart attack," the resident finally said in a low voice. "You can never be sure until you test, but these are the classic symptoms of a peptic ulcer, a bleeding peptic ulcer. This can be very serious. You can lose so much blood that you can pass out and die from that. A little bleeding doesn't mean that that's happening—yet. But I can call it an emergency and admit you, if you want."

"Would Medical Assistance pay for it?" Tynan, one of the top administrators of the agency that made the rules for Medical Assistance, asked the young doctor.

"I thought you guys were the lawyers," the resident responded. Then he turned to the old man. "They have to take you in here if it's an emergency. Most people don't need an immediate operation. Then it's treatment, long-term therapy, that you'll need. You need a doctor, sir, and I think you need to see him every week. But if you want, I can make them take you in now. Even a couple of days might help some."

Tynan and Bobbi Jo looked expectantly at the man.

"No, don't put me in," the man said. "I got someplace to go."

"Do you understand that you need treatment?" Tynan asked before the doctor could.

"Yes," the man said, looking him directly in the eye, "I know that now. I been looking away from a lot of things in the past. But I'm going to take care of all that now."

Since there were no admission papers, discharge was immediate, painless and free. Tynan thanked the doctor and asked him for his name, but the doctor just shook his head and smiled. "You never saw me," he said. "You lawyers know the drill."

The old man really did look much better. He said he felt okay. "You two are nice people," he said, "help out a man like me. I'm meeting more and more nice people all the time. People helping me who I never thought would."

He walked away in the direction of Calvert Street. Before he left, Tynan told him to apply for Medical Assistance.

"Here's my business card. If you have any trouble at all getting your Medical Assistance card, you just come see me. That's something I can definitely help you with."

The two state employees walked back toward the dirt parking space under the freeway in silence.

"You're a kind man, Leonard."

"I never answered your question in the restaurant, Bobbie Jo."

"About Mallory? You've got to get rid of him, Leonard."

"I know."

There was a thin layer of red dust on Tynan's BMW, but it didn't seem that important anymore.

12 THE KINK

Startled, Doxie held the shrieking receiver at arm's length. His bandaged hand began to throb. He put receiver down gingerly on his desk and quickly paced to his office doorway. He looked across the waiting room toward his private secretary. He didn't even have to ask the question.

"The mayor," she nodded emphatically.

He returned to his desk, sank down in his heavy swivel armchair, and listened from a distance of four feet to Crosley Pettibone's fulminations against the Legal Assistance Society. A bead of sweat rolled down the smooth, round, brown dome of his bald head. Doxie couldn't tell what Mayor Pettibone was upset about, but it was obvious that the Society's special relationship with the mayor was over.

"Doxie! Doxie!" For the first time, the voice required a response. Doxie shot out of the swivel chair to grab the receiver.

"Yes, Mr. Mayor."

"Do you understand how bad it will be? I will crush you, I will rush you, I will ruin you, I ...."

"Why?"

The voice was suddenly stilled.

163

"Well, you know ...." the voice began again, weakly.

"No. I don't really know, Crosley."

"You don't know what your own lawyers are up to?"

"No, I don't, Crosley. Not everything. Why don't you tell me what you are so upset about."

"You really don't know?"

"I promise, Crosley, I don't know. You can tell me, though. Why don't you tell me?"

"Have you ever heard .... Have you ever heard of 442 Jasper Street?"

Pettibone had just learned that 442 Jasper Street was not really in Susumee Development's hands, and that a client of the Legal Assistance Society still had control of the house, and that he would not negotiate a price. The mayor felt as if he had been stabbed in the back by his closest friend. Legal Assistance, it was obvious, had arranged a scheme whereby their client pretended to sell the property to the developers. Then, after Pettibone had announced the project publicly, staking his whole reputation on the project, Legal Assistance had sprung its trap. Susumee didn't own the property after all. And 442 Jasper Street was now worth a small fortune. Lawyer Sport Norris was ready to jack the price up, using as a lever the fact that it was the last unpurchased parcel in the tract, and grinding that lever against the fulcrum of Pettibone's public humiliation. Pettibone had always hated lawyers, hated the way they cleverly hid behind words. But this time, Sport Norris had been too clever. He would be made to pay the price.

"Now we are getting somewhere, Crosley. Explain to me about 442 Jasper Street."

It took Doxie half an hour to calm him down. Doxie assured him that Legal Assistance lawyers did not use unethical tactics.

"... but many of our clients are illiterate and will sign

anything. This wouldn't be the first time, Your Honor, that people who didn't know any better signed papers meant for someone else. Some business people are so anxious to get a signature on a piece of paper they don't even question who is doing the signing. We have a dozen cases like that in our Consumer Law Unit every month."

Gradually, Doxie convinced the mayor that the Legal Assistance Society would never have engineered a scam to jack up the price of 442 Jasper Street. He convinced the mayor with quiet but forceful logic, basing his arguments on the facts which he was making up as he went along. He had tried several times at the beginning of the conversation to ask for time to collect the actual facts, but since the mayor wouldn't allow that, Doxie just gave him the next best thing.

Of course, Doxie was absolutely correct that no Society lawyer had any plot to enrich his clients at the expense of Pettibone's public humiliation. He was not so lucky, however, with his next set of guesses. Mayor Pettibone began questioning him closely about why they were representing a man who didn't really have a legal problem.

"He doesn't have a problem at all, Doxie, except how much of a windfall he's going to get because his house is in the way of all my plans!"

"Well, you know, Mr. Mayor, the poor are poor partly because they have come out on the short end of the stick in every transaction in their lives. You know yourself how many people over the years have been cheated out of valuable property by clever people working for wealthy interests. I recall that your mother once had that plot of land ...."

"Yes, yes, I understand," said the mayor, hoping to forestall the retelling of a story that had been a source of shame to him since childhood.

"It was sold for some worthless stock, I believe."

"Let's not talk about that."

"We feel," Doxie continued crisply, relishing the role of advocate, now that the mayor had conceded him the right to act in that capacity, "that our client has the right to ask for whatever price he can get for his property, even though it may be valuable just because of a lucky break—just as any rich client would undoubtedly do."

"Money, then." The mayor breathed long and mournfully into the phone. "Well," he sounded resigned, "this venture has plenty of money. Your guy got a lucky break. Keep my mistake out of the press, and the deal will go a lot better, take my word."

"You can be assured of that, Your Honor. If your people make a good offer, considering our client's unusual degree of leverage, I'm sure we can make a quick and quiet deal."

"I'm sure also."

They were both wrong. Charles was at that very moment entering the front door of the Society's building, intent on seeking Sport's advice on how he could move into the house permanently. He had decided that the house meant a lot more to him than the outlandish amounts of money that were being offered to him by people he didn't even know. Although he came to tell this to Sport, he was held up at the reception desk. The desk was being covered temporarily by a legal assistant, since Linda had been given the rest of the day off to begin her search for child care.

"Mr. Norris is on the phone right now. Would you have a seat?"

It was an urgent call from Doxie. Sport ran up the back stairs as Charles settled into a chair in the reception room. Sport met Angela coming up the steps. Doxie's sec-

166

retary nodded them right into the Director's office. Doxie immediately began to pepper him with questions. Did he have a client named Charles Gage? Was he financially eligible for our legal services? Exactly what kind of a case did he have?

"What are you getting at, Doxie?"

"What I'm getting at is," Doxie cut him off rudely, "is a question of whether this Mr. Gage is really an eligible client, given the valuable property he owns ...."

"It was last appraised at $5,700."

". . . and whether this is the type of case, a real estate negotiation, that we should be involved with in the first place."

"Charles Gage came to me with a will question. The executor's lawyer was offering to buy out his legacy. It looked very suspicious to me, like another instance of slick people trying to take advantage of a poor client. And I was right. That was exactly what it was."

"I see," Doxie said, seeming to relax more in his chair. "I'm glad we had this discussion. I did have certain concerns about this client. The mayor, who, as you know, is one of our funding sources, is absolutely committed to this Waterside Towers Condominium development. His whole career is riding on it. It's named after him. I agree that it is our duty to get all the money we can out of Mr. Gage's stroke of good fortune. But it would be quite counterproductive, quite counterproductive, to Mr. Gage's own interest if it became publicly known that the mayor had jumped the gun and announced the project too soon. In other words, the mayor doesn't want to be made to look like a fool, and it will be in our client's interest to go along with that wish. So, are we in agreement?"

"Nobody wants to embarrass the mayor, Doxie. But you don't understand. Charles really wants that house."

The 400 block of Jasper Street had two more squares dug out of it, each surrounded by Pettibone signs. Angela pulled the car up to the blinking orange lights of the traffic barriers in the curb lane and cut the engine. She, Sport and Charles stepped out into the wave of heat rising from the sidewalk. Angela pulled Sport's arm back as Charles rushed ahead with the key.

"He wants to live *here?* Instead of taking a fortune from the mayor?"

"Shh."

Inside, the air was close. Only a small fraction of the evening sunlight penetrated the narrow windows. Angela admired some of Aunt May's dark antique furniture. She didn't think too much of the house itself, but she tried to see it through Charles's eyes.

"It must be exciting to own a house."

"The first thing you need to do," Sport told him, "is to make a list of everything that needs to be done, and everything that needs to be paid, before you can move into the house. I know some good roofers. I can help you get some estimates."

After they had opened all the windows wide, Angela asked Charles to come outside. They sat on the marble stoop, watching the stream of foot traffic into the liquor store across the street. Two old drunks sat on a stoop across the street, engaging in a bumbling, repetitive argument with a shriveled hag almost as old as themselves. "Listen here ... listen here ... I'm telling you ... I'm telling you ... no, no, no ...."

The incessant nattering of their voices provided a steady background drone.

"Do you recognize those men?"

Charles stared sadly at them without answering.

"How do you know," she asked, "that you need this house?"

"House? House found me."

"But how do you know that you need it?"

"Didn't want it. Sport made me look at it." He turned toward her. "He made me take a good look. One real good look, and I needed it bad."

"Why didn't you know what you needed before?"

Charles let his gaze drift toward the drunks, who were still nattering away. He shook his head. He could not answer the question. "I'll show you the house," he offered instead.

This time, Angela noticed the crystal doorknobs, the dark, varnished doors, the tiny marble tiles in the small foyer. A faint breeze now came in through the windows and stirred the stifling smell of old, hot wood.

"This was her living room," she observed, standing in the ten by twelve room to the right of the foyer, at the front of the house. Charles stopped, looked at her.

"See?" Angela gestured at the large pieces of furniture shoved together and covered with sheets. "Sofa, two comfortable chairs, coffee table."

He doesn't even know what a living room is!

"Living room here." Charles repeated, as if he were taking notes.

Dining room. At first, she wasn't going to say "dining room" to him. It seemed impossible, a man like Charles having a dining room. But he did have a dining room. So she did say it, and he echoed her again. He had a kitchen. Bedroom, bedroom, bathroom. He needed her to explain to him what he really had. Every word she said about the house was a revelation. At the same time, he repeated Sport's quiet suggestions about the roof, water service, electricity.

"Did you always know," she whispered to him when Sport was out of the room, "that the house was going to be so much trouble?"

169

"No."

"Are you sorry that you took this on? You could get a lot of money from just selling it to the mayor."

"No, no, no, child. This house, this is what I want."

"You're not the kind of person who adds up all the costs first, are you?"

"I'll be all right." He met her eyes easily.

The security and peace that Charles felt inside the house was contagious. They studied every room, every stick of furniture. She helped Charles plan, her ideas flowing freely and naturally now. Something had been hidden here all these years, waiting for him to come back and find it. And he had. Angela and Sport glanced furtively at each other in the dim light, both wondering how much this house was going to cost them. But the house itself, the weight and certainty of that house, steadied them. All three of them fell into a strange, contented silence, as the sky outside the windows changed from pink to purple to grey. The circle illuminated by the flashlight became sharper. They edged around the old furniture in the darkness, their faces illuminated only occasionally by the curious light, searching for treasures not easily found nor always appreciated.

13 DISCOVERY

None of Sport or Angela's requests for information had put the department in any immediate jeopardy of losing the crawlspace suit. The Legal Assistance Society had filed Interrogatories, and Requests For the Production Of Documents, so numerous, broad and wide-ranging that they required the production of almost every piece of paper generated in the department over the last five years. The standard defense to such massive requests was the massive bequest. This was a simple move. The defense sent a reply that basically said that the files were open and the plaintiffs could come and dig in them at will.

The agency using this defense almost always offered to provide an employee as a guide to the files. Bobbi Jo Ludell met Sport and Angela at her office door as soon as they arrived to study the files. She immediately pointed to a group of steel filing cabinets in a corner of the waiting area, near her desk.

"That's 1988."

She walked them to Gotterdung's outer office.

"That's 1989."

She pointed out groups of filing cabinets in seven other locations on the sixth floor. "There's a whole bunch more

171

in the records room on the fifth floor," she added, walking away from them. "And don't forget the records storage warehouse in Jessup."

In the massive bequest gambit, there was always the remote danger that the plaintiffs would stumble onto something significant, but the likelihood of that was low. Jody Hechtmuller had laid this massive bequest on Sport and Angela from the beginning. There was little to fear from them digging through the records themselves. Of course, if Mayor Pettibone carried out his threat, and sent city auditors to aid them in the discovery process, Jody would have to watch everything more carefully.

On the first day, Angela found a seven-year-old study which projected a slow but steady increase in the number of people eligible for Medical Assistance. She knew that the study's projection contrasted sharply with what had actually happened in the last seven years. Later statistics showed that there had been a sharp dropoff in eligible people five years before (coinciding with former Secretary Fiore's discovery of the power of the computer spreadsheet) followed by a Medicaid population that was basically stagnant until the present time. The study suggested that only something highly unusual (such as a crawlspace plot) could have suddenly cut down on the number of people eligible like that.

"Good. Good." Sport acted only mildly enthusiastic when she showed him this. "This is a fact we can use at trial."

"A fact?" Angela was incredulous. "This is the whole case, isn't it, Sport?" But Sport could see that she was restraining herself a little now. Two years of litigation experience had slowly taught her that nothing in law is simple.

"Just wait. You'll see at trial how they get around something like this. They'll say the study was preliminary, or

172

the analysis was flawed, or the projections were made by someone lacking in overall expertise. It's a piece of evidence for us, but it won't carry the day."

"Won't it at least prove to the judge that the bureaucracy doesn't know what it's doing?"

"All the judges already know that, Angela."

They hadn't been able to see the individual clients' case records. The old client records were stacked to the ceilings in some local offices, while they were thrown directly into the Dumpster in others. Just a handful of these records from a few different time periods would have conclusively proven Sport and Angela's case. The old records would have shown the imaginary crawlspaces and basements printed right on the forms, and the newer records would have demonstrated that everybody got one whether he lived in a house trailer or the top unit of an eight-story apartment building. But Jody would not let Sport or Angela see even one of these records.

"Both federal and state law," he told them, "require us to keep these records confidential."

Angela and Sport had offered much earlier to look at copies of the records with the clients' names whited out, but Jody still would not agree. They then proposed that an agency employee go through the records to collect certain statistical data that they needed. Jody said that this would cause a financial and administrative burden that the department could not bear. When they offered to reimburse the department, he said that he was unsure if this was appropriate anyway. He did say that he would get back to them with a cost estimate, but he never did.

All of this legal thrusting and parrying and dragging of feet was centered around the one point on which this lawsuit was going to be either won or lost. Once the case was certified as a class action, Sport and Angela would be the lawyers for the whole class of people who applied for Medical Assistance and who were turned down because of their crawlspaces. As their lawyers, they would have the right to see their files. As soon as they saw the files, they could prove that the department had been acting illegally for years, turning down thousands of eligible people on the basis of the phony basements. But for now, they could not see the files, because the class was not certified. They could not get the class certified because they could not prove to the federal judge's satisfaction that this was happening to thousands of people. They couldn't prove that this was happening to thousands of people because they couldn't see the files.

Although it had at first seemed like a simple thing to come up with a new client who was suffering from a phantom basement, weeks had now gone by without a sign of a real, live Medical Assistance rejectee. Both sides were suffering from the suspense. Sport and Angela were just starting to fear that the unthinkable was really happening, that the department had found some way of smoothing things over for a few weeks, and that no new client would come. The small doubt that still remained in Judge Barnett's mind would be magnified when they couldn't come up with one example of the 42,000 clients supposedly wronged by the department. He wouldn't sign the order. The case would be dismissed as moot. The department would find even more subtle ways of chopping people off the Medical Assistance rolls, and no one would ever entrust either one of them with a major case again.

Mayor Pettibone had promised that city auditors would be sent to help the Legal Assistance Society in the discovery process, but that promise was made before the mayor discovered that Sport and Angela were representing Charles Gage. Two city auditors were scheduled to meet with Sport and Angela the next day in the records room on the fifth floor of the Department of Public Welfare building, but the only representative from the city who showed up was Fosback.

"There will be no auditors," he quickly announced, "no support at all for the Legal Assistance Society in the *Throckmorton v. Gotterdung* suit."

Jody Hechtmuller smiled. He had come to the meeting to negotiate with Sport about which records the auditors could and could not see.

"I guess you don't need to talk to me now."

"Just one thing, Jody. The photocopy machine. We're supposed to have complete access to the one in room 515. But someone was using it all day yesterday."

They walked to the copy room next door, where a short, portly man was busily photocopying a huge stack of documents. Something about the man's appearance made Sport uneasy.

"This machine is reserved," Jody called out brusquely, "for the Legal Assistance Society's use only. No one else is authorized to use it today. I want you to clear out now, Mr. Mallory."

"You have no right ...."

Hearing the name, and seeing the man turn, with his goatee, his receding hair, his papers stacked up behind him, and his belligerent attitude, brought back to Sport the moment when he had seen the man before, in the clerk's office of the federal courthouse. On wobbly knees Sport turned to go. But the light of recognition lit up Mallory's dour features.

"Counsellor Throckmorton!"

"This is attorney Sport Norris," Jody spat out disgustedly.

Mallory ignored him. "Well, doesn't it seem that every time the common man seeks access to the justice system, bigshot counselor Throckmorton must have his way, and bigshot Counselor Throckmorton's cases must be given priority?"

"Mr. Mallory, my patience is running out. You have thirty minutes to clear everything out of here so Mr. Norris can use the machine." Jody motioned for Sport, Angela and Fosback to follow him out of the room. He knew they'd have to leave or Mallory would never back down.

"Norris?" Only Fosback, the last one in line to leave, heard Mallory grumbling as they left the room. "If his name is Norris, why is he signing the name Throckmorton to all those court papers?"

Fosback froze in the doorway, his keen ear for human weakness sudden sensitized. He turned back quietly. "That attorney," he whispered, trying to catch Mallory's eye. "What did you see him sign?"

The morning of his scheduled deposition by the Legal Assistance Bureau, Leonard Tynan performed a number of routine chores in his office, completely unconcerned about the prospect of being grilled by Sport or Angela about the crawlspace suit. He wasn't any longer particularly worried about the lawsuit. He knew that he would have to admit today that the department had perhaps gone overboard in the past, perhaps cut people off Medical Assistance too quickly, but he wasn't afraid any more of admitting the errors of his predecessors. Thanks to his diligent attentions to the problem, the department's policy was now so vague and ambiguous that no one could prove that the current procedures were illegal. The crawlspaces no longer appeared on the forms at all, and they were not even mentioned any more in the instructions to the eligibility workers.

Tynan now believed that he could accomplish everything he wanted, as long as the crawlspace suit was thrown out of court. His new policy would slowly allow thousands more people onto the Medical Assistance rolls, but this would happen in a way that the department could comfortably handle. Only a trickle of the 42,000 people previously turned down would find their way onto the rolls this year. The department could afford to pay them. And when more came in the years after that, he had a plan for the department to cover them too. Eventually, within six or seven years, everybody would be covered—and without any embarrassing revelations, or budgetary shocks.

Tynan felt that he had this matter under control. He was also supremely confident in his careful preparation for the deposition, and in his raw verbal jousting abilities. He had been bested before, but never by a lawyer.

But the department now had a more powerful enemy than any federal judge. Joe Keane had the department in his bulldog grip and was starting to grind away slowly at its vital organs.

Tynan had realized from the beginning that the full story of the crawlspaces might leak out; but he had counted on it coming out slowly, in dribs and drabs, long after the drama of the lawsuit was over, when nobody cared anymore, after the elections. That hardly seemed likely now. He glanced at Keane's current column in the *Free American,* headlined:

BASEMENTS 'CRAWLED' ONTO WELFARE FORMS ON THEIR OWN?

This reporter has learned, from sources familiar with the Department of Public Welfare's attempts to weasel out of its responsibility to the old, the poor and sick of this state, that the department will admit to the Legal Assistance Society's lawyers today that it used to assign phony basements to thousands of Medical Assistance applicants in order to keep them from getting the medical care they were entitled to by law. Last week, the department admitted for the first time that an application form was used which automatically assigned a basement to every poor piker in the Free State. The basement was printed right onto the form. These compassionate bureaucrats refused to admit this until this reporter stole a copy of one of these old forms and threatened to print it in this newspaper. Now, they say they have no idea how these basements got there. Well, I know how they got there.

The column went on with Keane's speculations about how and why Secretary Gotterdung and his Assistant Secretaries had ordered this, and how they might think that this was the appropriate thing to do from "their comfortable, safe, Blue-Cross-protected point of view. But," he concluded:

their concern for their fellow man, and their basic respect for truth, are no more highly developed than that of those other creatures who slither around in all of our basements and crawlspaces, only to scurry for cover when someone flicks on the light. Flick!

Gotterdung erupted. "That bastard's killing us! We didn't even do it! How come he knows everything else, but he gets it wrong about who started this mess? I'd like to let him have it. Put out a statement, Leonard, showing that Fiore did this. My wife will hate me, but I'm tired of taking the heat for that dead old coot."

"Can't you see?" Tynan spoke quietly. "He's baiting us. He's making things look just a little bit worse than the truth, trying to force us to tell what we do know. He knows that we inherited these crawlspaces."

"But if we say nothing, everyone will believe that you and I invented them."

"They might."

"Jeez!"

Gotterdung sulked in a chair. He was worried about Joe Keane affecting his plan to become Slidell's lieutenant governor.

He had just gotten off the phone with Slidell.

"You screwed up the plan," Slidell had growled. "But it can still work if you keep your mouth shut. That lawsuit—what's it about?—crawlspaces?—that doesn't help either. What would it take to settle it quickly and quietly?"

"At least five million dollars a year."

"Oh. What are the chances of winning it in court?"

"It's a crapshoot." Gotterdung had no idea.

"Keep a low profile on that."

"Okay."

"You know what I mean? Don't be out in public defending it, in case what you're doing turns out to be illegal. Do you understand?"

Gotterdung later repeated to Tynan something that Slidell had suggested. "Maybe we should pretend we are the ones solving the crawlspace problem."

"Right. We're not trapped. Let me put out a statement. We'll have to admit that those forms used to have those automatic basement deductions. But we'll take credit for stopping that. 'We've been trying to eradicate this eligibility problem for a number of months. We've now gotten rid of all the illegal barriers that were keeping people from the medical care they needed. People are coming back onto the rolls. But we have to move cautiously, to conserve these tax dollars for those who are truly needy.'"

"Yeah. Yeah. Great. Handle it."

Tynan did not tell Gotterdung that he had already sought out Slip, locating him finally in Eddie's Restaurant. It was suspicious for someone of the rank of Assistant Secretary to be privately conferring with powerful politicians. There was never an approved reason for Assistant Secretaries to contact politicians on their own.

For Tynan to see Slip on his own, and to seek him out at the restaurant instead of his legislative office, was the political equivalent of walking in your neighbor's back door without knocking. It boldly announced a new presence and attitude to be reckoned with. Slip appreciated boldness when it was coupled with intelligence. Too many of the intelligent people he knew retreated into safe little roles in the professions and wasted the rest of their lives building walls around their success. Too many of the bold people had nothing in mind but greed. Tynan's attitude grabbed Slip's attention immediately.

"I think you should know that the department is in a state of turmoil," he began. "There's a very real possibility that it could be burned very badly in this crawlspace suit. And Secretary Gotterdung is no longer capable of carrying out any rational plans. He doesn't think about the consequences of his acts."

When he saw Slip's green eyes focus their way out of the calculated lethargy of his face, Tynan knew that he had hit paydirt. He took a sip of his hot tea and watched to see how the legendary senator would react.

"How much do you know?" Slidell's bluntness was startling.

"I know that he doesn't want to release the study, and I know that he's working for you on this." Tynan hadn't meant to be this candid.

"What did Gotterdung do that's going to get him in more trouble?"

"It's a long story. Something he did at his news conference."

"We have time."

Tynan explained about Gotterdung praising Mallory at the press conference.

"It's a contradiction," Slidell admitted, but he shrugged. "It can be explained away."

"Gotterdung's credibility with the public is shaky already. He doesn't need another contradiction on the record. But the frightening thing is *why* he said that."

"Yeah. Why did he say that? I can't see any reason for that."

"He said it—for fun."

Slidell jiggled the ice around in his diet soda. "So, in the process, he screwed up the department's big effort to get rid of its pet turkey." He took another sip, staring at Tynan, measuring him. "You're smart enough to know, Leonard, that this trading of public insults between Gotterdung and the mayor was not part of my original plan."

Tynan met his look without responding.

"Gotterdung screwed that one up too," Slidell admitted.

Still, Tynan didn't respond.

"And the next logical step for me might be to think about replacing him—*with you.*"

Tynan delicately sipped at his tea.

"But I can't go back on my word to him," Slidell finished.

"I wasn't going to ask you to do that."

"Oh no? What is it that you want?"

"Tell me why you are holding up Pettibone's project. I can help you. I can keep Gotterdung pointed in the right direction."

"And you get ...?"

"The department holds together, provided I can also

save it from the crawlspace suit."

"And *you* get?"

"I get to be the next Secretary of the department if your plan succeeds and you become governor."

Slidell sat back, seeming to measure the value of what he had been offered.

But Tynan wasn't finished. "But anything I do has to be kept a secret, even from Gotterdung."

"That way," Slidell stared at Tynan. A frown creased his forehead. He knew that he had met his match. "... Pettibone will have nothing against you. If my plan succeeds, I make you Secretary. If it fails and Pettibone wins, he gets rid of Gotterdung and makes you Secretary. You win either way."

Tynan shrugged. "I don't do this for fun."

Gotterdung did not like the feeling he was getting that Tynan was taking control of the department, but Tynan's advice had always been good. After their conversation about the crawlspace lawsuit, Tynan began ushering him out of the office on the pretext of preparing for his deposition. Gotterdung stood up meekly.

"Go ahead," he said, standing in the doorway as if it had been his idea to leave. "Handle that asshole Keane however you want. Handle the deposition however you want." Tynan didn't say anything. "Handle it," Gotterdung said again, weakly, then disappeared out of the doorway.

After he left, however, Tynan didn't think at all about Keane, or about the deposition coming up. He decided to spend a few minutes congratulating himself. He had maneuvered himself into a no-lose situation. He knew where all the bodies were buried. No matter what the outcome of his boss's political plot, he would come out ahead. He was starting to think of the possibility that he was a new, superior type of politician.

Two years before, Charles Gage would have passively endured the elevators. Even then, the elevators were already slow, and exhibiting a tendency to stop between floors. But before Mallory had been put in charge of building maintenance, they had at least generally traveled in one direction to the ceiling or basement, then slowly oozed back the other way. After only a few months of Mallory's administration, however, they began to exhibit behavior not mentioned in any of the engineering literature. Buttons would light up to indicate that a floor was punched, then mysteriously go out. Buttons not punched would light up on their own. Elevators would take themselves out of service, or change their minds in the middle of a run. They might or might not go to any given floor, and the doors might or might not open when they got there. The employees had learned to take along a book or a snack. No one ever entered an elevator who thought he might have to go to the bathroom soon.

Charles had become a more patient man since he had learned of Aunt May's act of faith in him. He knew now that she had shown good judgment in leaving her house in his care. He had learned from the house, and from working with people like Sport and Angela and the doctor in the emergency room, that problems were complicated, but that he could solve them if he worked on them steadily, one part at a time. He had learned to ask for help, and to expect it, and to wait for it.

When he stepped onto the elevator in the lobby, it was already packed. The crowd crushed back even a little further against itself, wordlessly making a little sliver of room for him. He backed in. Somebody said "Watch yourself," and the two metal doors with their rubber gaskets clattered shut close to his face. He pulled his head back and stood erect, in a posture that made his stomach hurt.

Every button up to the sixth floor, his destination, was already lit. After the doors closed, the car waited, as if to gather its strength, then shot up to the fourth floor. Those who wanted to go to the fourth floor positively crowed, while the second and third floor passengers grumbled and moaned.

The elevator stopped on the fifth and sixth floors, but the doors didn't open on the sixth, which was Charles's destination. It then descended directly to the basement, where a large crowd of people was anxiously waiting. When it stopped at the first floor lobby again, Charles got out. He had been gradually moved to the back by the reshuffling of people at each floor, and now he had to excuse himself a number of times to get people to let him go by.

"Sir," a woman carrying a paper plate, and wearing bedroom slippers, called out, "this is the same floor you got on."

Charles looked back only after he was well clear of the doors. He saw a carful of numbed people framed in the doorway.

"Why don't you all use the stairs?"

He walked up to the sixth floor and found his way to Assistant Secretary Leonard Tynan's office. He gave Bobbi Jo Tynan's own card.

"I'm a friend of his."

Bobbi Jo looked down at the card with suspicion.

"And what should I say your name is?" Her voice was snippy.

"We met last week at the hospital. Sacred Heart."

"You met him ...?"

"You too. Remember? Picked me up off the street."

"Oh. Oh, yeah. How are you doing?"

"Pretty fair."

"He gave you his card. I remember. But you know, he's due to leave for a meeting in another office in about five minutes. Maybe I can get him to see you anyway."

She did not ask Charles to have a seat. The seats were deliberately arranged at the far wall of her office so that she might buzz Tynan and talk to him out of earshot of visitors. But if she spoke to Tynan while Charles was still standing at her desk, this would put pressure on Tynan, as his questions and responses over the intercom would be heard immediately by the visitor. It was like allowing the visitor halfway into the office. Bobbi Jo always did this for someone she wanted Tynan to talk to.

"It's who?"

"That man we took to the emergency room last week. You remember, picked him up off the street downtown."

"Oh. Oh, yes, that's great. Um, I'm getting ready to leave for this deposition right now. Well, send him in. Maybe I can take care of his problem in the one minute I have."

"You're looking better!" Tynan said right away, standing up, shaking Charles's hand and waving him toward a chair right across from his own. "Have you seen a doctor?"

"No. Why I'm here. I need Medical Assistance."

"Well, you certainly came to the right building! Actually, you should go to your local office. But maybe we can do it right here, have somebody walk you through the process. Make it easier."

"I already applied. They turned me down."

"They did! Why ...?" Tynan's ebullient momentum carried him that far before the terror struck. He mentally froze. His heart jumped crazily. Sweat began rolling down from his armpits. He knew what was coming next, he could hear it coming, but he couldn't deflect it.

"They say something about ... something about a *base-*

ment. I don't know about no basement. I got my papers right here ...." He reached into his back pocket.

Tynan held out his hands against the papers as if warding off an evil curse. Sitting in front of him, he realized, was the missing piece of the puzzle that the Legal Assistance Society was trying to put together to lock him and the department together in ignominy. This man sitting in front of him was a live crawlspace client, and he was trying to personally hand him his application, not two minutes before he was going off to a deposition in the case. Once he touched those papers, deniability was gone. He couldn't take these papers. He couldn't be aware of this. Most of all, he couldn't know this man's name.

"You said if I had problems, come to you."

"I know. I know." Tynan still had his arms out in front, his fingers spread. If only this man had come ten minutes later! Why couldn't the elevator have jammed when it would have done somebody some good? He tried not to look Charles in the eye, because he didn't want to think of him right now as a human being. But he couldn't help but picture the man's pain, and remember the way he had lain twisted on the sidewalk. He couldn't run out on him.

But if he took his appeal here, and now, it would ruin the defense of the crawlspace suit. He would have failed in his mission for Slip. His crawlspace coverup would be exposed to the court and the press. He would forfeit his political future. Charles's eyes caught his for a moment. Tynan was forced to acknowledge his presence. But he steeled himself to do what he had to do. His whole future depended on getting this man out of his office without learning his name.

14 THE OBVIOUS

Tynan had wanted the deposition to be in his own office, but Sport had insisted that it take place in the conference room of the Legal Assistance Society. Jody Hechtmuller was there. Angela was there also, though Jody had insisted that only one attorney for the plaintiffs ask the questions. It was actually unusual, and quite unnecessary, for two attorneys to be present for the same side. It was almost never done in private practice, since it was hard to justify charging the client for the attendance of a second attorney who only watched. Although there were no financial pressures from clients at the Legal Assistance Society, Angela and Sport usually avoided doubling up. They wanted to avoid the appearance that it took two Legal Assistance attorneys to equal one regular one.

The crawlspace suit seemed to be in danger of a sudden death. Jody Hechtmuller, sensing that Sport and Angela were having trouble finding a live client, asked the court to hold another hearing on the class certification issue. Ominously, Judge Barnett granted a hearing. The department would have a chance to point out that not one of the supposed 42,000 victims had stepped forward to be represented by the Legal Assistance Society. There

187

was no reason for Judge Barnett to hold another hearing except to deny the class certification and get this politically sensitive case off of his docket.

Keane, the *Free American* columnist, was not making things any better for the plaintiffs. The information that he was digging up (or making up) about the department's past practices was devastating. Everyone in the city now believed that the poor had been done a dirty deed. But Tynan and Gotterdung were defending the department very cleverly. They managed to convey the impression that the department had indeed been a cesspool of double dealing when they took it over three years before, after Bob Fiore died, and that they had been working righteously on straightening things up ever since. (They said that they could not, of course, go into any specifics, because of the pending lawsuit.)

Angela had visited Keane in his office. It was a tiny cubicle partitioned out of a large, beige, air-conditioned room. Keane filled up most of the space between his desk and the back wall.

"If the class isn't certified," Angela explained, "99 percent of these people will never get medical care. I know that it might seem strange for a lawyer to be asking you for this, but we need access to your sources of information. A lot of people will get sicker if we lose this suit."

Keane stared at her intently through his thick glasses. "No can do," he said finally.

Keane could feel the heat of Angela's desperate fervor. He considered for a moment jumping off his journalistic high horse. But if he did that, he didn't know where he would land.

"All I can do is help you by writing, as a journalist. But I can't reveal my sources. I write whatever I get. It's all in the paper anyway."

"But we do need access to your sources. Please."

"Why don't you just hang out at a social services office and sign someone up?"

"Can't. Legal ethics. We're not supposed to stir up litigation. Believe it or not."

Keane shrugged his massive shoulders. He kept the conversation going for over a quarter of an hour. He said he would do what he could without revealing his sources. Then he asked her for a date.

But having the lawsuit followed in the papers was really only making things worse. Every time Keane focused on a dirty deed of the past, Tynan would pretend to be proud that this, too, had been corrected by the compassionate and professional men now running the department. All of this publicity merely highlighted the fact that the lawsuit, which concerned what was happening *now,* was stuck in the mud.

If the federal court case was stalled much longer, the department would slip out of the grip of the law's logic. Using the pressure of the lawsuit as justification for more funding, the department probably would get an increase in its budget big enough to pay for a few of the additional people who deserved to be on Medical Assistance. Starting in the next year, all those applicants who appealed, or complained, or were obstreperous enough, would probably get their Medical Assistance cards. Most of the others would never be heard from; the department would escape the supervision of the federal court; and its officials would keep their jealously guarded prerogative of dealing with the poor as they saw fit.

"The statistical evidence proves that we're right," Angela argued in an emergency litigation meeting with Sport and Doxie. "Judge Barnett's failure to certify the class is just a little whim of his. This is a legal system, isn't it? Let's make him give us a legal answer. If we don't like it, let's appeal. Isn't it that simple?"

189

"We said we'd get him a live plaintiff. That would take some of the heat off him," Sport replied. "If we throw it all back on him now, we'll be going back on our word. We'll seem like bad sports."

"Bad sports! Is *that* the reason we're not pushing for a ruling on our motion?" She looked from Sport's blank face to Doxie.

"Old Tom Barnett doesn't feel comfortable with statistics," Doxie said. "He said that he wants to see a real person, and we said that we would get one. He's going to feel like we were too lazy to humor him."

"What difference does it make how he *feels!*" Angela lashed back. But the silence of the other two made Angela think hard about what she had said. The meeting dissolved without any agreement on a plan of action.

Keane then raised the stakes. Three days after Angela had visited him, his column read:

COME FORWARD, MY CHILDREN, AND BE HEALED

We know that you exist. So do those self-satisfied bureaucrats over at the Department of Public Welfare, but they have already denied you not once but twice. They've asked for a court hearing next week so they can deny for a third time that you exist. And if they succeed, and the judge turns you down, you won't feel the hands of a doctor working on you until they're cutting up your body for the medical students.

Legal Assistance needs someone who has recently been denied assistance to come into their office and sign some simple papers. That is all it will take to help thousands of people just like yourself. But no one has come, for weeks.

Where are you?

190

"Where are you?" Jody Hechtmuller quietly taunted, as he and Leonard Tynan arrived at the Legal Assistance Society for Tynan's deposition. He knew that Sport and Angela wouldn't even be going through with this deposition if they had found another actual client. As far as Jody could tell, Sport's not finding anyone had simply been an incredible piece of good luck—nothing to be counted on to last. But when no one had shown up, even after the Keane column, he told Tynan that he thought their luck might hold. There was a good chance that Legal Assistance's case would find its way to an early grave.

When Jody saw Angela enter the office too, he raised an eyebrow. This was supposed to communicate surprise that she had little enough else to do but watch Sport take Tynan's deposition. It was nothing personal; it was nothing more than another standard piece of professional intimidation. But Jody had no idea of the fervor Angela had for this case. She could not bear to wait a whole week for the court reporter to type up Tynan's deposition testimony. She couldn't even wait until that afternoon to hear Sport's description of the event. She wanted to see Tynan under oath, in person, live, now.

Jody didn't understand why Tynan looked nervous.

"Is there any subject you are worried about?" he had asked in the car.

"No."

But Tynan said nothing else during the whole drive downtown. This was not the Leonard Tynan that Jody was used to. Tynan was a good client to represent because he was adept at explaining, rephrasing, shifting the emphasis, distracting, misleading and concealing, but he would never tell an outright lie. There was little point in having so much intellectual skill if you were willing to make up the facts too.

191

Tynan rose to Sport's challenge throughout the three-hour deposition. Many of the questions were about the various subtle changes in departmental policy that had taken place since the crude old days of Fiore, when the illegal basement deductions were printed right on the forms. Tynan admitted his part in most of these small changes, even providing Sport at times with information just a little more candid and honest than he had ever provided Jody, his own lawyer, in the privacy of his own office. It was an attack of "the whole truth." Jody was used to a witness's story shifting and changing a little bit as a case progressed. Tynan had shaded things when he first spoke with him, but that version of the truth was not needed any more, since Jody was already on board and committed. This current version was not only more honest but was more detailed. Tynan described to Sport the successive steps by which the illegal crawlspace deductions had been taken off the forms, taken out of the policy manual, taken out of the list of directives, taken out of the supervisors training manual, and taken out of the new workers' orientation program.

"Taken out of everywhere where it could be seen, but not taken out of the way the department operates, or the way it treats its clients. Isn't that right?" Sport had badgered.

"That's what you say, but I haven't seen any proof of that."

"You haven't seen that?"

"No."

"Have you investigated what the local offices are actually doing?"

"No."

"Why not?" The real reason, they both knew, was that Tynan didn't want to know what the local offices were doing.

"It's not necessary. We've eliminated all instructions that were wrong about crawlspaces."

"But don't these recent statistics indicate to you that the local offices are still following the old instructions?"

"I wouldn't know."

"Don't your own statistics reveal a sudden and unexplained drop about five years ago in the number of people found eligible for Medical Assistance?"

"A sudden drop," Tynan suggested.

"And an unexplained drop?"

"I wouldn't necessarily characterize it that way."

"Does that mean you have an explanation?"

"No."

"Then it's unexplained," Sport said.

"No. There might be an explanation. But none was ever presented to me."

"Did you ever ask for an explanation?"

"No."

"A drop of 42,000?"

"Yes."

"But your own department's report projected an *increase*."

"I don't know that."

"Here. Here's the document we marked Plaintiff's Exhibit Number 177. Do you recognize this document?"

"Yes. Okay. Yes, it says an increase."

"Doesn't this paper indicate to you that a large number of people who are eligible today are not getting Medical Assistance?"

"No, it doesn't say that at all."

"But that statistical projection was valid at the time it was made?"

"It is valid as far as it goes, but you can't draw all these dramatic conclusions about the existence of thousands of people from these papers."

"Oh. Well, why do you collect these statistics?"

"We use them for planning, budget projections—things like that," Tynan explained.

"You submit them to the General Assembly with your budget requests?"

"Yes."

"You use them to plan the location and staffing of your offices?"

"Yes."

"You submit them to the federal government?"

"Yes."

"You include them in your Annual Report?"

"Yes."

"These statistics are useful for almost any purpose, you're saying, except for what I'm trying to use them for?"

"I didn't say that." Blandly.

"What are these statistics good for, then?"

"Haven't we just gone over that?"

Sport dropped his yellow pad on the desk. He stared at it for a moment, then started to gather his papers.

"That's all I have for Mr. Tynan today." He spoke directly to Jody. Sport was not disappointed in the answers he had gotten from Tynan. The purpose of a deposition was not to obtain dramatic confessions, or stunning revelations. Sport's method was to question the witness about the lawsuit from every possible angle, to collect a mountain of detail, to hem in the witness with a hundred small admissions. This painstaking process sometimes led to the discovery of new truths helpful in proving the case. And it always limited the amount of new fiction that the witness could come up with at trial. But the well-prepared witness rarely revealed at deposition anything that the other side didn't already pretty much know.

Tynan pushed his chair back from the table very casually. But Angela noticed how much he was perspiring, and she saw him glance furtively over at Jody Hechtmuller and motion with his eyes toward the door.

"Okay, I guess that's a wrap," Sport pushed back his own chair.

"Wait," Angela interrupted. She leaned close to Sport. "There's something wrong." She had her hand on his arm. "He's too relieved. I know he's hiding something."

"Just a moment, please." Sport suddenly gestured for Tynan to sit down. He seemed reluctant to do it. Sport was now sure that he was hiding something. But he had asked him every conceivable question, approached the lawsuit from every possible angle.

"What haven't I asked?" he whispered to Angela.

"He's really worried. It must be something personal. Something he personally believes ...."

"You know him. He personally believes whatever it is convenient for the department that he believe."

"But what if he *knows* something different?" Angela asked.

"Would he admit it anyway?"

"Would he be so worried if he was willing to lie?"

"But what is he afraid of?"

"Something simple. Something he can't quibble over."

"What?"

"I don't know. You came at this from every possible tricky angle. Why not try the obvious?"

"A few more questions, Mr. Tynan," Sport commanded. "Are you personally aware of any applicant who has been turned down for Medical Assistance because of the existence of a crawlspace or a basement since the filing of this lawsuit?"

"I don't know the name of any such person," Tynan responded edgily. "I have the feeling," he added quickly, sarcastically, "that if you knew even one name yourself, we wouldn't be here."

This last comment struck a wrong note. Tynan looked embarrassed after he said it. Sport wondered why Tynan was trying to draw attention toward the lack of a name. There was nothing to be lost by exploring this further.

"Forget the name. Do you know of any such case, though?"

"No such case had been presented or described to me by any employee," he responded.

Jody stood up. "Is that enough? We've already gone over the projected time for this deposition."

"Your client didn't answer the question."

"The projected time ...."

"We've already seen from Mr. Tynan's testimony that projections are often wrong. Sit down, Mr. Tynan. Again, do you know of any such case?"

Tynan remembered the disgusted look that the old man had given him as he had glibly shown him the door. The man was old enough to be his father. Tynan had not felt so vulnerable, and so guilty, since he was a child. On a physical level, Tynan was still capable of holding himself together and pretending that their meeting didn't happen. Pretending that he had never met the man would be in the best interest of the department. It would be in his own political interest, and it would protect his own reputation as a decent and compassionate human being. But he had a strong premonition as he sat across the table from Sport and Angela: if he denied that man's existence now, he would never be able to tell the truth again.

"I don't know his name, but I know that the man you are looking for does exist."

15 CONFESSIONS

It was to be their first date. It was a bold step, and they had not tried to hide it. They were meeting in a restaurant in Little Italy, not far from Fells Point. Elena waited there impatiently. Slip was supposed to be there at eight, but he was almost forty minutes late.

For weeks, Slidell had worked at the soup kitchen every morning. He always arrived early and took a place on the line with hardly a nod to Elena. But when he left, he lingered at the door. And every day, they met for lunch. They talked about people—the soup kitchen clients, the charitable benefactors, the local religious and political figures. Watching Slidell's experienced green eyes, Elena was intrigued that he was not yet jaded. He laughed with her at the mysterious web of craft and coincidence which held the world together. Slidell's conversation was knowledgeable and worldly. At the same time, he was shy with her, like a young suitor. She had never accepted this kind of admiration before. But they seemed perfectly matched.

"Samuel, aren't we acting just as crazy as any of these people we talk about? Shouldn't we admit that we need things too?"

Slidell nodded gravely. But they still hesitated, afraid

197

to step out of their special roles, afraid they would not be able to step back.

Elena had not become a nun because she believed in meaningless self-sacrifice. The face of Jesus which she saw in the lined and wasted faces of the alcoholics was a decidedly human one. She wasn't trying to uplift those faces, but to understand and help them. Mostly, she wanted to draw from them a clue to the mystery of why life was so much deeper than anyone seemed to want to admit. Elena had been stunned to meet in Slip another person who recognized the value of those faces.

Of course, Slip approached the whole task from a different angle. He sifted and measured and weighed the needs and desires of that sea of faces, touching each one of the thousands of persons who trickled through his manipulating fingers like grains of sand. People could feel his fingers on their lives, and they recognized the deft touch of a master. He shaped their lives because he had a knack for doing so; but he also needed them sifting through his fingers, as badly as Elena needed to see her alcoholics' faces.

Slidell was the first person on the earth whom Elena had actually noticed, besides her mother. Talking with him made her understand how lonely she had been. It also made every other part of her life more difficult. Before she knew Slip, all of the people outside of her beloved sea of Jesus-sotted faces were just plastic chessmen to be knocked down, won over or gotten around. Slidell was different.

Two days before, they had lingered in Eddie's lunch room until it was virtually empty.

"I guess we should go."

"Samuel, do you feel ...?"

"What?"

"Never mind. What I was going to say was outrageous.

Samuel, I admire you more than anybody I've ever known."

His fingertips were just touching the tablecloth.

"Outrageous. I think I know what you mean. I have no right ...."

"Don't *we?*" She touched his fingers. "Don't we have the right to be ordinary?"

"Elena, I shouldn't."

She pulled her hands back. "I'm sorry. I've never had a feeling like this before. I was just ... guessing. About you. About how you felt."

"Elena," Slidell's words came slowly, "you guessed right."

"Oh, I thought so! You see everybody else around—it happens, doesn't it? It's an ordinary thing, isn't it? Not strange. It's okay for us too, Samuel, I'm sure."

But Slip looked different when he finally walked into the restaurant that night and came up to her table. He stood silently, his hands nervously pulling at each other. He looked worse than nervous.

"Why don't you sit down. Are you tired?"

He shrugged, still standing.

"Something came up I didn't expect so soon. A meeting. Highlandtown. Unions."

"What about?"

"Setting something up."

"I admire what you do, Samuel. People criticize you, but you help them. I've seen it."

"I wish ...." Slidell's voice cracked. Averting his eyes, he slumped into the booth.

"I'm fifty-two years old," he started again. "I was up all night last night, thinking about why the world is not as good a place as it could be."

"What's wrong? Whatever it is, I can help."

"Elena, believe me: I would have been a different person, my whole life, if I would have known that I was eventually going to meet you."

"What is it?"

"You can't fix it, and I can't either."

"Come on, Samuel, we're both grownups. How bad can it be?"

He put his hand on her arm.

"I did it because of promises I made long ago, before I met you. You weren't supposed to come along. You weren't supposed to make me doubt my whole life."

He had her complete attention.

"Are you going back to your wife?"

"Waterside Towers. I'm going to let it go through. The whole neighborhood will be gone."

She shrunk back from his touch. She stared at him for a long time, taking small, compulsive gulps of her wine. It was an ordinary red wine.

"Why did you lie?" The voice she finally found was tiny.

He just looked at her, breathing in sighs.

"My God!" she whispered, her voice even smaller. "You *didn't* lie. It was *me*. You always keep your promises, but you never made any promises to me. It makes sense. It makes sense. Why should you owe me more than anyone else? Why should I have thought I was special? That's the mistake I keep making over and over, isn't it?"

She slid out of her seat and rushed out of the restaurant, leaving him slumped alone at the table.

"I've just talked to my client." Sport's voice sounded uncomfortable but firm. "What he said makes me think that you might have misunderstood."

The word "misunderstood" grabbed Doxie's attention immediately. The word had come to have a special meaning among lawyers. Although misunderstandings between *clients* were practically the lawyer's stock in trade, true misunderstandings between lawyers about things they had previously agreed upon were rare. But it was a word you heard all the time. When used by one lawyer to another, concerning an agreement that they had made with each other in the past about any important matter, it was the equivalent of an announcement that someone was about to be stabbed in the back.

"Oh?" Doxie's eyebrows rose with the intonation of his voice.

"This is about my client Charles Gage, the guy who is going to inherit 442 Jasper Street." Sport had brought Angela with him to this meeting up in Doxie's office. "He really doesn't want to sell the house at all. He's turned down $40,000. He says that he never wanted to sell it. And, to tell the truth, Doxie, he never told me he wanted to sell it. He first came here with the papers from his aunt's estate. The attorneys for the *executor*, Peck, Peck and Peck, were offering him money if he would assign the bequest to them, but he didn't want to do it. He never said that it was the *amount* of money.

"I've been with him to the house. He has a real reverence for it—I think because of his aunt. All he talks about now is fixing it up. He has some real rational plans ...."

Doxie smiled, relieved that this was all it was. "You know," he said, "I'm in direct contact with the mayor on this. In the light of all the millions that are to be made on this project, $40,000 does seem a little miserly. What do you think we can get for Mr. Gage?"

"Doxie, I'm trying to tell you. He doesn't want to sell."

"Heh, heh, heh," Doxie leaned back in his chair. He stated next, as a fact, something that he only hoped was true. "I think this is a case of the clever client fooling even his own lawyer about his intentions." Doxie smiled patronizingly at the two young lawyers.

"If you met him, Doxie," Angela piped in, "you would know. Charles is intelligent, but he is not a tricky man. He really loves that house. He doesn't want anything else but to fix it up and live in it."

The Director slowly brought his chair back to a level position. "If this is true, Mr. Gage would be throwing away the magic lamp that could *instantly* take him out of poverty. The mayor will be furious. Pettibone will be sure that I lied to him.

"Sometimes," he added, "we have to *guide* our clients toward what's in their best interest. What efforts have you made to make him understand how much his life can change with a decent settlement?"

"I've talked with him over and over again, Doxie. Maybe the problem is, he's been poor for so long that he doesn't even realize it. The way he looks at it, he had nothing before, and now he has nothing, plus this house that he thinks of sort of as an ancestral home. He's very happy with it."

"Is he on welfare?"

"Off and on. He works day labor when he can."

"Sixty-one years old and working day labor! He's got to sell that house! He's crazy. You know what this whole thing's going to do to us? Nobody's going to believe that this was just Charles Gage's decision. We're going to be blamed for ruining the whole Waterside Towers project. When Pettibone becomes governor, he'll close us down. Do you think this is all worth it because Mr. Gage has a sentimental attachment to an old run-down house?"

"I have to do what my client wants. I can't pressure him to sell just because it will keep the Society out of trouble. I have faith in him. He is not doing this for the money."

Doxie hunkered down into his chair, as if he were already under attack by the mayor. He clenched his jaw muscles. He shook his head and mouthed the word "damn." He sighed.

"Of course, you're right. We are his lawyers. He is our client. We cannot sell Charles out."

Sport leaned forward, ready to get out of his chair and leave.

"One thing, though," Doxie added. "Let me try to talk to this Charles Gage myself."

Charles was waiting in the reception room in the basement for Sport and Angela to return when a young woman dressed all in dark blue came through the glass doors and announced that she had an appointment to see an attorney. From her determined look, Charles thought that this woman might be a match for Linda. As the woman approached the reception desk, he sat back and watched. Linda had lost a little of her steam since M. C. had been sent to day care. She didn't try to obstruct Charles any more, since he was known as a legitimate client. But on her particularly strong afternoons, he noticed, she could give a newcomer as hard a time as anyone was likely to get anywhere.

Linda was taking a rubber band off of a pencil. She did not look up from her task, nor did she in any way acknowledge this new woman's existence. The new woman announced again that she had an appointment. Linda lifted her gaze to waist level but didn't say anything. Charles began to laugh.

"Don't worry, miss," he laughed again when the young woman glared over at him. "She does everybody like that."

Still without looking up, Linda punched some buttons and spoke into the phone. She then looked directly up into the woman's face, as if to say that *now* was the appropriate time to make eye contact.

"He's with another client," she mumbled, leaving Elena to guess what she was supposed to do next. Elena decided to sit down next to Charles.

Charles nodded in the direction of Linda.

"She's a right cheerful soul."

Elena had been too proud to ask Slip for the details of the plot. It was enough to know that the study was just a device that he was using for some political end. She realized that Gotterdung also was in on it, and that Slidell and Gotterdung were just holding the study back for their own advantage until *they* were ready for Fells Point to be leveled.

After Slidell confessed to her, Elena had a difficult night. She sat on her bed, closed her eyes, and tried to find the line between what she had imagined the world to be and what it really was. She forced herself to focus on one absolute fact: Slip had never *said* that he was going to save the neighborhood. This truth was like a clear, cold serum permeating her brain, illuminating in an especially humiliating way her fantasies, her delusions, and her silly, silly hopes. But early the next morning, she called the Legal Assistance Society.

Elena laughed too long at Charles's remark, then held her hands to her face as tears began rolling down her cheeks. Charles looked at Linda, who lowered her eyes.

"Give her something!"

Linda put her hand on a box of tissues on her desk and shoved it six inches closer to Charles. He reached over and grabbed it and offered it to the young woman. Then he sat down, with a sudden, sharp intake of breath.

Elena thanked both of them, blew her nose, stopped sobbing. She held out her hand to Charles. "I'm Sister Elena."

When Linda heard that the woman was a nun, she chortled. Charles stared her down. "Seems like all kind of people need lawyers now."

"I'm trying to stop this development project that's destroying my neighborhood. I know it's wrong, but I don't know if I have a legal case or not. Why are *you* coming to Legal Assistance today?."

"I got this house on Jasper Street. Got it from my Aunt May. In a will. People trying to take it away. These people here trying to help me keep it."

"I've been running a soup kitchen down on Jasper Street for a few years."

"Oh! I know your place. I ate there some times. Good food."

"Thank you."

"My Aunt May was a good woman. People like me, we just go along and grab whatever comes to them—but Aunt May, she did the right thing every day of her life, whether it was easy or not. And she was a kind woman too, like you."

One of the legal assistants appeared in the reception room. Elena stood up to meet him. As they began to walk down the corridor to the offices, she turned back momentarily to Charles.

"Please take my card, and call me if you need anything."

"Okay, Sister. Need me, I'm at 442."

Doxie was eager to get to Charles before his two young lawyers did. He was afraid that Sport and Angela would blow Charles's chance to collect a fortune. Doxie arrived in the basement reception room two minutes after Elena walked out. He wanted to judge for himself whether Charles was a supremely cagey old guy who had fooled

205

even his own lawyers, or an old fool who didn't recognize that he had stumbled his way into a fortune. But the only judgment which he made immediately was that there was a very sick man sitting on the chair in front of him.

"Is this Mr. Charles Gage?" he spoke in the direction of Linda. Linda never failed to cooperate with Doxie. She was a nasty person, not a stupid person. She met Doxie's eyes and nodded. Charles was leaning forward, his back very rigid, his hands over his chest, his eyes closed. The tension of his posture and the strained look on his face were those of a man in pain. Doxie approached without speaking and quietly sat down on the plastic chair next to him.

Charles's spasms were coming more often now, once or twice a day. He didn't know what else to do about his medical problem. He had applied for Medical Assistance again. When his application was turned down, he had even visited Mr. Tynan, the man who had helped him when he had fallen down in the street. Tynan had acted very rude in his office; still, Charles had done exactly what he had said to do. Presumably, it was just a matter of waiting now. Soon, he would have his Medical Assistance card.

"Sir, are you all right?"

"Oh. Okay now."

"My name is Doxie Clearwater. I'm the Director of the Legal Assistance Society."

"They told me you were coming. Want to talk to me about the house."

"Do you think you can make it to the lobby now? We have a public elevator that goes to my office on the third floor."

Angela hurried into Sport's office and closed the door. "Doxie has taken Charles upstairs. He'll harangue him for a while.

"You are a good lawyer, Sport. I was getting ready to rationalize for you if you traded poor old Charles's house for everything else."

"I couldn't do that."

"I believe in you, Sport."

He looked at her sharply.

She turned aside, looked down, turned back to face him.

"One of the things I've learned from you is to go over everything carefully, check the details."

The fear visible on Sport's face made it all the more difficult for Angela to continue. "Our photocopies of Mrs. Throckmorton's affidavit are not signed at all."

"The original filed in court is signed," he said, too quickly.

Sport focused his eyes on the top of his desk. His first reaction was to blame Linda for her recklessness with the notary stamp. But he knew that it was his fault. And he could not lie to Angela.

"It's worse than you think," he warned her.

"I know. I looked at the court file today before the hearing. I saw that signature."

The words she used, *that* signature, told Sport everything. He looked sadly at his earnest, pretty colleague.

"I don't want to discuss this part of the case any more."

She jumped to object, then stopped herself. It did not look easy for her. She looked past Sport and out the tiny window to the sky. "Okay, no more questions. I'll worry about the other 41,999." She sighed as she left, a dispirited sound that made Sport realize how much he would miss her admiration.

Though the initial presentation of the case against Mallory had taken only a few hours, there had now been seven full days devoted to Mallory's smokescreens and counterattacks. The longer the defense's case went on, the foggier would be the hearing examiner's memory of the actual things that Mallory had done wrong. Worse, the longer the hearing went on, the more likely it was that the hearing examiner would pick up that stack of memos that Bobbi Jo had typed, see that they were all the same, and think that it was Tynan, and not Mallory, who was crazy.

An employee in these discharge cases was generally allowed as much time as he wanted for the presentation of the case. Van Hoof, the hearing examiner, looked at his watch and rolled his eyes as Mallory's defense stretched on for days, but an employee was generally allowed to keep on going until either he was exhausted or he had run into problems with his own lawyer.

It was easy to tell if it had anything to do with the lawyer. A defense that blossomed larger and larger, raising more and more issues over a period of days, but which then suddenly ended in mid-issue without so much as an explanation or apology, was a sure sign that the lawyer was no longer being paid, or that he had someplace better to go.

On the morning after Gotterdung bungled the press conference, Mallory's attorney, Anthony Stem, immediately dropped his loquacious, rambling defense. That defense had served its basic purpose, which was to drag things out until something better came along.

"Your Honor, in light of the extraordinary remarks made by Secretary Gotterdung about this case on television yesterday, we have to insist that he be subpoenaed to this hearing."

"What remarks?"

"Your honor, Secretary Gotterdung, the very official who signed these charges against my client, yesterday made a speech in which he praised Mr. Mallory for being his most productive and conscientious employee.

"And in the light of this statement," Attorney Stem continued, "we must insist that the Department of Public Welfare produce him for testimony and cross examination. If we can't question, him, Your Honor, I think the only alternative is to dismiss the charges altogether."

"Counsel?" Judge Van Hoof turned to Jody Hechtmuller. "Objection?"

There was a noticeable pause. Gotterdung had blown this case on his own. A certain poetic justice would be served by having him dragged in to explain himself.

"Are you sure, Mr. Hechtmuller," Van Hoof persisted, "that you don't object to this?"

"Oh, all right, Your Honor, I object."

"Your Honor, he doesn't really mean it."

"No. I mean yes, I do mean it. I have a duty to the department. As a matter of principle, we oppose this."

It was a matter of principle. Once word got out that Mallory had subpoenaed the Secretary, the floodgates would be open. Every state employee would feel it necessary to subpoena his department's Secretary to every hearing.

Van Hoof's usual policy on evidentiary rulings was to deny all inconvenient requests. But Stem, Mallory's attorney, was arguing ferociously. "Your Honor, I think that you must dismiss the case if you allow Secretary Gotterdung to say one thing about Mallory in public, then say a completely different thing in these official charges here. As you can see, Secretary Gotterdung himself personally signed the papers charging Mr. Mallory with incompetence."

Van Hoof felt trapped. To subpoena the Secretary himself would have risked violating one of Van Hoof's cardinal rules of jurisprudence, adapted by him for legal use from the Hippocratic oath: first, do no harm—to thyself.

"Your Honor, the department is willing to have the Assistant Secretary for Administration, Leonard Tynan, testify without the necessity of a subpoena. And we can do it this morning. Assistant Secretary Tynan actually runs the department on a day-to-day basis, he attends all departmental meetings, and he knows what the Secretary's plans and policies are. And I know for a fact that he drafts most of the Secretary's speeches."

As soon as he saw Van Hoof's relieved smile, Jody knew that he had won the battle. Secretary Gotterdung would not be subpoenaed to the hearing. Still, Leonard Tynan would have to testify, and Tynan had shown lately a dangerous propensity to speak the naked truth. Altogether, the prospect of winning the war with Mallory was fading fast.

The phone call from Mrs. Brazelton came five minutes after Angela left Sport's office.

"Mr. Norris, when filing away those pleadings on the *Throckmorton* case, I noticed something. On the photocopies of the affidavit from Mrs. Throckmorton ...."

".... there is no signature," he finished her sentence.

"Yes, and I was wondering ...."

"It's all right," he interrupted her again, noticing how his own fear perversely infused his voice with a smooth, calm, false resonance of assurance. "We had a little problem with our notary. She's an employee here, and didn't really understand what to do at the time."

"But that doesn't solve ...."

"I explained it to the judge at the hearing, Mrs. Brazelton," Sport lied. "We could file new affidavits for Mrs. Throckmorton, but there wouldn't be any point, since we have conceded that she has now been given a Medical Assistance card."

"So ... her situation is irrelevant now?"

"Right. Mrs. Throckmorton is okay. We're now arguing only about the other 41,999 people."

"Well, if the judge says its okay .... I just like to check over these things carefully."

"You were right to bring it up, Mrs. Brazelton. It was an error. But it just makes no difference now."

"All right, Mr. Norris. Thank you."

Shaken by his own lies, Sport vomited into his trash can. He was hanging his head over the edge of his desk, wiping his mouth with a handkerchief when Charles walked into his office a minute later.

Jody Hechtmuller was not happy to see Tynan testifying at Mallory's hearing. After Tynan's performance at the Legal Assistance deposition, Jody no longer had any confidence in him as a witness. He didn't know if there would be another embarrassing revelation. He had no idea what surprise truth might pop out from Tynan's mouth now.

But Tynan had a lot more at stake than Jody. Three years of hand-to-hand bureaucratic battle with Mallory had preceded this removal hearing. He knew he wouldn't have the strength to go through such a nerve-wracking campaign again. He would have been gratified to see Gotterdung himself brought to the hearing and cornered into admitting how little he really knew about the department. But the important thing was to win the case against Mallory. If the department couldn't remove Mallory, it couldn't remove anybody. And if it couldn't remove anybody, there wouldn't be any use in his working there any more.

Chills ran down Tynan's back when he saw Van Hoof busying himself, during a fifteen-minute break, by leafing through the stack of memoranda which Mallory had thought that he had written, but which had actually been composed by Bobbi Jo with the help of 512 kilobytes of her computer's memory. Van Hoof leafed more and more slowly. As his expression slowly changed from idle boredom to quizzical interest to alert concern, Tynan's heart rate rose accordingly.

"Counsel?" Van Hoof tried to get Attorney Stem's attention while at the same time continuing to scan the pages. There was no question but that Van Hoof had noticed that all of the memos were identical. "Counsel?"

It seemed horribly unfair that Mallory hadn't even bothered to read the memos when he sent them, and that Stem hadn't even bothered to read them when he introduced them into evidence, but Tynan had always been willing to readjust the scales of justice. He now readjusted the position of the water pitcher that sat on the table between him and Jody Hechtmuller, causing it to spill its contents onto Jody's papers, across the table and onto the carpet directly in front of Van Hoof's desk.

Tynan was the first one up, collecting ice cubes on the floor and plinking them into the pitcher.

He turned to Van Hoof. "Are there any paper towels down the hall?"

"I'll get some." Van Hoof bustled out.

On his way back down the hall, Van Hoof was intercepted by Tynan. "It's under control in there. We probably won't need those."

Van Hoof's path was blocked. Tynan took the towels but stood in his way.

"I see you've discovered Mallory's memos." He kept his voice low so Van Hoof wouldn't have to worry about the lawyers hearing. "He's sent that same memo over eighty-five times. Only the first sentence is different."

"Yes, I ...."

"I hope you won't bring that up." Tynan's whisper was conspiratorial. "It's so pathetic—he thinks that's his work product. We do want to fire the man, but we don't want to *humiliate* him."

Van Hoof looked past Tynan to make sure the lawyers weren't observing this conversation. "I see what you mean. A little discretion is called for. I'll make sure nobody mentions them. I don't want anyone made a fool of at my hearings."

Stem spent a moment making Tynan admit that the Statement of Charges, and the Secretary's public praise of Mallory's abilities, were both made by the Secretary, and that they contradicted each other.

"Which one of these statements, Mr. Tynan," Stem intoned, "which one of these contradictory statements represents the true opinion of the Secretary, and the department, about Mr. Mallory's work performance?"

Jody immediately objected, causing a long, philosophical dispute to arise over whether the Secretary's opinion was necessarily the same as the department's opinion, or whether a department could have an opinion without any person in particular holding it, and whether one person's private opinion could detract from the department's opinion, if a department could have an opinion. Tynan ended all this discussion by blurting out, completely out of turn.

"Secretary Gotterdung's personal opinion is exactly the same as the department's official position."

"And what is his true opinion?" Stem jumped in before Jody recovered enough to slow things down.

"He thinks that Mallory is a horrible worker. He knows that the word 'Mallorying' has come to be a synonym around the department for avoiding work."

Mallory cringed in his seat. This may have been the first time that he had ever been seen to react appropriately to managerial criticism.

"He's making this up!" Mallory stage-whispered to Stem. Stem put his hand up to quiet Mallory and to as-

213

sure him that the case was in his skilled professional hands.

"Well, this means that you can't explain Gotterdung's statement at the press conference," Stem continued. "Clearly, only the Secretary himself knows why he made a public statement which differs from his own opinion of Mr. Mallory's abilities."

A basic rule of cross-examination is never to ask a question you don't know the answer to. Another cardinal rule is never to ask a question that begins with the word "why."

"Tell us then, Mr. Tynan. Why, having signed charges for Mallory's removal because of alleged poor work performance, did Secretary Gotterdung hold a public press conference and specifically single him out as one of the best workers in the department?"

"He did it," Tynan flatly replied, as the stenographer labored to record every syllable, "as a joke, so everyone in our department would know he was making fun of the mayor."

"Sit back." Charles's hand was on Sport's chest, pushing him back into the chair. Sport was still trembling.

"I may be in some trouble," Sport said quietly. "I did something wrong. I just wanted to tell you ... in case some time in the future I'm not your lawyer any more. Angela is really good. Better than I am. She believes in you, and in your house."

"What kind of wrong?"

"Legal wrong. Something I did. I might be disbarred, lose my job. I was only trying to help, but ..."

"You sold my house?"

"No. No!"

And the very thought of betraying Charles loomed

so monstrous that what Sport had really done seemed suddenly small, or at least manageable, and he confessed to Charles right away.

16 EPIDEMIC

"It's time that cooler heads prevailed." The editorial in the *Baltimore State,* after summarizing the battle between Mayor Pettibone and Secretary Gotterdung over the Waterside Towers project, gushed with relief that Senator Samuel Slidell was "making himself available to mitigate this unfortunate governmental crisis."

The same day, the *Free American* carried a story about the construction unions' complaints, "first brought to public attention by the ever-attentive Senator Slip Slidell," that they were unfairly locked out of the jobs which could be provided by the construction of the Pettibone Waterside Towers.

It was only after Pettibone read these stories that he realized who his real antagonist was.

"Get over here!" he screamed at Slidell over the phone.

It was a plan to humiliate him politically, and it was going to work. He had to go along. The only other choice was a public airing of the whole affair, and he could not bear that. To expose Slip's scheme, he'd have to admit that he'd been tricked by it.

The meeting itself was short and without any of the usual phony preliminaries. Slip insisted that no one else be present.

"I'll destroy us both before I'll give you any credit for this project," Pettibone promised.

"I'm not looking for praise," Slip said. "I'm looking for jobs."

"Let me guess. Union jobs. *Pick and an axe / Pick and an axe / Stab in a back for Mister Tax.*"

"What was that?" Slip sat forward, suddenly curious.

"Nothing."

"I thought you said something about tax."

"No, I didn't."

"I thought you said something."

"No, I didn't. What do you want?"

Slip hadn't gotten as far as he had in politics by being the kind of person who liked to rub it in. He never thought for a moment about forcing Pettibone himself to make the announcement. He did insist that announcements be made within a week that union contractors and subcontractors would be getting 65 percent of the work on the Crosley T. Pettibone Waterside Towers Project. A union man of Slip's choice would be allowed access to all meetings of the development team in order to make sure that this commitment was honored. Then, within ten days of these announcements, Gotterdung's Department of Public Welfare would complete and publish its study, thus clearing the last legal barrier to the project getting started.

"What! Why ten days!" Pettibone surged out of his seat.

"Well, Crosley," Slip's expression was a little sheepish, as if he knew he was delivering a slightly damaged product. "It seems there is a slight problem with the study."

"What's a 'slight problem?'" Pettibone put his hands out defensively, as if suspecting another twist of the knife.

"There is this group, CORP, Coalition of Real People ...."

"I've never heard of them."

"A new community group in Fells Point. Headed by a nun who runs a soup kitchen there. They've gotten wind," Slip had no intention of mentioning how this had happened, "that the study might be a phony. They're putting pressure on the department, and on Gotterdung. They want to be involved in the study. I'm sure they want to make some political statement on the evils of this type of development compared to ... smaller-scale projects."

Slip was politic enough not to bring up the criticism that had dogged Pettibone since his first days in office, charges that he spent city and federal money on large-scale amusements and luxuries for the rich.

"But the law doesn't say," Slip spoke authoritatively, "that the community has to be involved in the study. And I guarantee you that CORP isn't going to be involved. But Gotterdung does have to come up with some minimum kind of study, with some real numbers, etcetera. He can't get away with a phony study any more. It will take a couple of weeks."

"Why didn't he start it before?"

"There was no reason to, Crosley."

Later that day, Charles was visited in his room by Fred Lowell, a real-estate broker. He said he had been hired jointly by Bold Tip Development Company, Susumee Development and Builders National Bank.

"We want to buy Aunt May's house directly from you, to save ourselves the money we would have to pay if you sold your house to a speculator. We'll be happy to add to our offer most of the profit that would go to a speculator. That way, the real profit on the deal will go directly to you.

"I'm offering $100,000, and I think that's more than double the last offer that was made to you."

But he wasn't sure that Charles heard him. Charles

was lying on top of his bed, though it was the middle of the afternoon. He was fully clothed, and Fred Lowell noticed that his shoes, set down neatly next to the wall across the room, were covered with mud. Although Charles acknowledged him at first, he had watched Lowell's presentation with the squinty, glassy gaze of someone who is not really there, or will not be there for long. He didn't even blink at the mention of $100,000.

"Are you okay?" Fred tried to suppress an unkind thought. If this man dies, it might take forever to figure out who inherits the property *from him.*

"Stomach." Charles was whispering. "Worked all day yesterday, the day before. Couldn't get up today."

"Man, you don't look good at all. Why don't you see a doctor?"

"I'm gonna try."

"Do you think you want to talk about this offer today?"

Charles shook his head. He seemed weak, but his eyes met Fred's directly.

"Okay. You get yourself some help. I'll leave my card here, and I'll be back again. Please don't sell the house to anybody else while I'm gone."

"No."

Jimmy was in the hallway just outside Charles's door, leaning back against the wall. Fred Lowell nodded briefly as he passed. He was sure that he could have gotten Charles's signature on a $100,000 contract of sale if he had really pushed it. But Fred was also sure that his clients would go to $200,000 if they had to.

The worst part of the humiliation Pettibone had undergone at Slip's hands was the fact that he couldn't even complain about it. Susumee and Bold Tip made their announcements within twenty-four hours of the meeting between the mayor and Slip. The *Free American* not only praised the inclusion of local union labor in the deal, but also lauded Slip for having a "practical, local, workingman's perspective" about these "grandiose projects." Slip Slidell, who had done nothing for the project except slow it down, was now getting half the credit.

Fosback was the only aide authorized to tell the mayor bad news. "Oswald Fundertow called, sir. He wants to talk to you. He said that Bold Tip is, um, not accustomed to using union subcontractors. And ..."

"One short, one sweet message for him," Pettibone interrupted. "No one is backing out. Plan to start demolition of the vacant houses within ten days. Get the banks recommitted to the financing within the week."

"And you," Pettibone's voice dropped low and quivered with dead earnestness, "you personally make sure that Charles Gage signs off on 442 Jasper Street."

It was Sister Elena's idea to sue. When Legal Assistance had declined to represent her group, she talked to the parish priest who had once been smitten by the fire in her eyes. She asked him to find a lawyer among his parishioners. The young priest jumped at the chance to do her a favor.

She saw now that she had always used people. One of the main attractions of her calling had been its license to use people for God's ends. She had once felt like a tool of God, and she had been as singleminded and irresponsible as anyone totally given over to the will of another. She had felt that she was specially blessed. But when Elena now pictured her previous self, she saw only an arrogant and limited woman.

Her attempt to go back to the soup kitchen after her legislative humiliation by Slip hadn't really worked. She couldn't go back. She didn't believe any more that begging for food to feed the hungry was enough. The second time, when Slip came back and pretended to team up with her, she had believed that she had gained real power. This had been like an intoxicating drug. Under the influence of that intoxicant, she had crossed with Slip several thresholds, thresholds over which she could never step back.

It would be a more satisfying profession if the lawyers who screwed you would just laugh right in your face. Instead, Sport had come to anticipate the "forgotten" commitments, the promised papers that never quite got signed, the checks with the sudden last-minute deductions—all the "misunderstandings" that seemed to be a certain type of lawyer's stock in trade. These lawyers often claimed to be forced to act irresponsibly because of their clients, but the truth was that they were always representing this type of client because they were the same type of people themselves. They, too, felt comfortable with the lost paper, the missing expense voucher, the new refrigerator that turned out to be used.

There had been fair warning that he should have kept a closer eye on Peck, Peck and Peck. As executors of Aunt May's estate, they were being paid to carry out Aunt May's wishes. Their duty was to account for all of her assets, register them in court, pay the debts, then distribute the rest. In the meantime, they were supposed to conserve the property and pay the taxes. The paperwork required was no more complex than what could be done by an average high-school graduate who could read. In fact, it was almost always done by a junior secretary in the typing pool. It was easy, profitable, coveted legal work, generally netting the lawyer about 10 percent of the dead person's lifetime accumulation of property.

But there had been no reason for Peck, Peck and Peck, if they were impartial executors of Aunt May's will, to ask Charles to sign a paper selling his rights to the Jasper Street property. There was no reason, that is, unless the law firm was being paid to procure the property for someone who knew its true value. When Sport had called Andrew Peck about that, he received the sort of response that put him on notice that the Attorney's Canons of Ethics was not a publication in popular demand at the checkout table of the law library of Peck, Peck and Peck.

"Don't you think it's a conflict of interest," Sport had complained, "for the executor to be trying to buy out the inheritance of one of the beneficiaries—especially before the property has even been appraised?"

Andrew Peck was unrepentant. "This isn't John D. Rockefeller. We just use the latest tax assessment."

"But why did you send him a paper that looks like he's supposed to sign it and send it back to you, when in reality it's a sale of his rights to the house?"

"Don't make this sound like we're con men," Peck scoffed. "We just had an offer and passed it on."

"It's typed on your own letterhead."

There was a slight pause. Andrew Peck's voice sounded both annoyed and bored when he spoke again. "Did we do that? Maybe we were just trying to speed things up. Look, I can tell that you've told your client not to sign, so let's not beat a dead horse into the ground. He can forget the offer. Maybe he'll get a better one, maybe he won't."

"I'm going to follow closely the administration of this estate."

"Good for you," Peck patronized him.

"I'd appreciate it if you'd send me, as attorney for Charles Gage, a copy of any reports that you file in the Orphans Court in this case."

"Can't do that. Expense. Postage. You know."

"I understand perfectly now."

"Good for you."

Later, Sport called and pressed Peck on why he had not ordered an appraisal of Aunt May's house and filed it in court.

"Small estate. We don't do that. We use the tax assessment." Peck sounded both bored and disgusted.

"So you're saying the whole estate is worth less than $20,000?" There was nothing in the estate except the house, the furniture and about $3,000 from Aunt May's passbook savings account. Peck had to say that the estate was worth less than $20,000. If he didn't, he would be admitting that his own offer to buy the house from Charles for $10,000 had been a form of fraud.

"I'm saying something like that." Peck made his voice sound as if he were very tired of the conversation.

"If it's a small estate, then why didn't you file it under the simplified proceedings in 8.601 as a small estate?"

There was a very long pause on the line this time. The simple truth was that executors weren't allowed to charge *any* fees, under Section 8.601, for small estates. There was no chance that Peck, Peck and Peck would ever use a procedure that would be of no profit to them.

"If you have any *specific* questions, just give me a call," Peck said slowly, then hung up.

Despite all the reasons he had to keep a watchful eye on Peck, Peck and Peck, Sport hadn't seen the next move coming.

Aunt May, being dead, had not gotten around to paying her property taxes for the coming year. Her property tax account was delinquent $278.96. Normally, the city was the picture of forbearance with small homeowners, and especially with their estates. When an estate held the property, the city was content to file the bill in the Orphans Court, secure in the knowledge that no one could finally get the property until the taxes were paid. In the case of 442 Jasper Street, the tax bill had been filed in the Orphans Court as a matter of course within two months of Aunt May's death.

But the city's legal department now heated up the tax collection procedures on the property. The object was to demonstrate to Charles that a lot of bad things, including a forced tax sale, could happen very quickly if he didn't agree to sell for a reasonable price. The estate was given notice of a tax lien and proposed tax sale. Normally, this would be no more than a minor annoyance to the executor, who would simply write a check from the remaining money in the estate to cover the bill. But when these tax notices had fluttered down onto Andrew Peck's desk, he had seen them in another light entirely.

Ever since Charles Gage had refused to sign the paper giving up the property, Andrew Peck had regarded this estate sourly. It was not just that he wouldn't make much money on it. It was also a constant reminder of the one big chance that got away. Now, when Peck saw the tax notices suddenly stacked up on his desk like so many unexpected presents from City Hall, he realized what a wonderful, central position he was in. The procedures leading to a forced tax sale of the property by the city were already in place and would operate automatically if the taxes weren't quickly paid. At a forced tax sale, the mayor's allies could buy the property without worrying about Charles's wishes. Andrew Peck, and only Andrew Peck, could thus hand over the one thing the mayor needed and was willing to pay almost anything for. And all Peck had to do was—nothing.

On one of his trips to check his property, Charles had picked up a tax notice posted on the front door. He brought it in to Sport. Suspicious, Sport began to try to get Andrew Peck on the phone. His thirteen unreturned calls were enough to confirm those suspicions.

It was completely unethical for Peck to ignore the tax bill and let the property be taken by a tax sale, but that was exactly what Peck was apparently going to do. There was a kind of perverted logic to it. As the executor, Peck would normally collect his ten percent commission on everything *except* the transfer of real property. He would not normally make a penny of commission on Aunt May's house. As a result, this was the kind of estate that he would describe to his friends as a charity case. This meant that his secretary would do about four hours of work, and he would collect about $400 from the estate. His executor's fee would be based on Aunt May's bank account only. But if the house were sold, even by a tax sale, the house would count as a liquid asset, and Peck would get ten percent of its selling price.

Sport sent Peck three certified letters in three days, reminding him in the strongest terms of his fiduciary duty to conserve the property, and threatening him with every possible type of lawsuit if the estate didn't pay the taxes. There was no response. Peck was clearly going to let it go.

Late that night, when he should have been preparing for his oral argument in the crawlspace suit, Sport sat in his office, scribbling a request for an injunction against Peck, Peck and Peck. He didn't have time to write in the elegant legal style that he was so proud of. After he finished the rough draft of the statement of facts, he put down his pen. All of this writing would be for nothing if he couldn't devise a scheme to persuade the Word Processing Center to type it the next morning. As he was plotting his typing strategy, the phone rang.

"This is Sport Norris."

"Hello, Mr. Norris."

"Who is this?"

"Let's say, a friend."

"I'm too tired and busy to play games."

"I'm talking about a forged signature on a document filed in federal court."

Sport's stomach muscles clenched. He couldn't speak. "Mr. Norris?" But he had to.

"Who is this?"

"Never mind that."

"The judge is aware," his own voice was weak as he repeated the lie, "...of the, of the... technical problems of that affidavit." Caught off guard, he couldn't pull it off as he had with Mrs. Brazelton. He was caught.

"I'm not interested in whether the judge cares." Sport realized that his caller actually believed him. The caller did not know everything. He was guessing. Sport gasped in relief.

But he had not denied that the Throckmorton signature was a forgery. That was a mistake. The caller had probably already learned what he needed to know.

The caller was now silent, again waiting for Sport to crack, to say something stupid. Sport realized that the caller had no well-developed plan. He was relying on Sport being afraid.

Sport quietly put him on hold. He stared at the light for that line intensely, for several minutes, until it blinked off. He watched the phone quietly, awaiting another ring.

A sudden rap on the casement window high up on the wall jolted him out of his seat. He stood up and squinted up at the light. Charles's face was outlined against the skyline. He was lying on the sidewalk to get his face close to the glass. Sport stood on his chair and pulled the window open.

"What's the matter?"

"Door locked."

"Wait."

He navigated the empty halls and stairwells to the first floor entrance, where Charles was waiting. Charles followed him back down to his office. Walking down those gloomy halls once again, with an impoverished client behind him, once again, Sport was attacked by despair. He felt as if he had been trapped for his whole career in this tiny little underground office, and that all the injustices of the world had been dragged down the halls and piled on his desk. He had tried to do his part to lighten the load of human misery, but now he was just being punished for it. He walked ahead of Charles and did not look at his face until they were in his office.

Charles's clothes hung loosely from his shoulders. He looked very weak. He stared ahead, mouth open. Sport waited for him to start.

"Are you here about the real-estate taxes on the house?"

Charles nodded yes. Sport realized that Charles was different from most of his other clients. He never complained. He blamed no one else for his misfortunes. He understood what he wanted for himself, and how much it would cost.

But he looked like he was dying. His cheekbones pressed out against the thinning flesh on his face, and his eyes were not focusing well. He seemed halfway gone. A sudden loneliness filled the room.

"Don't worry." Sport whispered into the silence. He felt like a hypocrite. He didn't know, himself, if he could go on.

"You been good," Charles croaked. "Good to me."

"Thanks." But Sport was at a loss for what to say. What to do. Until he realized that there was no choice. His voice then regained some of its strength.

"I'm going ahead with the lawsuit against Peck, Peck

and Peck. I'm going to save this house for you. They might come and get me. They might come and take me down. But I promise I'm going down fighting for you, and for Aunt May's house."

Sport stared grimly across the room at his client.

Charles slowly reached over and dropped a wad of bills onto his desk. "For the taxes," he said. "Day labor. Can you give me a ride home?"

Crosley Pettibone got down on his knees in his office and pounded his fists into the oriental rug when he learned from the television news that the Waterside Towers project was tied up in controversy again.

Without the ability to distinguish between a noisy PR stunt and a serious legal threat, the television news stations afforded CORP's lawsuit attacking the study the same excited coverage that they had given to Pettibone's original announcement of the project. But, as a legal challenge, the suit was really weak. It was questionable whether CORP even had standing to sue. Although the lawsuit claimed that the study could not be valid without citizen participation, there was nothing in the law itself that even remotely suggested that. Even weaker was CORP's claim that the results of the study would be skewed by the lack of citizen participation in an open study process. The plain fact of the matter was that the results of the study were irrelevant. No matter how the study was conducted, and no matter what the study found, Waterside Towers could go forward the second the study was *completed.*

Sister Elena's volunteer lawyer, found through her contact with the young parish priest, had drafted a complaint so cleverly written that all of these technical problems were obscured, written around, camouflaged and evaded. Upon reading the complaint, one would get the idea that the legislature had ordered a comprehensive scholarly study and public referendum on the subject. The word "study" had never been so stretched out, magnified, or blown out of proportion in its whole etymological history.

The complaint was delivered to the media before it was ever filed in court. It was effective in focusing attention on the issue, and on the CORP demonstration in front of City Hall. It also had some legal effect. The papers requested Judge Sanders of the Baltimore City Circuit Court to issue, *ex parte,* a three-day injunction prohibiting work on the project from starting. An *ex parte* injunction was an order that was issued without even consulting or notifying the other side to the controversy. It was appropriate only in an emergency situation.

Although the suit claimed that the department's inadequate study had created an emergency, Judge Sanders found this hard to believe. He decided to make a phone call, as a matter of courtesy, to the department's lawyers. All he wanted was a general statement denying the charges. Then, he would feel justified in denying the request for an injunction.

He telephoned Jody Hechtmuller, who had to be pulled out of the middle of Mallory's hearing to accept the call. Jody had been dueling with Mallory's attorney all afternoon about the meaning of Leonard Tynan's testimony. Judge Sanders told him that a complaint had been filed which claimed that the study being conducted by the department was bogus.

"Your honor," Jody protested, "there are no statutory requirements at all saying that any special parameters have to be met. It just says 'a study.'"

"Oh. You seem familiar with this matter. I must have called the right lawyer, for once."

This was a setback for Jody. Judge Sanders would now

require him to say something substantive.

"There are no requirements for this study," Jody repeated, lamely.

"No, I guess there are not," Judge Sanders sounded as if he was reading the new statute for the first time. "As long as it's a real study. Not a joke."

This last word cut Jody to the quick. It caused him to succumb also to the epidemic of truth that had been slowly breaking out in the higher levels of the department in recent days. He found himself unable to blandly assure Judge Sanders that the study was any more than a joke.

"I can't argue this over the phone, and I'm in the middle of another hearing right now," he managed to say.

"Well, CORP is asking for an injunction. I hate to do something like that, stop the study, and the project, based on their say-so. Just tell me it's not a joke, and I'll deny the injunction, and we can all go home happy and argue about this in my courtroom in the morning."

"I can't say that," Jody admitted. Realizing how bad that sounded, he quickly tried to cover it up with a more general statement. "I can't say anything."

"Well, you seemed to know an awful lot more about this business a minute ago. If you won't say that the study isn't phony baloney, maybe I'd better issue this injunction, just for twenty-four hours, until you can get together with your client and see what the story is. It's already three-thirty. I don't see how any major construction projects were going to get started that quickly anyway."

"I'm not in a position to say anything to stop you."

"I'm very surprised by that."

Judge Sanders' 24-hour injunction made the television news because Sister Elena had marched on City Hall with over 30 CORP members. They carried signs accusing the Department of Public Welfare of conducting a fraudulent study. They also accused Mayor Pettibone of being personally indifferent to the fate of the hard-working people of Fells Point. Technically, the Mayor had nothing to do with the study; but Sister Elena wanted to focus public attention on City Hall's involvement in the whole Waterside Towers deal.

Sister Elena knew that a demonstration would get an enraged reaction from the mayor, and that the reaction itself would make news. For this reason, she directed most of the group's criticism at Pettibone, even though Pettibone had no control at all over the study. To make matters worse for Pettibone, CORP hadn't been able to come up with any good rhymes for "Secretary" or "Gotterdung." So the news footage that actually aired was of a street interview with Sister Elena during which her voice was completely drowned out by chants of "Mayor don't care, Mayor don't care" from the wall of angry pickets behind her.

Fosback rushed into Pettibone's office. The television station on the mayor's desk was carrying the live footage of the chanting crowd in the plaza. When he saw the mayor on all fours on the carpet, he stopped. Pettibone was not even trying to hide his rage.

"Unfair! Unfair! I can't ...."

Fosback stubbed out his cigarette and reached a trembling hand down toward Pettibone. The mayor let Fosback help him off the floor. There came a moment when it seemed safe to talk.

"It's that nun," Fosback offered. "We can talk to the Archbishop about her."

Just at that moment, however, the words "poppy-eyed egomaniac," came from one of the protesters being interviewed on the TV screen.

"He doesn't mean you, sir!"

"So unfair, so unfair / Pulled my mother by the hair."

Fosback's reason for coming in was to see if the mayor

wanted to take the opportunity to respond live, on camera, to the questions being raised by CORP. He now decided that this would not be a wise thing for the mayor to do in his present state. But Pettibone was not in the mood to be handled.

"Get the press in here. All of them. Now."

Once the TV lights were on, Pettibone refrained from repeating any of the little rhymes that circled around inside of his head. But he did blast Sister Elena, and CORP, and Keane. He accused the Legal Assistance Society of encouraging CORP's suit, and of bringing other cases, such as the crawlspace suit, which, he claimed, "do nothing but prevent government officials from doing their jobs.

"I will no longer let the city subsidize this kind of negativism. From now on, I will do everything I can to cut off all funding for the Legal Assistance Society."

The television interviewer immediately asked him his reaction to being called a "poppy-eyed egomaniac."

It wasn't necessary for Pettibone to actually say anything for his reaction to be evident. On thousands of television screens across the city, he could be seen to turn his back to the eagerly extended microphones. Fosback and a few other aides rushed toward him, but then they were seen to back away quickly, and the looks on their faces conveyed more to the television audience about the mayor's reaction than any press release could ever do.

"Mayor Pettibone? Mayor Pettibone?" The interviewer himself had been frozen for a moment, but then his journalistic insensitivity training kicked in. He saw that even the mayor's inability to turn around and answer the questions was news—and the kind of news that couldn't be conveyed in print. The longer that Pettibone's back was turned, the longer he stood hunched over in a defensive position, like a little boy expecting to be hit hard by his mother, again, the more of the man's inner soul might be

232

revealed to the world.

But Pettibone did turn back. He ignored the previous question, though the twisted look on his face made it obvious that he had been affected by it. He had gained a bit of control over himself. He would not scream or cry. But Pettibone's entire political career had been based on his aggressive intolerance for being told that he was wrong.

"Smash their heads, smash their heads / Do they do it in their beds?"

"Mr. Mayor, are you all right?" Fosback had seen it coming. He drowned out Pettibone's poetic efforts with his shouted question. He tried to push the mayor out of reach of the microphones, but Pettibone stiff-armed him and lurched unsteadily into the gaggle of reporters. There, in a strained, abnormally high-pitched voice, Pettibone announced: "Construction on the Mayor Crosley T. Pettibone Waterside Towers Luxury Condominium Development will start early tomorrow morning. No questions."

The truth, Tynan was finding, was almost addictive.

"But, Mr. Tynan, isn't it true that Secretary Gotterdung assigned this very important relocation study to Mr. Mallory?"

"That was a joke too."

For the past two weeks of hearings Mallory had been slouched down, passively watching the proceedings when he wasn't testifying himself. But his chair suddenly crashed to the floor as he stood up angrily after Tynan's last remark. Mallory stepped quickly away and burst through the door into the hallway. Stem chased after him, catching up with him near the elevators.

Mallory brushed Stem's hand off his shoulder. "I don't have time for you, counselor." He banged open a heavy metal door and ran down the fire stairs, away from his lawyer.

When Stem returned to the hearing room, Tynan had already left the witness stand and was trying to get to the door. But Stem insisted that they continue the hearing. Tynan had to take the stand again.

"Are you saying under oath, Mr. Tynan, that Secretary Gotterdung's public statement about this relocation study was not made in good faith?"

This question cut to the heart of the truth that Tynan had been trying to avoid. He would not avoid the truth today, though he was not sure why. His attack of truthfulness at his deposition the day before was due to that sick old man whom he took to the emergency room. But there was only Mallory involved here. Mallory wasn't worth publicly insulting Gotterdung and ruining his own carefully plotted political future. Yet Tynan knew that he still could not lie.

"The Secretary's statement was not made in good faith."

Stem went on for half an hour, forcing Tynan to admit enough to discredit Gotterdung completely—and assure that Tynan would be fired as soon as word got out. Unfortunately for Stem, not one word of it helped Mallory's case.

"I simply cannot accept, Your Honor," Stem expounded, trying to undermine Tynan's testimony, "that the department could be so corrupt as to flout the express command of the legislature to do a study. This is too fantastic a story! I can't believe it!"

But everyone else in the room apparently could. All of them had had enough experience in government to realize that the department really could be that corrupt, that there really may have been no serious plans to do a study—and that the Secretary was not only short-sighted and stupid, but that he also had a sense of humor primitive enough to think the whole thing was funny. The case against Mallory was holding up.

Stem insisted again that Gotterdung himself must now be called to testify, but Van Hoof would not do it. Tynan had supplied the missing fact which explained these strange events to everyone's satisfaction: Gotterdung was a jerk.

Jody Hechtmuller and Stem, each intent on packing up his books and papers, found themselves together at the hearing table after the session had concluded for the day.

"Quite a day, huh?"

Jody nodded. "Where did Mallory go?"

"He wouldn't tell me. To tell you the truth, he's getting kind of unfriendly lately."

Jody smiled drily. "You're becoming an authority figure in his life. I don't think Mallory's too fond of taking orders."

Tynan walked up the sidewalk back to his office. He looked at the turquoise and steel Department of Public Welfare building at the top of the hill. When Gotterdung found out about his testimony, his career in that building would be over. He wondered how he had been infected by this epidemic of truth.

Bobbi Jo jerked open the thick plate glass doors at the front of that building and clattered quickly down the sidewalk toward him on her high-heeled shoes. He smiled as soon as he recognized her. She flapped her skinny arm in the air to get his attention. He realized then that he had done it for her.

"I'm glad I caught you," she huffed. "He's in there!"

"Who?"

"Mallory. He came back to the office a half hour

ago! He got out a new file, and he put a label on it that says 'Study'! I don't like it, Leonard."

17 A LIVE PLAINTIFF

A: I don't know his name, but the man you are looking for does exist.

Q: How do you know this?

A: I met him.

Q: Where did you meet him?

A: I met him when he fell down on East Saratoga Street.

Q: What happened?

A: He was sick. I took him to the hospital.

Q: You didn't learn his name?

A: No, he wasn't admitted.

Q: How do you know he was an applicant for Medical Assistance?

A: He told me at the hospital.

Q: How do you know he was turned down?

A: He told me.

Q: At the hospital?

A: Yes, and in my office.

Q: In your office? This man was in your office?

A: Yes.

Q: Why?

A: I told him if he had any more problems getting his Medical Assistance, to see me.

Q: And he came?

A: Yes.

Q: And he said he had been turned down because of a basement or a crawlspace?

A: Well, his exact words were: "something about a basement."

Q: Did he show you his denial letter?

A: Yes, but I didn't look at it.

Q: You didn't look at it?

A: No.

Q: Why didn't you look at it?

A: Well, one reason was that I was in a hurry.

Q: Why were you in a hurry?

A: To get here.

Q: Here? You mean this deposition?

A: Yes.

Q: You saw this man just today?

A: That is correct.

By Mr. Hechtmuller (by agreement)

Q: Is there a process for appealing a decision that you are not eligible for Medical Assistance Benefits?

A: Of course. You can file an administrative appeal.

Q: Is it just a paper appeal, or what?

A: Eventually, you can get to a hearing before a hearing examiner.

Q: These hearing examiners are sworn to follow the law?

A: Of course.

Q: Is there any law that allows fictitious basements to be used as a basis for denying benefits?

A: No.

Q: Any regulation that allows it?

A: No.

Q: Is there any written policy that allows the use of fictitious basements to deny Medical Assistance benefits?

A: No.

Q: So if this man is truly denied benefits because of a fictitious basement, the hearing examiner will overturn that decision?

By Mr. Norris:
Objection. That's not even a question. Don't use our deposition for your argument, Mr. Hechtmuller.
Mr. Tynan: I don't know what they will do. They should overturn it.

By Mr. Hechtmuller:
I'm trying to establish that there are normal channels by which this man could have any error corrected.
Mr. Tynan: Of course there is a process. And he used it. He filed an appeal.
Q: He did already file an appeal?
A: Yes.

By Mr. Norris:
Q: How do you know that he filed an appeal?
A: I helped him.
Q: How did you help him?
A: I gave him the form.
Q: Did you give him any other help?
A: Yes.
Q: What other help did you give him?
A: I wrote his appeal for him.
Q: What exactly did you write?
A: "I am being illegally denied because of a fictitious basement."
Q: How did you do all this without finding out his name?
A: I put my hand over the top of the papers so I wouldn't see it.
Q: You did this because you wanted to be able to deny

that he existed?

A: I wanted to be able to deny that I knew his name.

Q: So you succeeded, at the cost of sending him away?

A: I sent him to get his problem solved, by the normal remedial procedures.

Q: This didn't seem callous to you, not even asking his name?

A: Look, I'm not crowing over this. Fifteen seconds after he left, I ran out after him into the hall, but he was already gone.

Tynan's deposition proved that there still were people being denied Medical Assistance cards because of phony crawlspaces, but it hadn't led to the discovery of the one thing that Judge Barnett really wanted—one more actual, identifiable person with a real name and address.

Angela's assignment had been to prepare for the worst, in case no live plaintiff appeared by the date of the hearing. She found precedent cases which said that a class could be certified, even though the original named plaintiffs had been paid off. And they could also use Tynan's deposition—if they could figure out whether it helped or hurt their argument.

She and Sport rehearsed their legal argument up until the second they had to leave for court. They took turns playing the part of the judge and asking all of the hard questions. They then took turns playing Jody Hechtmuller's part, anticipating what he would say. Sport and Angela had just finished a last, tense run-through of all the possibilities that could occur at the crawlspace hearing, and Sport had just picked up his briefcase to walk to the courthouse, when the phone rang. Angela completely ignored it and walked out of the doorway and down the hall. Sport, however, was too much of an optimist to just let a phone ring. He picked up the receiver.

"Call on 46," Linda said. "He says he's a friend, and you'll know what he wants."

Sport chased down Angela in the hallway.

"I've got to stay here a minute. It's a call ... it's a call I've got to take." His voice was not steady.

"Let's just walk out now. You can call back later."

"It's important, Angela. I can't do the crawlspace argument with this thing hanging over my head. I think you had better argue it alone."

"But this is *your* case."

"I may have taken it as far as I can. I may have to let you do it from now on."

"What's happening to you, Sport?" Her voice dropped to an urgent whisper.

"I can't tell you that."

"Does it have anything to do with Mrs. Throckmorton's affidavit?"

"Goodbye, Angela. Give 'em hell."

As Jody Hechtmuller saw it, this was his only chance to win the crawlspace suit for the department. But it was a good chance. Other judges had certified class actions in situations like this. But Judge Barnett clearly had doubts. All Jody had to do to win the case was to magnify these doubts. The statistics were pretty incriminating, but if Jody could cast just the slightest bit of doubt on the statistics, and convince the judge that they had really changed the policy, Sport and Angela might be left looking like fanatics, fighting viciously for benefits for a group of people who might not even exist.

But the wild card in the situation was Tynan. Tynan was still unquestionably loyal to the department. He was trying to save its ass (if a department could be considered to have an ass) as much as Jody was. But recently he had been speaking with a naive candor that was a frightening thing to see in a government official.

As soon as Jody entered the courtroom, Angela stood up and rushed toward him with a stapled sheaf of papers in her hand. He hesitated to look down and read the caption on the first page, fearing that it was an Amended Complaint on behalf of a new, real client. When Angela noticed that he was frozen, and wasn't reading the papers she had put in his hand, she prompted him.

"Supplementary citations to section four of my brief. I sent you a letter that I would give them to you today."

"Oh. Right." He slid them onto the counsel table without really looking at them. He wanted the argument to begin. As a government lawyer, he had spent his career filing various motions and requests, the main purpose of which were to slow down, delay and discourage the other side. At long last, he now had a case where he was the one trying to move things along. It felt good.

"Your Honor, as much as I hate to admit it, I think the Legal Assistance Society has already won this case. They just don't realize it. But everything that they could realistically hope to achieve by a judgment from this court has already been accomplished. As a result of this lawsuit the department has overhauled its whole regulatory structure and written a new policy manual, and it has promised to make sure that these fictitious crawlspaces will never be used again.

"Asking for more now is really overkill, litigational momentum gone mad—and perhaps a bit of lawyer's pride." Jody paused for a half second, as if to give Angela a chance to digest this pearl of insight from a wiser soul. "I won't talk about the past. We have been at fault in the past. But right now, there is no reason to think that there is *anybody* being hurt by these alleged phantom ...."

"Your Honor," Angela cut him off. She realized that they were just beginning to get into the meat of the argument. The technical legal points had been well argued by both sides, but Judge Barnett still had that leeway. It was this leeway part of the case that Sport was supposed to argue.

She had stopped every block on the way to the courthouse to turn around and look for Sport, but he had not made it. Deliberately, for the sake of her crawlspace clients, she did not let herself think about what that phone call might be about. Instead, she primed herself to say what Sport would have said in court. She made herself forget about him.

If he were there, Sport would have quietly awaited his turn to refute Jody's appealing, but basically phony, argument. Angela held herself back, trying to do what Sport would do, during the beginning of Jody's rebuttal, but she realized right in the middle of it that this was not her style.

"Your Honor," she interrupted, "Mr. Hechtmuller is wandering away from the facts and into the arena of pure wishful thinking. The fact is that 45,000 people did have their benefits cut off because of these illegal crawlspace deductions. The fact is that only 1,500 of them have been made eligible since the first of the year, when this illegal practice was first exposed. The fact is that, statistically speaking, at least 25,000 of these people are still living in Maryland, are still sick, are still poor, and still have not gotten any medical care through Medical Assistance. The fact is that the department won't give us the names of any applicants. They say that they don't have the manpower to give us any meaningful statistics. They won't let us look at their records. They haven't looked at the records themselves. They've closed their eyes to the problem, they've effectively blindfolded us—and what they're trying to do now is blindfold this court."

Judge Barnett had been staring intensely at each of the

two lawyers in turn from behind the bench. A modern affair, all sharp angles and light wood (and inconspicuous bulletproofing), the bench elevated Barnett far above the level of the two lawyers who stood respectfully below. Barnett was impressed by Angela's comeback to Jody's very good argument.

Judge Barnett was fifty years old. Before he came to the bench he had always been regarded as somewhat too scholarly and intellectual for the rough and tumble world of commercial litigation. He felt more comfortable in the role of judge than he ever had as a lawyer. He was basically a modest man who tried to understand first the plain meaning of the law, and then the complications, and then the subtleties. Only when it was shown beyond a doubt that there was no answer in the books did he feel that he had a right to consult his own opinions.

Barnett recognized Angela's gambit even as it began to work on him. There might be judges who didn't mind being called harsh, or strict, or arbitrary, or even pig-headed, but there was no such thing as a judge who liked to think of himself as a dupe. Angela had said that he was being made a fool of by Jody. And Jody really had no hard evidence that these thousands of people did not exist. The department did seem to be keeping a tight lid on the facts, then claiming that there were none. Jody was asking him to assume that everything was just fine, based on some paper changes in procedures that hadn't yet seemed to have any effect.

"Your Honor," Jody sensed that Angela's interruption had scored points. "There's no way that the department can prove that these people *don't* exist. But Miss Watkins is asking you to believe in something that you haven't seen, and that the whole department hasn't seen either. Undoubtedly there were large numbers of people affected over the years, but that was in the past. You just can't say that the situation is the same now. People move away. They come out of poverty sometimes. They get their own medical insurance. They get well and don't need medical care ...."

"They die," Angela interjected.

Jody shot her a malevolent look. But he knew enough not to try to keep going. He sat down, and let the rest of his argument go. The judge had heard enough, he decided. Let him make the decision.

After an agonizing moment's silence, Judge Barnett spoke up tentatively. "Is there a Mr. Leonard Tynan here?"

"The reason I ask," Barnett continued, after Tynan had been identified, "is that I'm very curious about his statements in the deposition about this applicant whom he aided with his appeal."

Angela's heart sank when she heard these last few words. If Barnett couldn't see that Tynan had practically pushed that old man out of his office *instead of* aiding him, then he really must have succumbed to Jody's rosy view of the department's intentions. If so, there was little hope.

"I think," Barnett continued, "that it might be helpful to the court to hear a few more details of that transaction. Mr. Hechtmuller, would you be interested in calling Mr. Tynan as a witness?"

Jody was on guard. The judge's comment about Tynan "aiding" that old man had sounded to him like a false note, a deliberately over-polite and naive-sounding view of the event, a view that was not in keeping with Barnett's otherwise worldly demeanor. He didn't see how he had anything to gain from Tynan testifying about this incident. It was in his interest to keep this mysterious old man as abstract as possible—not a poor old man sent around in circles by devious bureaucrats, but an applicant, a *unit* denied benefits by mistake but later given adequate instructions to get the problem straightened out. Anything Tynan said would make this old man seem more real to the judge. Or, worse, the new Tynan, sitting impassively next to him, might blurt out some damning new truth.

"The state wouldn't be interested in that, Your Honor."

"Miss Watkins, would you see any benefit in calling Mr. Tynan as a witness," the judge persisted.

Angela felt her own reaction immediately, then she controlled it, then she decided that it was right. "No, Your Honor," she said simply. Tynan had been thoroughly grilled by Sport at the deposition. She was sure that he had told the truth, and the whole truth, about this incident at the deposition. She knew that Barnett had read the whole deposition. "In fact, if it makes things any easier," she added suddenly, "we would stipulate that Mr. Tynan's testimony at the deposition about that particular applicant was truthful and complete."

Barnett was clearly disappointed, but Angela did not regret her decision. This was one of those times in court when both lawyers are for the moment on the same side, and the opponent is the judge. This was the second hearing on the matter, and both the legal and the human sides of the case had been argued over and over. It was time for a decision, and that was the judge's job. The judge could always call Tynan as the court's witness, but he would run the risk of making himself look like a fool. Barnett was peeved that Angela hadn't given him an out by calling Tynan to the stand, but Angela did not back off. Jody stuck by his position too. The silence in the room was the sound of Barnett feeling their pressure.

It continued for two long minutes. "All right," Barnett finally said, "I'm ready to make my ruling." They waited through another minute of silence. Jody was content that he had given it his best shot. Angela was mentally listing the things she hadn't said.

"A class-action suit is an important legal tool. It not only saves the court's time but, more importantly, it also can provide justice in a timely manner to a whole class of people who have been wronged. But a federal judge must be extremely careful in certifying a class in a case such as this. Since the only remedy in a case like this is a court order issued against a branch of the state government, followed by court monitoring and supervision, the end result requires a federal judge to be closely involved in running a part of the state government. This is abhorrent to our federal system of government, and so a class action of this type should be employed only when it is crystal-clear that all of the requirements of the rules have been met."

Angela looked down at the papers on the counsel table and fought back tears as Judge Barnett then went on to paraphrase Jody's argument, using polite legal terminology instead of Jody's patronizing shots. Angela saw that all of her efforts had been to no avail. She had not been good enough to stop the truth from being smothered under a mountain of lies. The case would just dribble away, and there was nothing that she could do about it. She was so angry at Barnett that she interrupted him. When he asserted that the evidence failed to demonstrate that the class definitely existed, she declared: "Your Honor, the evidence that there are at least 25,000 people in this class is uncontradicted."

Judge Barnett looked up from his notes at her, took a breath, and continued without acknowledging her. He got no more than two or three sentences when she did it again. In the back of her mind, she knew that this was not productive conduct. Barnett dropped his notes and stared at her. Meanwhile, Jody squirmed, because he didn't want anything to interrupt the flow of the decision, which had been definitely going his way. Angela's interruption trailed off, but Barnett didn't start again.

There was a sudden thump at the side of the room as Sport burst through the swinging door. His clothes and hair were disheveled, and the armpits of his suitcoat were outlined in dark crescents of sweat. He walked quickly across the front of the courtroom toward Angela, a look of utter dismay on his face. Angela stared at him and experienced a moment of despair. Everything important in her life was going down the drain.

"Your Honor," Sport began speaking, too loud, before he was even fully into the room. "I have to tell this court about something that I am ashamed of."

Jimmy had found Charles lying on the floor next to his bed. Charles had probably tried to get to the toilet when the bloody retching started, but he had passed out. Jimmy found a napkin and cleaned off his face, but still Charles didn't wake up. He picked him up, put him back on the bed and did his best to clean his pajamas and prop him up. Jimmy waited to see if this would take care of things. He walked around the room and tried to think, but Charles still didn't wake. Finally, he ran down the hall and woke up Miss Agatha, who came into the room, took one look at Charles, and said to call an ambulance.

Miss Agatha stuffed all of Charles's papers into Jimmy's pockets. In the Sacred Heart emergency room, they rolled Charles's stretcher away immediately. The ambulance attendants asked Jimmy a lot of questions, and he was proud that he could help. But near the emergency room, a lady sat him down at a desk and asked him a lot of questions about Charles that he didn't know the answers to.

"Does he have any kin?"

"He used to have an aunt named May."

The lady took all the papers from him and looked

through them wearily. Later, a man who said he came from surgery walked up and handed him Charles's shirt and pants.

A few hours later, the doctor, a thin young man with glasses taped on, came out and tried to explain to Jimmy what he had just done. He drew a little picture of a stomach and a duodenum, but Jimmy couldn't seem to get it into perspective.

"His stomach was bleeding," the doctor finally said. "We had to cut part of it out."

The doctor looked tired, and his hands were shaking, but he waited a moment patiently for Jimmy to ask the obvious question. He waited in vain.

"He lost a lot of blood. It's 50-50 whether he will make it or not."

"Thank you," Jimmy said.

"You can go and look at him in the recovery room, but don't try to talk to him."

"Thank you."

"Listen. Doesn't he have any family or other friends?"

"He has lots of friends." Jimmy reached into Charles's coat pocket and pulled out a small pile of business cards. The doctor took the cards for a moment and quickly thumbed through them.

"Does he really know all of these people?" the doctor said, surprised.

"Charles knows a lot of people."

"Why don't you pick one, one who you think would care, and call him."

"Thank you," Jimmy said.

Two hours later, after Jimmy had long since disappeared, it was a social worker who pulled Sister Elena's card from the pile and called her. Sister Elena did not recognize Charles's name, but she came. She guessed that it was one of her alcoholics, dying from a bursting vein or esophagus, the predictable result of a hardened liver from a life of booze. They let her into the intensive care room. Charles's drawn, unconscious features were barely recognizable as those of the strong and dignified man who had once helped her get past the receptionist in the waiting room of the Legal Assistance building.

There were tubes up both of his nostrils and a tube coming out of some bandages in his stomach area. An intravenous needle hooked to three hanging plastic bags was strapped to his arm. A tube going under the sheet at his crotch area led to a lower bag strapped to the bed. A monitor connected to him showed his heart rate and illustrated the heartbeat with a little spike on a screen. Poked, prodded and stretched between these instruments was an incredibly thin and very exhausted-looking body. Its rich brown skin color had faded to grey. The nurses told Elena that he had briefly regained consciousness in the recovery room and was sleeping now. He was in intensive care to watch for complications. He might be a diabetic. There was no medical history to go on.

"Even if he wakes," a nurse advised, "don't expect him to talk."

There were other patients in this dimly lit area, other tiny monitors blinking silently across the room, but Elena was the only visitor there so early in the morning. It was a shadowy room of souls being mechanically held back from going over the edge into death. Elena had never had to think about death before, in the sense of where it actually happens, and how. She stood now at the side of Charles's bed and was overwhelmed by the silence of that process. She had lately been very confused and disheartened about what she was doing with her life. She felt that she could die easily now, without any fear. And it didn't seem fair that this kind old man with an evident purpose in life would have to go first, while she stood next to his bed, wondering why she had been born.

Nobody in the lobby, or in the admissions office, could understand Jimmy. This had the effect of making him talk louder. Nobody would look at the card in his hand. When he refused to leave and started yelling at the ladies trying to silence him, they called the police. At the station, the police did look at the card, and they told him to call Sport immediately.

No one in the courtroom had the nerve to stop Sport from recounting the story. He described how, weeks before, he had collided with Charles in the hallway of the Legal Assistance building, at the very moment that he was leaving the office to file this crawlspace suit.

"I'm coming now from seeing him in the hospital. He's recovering from emergency surgery for a bleeding ulcer. He's had it for over a year. He has a 50-50 chance of recovery. The nurse told me that this just doesn't happen any more. This is a treatable condition."

"Your Honor," Jody interrupted. "Mr. Norris is obviously upset, but I don't think this has anything to do with this case."

Judge Barnett held up his gavel awkwardly and cleared his throat, not quite meeting Sport's eyes. Sport did not take the hint. Nor would he look at Angela.

"A treatable condition. But he didn't have a doctor. He didn't have a Medical Assistance card. Somebody at the hospital handed me all of his papers, the same ones he tried to show me on that first day. He came to me to get a Medical Assistance card, but I wouldn't listen, and now he might die. So much ego involved. I'm sorry.

"Your Honor, these people *do* exist, no matter how *convenient* it may be to deny them."

Judge Barnett dropped his notes. It was one thing to

take the risk of being made a fool of by Hechtmuller and the department, but it was quite another thing to risk sending real people away to get sicker, and to die. Jody could feel the change of mood, and he rose to speak. He wisely began in grave tones of sympathy towards Sport's client and friend, but then he slowly turned the focus toward his argument that this had nothing to do with the requirements of this case. He was interrupted by simultaneous outcries from Angela and Tynan.

"Your Honor, we move to allow Charles Gage to file an Amended Complaint in this case right now," Angela snapped.

"Tell me what this man looks like!" Tynan yelled across the counsel table.

Jody Hechtmuller requested a recess, and Barnett granted it immediately.

Jody wanted time to try to cut a deal with Sport and Angela. Unless Sport's story, or this Charles Gage character, were shown to be completely fraudulent, Judge Barnett was certainly going to grant him status as a named plaintiff. That was the whole ball game.

Sport still looked shaken. Angela stood in front of him and slowly pushed him backwards until he was sitting on the counsel table. He absent-mindedly handed over the sheaf of papers from his inside coat pocket to Jody. Normally, Angela would jump to peer over Jody's shoulder, but she looked only at Sport.

"The 'friend' on the phone" she whispered urgently.

"Just Jimmy," he said loudly.

"Jimmy's out," he continued. "He just got a little too excited." Sport was still breathing heavily himself. "I guess I made a fool of myself. I don't care. You couldn't do much worse for a client than I did for Charles over the last few weeks."

"*We* couldn't do worse," she corrected him.

Anyone who was looking would have seen that Tynan also was very disturbed, but no one was looking. Jody and his two assistants were intent on opening up the new papers and spreading them out on the table. Sport and Angela were absorbed in each other. Judge Barnett had already left to hear criminal motions in another courtroom. The court reporter was idly checking his equipment. Tynan stared blankly at the others, then bolted out of the room. One minute later he emerged from the courthouse at ground level and began retracing Sport's journey through the simmering, humid streets.

At the hospital, he first tried to pass himself off as a public official interested in Charles's case. When the social worker learned about his position, though, all she did was eagerly open up a file she had started on Charles's Medical Assistance eligibility. She wanted his assurance that the bill would be paid. He hung around just long enough to get wind of where Charles was actually located, then said he had to go the bathroom. He leaped up the steps to the fifth floor. Peeking out of the stairwell door quietly, he had a chance to observe the nurse's station without being seen. Even though it was an intensive care unit, there was actually only one nurse present, and she was at the nurse's station, facing away from him, with her head down, apparently making notes in a chart. Tynan eased out of the door and slipped very quickly by the station without making a sound.

He waited a moment for his eyes to get used to the gloom. He did see that there were no nurses present. There were five beds hung with tubes and monitors and machinery. The venetian blinds on the three windows overlooking the silent traffic on Charles Street five stories below were mostly closed. Tynan realized that he'd have to walk up and look each one of these patients in the face. The first was a very old white woman with a bun of yellowing hair. He was grateful that she was not awake. An incredibly thin, elderly black woman was in the next bed. Her eyes flickered open, but not long enough to notice him. He felt a small bit of relief that these were obviously people over 65, not clients of his department, not crawlspace people. At the next bed, he peered down into the face of Charles Gage.

It was unquestionably the same man that he had helped out of the gutter the first time they met, then shooed out of his office the next. Of course, he looked much worse now. Charles's eyes opened, and turned toward him, but it was hard to tell if there was any recognition behind the glassy blankness of his stare.

"Don't try to talk," Tynan whispered. "Your lawyer's been here. He's worried about you. We're all worried about you. You know that, don't you?" He stared into Charles's eyes.

"Sir, you are not allowed in Intensive Care."

"I need to talk to his doctor." There was one doctor present in the station now, busily checking the charts. Tynan guessed that Charles didn't have any particular doctor, and that any doctor would do. He spoke directly to the doctor, who hadn't yet glanced up from his charts.

"Doctor, what is the prognosis for Charles Gage?"

The doctor picked up a chart and walked up next to Tynan at the counter. "I can't give out that information to you," the doctor stated softly, "unless you are a close relative. Are you kin to him?"

"Yes."

"Wait a minute. Wait a minute. Wait a minute!" Jody mumbled to himself. The papers which Sport had retrieved from Jimmy's pockets were spread out all over Jody's counsel table. The recess had been extended to three

254

hours, as Judge Barnett sent word that he was booked for the rest of the morning. Jody was starting to feel that things weren't so hopeless after all. For one thing, there were some technicalities he could raise, such as the fact that Charles would now surely be eligible for Medical Assistance—once his huge hospital bill was thrown into the equation. No matter how many crawlspaces the department might have assigned to him, the multi-thousand dollar bill from Sacred Heart would wipe them out in a second. He would be so far in debt that no number of crawlspaces would disqualify him. Therefore, he was not really a proper plaintiff for the crawlspace suit.

On the other hand, one of the papers showed that Charles had been offered, just yesterday, $100,000 for a piece of property he owned. Of course, no one who owned a piece of real estate worth $100,000 could be financially eligible for Medical Assistance.

Tynan came back into the courtroom, the crisp edges gone from his clothes; he could have been walking in a swamp. Jody had no idea how long he had been gone. Jody hurriedly showed him some of the papers and they held a long, whispered conversation. Then Jody looked over to the opposing counsel's table.

"Let's talk settlement. Consent decree," Jody offered. He was talking quickly. "Six months retroactivity. We'll recalculate everybody who applied in the last six months, with an order to our workers absolutely prohibiting any deductions being made for crawlspaces or basements."

Angela had never guessed how good it would feel to see the enemy crumble right before her eyes. It was even better than having the judge do it. Up until an hour ago, she would have happily settled for what Jody was now offering.

"No. You have to go back further."

Jody did make one good point.

255

"Look how bogged down the department is already. Forcing it to recalculate five years' worth of applications will result in complete chaos. It won't really do anybody any good."

Angela had to try hard to look dissatisfied and skeptical.

Judge Barnett agreed to wait another five minutes before coming back on the bench. Angela told Jody that they'd accept an eighteen-month recalculation, if the department made a public announcement of its new policy, and actively encouraged people who had been cheated by the crawlspace deductions to reapply.

Tynan looked preoccupied. It was clear that Jody was making up their counterproposals and simply running them by Tynan, who seemed to nod vague approval every time. Tynan did leave at one point to make a phone call. When he came back, he blurted out: "The bastard says he'll do it." Jody was so engrossed in the details of the settlement he didn't even blink at Tynan's language. They agreed to stick to their position that eighteen months was too far back to recalculate everybody's application.

"You're forcing the judge to decide this," Angela threatened.

"You seem to be forgetting that it could still go either way," Jody countered. "This Charles Gage has had a $100,000 legacy waiting for him for months. He may never have been eligible."

It seemed that the judge would be forced to decide it. They sent word through the judge's law clerk that they could not reach an agreement.

By the time that he returned to the bench, Angela had crossed out Mrs. Throckmorton's name on an extra copy of the original complaint, substituted Charles's name in ballpoint pen, and interlineated Charles's specific fact situation. She wanted a specific document with a specific motion on it to be sitting on the judge's bench when he returned.

"Your Honor, we could not wait to have a neater motion typed up tomorrow, since there is no assurance ... there is no assurance of anything. He could be dead by tomorrow."

"Your Honor, there's no signed affidavit accompanying this complaint," Jody complained. "This is hearsay, an anecdote. This is not something that deserves serious consideration as a motion."

"Then I propose, Your Honor, that we all walk down to the intensive care room at Sacred Heart and swear Charles in."

"Your Honor," Jody stood up, "just one minute of argument, please, before we all get carried away on a tide of sympathy for this evidently very sick man.

"Charles is a very sick man," Jody continued, "but he is not now, and has not been for some time, a poor man. Just during the recess, Your Honor, I have discovered in these papers evidence that he is the owner of a property..."

Tynan rose out of his chair and pulled Jody all the way down into his chair by his coat sleeve. They argued in whispers. Tynan was shaking his head, upset. Jody seemed to be explaining things to him, talking with his hands and shrugging his shoulders. Tynan nodded again, and again, then stage-whispered one final curt order to Jody. Jody then stood up. He looked relieved.

"Your Honor, the department has found itself able to accept the terms offered today by the Legal Assistance Society for the settlement of this suit."

Sport sprawled back in his chair, strangely quiet, as Angela and Jody Hechtmuller put the terms of the settlement on the record before the judge. In three minutes they were done, the judge had gone, the court reporter was packing up his machinery. Angela turned back to Sport and sat on the counsel table, facing him. She had never seen him so exhausted and out of control.

"What's wrong?"

"Charles tried to tell me from the beginning. I remember. Everything I've done on this case from the beginning has been wrong."

"Sport, I had lost this case this afternoon, before you came in."

"Well, it's over."

"We are just the lawyers, Sport. We may not have done so well, but our *clients* did. *They* won! The 42,000 people! Charles. Mrs. Throckmorton."

At the sound of that last name, Sport grimaced and bowed his head. Angela slid off the table and sat in the chair next to him. He looked up when she put a hand on his arm. A silence grew between them stronger than the rustling papers and snapping briefcases at the other counsel table.

"Angela, I have to make a confession to you. You already know..."

She leaned very close. "I think I know," she whispered fervently. "It's been so hard, not being able to talk to you about it."

"Angela..." He held onto her hand, his eyes desperate.

"Don't say any more. Mrs. Throckmorton's signature. I knew you did it. It's okay, Sport. You won for her. You did the right thing for her." Her grip was tight. "I think it's bothering you, and I don't think it should."

"You don't understand, Angela" Sport moaned. He threw his head back, unable to meet her eyes. "There is no Mrs. Throckmorton."

18 GLASS HOUSES

When Tynan phoned Gotterdung from the federal courthouse on the day of the crawlspace settlement, he dutifully informed the Secretary of every detail of the settlement proposed by Legal Assistance. One of the details was Angela's insistence that the Secretary himself make a public, televised statement that the agency had miscalculated Medical Assistance eligibility for the past five years, and that anyone who thought they had been wrongfully turned down should reapply. Legal Assistance was demanding no less than a public confession of error.

"Ha ha. No problem," the Secretary had laughed. "I can turn this around, make it look like we're the good guys again."

"Sure you can."

"With the help and advice of the Legal Assistance Society," Gotterdung began his televised speech, "the Department of Public Welfare has discovered that there was an error in the way we calculated eligibility for Medical Assistance benefits." This opening was Gotterdung's own idea. Act as if it had been a cooperative effort with Legal Assistance. Characterize the whole thing as a calculation error. Gotterdung's plan thus far was no different than

Tynan's would have been. His next idea was also a good one: get the worst of it over with quickly.

"This is an announcement to anyone in the state who has been turned down for Medical Assistance in the last five years. We were calculating your grant wrong. We were subtracting for basements and crawlspaces that, in most cases, didn't exist. We might have turned you down because of this wrong policy. If you think you might be eligible, you can apply again. If you apply again, we will use the correct calculations." Gotterdung read these words from a separate piece of paper. These words had been written by Angela. She had never dreamed that Gotterdung himself would read them on television. But this humiliating requirement had found its way into the settlement agreement, all without a peep of protest from Leonard Tynan.

Gotterdung hadn't counted on Keane being at the announcement. It wasn't supposed to be a press conference, but Keane pushed his way to the front and interrupted.

"How much is this going to cost?"

Gotterdung was ready for this one, but he made a strategic mistake by answering it. He had been advised by his public relations officer just to read the statement. No questions were supposed to be allowed. But Gotterdung was so proud of *knowing* the answer that he couldn't resist reciting it then and there.

"It will cost anywhere from eight to twelve million dollars," he replied somberly. "And I am determined that the money will not be taken from other programs. It will be in the department's next budget request, no matter who the next governor is. I have no doubt that both of the candidates will have the compassion to find the money for this basic medical care for our neediest citizens." Gotterdung had already cleared this with Slidell. Slidell would announce that, if elected, he would be compassionate enough to come up with the money. Pettibone would not be left with much of a choice. As he boxed in Pettibone again, Gotterdung felt an inner glow of satisfaction that things were finally going his way.

Since Gotterdung had answered Keane's question, all of the other reporters felt free to yell out questions of their own. No one in the room had much respect for Gotterdung. Everyone knew that the department had been sued by Legal Assistance and had been stoutly resisting the suit before being forced to settle. They knew this because Angela had called them up and told them just that afternoon.

"Didn't you deny that this miscalculation existed, up until yesterday afternoon?"

"Weren't you saying that people who lived in third-floor apartments had basements? That's not a 'miscalculation,' is it?"

"Legal Assistance filed papers in court saying that you stonewalled them on getting information. How can you say you cooperated with them?"

Gotterdung was not the type of person to turn and walk away from a challenge, but his speaking skills fell far short of what was needed here. So he stammered and blustered. He denied knowledge of things everyone knew he knew. He appeared petulant, ignorant, and guilty of hiding things even now. The impression given on the television screen was that of a large, ignorant and fairly uncaring man who had been caught covering up the misdeeds of his department. This impression was accurate. Across town, in Eddie's restaurant, Slip once again put his face in his hands.

"What about this study that's holding up the Mayor's Waterside Towers Project?" someone yelled. "A group called CORP filed a lawsuit yesterday. They say that the study is a phony. Is it a phony study?"

"Of course it's not a phony study." Gotterdung was glad to be on familiar ground. He knew that the deal between Slip and Mayor Pettibone was done. All that he had to do was deliver the study.

"Why don't you just read it?" Gotterdung sneered.

Like many persons whose analytical powers are overshadowed by their egos, Gotterdung didn't always distinguish between what he intended to do and what he had actually done. When Slip had called him and told him to release the study, he had said fine, he would do it right away. But he was used to having details like this taken care of for him by office secretaries and assistants. And Tynan, who would normally remind him of something like this, had been in court all that day on the crawlspace suit. As a result, Gotterdung had done nothing at all about the study; he simply assumed that, because he had wanted it to be completed, it had been done.

"But your Public Information Office just issued a statement saying that the study had not yet been published. If it is finished, why won't you give it to Judge Sanders, so he can let Pettibone start work on Waterside Towers?"

"Let me tell you about that study."

Word that Mallory had actually begun work on the study had spread down the corridors of the department as fast as the clatter of Bobbi Jo Ludell's sequined high heels. By the time Tynan had returned from the Mallory hearing on the day before, everyone in the building knew. Many of the departmental employees believed that Tynan had finally found a way to put enough pressure on Mallory to get him to do some work.

But it was not pressure, but ridicule, that finally got Mallory started on the study. Mallory was completely unaware of the importance of the study, or of the CORP lawsuit about it. Even if he had known, it would have had no effect on him. He would have enjoyed frustrating everyone. But the one thing which he did not enjoy was being referred to as a joke.

The minute she saw Mallory setting up a file for the study, Bobbi Jo had left the office to warn Tynan. She didn't know what else he had done, because 4:30 had arrived, and Mallory had gone home by the time she and Tynan huffed back into the office. Mallory's file cabinet and desk were locked. The next morning, Bobbi Jo spied on him. She found out that his old habits had proven hard to break. He had done absolutely nothing else. He did leave the study folder out on his blotter for most of the morning, but he put it back in his drawer after lunch, still empty, as if he had exerted himself enough on that project for one day.

Of all the unfortunate consequences of his mental and emotional limitations that visited themselves upon Gotterdung that day, the most damaging was his belief that Mallory was actually working on the study. Like everyone else in the building, he heard the news that Mallory was working on it. He assumed that there was some connection between this fact and the deal that Slidell had made with the mayor to release the study. There was no basis for this assumption; but without Tynan around to help him think, Gotterdung tended to jump to conclusions.

"The study," he stated boldly, "is not connected to any lawsuit that may have been filed downtown. But it is going to be completed and released by the end of the day."

Still, the reporters wouldn't let him go. There was a quickened sense among them that this man was making up his facts as he went along.

"How many pages are in the report?"

"Was there citizen input?"

"How long did it take to prepare?"

"Who worked on it?"

"Were any homeowners in the Fells Point area interviewed?"

"What kind of statistics were generated?"

Gotterdung quickly reached his breaking point.

"I don't have that infor...."

"None of your business...

"You'll find out when the study is officially released.

"You have no right .... You'll find out when I'm good and ready!"

Gotterdung had excluded his press officer from his preparations from the press conference. The press officer now stood to the side of the podium with a small smile. His boss was doing a good impersonation of a tongue-tied bully. Finally, he could stand it no more, and he went up to the front and pushed Gotterdung away from the microphones, just as a matter of professional mercy.

Across the city, Slip felt his own stomach churning. He searched his conscience to see if he really thought he had to keep this buffoon on the ticket. He swore that he would never make an important deal again with anyone he didn't really know. On the screen, the local anchorman began wrapping up the story. But then, the camera suddenly cut to an even more startling scene.

The moment Gotterdung left the press conference, the camera lights went off. A PR officer was not worth live coverage. Gotterdung stormed out of the office trying to flee from the reporters. Some of them turned and persisted in peppering him with questions. He knew that he had blown the news conference, and he didn't even understand why. Slidell and Pettibone would both consider him an idiot now. But he still was in control of the one thing that they both needed, the study. He vowed that he would deliver it as promised.

He raced down the hallway toward the elevators. He pressed the "down" button, but it just flickered on, then off, then on, then off. He ran to the fire stairwell and leaped down the stairs to the fifth floor. It was 4:29. Many of the state employees had already gone home for the day. He turned in to the Statistical Unit and bounded right past the startled Division Director. After a few more lunging steps, he turned a corner and stopped, breathing heavily, in the doorway of one of the cubicles within. There, he observed Mallory, precisely at the stroke of 4:30, click closed the lock to his file drawer.

Mallory did not acknowledge *anybody* after 4:30. He barely glanced at the Secretary, then turned to pick up his neatly folded newspaper from his desk.

"Mallory!"

Gotterdung assumed that the quivering anger in his voice would stop Mallory in his tracks. But Mallory may as well have been deaf. He methodically picked up his wallet and his keys and turned to walk out of the cubicle as if he were blind to Gotterdung's hulking presence. It took a few seconds for Gotterdung to fully comprehend just what was happening, just how insolent this man could be. His entire body tensed with the effort of holding himself back from landing a punch right in the middle of that round, pink, smirking, goateed face. But he fought with himself for control of that urge. He needed that study right now. He would make sure Mallory was washed out tomorrow. But the study was what he really needed now. He fought to keep that rational fragment in the forefront of his mind.

But then, Mallory started to walk right past him, as if nothing had happened. He had the key to the file cabinet. The study was in there. When Mallory tried to maneuver himself out of the doorway, Gotterdung blocked his way.

"I want that study, now," Gotterdung commanded.

Years of practiced passive defiance made Mallory's response flow naturally and freely: "Excuse me. I'm on my own time."

"The study about Fells Point. Just hand it to me."

"It's in my file cabinet. I'll hand it to my supervisor tomorrow morning."

"Give it to *me. Now.*"

"If you want something from me, speak to my supervisor about it during work time."

Gotterdung was seething. He made a desperate attempt to hold himself back. He forced himself to try one more time. "This is an order. You realize who I am, don't you?"

"Yeah. You're Gutterschmidt, or whatever ...."

"Give me that key ...." Gotterdung grabbed for Mallory's arm, but Mallory clenched his fist over the key and curled his arm to his side. Gotterdung started pulling on his arm, but Mallory pivoted and turned his back to him, breaking Gotterdung's hold. Gotterdung lost control and pushed him roughly into the filing cabinet. There was a hollow metal thud, and the cabinet rocked from the collision with Mallory's stomach. He pushed him again, but Mallory still wouldn't turn back around. Gotterdung was screaming, "Give it to me! Give it to me," pounding on Mallory's back, and launching vicious hooks to the side of Mallory's head, when he noticed that the cubicle was unusually bright, and he realized that the television camera lights were on again.

"Why, Sport?"

Through Sport's tiny casement window up by the ceiling, Angela could occasionally see the feet of passers-by on the sidewalk above. Now a maverick ray of late afternoon sunlight lit a casement-shaped rectangle at the top of the pine paneling that served as one wall of his office. Sport was standing behind his desk, against the concrete wall, in the fluorescent gloom.

"I was thinking about all those people, thousands of sick people. The Department of Public Welfare tricking them all, turning them all away."

"You planned this out?"

"I was just writing a dummy complaint after they paid off Mrs. Jackson. I just made up the name Virginia Throckmorton to fill in the space until we got a real client, and ... I don't know what happened."

"So you just ..."

"I just kept on going, as if Mrs. Throckmorton were real. Linda was just learning about being a notary, so I told her it was okay to notarize Mrs. Throckmorton's signature, even if Mrs. Throckmorton wasn't there."

"But the signature lines on the photocopies were blank."

Sport shrugged. "I always meant for the photocopies to be blank. That could always be explained. Only the judge would see the funny signature. But I didn't plan to sign it in front of Mallory. I'm sorry."

"I admired you so much."

"I thought I was taking all the risk. I never thought about you."

"I would never have done this, not for a million sick people."

"Your best bet is to keep as far away from me as possible, Angela."

"No. That will never happen."

There was a catch in her voice when she said this, but when he looked up she was clear-eyed and staring back at him calmly. The office had grown even dimmer, but the rectangle of light had flattened itself into an orange lozenge that stretched across the wall and streaked across the gloss of her hair. He knew that he would never find a better friend.

267

It was Fosback's dream of redemption come true. Ever since he had been the messenger for the original bad news that Gotterdung would not do the study for Pettibone, he had been forced to take the blame for the foul-up of the Waterside Towers plans. As the foul-up had grown worse, Fosback's fortunes fell. The mayor even made him conduct interviews for the selection of his own replacement. Fosback fought back, frantically shoring up his own position by undermining that of his rivals. He traveled throughout the city offices, contacting his extensive network of acquaintances in city government, gathering dirt on the candidates for his job and creating rumors and doubt where there was no dirt to be found. These were just defensive measures. But the dirt he dug up on Sport was so fertile it revived his faith in the usefulness of a cynicism as deep and broad as his own.

Pettibone agreed that they had to meet with Sport right away.

"We've made every reasonable effort to work with you, and your client," Fosback began bluntly.

"The developer's offer for your client's property now stands at $125,000. That's ten times what we paid most homeowners in the area. It's twenty times the assessed value of the property before the Crosley T. Pettibone Waterside Towers Luxury Condominium Development project was planned. Your client's aunt bought it for $1,200 in 1946. Everyone else accepted much lower offers without much fuss. We know that you are advising him to hold out. But this is a game that both sides can play. If you're not reasonable, this thing can be made to backfire in your face."

Sport smiled back comfortably. He was having a wonderful day. He had been to the hospital and learned that Charles would recover. The news coverage of Gotterdung pummeling Mallory had attracted even more attention to Gotterdung's announcement about the crawlspaces. The headline in the Baltimore *State* had read:

OFFICIAL ADMITS DECEIT, THEN
PUMMELS UNDERLING
-Also enjoined for allegedly false study-

The *Free American* had waxed more poetic:

CHEAT THE POOR, HIT THE WEAK,
FLUNK THE STUDY
-One, two, three: Gotterdung strikes out-

Keane, as usual, had seen the events from a slightly different angle. His column about Charles was captioned:

AGENCY PLEADS WITH JUDGE TO LET
POOR MAN ROT
-Charles refuses to die, foiling Department's
legal strategy-

Governor Mallard had asked for Gotterdung's resignation immediately after the fight scene hit the television screens. He had it by noon the next day. Tynan was made Acting Secretary. One news story mentioned that Tynan "was widely given credit for the humane compromise that was finally reached in the Medical Assistance suit." The press reports expressed a general feeling of relief that the system had finally rid itself of that governmental disaster, Brendan Gotterdung. Editorials exhorted Tynan to straighten out the mess he had inherited.

If Charles wanted just money, he couldn't have found himself in a better position. Sport had no doubt that Fosback's offer would double before the meeting was over, and he knew that $250,000 could set up Charles for life. But, just that morning, in the hospital, Charles had shaken

off Sport's apologies, whispering vehemently: "No. The house. You got me the house. Better."

"I want you to know that we appreciate your offer," Sport began. "But I have to obey my client's wishes, and he really is not interested in money. That house has a lot of sentimental value to him, and he plans to live there when he recovers. I wish we could deal; I see you're ready to deal. But he wants to keep his house." Sport knew that he should have stopped there, but he was feeling especially cocky. "You don't have condemnation powers, I know. And, after today's headlines about contempt of court, I don't think you'll ever get them."

Fosback tapped a cigarette out of a fresh pack and lit it. He turned on his portable ashtray, tapped another cigarette halfway out and leaned toward Sport.

"Smoke?"

"No. No thanks." Sport pulled back.

"I thought you smoked."

"No. Not any more."

Fosback exhaled very slowly.

"You get a lot of interesting clients at the Legal Assistance Society?"

"Yes."

"Live all over the city?"

"Yeah."

"I know you needed one real bad for that crawlspace suit."

Sport's eyes narrowed.

"My job is liaison. Contact with all kinds of people. You hear the funniest things. From what I hear, you signed Mrs. Throckmorton's signature on her affidavit."

"That's all been explained." But Sport's voice was tiny.

"And her address is a house on West Ostend Street that has been boarded up for the last three years."

"What's your point?" Sport managed.

Fosback ground out his cigarette slowly, with obvious satisfaction. He started tapping another one out of the pack, taking his time.

"Get to the point," Pettibone commanded.

"We've got three letters here." Fosback fingered a folder on the edge of Pettibone's desk. "One to the bar association, one to Judge Barnett, and one to the federal prosecutor's office requesting an investigation of possible perjury by a member of the bar. All signed by the mayor. He's holding up mailing them for one reason only. Do you know what that reason is?"

Sport just stared at him.

"Because I asked him to. I told Mayor Pettibone that I don't know if this Sport Norris is really a forger and perjurer. Maybe he's not that kind of person at all. Maybe he's a cooperative gentleman." Fosback smiled.

"We're not trying to grind your client down, Sport. We'll offer him his share. I'm authorized to offer as high as $150,000. I may be able to squeeze out even a few pennies more. It's this unreasonable refusal to negotiate at all that makes us feel—well, that makes us feel that you really aren't worth saving."

Fosback sat back to let the shock sink in. Pettibone stared at Sport without a trace of sympathy. Sport tried to keep himself from shaking.

"We could go to $160,000. I'm giving you an extra $10,000 right now, just to show that we're being reasonable."

"You don't understand Charles, or his dream."

"We want your agreement right now."

He had already failed Charles once. He could not fail him again. He remembered Charles's words in the hospital, refusing his apology. *No. The house. You got me the house. Better.* But he had never planned to suffer for a client in the way that he was now going to have to suffer

271

for Charles.

Since Angela wasn't there at the meeting to represent him, Sport didn't have the option of remaining silent while his lawyer feigned dumbstruck, astonished innocence. He couldn't do that himself. He couldn't modulate his voice well enough to pretend that he had no idea what they were talking about. Pettibone and Fosback could see right away that he was guilty.

"It doesn't matter where she lives." His mouth was so dry he had to push the words out.

"So you're willing to undergo an investigation?" Fosback replied acidly.

"You'll both be disbarred, of course." Sport rasped. A flat-out counterattack was the only move available. "Threatening to use criminal proceedings to gain an advantage in a civil case. Conspiracy. Blackmail. You two will both be finished, if you don't finish me off completely." Sport's voice crackled with an icy malevolence. "Are you really sure that you can prove this? Are you *positive?* Because if there's a slip-up, both of you will slip down the drain."

Sport's threat took Fosback by surprise. He had worked in the city government too long to believe that slip-ups didn't happen. And the very word Sport used, "slip," made Pettibone's stomach queasy.

"Well, you had better be *absolutely* sure, and *absolutely* positive."

"We know what we're talking about." Pettibone's ice blue eyes stared at him, implacable.

"You both must be quite sure, to stake your reputations on it."

"We are," Fosback replied.

"We are," the mayor said.

But of course they weren't.

"We'll give you exactly forty-eight hours to accept our

offer." This was a tactical retreat, though Fosback tried to disguise it with an aggressive tone. Fosback had decided to double-check his information before going ahead. This would give Sport time. Excusing himself with a jittery nod, Sport ran out the massive street-level doors of City Hall and up Calvert Street to the back door of the Legal Assistance Society.

Angela listened gravely.
"What do you want me to do?"
"I don't know. Save me."

19 RECOVERIES

The surgeon came in to speak to Charles. "I've been reading about you in the paper." He dropped that part of the paper containing Keane's column on the bed. He seemed pleased at the note in the chart that Charles hadn't had any alcohol for the past ten years.

"I thank you for saving my life."

The surgeon smiled, pushed his glasses back up onto the bridge of his nose, and shrugged. "It's my job," he said. "But this whole thing would have been unnecessary if you had visited a doctor and taken care of yourself."

"It's a fine job. You did a fine job."

"Thank you. I usually don't get to know," he motioned down toward the paper, "who I'm cutting on. They're just bodies, almost, sometimes. It all goes so fast."

"You're real good at it."

The surgeon resolved right then to come and visit Charles when he could, but by the time he got another break in his schedule Charles had already been discharged.

Judge Sanders' injunction against any construction or demolition work on the Pettibone Waterside Towers project was only supposed to last twenty-four hours.

The Crawlspace Conspiracy

Sanders had little patience with CORP or its wild allegations, but no one had shown up that first day to deny any
of these claims—and Jody Hechtmuller had refused to
deny them even over the phone. Sanders had assumed
that the mayor, and the Department of Public Welfare,
and all the development and construction companies
would be represented in his courtroom at ten o'clock the
next morning, the scheduled time to hear the motion, and
that they would give him a sufficient reason to lift the
injunction.

By nine o'clock the next morning, however, CORP had
filed a motion that all defendants be held in contempt.
The motion quoted Pettibone's threat to begin the project
that morning. At ten, CORP's lawyer came into Sanders'
chambers with a CORP member who owned a video camera. None of the defendants, or any of their lawyers, had
shown up on time.

Judge Sanders was irritated. He let the CORP man testify in chambers and show his videotape right away. The
man testified that he had been out at the site of the proposed Pettibone Waterside Towers project since seven-
thirty that morning. One row of houses on the very edge
of the proposed project site had been empty for over eighteen months. The opening shots showed that these houses
were protected from human infestation by high barbed
wire fences topped with concertina wire.

The video showed a gate in the fence being unlocked
and opened, and a huge crane being driven onto the site.
What followed was a lot of extremely slow fiddling
around with cables and a wrecking ball. The wrecking
equipment was eventually set up near the old three-story
brick houses. The cameraman fast-forwarded through
most of this as he showed it to the judge. He switched
back to normal speed when the crane finally swung,
knocking a five-foot chunk of cornice off the edge of one

275

of the houses. The camera then followed several more destructive swings of the ball. It then shifted focus to a small pickup truck parked near the crane. Although the camera was jiggling now, it became apparent that the cameraman was trying to focus on the name painted on the side of the pickup truck. The name "Susumee Development" just barely came into view, and into focus, before the door of the truck opened and the camera's field of view swung around a hundred and eighty degrees. The picture then started bucking and careening wildly, giving an occasional lurching glimpse of the ground, which seemed to be moving past at high speed.

Judge Sanders had seen Pettibone on television the evening before, promising that construction would start immediately. But Sanders had not gotten to his position as a judge by thinking the worst of people in high office. He had assumed that Pettibone was only blustering, and that Pettibone's lawyers in the City Solicitor's Office would dutifully get the injunction lifted before any construction work would begin. This morning, Sanders was more than disappointed in Pettibone. He was enraged. He stormed back to the bench, waiting to lash into the City Solicitor, but no one was in the courtroom to represent either the city, or the state, or the developers. The City Solicitor assigned the case was quite used to being waited for by the city judges. She wouldn't arrive in court for another ten minutes. The attorney that Jody Hechtmuller had assigned the job of defending the Department of Public Welfare was still in his office, putting the final touches on a Motion to Extend Time to Answer. Ken Kiger of Susumee Development assumed that the mayor's lawyers would take care of this, and he thought that he wouldn't waste money contacting his own lawyer. Bold Tip's law firm in Chicago was just then opening the envelope of legal papers mailed yesterday from CORP.

"Get the court reporter in here!" Sanders bellowed. He started and ended the hearing in three minutes, without giving anyone else a chance to speak. He put on the record everything that he had seen on the television news and on the CORP videotape. In the process of putting everything in the correct legal terminology, and in clarifying the exact legal procedure he was following, he cooled off a little bit. When he had started talking, he had intended to hold Pettibone in contempt of court immediately. He knew that Pettibone deserved it, and that "contempt" was the right word. By the time that he finished his procedural statement, however, he realized that he was a judge, and that the very essence of these judicial powers included the requirement that he was not allowed to fly into a rage, like a madman, like Pettibone. He knew that Pettibone had a right to be heard, even though Pettibone wouldn't listen. So, instead of immediately holding Pettibone in contempt, he gave the mayor until 4:30 that afternoon to show cause why he should not be held in contempt. He had his own clerk personally deliver the message to the City Solicitor's office.

Pettibone hated nothing more than learning from a news reporter about something that was going on inside his own administration. This happened a lot when legal matters were afoot, since most of the City Solicitors regarded the city as just another client, no more deserving of communication than any of their private clients. One of the justifications for Fosback's job, in fact, was the need to improve liaison between the mayor's office and the city's lawyers. This was a part of his job which Fosback performed without too many hitches, and he did this assignment well enough under ordinary circumstances. But, despite his access to the very latest in communications equipment, including call forwarding, call waiting, call parking, caller identification, 24-hour beeper, home and office fax machines and free 24-hour use of his cellular car phone, it still often took him several hours to transmit fast-breaking case developments to the mayor.

On the morning when Judge Sanders ordered Pettibone to show cause why he should not be held in contempt, Fosback had been consumed with his plan to get back in the mayor's good graces. He was busy double-checking the facts behind his scheme to blackmail Sport. He hadn't bothered to call in to the office to pick up any of the routine legal communications. As a result, Mayor Pettibone was never told that he was due in court late that afternoon on a contempt of court charge—until *Free American* columnist Joe Keane blustered his way into his office at three o'clock, and taunted him with the news. Fosback had the misfortune to be present, and to appear to be walking into Pettibone's office at Keane's side.

The sound of Pettibone's eruption could be heard even through the three-inch-thick mahogany doors. Those doors flew open, and Fosback ran out. Inside, Keane stood his ground as Pettibone swept all of the papers, the files, and the blotter off of his absurdly oversized executive desk. Keane then stepped closer to the mayor. Keane's bemused expression could be seen even through the thick lenses of his glasses.

"Even your old buddy, Judge Sanders," he baited the mayor, "seems to doubt that you have much respect for the law."

Pettibone picked up a ceremonial inkwell set and winged it at him. "Get out! Get out!" he yelled, but Keane was the kind of person who reacted to danger by charging ahead. He stepped even closer to the desk. Pettibone stood up and picked up a lamp by its base. He rushed toward Keane, but he was stopped short by the lamp cord.

"Do you think you'll go to jail, or will Judge Sanders

just give you a fine?" Despite his smart words, Keane was keeping a close eye on Pettibone's hands. But his journalistic mind was still functioning well. He wanted to find out just how monstrous this man's ego was. Pettibone was swinging the lamp in his direction now, but slowly, as if he were in a trance. *"Stick in a knife / Stick it in your wife."*

"What?" said Keane. "Say again?"

Ken Kiger had not become a millionaire during Pettibone's administration by telling him that things could not be done. A lot of contractors cut corners on construction, always trying to substitute cheaper, shoddier building materials—or cheaper, new products just out on the market that were always guaranteed to be "just as good," but rarely were. Kiger's companies cut about the same amount of construction corners as the others. Their roofs leaked like everyone else's, and their buildings held up just about as well. But Kiger had learned to cut different and bigger corners under Pettibone. He had cut legal corners and contractual corners and financing corners, always because of Pettibone's insistence on plowing ahead at full speed. He had always been comforted by Pettibone's word that those who cooperated with him would not be left out in the cold.

Kiger was perfectly willing to begin tearing down the empty houses in Section A-6 of the Mayor's Waterside Towers Project, if that was what Pettibone wanted to do. He didn't even bother to check with Bold Tip, the developer for whom he was supposedly working. He wasn't even sure who owned the empty houses. He had his men cut the locks on the gate to the chain link fence and bring in the crane, which he had rented the night before after he had seen Pettibone on television vowing to begin the project. He had personally chased away that little creep from CORP with the camera.

His foremen were loyal to him and were equally bold. He had a good relationship with all of them because he paid them well and expected them to know what they were doing, and because he knew what he was doing himself. For this reason, he was surprised when the foreman of the demolition project called him about a half hour after it started and told him that he had to call it to a halt.

"Pettibone wants it done. I want it done. Right now. What's the matter with you, Mike?"

"I want it done too, Ken."

"Then do it, Mike. don't let anything stand in your way."

"What you're telling me, Ken, is to bulldoze over a nun. Carrying a court order."

Elena and fifteen other members of CORP had infiltrated the demolition site. The Susumee workers waved their arms and whistled and shouted that they must get out, that this was a "hard-hat area," but this did not intimidate the CORP people. They all carried identical posters. Each poster was a huge photographic blowup of Judge Sanders' actual court order, complete with his characteristic illegible signature. The press had been notified, of course. The pickets were sometimes lost from view behind the swirls of dust created by the trucks and the wrecking ball. But they stood their ground, stopping so close to the crane that the operator refused to operate it.

"Call the police."

"Ken, they got a court order telling *us* not to do this."

"Shit! Well, they're trespassing."

"Ken, so are we. Bold Tip owns Section A-6. Do you think with all this shit flying that Bold Tip is going to back us on this? Anything goes wrong here, anybody gets hurt, we're going to be left holding the bag. No authorization from the owner."

"But Pettibone ...."

"We don't work for him. Anything happens, city's not responsible. Bold Tip's not responsible. You are."

Kiger stared ahead blankly. He had always been richly rewarded for taking risks for Pettibone. Pettibone had always come through. But the mayor did seem to be going off the deep end now. Of course, the deep end was where the real treasures were hidden. If this brazen move of Pettibone succeeded, Pettibone would control everything. And he would owe it all to Kiger. The idea was very tempting. But Kiger realized in the end that he really didn't have any choice. Mike was not asking him; he was telling him that the men would not go ahead.

"You're right. Send the men away. Pull out all the equipment. If anybody asks why, tell them we're pulling back to get clearer instructions from the owner, the Bold Tip Development Company."

Acting Secretary Tynan could not pretend that the study had already been done. Everyone in the city had seen on television that the study file was locked in Mallory's file drawer, and everyone in the building knew that there was nothing in it. So Tynan's first official act was to order an actual study done.

"What kind of a study?" Tynan couldn't tell if the Special Projects supervisor was being sarcastic.

"A quick study."

"But what do you want in it?"

"I really don't care. Whatever you can come up with in three days."

"Statistics? We could ...."

"Do something in three days that meets the minimum dictionary definition of 'study.' But don't release it. Don't show it to anybody until I tell you."

He asked for an informal meeting with Sport and Angela about the crawlspace settlement.

"In some of our local offices," he told them, "they have actually kept the records of past applications in some order. Even though you agreed that we only have to go back eighteen months, we are going to go back three years in those offices. In the other offices, it's just impossible to go back more than eighteen months."

"This is in return for what?"

"Nothing. I wanted to explain why you might see different results from different offices. I don't want to be sued on account of the differences."

The sensational footage of Gotterdung battering Mallory had attracted even more attention to the crawlspace suit, and to the CORP lawsuit, and the study. Tynan took it upon himself to re-announce the crawlspace settlement a few days later. He emphasized that the department was being even more generous than the official settlement required. After Gotterdung's performance, it was easy for Tynan to look like the moderate, sensible reformer cleaning up the mess left by his power-hungry predecessor. No one dug deeply enough into the administrative history to find out otherwise.

Slip dumped Gotterdung from his political partnership by phone, unceremoniously, just a few minutes after Governor Mallard called to dump him from the cabinet. But Slip had now lost control of when the study would be done. The whole state knew that it hadn't been done yet, and Tynan was in charge of it now. Slidell was now every bit as committed to the Pettibone Waterside Towers project as Pettibone was. He received frantic calls from his union constituents asking about the CORP lawsuit. This trickle of concern grew to a flood of worry after CORP members paraded around the Waterside Towers site carrying their enlarged copies of the court order. Slidell's allies wanted to make sure that the project was still on. Slidell told them not to worry. But there were problems. Some of the financing for the project had already disappeared in the confusion and delay. And Leonard Tynan, who now held the key to the project in his hands, was not known for giving away anything.

They met again in Eddie's restaurant. Tynan acted no differently than he had at their last meeting. He had too much natural grace to crow over the fact that he now held the key to Slip's political future. He didn't mention it. Instead, he talked of the general problems and concerns of the department and its clients.

"How is it that I can help you?" Slidell cut him off.

"The crawlspace settlement. We don't have the $8 million it will cost. We need the next governor to put it in his budget."

"You made the settlement without a funding source?"

"I always had faith that a source of funds would be found."

"You don't mean you *planned* all of this?"

Tynan sipped his tea.

"Have you ever thought," Slidell added, "about running on somebody's ticket for Lieutenant Governor?"

Tynan put his cup down.

"Stick a needle in his back / Stick it twice, if he's black."

Pettibone hoped that he pretty much had these little rhymes under control now. When he felt this one coming on at the beginning of his talk with Tynan, he put his hand to his mouth, looked down, and made sure that it came out no louder than a whisper. Pettibone was very fortunate that columnist Keane was generally regarded as a little crazy himself. His column the morning before had been brutal:

Thomas Keech

COURT CITES FOR CONTEMPT; MAYOR
REPLIES WITH DIRTY DITTIES
-Pettibone kowtows to Judge in the end-

Although Keane's blistering columns were widely read
and sometimes had a dramatic effect, they almost always
relied on facts dug out by the more conventional reporters. When Keane tried to report something that only he
saw or heard, people seemed to take it with a grain of
salt. Pettibone said a short prayer of thanks (also under
his breath) that no one else had been present during the
dirty ditties, and that the worst of the episode was over
by the time the security people had arrived. As for Keane's
allegations in the column itself, Pettibone had been able
to deflect them somewhat by putting out his own statement.

There should be no question that I, as
mayor, was disturbed by the illegal and
unwarranted order of Judge Sanders, which was
issued without the city government even being
given the courtesy of advance notice that there
was a problem. But the fatuous and obscene
little rhymes attributed to me by *Free American*
columnist Joe Keane are nothing but products
of his own overheated imagination.

"Since taking over as Acting Secretary, I've discovered,"
Tynan began, "that this study, which was supposed to
have been finished before any major development projects
are started, was actually not even begun. The CORP
people are wrong when they say that the study is a phony.
The truth is, there's no study at all. The 'study' that former
Secretary Gotterdung got into a fist fight over turned out
to be nothing more than an empty file."

284

"What do you want?" Pettibone barked.

"Let me tell you for a minute," Tynan began graciously, ignoring Pettibone's hurried tone, "about some of the priorities of the department, as I see them now." But the only priority that Tynan actually described was the crawlspace settlement.

"I need your pledge. If you become governor, you will find the money to put these people back on Medical Assistance."

"*Chain me up, chain me down / Whipping day will turn around.*"

Pettibone needed to become governor soon. He could not function in a situation where other people could tell him what to do—or, at least, he could not function without these little rhymes popping out. Having the governor's job would cure him of these rhymes. That was his plan. But now, Tynan was forcing him to sign away, in advance, some of his prerogatives as governor—before he even became governor. He tried to think rationally, and to appreciate that things could have been worse. For example, Tynan could have wanted to be on his ticket.

Pettibone had a lot of weaknesses as an executive, but one of his strengths was his conviction that something that was worth doing was worth paying for. Another was that he was willing to spend money on the poor. He did not mind pledging the funding itself. He promised Tynan he would provide the money if he was elected. But he hated the fact that Tynan was forcing him to do it. Whenever he thought about that, the rhymes came out.

The Special Projects supervisor came up with a surprisingly good study in the three days he was given. Using the statistics readily available from the census, from several different agencies and from the real estate market, the study estimated how many homeowners and how many renters had been displaced; and it made a reasonable guess as to how much each group had been financially hurt, and how many marginal renters had been made homeless. Tynan explained the study in Judge Sanders' court, and the judge was satisfied with it. He dissolved the injunction that afternoon. The study was delivered to Pettibone. The project was legally ready to go.

Upon returning to the state office building after his successful day in court, Tynan had to walk a gauntlet of enraged CORP pickets. "75 Extra Homeless—No Big Deal?" was their chant. He pretended not to hear.

The next day, Slidell announced officially that he was running in the Democratic primary for governor. In his announcement speech, he took credit for being the "cooler head" that had kept the Pettibone Waterside Towers project from sinking under the weight of the monstrous ego of the mayor.

The following day, he made another announcement.

"Mr. Leonard Tynan, the Acting Secretary of the Department of Public Welfare, has negotiated an agreement between both gubernatorial candidates. Under this humanitarian agreement, both candidates have now pledged to find the money to pay for the new Medical Assistance applicants, those people so wrongfully denied medical help by the fraud and corruption of the previous administration. It is obvious to me," Slidell concluded, "that a man of such demonstrated compassion, and obvious political abilities, as Leonard Tynan, is needed at an even higher level of government. For this reason, I am announcing today that Mr. Tynan has agreed to be on my ticket as my running mate, as a candidate for Lieutenant Governor."

Attorney Stem was ecstatic. Just when the Mallory case

had seemed to be degenerating into a time-consuming and unprofitable mess, his client had been physically attacked in front of an audience of tens of thousands by the very same governmental official who had been trying to fire him. Things couldn't have worked out better.

When Mallory did not show for the next day's hearing, Stem obtained an indefinite postponement on the ground that his client was probably in shock and seeking medical treatment. Stem asserted these speculative excuses as if their truth were self-evident. Van Hoof accepted them without a blink. Of course, it appeared from the videotape that Mallory had not suffered any serious injury from Gotterdung's brief attack. Neither Stem, nor Van Hoof, nor anyone else would have sought medical treatment for an equivalent injury suffered, for example, by bumping into a doorway at home. But the crucial fact was that these injuries did not happen *at home*. These injuries happened in a place where there was somebody to sue.

It was a week later before Mallory made it into Stem's office.

"Have you seen a doctor?"

"No."

"I know a good doctor you can see. I'll also set you up with an audiologist to test for possible hearing loss. And I think you had better see a psychologist too. We have a good lawsuit here."

"I guess maybe I *would* like to sue that bastard Gotterdung," Mallory admitted.

"That's the spirit. I advise you not to return from Accident Leave until after you've been evaluated by all of the physicians. Then we can take our time and negotiate about a date for your return to work. Just listen to me. Listen to all of the doctors I send you to. Pay attention and do exactly what I say, and we may get a hefty settlement out of this."

But Stem had made a fatal mistake.

"I hired you to shoot down all the plans they were making for me," Mallory said.

"And I think I've done that, Kevin. And we can go further now. Just follow my directions exactly."

"Now *you* are making plans for me."

"No ... no ...."

"I can't stand it!"

"Kevin, no ...."

"Your services will no longer be necessary," Mallory turned and walked out of the office, slamming the door behind him.

After sixteen years of employment at the Department of Public Welfare, Mallory had finally gotten what he had come for. When Gotterdung's blows rained down on his back and onto the side of his head, a deep inner connection with his boss, one that he had always longed for, had been made. Each and every one of his previous jobs had ended with his supervisor yelling and screaming and pounding on his desk. This job had taken sixteen times as long as any of the others before that connection had been made. But when it finally happened, it was at least sixteen times as good. The chance to fire his own lawyer had come as a little extra thrill. As he stomped out of Stem's office, he realized that this was one of the few times in his life that he had ever felt completely at peace with himself. Two days later, he mailed in his formal resignation letter to Tynan. He was free at last.

20 A PRICE TOO HIGH

Slidell had fantasized about this meeting, had tried to practice speaking from his heart.

"What can I do, Elena?" Were his smooth politician manners sucking the meaning even from this heart-jarring moment? He searched her eyes. "I've missed you so much. Everything is going even better than I'd hoped, but it doesn't mean anything to me any more."

"You're so skilled at dealing with people," she said. He couldn't interpret her tone of voice. "It would be a real waste for you to do anything else. I've come to tell you how much you hurt me. I don't think you can really understand."

Elena had created CORP and instigated the lawsuit and the demonstrations to stop Slidell and the developers. But before CORP's lawsuit had even been filed, she had realized that her main motivation was revenge. This made her feel really small. When the injunction had held, and Ken Kiger's crew had refused to smash through the picket line, spontaneous cheers had arisen from the CORP members, who made fun of the mayor in another series of televised interviews. But Elena had walked back to the soup kitchen that morning with her hand over her stomach, not sure at all how she felt. She stood up in her own closed room until evening, her eyes blank, seeing nothing. The thought that took root as she stood there in her unholy trance was that she was now corrupt. She now was as corrupt as any of the egomaniacs and poseurs involved on either side of this controversy.

This feeling of corruption and uselessness grew. She tried the next morning to serve food on the line at her soup kitchen downstairs, but the ravaged faces that used to inspire her now seemed vacant. The younger women and their children seemed to stare at her accusingly. The resonant thrill that she used to feel from helping these people was gone. She realized that this thrill had just been a form of corruption also. It would never come again. She did not want it to come again.

Elena tried to think of what she should do with her life now. The world was much more complicated than she had imagined. She cursed her parents for letting her believe that she was special. That idea seemed to be the root of all the evil in her life. It had infected everything she had done. When she tried out plans for what to do with the rest of her life now, she could see that all of them were corrupted and undermined by this pride. She couldn't bear to work out plans in her head. She did not trust her own inner voice any more.

She stayed in her room for two days with the shade drawn over the window, blocking out all the light. She guessed that she might die, or come in contact with God, but she was surprised that the vision that came to her was of Slidell. He was the only person who had ever become real to her. He had slipped through all of her defenses and made a mark on her that could not be rubbed off.

She had to admit this to him before she could go on to anything else. It almost made no difference what he said.

"You have ruined me," she said. Her speech was not

planned. She didn't mean that she was *blaming* him. Slip had rocked her soul, destroyed her old self. She was still scrambling to get her balance. A new self had yet to form. It had to be a person who knew everything that she knew now but was still willing to go on. She was afraid to let it happen, afraid of who this new self might be.

"I'm very sorry," he rasped gravely. His voice came from a private, pitiful part of his throat she had never heard from before. She thought this might be Slip with all of the politician taken out of him. "What can I do?" he continued. He was seated behind his desk. He opened his hands wide. "There's no limit." He was almost whispering. This was not his political voice at all. "Absolutely none."

"Help me stop feeling so worthless."

"You don't really think," he said, incredulous, "You don't think that *I* ...!"

"I've lost everything for you. I need it to have meant something."

"It was my fault, Elena. I was just weak. I needed you to believe in me. I couldn't stop it."

"You'll be governor soon. Do something that you wouldn't have done. Change. Promise me. This is my last request."

"I think about things differently now. I could change. Elena, if we could start over, we could have the kind of life we always talked about." His green eyes drew her in.

"Samuel, I would just be another consideration for you to juggle, along with everything else."

"You think that little of me?"

She didn't answer.

"You won't be with me, but you still want me to be the man you thought I was. Why?"

"I need to know ...." Her own voice now also seemed artificially high and unreal. She looked around at the other people in Eddie's restaurant. Her thoughts seemed so preposterous in this place with fake brick walls and neon beer signs and a lotto booth sticking out of the wall.

"Samuel, was it just a sick dream I had, about me and you? Is this just another sick part of it, that I want you to be better because we met?"

Slidell didn't say anything, and she could not read his eyes.

"Was I wrong that I thought that you loved me?"

"No, you weren't wrong. Oh God, you weren't wrong. Elena, I'm sorry."

After she was gone, Slip considered the trap that he was in. The more power he obtained, the less he would need to compromise his own ideas of what was really good for the people of Maryland. He could do as much good as anyone in the history of the state. But it would not do *him* any good. The woman he loved would never fall into his arms. She would never fall into his arms, because, if she did, she would never know if she herself was just part of the bargain, the icing on the cake, the tit for the tat. He wished that she had more confidence in herself, but then he reminded himself harshly why she did not.

Charles couldn't identify the source of tension in the room. "We didn't listen to you, Charles." Angela finished the long apology on behalf of herself and Sport. "And you almost died. We wanted to tell you right to your face that we are sorry."

"Don't worry," he waved off their concern. "You didn't do no worse than the others." Neither of his friends responded.

"And you helped me with the house," Charles added, dropping the words hopefully into the growing silence.

But the silence between them grew deeper when Sport

began to talk about the house on Jasper Street.

"I have a duty to convey this offer to you. The mayor has now offered $175,000 cash for 442 Jasper Street. As your attorney, it's not my place to tell you whether to accept or not. But it is true that you could buy a good house almost anywhere in the city—or in the state, for that matter—for that amount."

Sport and Angela had already practiced this conversation. They had thought hard about what they had to do, and they decided that Sport could never ask Charles to give up his dream of living in Aunt May's house just because of Fosback's blackmail. The fatal flaw in Fosback's plan was that he had assumed that Sport was just as corrupt as he was. It had never occurred to Fosback that Sport would put Charles's interests first. But Sport knew that he had to do this. He couldn't even tell Charles about Fosback and his blackmail. Just telling Charles would put him in the position of having to choose between his lawyer and his dream.

Sport and Angela had talked for hours, looking for a loophole so that they could tell everything to Charles. But they were grasping at straws. There was no way that either of them could tell Charles that his dream was in the way of their happiness. They couldn't put this kind of squeeze on the man they had already almost killed. They had to let him decide for himself.

The empty silence in the room was the sound of them letting Charles decide. Sport told Charles everything that he had to know. There was no longer any legal barrier to beginning construction on the Pettibone Waterside Towers project. All of the politicians were now lined up behind it. Aunt May's house was the only obstacle left. Theoretically, Bold Tip could build the project around Aunt May's house. It would probably cost them $500,000 to do it, and it would ruin the looks of the main entrance.

Pettibone probably wouldn't allow the contractors to do it. He was likely to do anything. The city had already sent out an inspector who had cited 442 Jasper for 17 Housing Code violations.

"We can probably fight those off with lawsuits. But Pettibone will then try something else, and nobody is on your side now."

"Except you," Charles smiled. But there was a second's pause before corresponding smiles showed up on Sport and Angela's faces, and Charles knew that something was wrong. They both assured him that they would back him and his dream of living in 442 Jasper Street. He didn't doubt them, his tough new lawyer friends, but their heavy mood took a lot of the fun out of his plans.

In the hospital, Charles had dreamed of Aunt May's house. In the dream, he explored every wall, every corner, every doorway, every bit of wallpaper and paint, searching for signs of her. He sensed her presence permeating the very plaster and wood and glass. There were places where he felt a warm glow emanating from the walls, and he knew that he had discovered in these places parts of her that had been left behind for him. Charles was convinced that he could have no higher destiny than to live in this house. It was not only the ecstasy of feeling Aunt May's soothing presence in the house, but also the chance of discovering his own character, and imprinting it alongside of hers, into those sacred walls.

"You're not happy about this any more?" he challenged the lawyers.

"Yes we are," Sport protested.

"No, we're not," Angela admitted.

"Why not?"

"I can't tell you, but it has nothing to do with you," Angela tried to assure him. "We promise we will do all we can to let you keep this house, whether we're happy about it or not. You have a right to this house, and we can make sure you get it. So it makes no difference whether we're happy or not. We're just your lawyers."

"Just my lawyers."

Angela's words took a little bit of the edge off of his dream. He had thought that he could happily explore the house alone for the rest of his life. He was surprised that it made a difference to him that his lawyers were acting like lawyers now. He hadn't known that Sport and Angela were part of his dream.

The next day, the pressure on him to sell the house intensified. Fred Lowell, the real estate broker representing all of the developers and contractors, visited him again. Charles liked Fred Lowell. Lowell asked Charles about his surgery.

"I do not like to drive hard bargains with a sick man."

"Doctor says," Charles confided, "eating, swallowing, and the rest—never be the same again." Lowell nodded.

"Took out a part of me. Had to do it. So the rest of me could live. Nothing like that ever happened to me before."

"Oh, it happens," Fred Lowell said. "I've had a couple of operations myself. You get used to these things. You have to. There's not really any choice."

"A lot of things I never knew before."

Fred Lowell offered him $185,000 for the house. He made a very persuasive case for Charles to accept the offer. Developers were willing to pay premium prices to those lucky holders of the last few properties on any project, he said. But there was a limit. Developers were bold, proud men, and there was a point at which they would take a loss rather than be made a fool of. It was possible to redesign the project around his house, and they would do that if they had to.

"Okay with me. Nobody else in those other houses

anyway."

It did not seem that Charles was bluffing. He seemed unaware of how ridiculous it would look, and how uncomfortable it would be, to have his house cut into the side of a mammoth modern condominium complex. But Lowell had not spent forty years negotiating over real estate for nothing. He eased into a long conversation with Charles.

"Wasted thirty years on booze," Charles admitted. "You ever drink like that?"

"Not me. But I have a son .... It's a long story. You've been there and back. Can you tell me why people do that?"

"I only know why I stopped," Charles began. It was over an hour later that Lowell left.

Fred Lowell reported to his principals the following day that no amount of money would suffice to pry Charles away from his attachment to Aunt May's house. And he infuriated Oswald Fundertow by insisting against all their arguments that Charles was not crazy.

Charles asked Angela to take him out to 442 Jasper Street the next day. All the way over in the car, she silently prayed that Charles would change his mind and sell out to the mayor, though she did not permit herself even to hint this to Charles. But she could not bring herself to fake any enthusiasm for the house.

"Not going in?"

"No. I'll just sit on the steps. I need to make a phone call from that booth across the street before we leave."

Room by room, wall by wall, Charles inspected the house gravely. But in ten minutes he was out on the stoop again.

"You not coming in?"

"No," she said. "I just can't."

Charles sat down. Angela made her way across the street

to the battered and scratched public phone in front of the liquor store. She punched in her own number.

"Linda, this is Angela Watkins. I need to know if there are any messages for me." To an infinitesimal degree, Linda had been more civil to her since M.C. had been banned from the waiting room.

"Messages? Uh-huh."

"Linda, I'm not asking you to do something like this every day. But I'm expecting a very important message. Would you *please* put the phone down and get those messages and read them to me?"

The message was that Tynan would see her right away.

She'd have to bring Charles; he could not make it home on the bus, and Angela could not wait another day to see Tynan. Tynan was their last hope.

Unless Charles agreed to hand over his rights to the property by the following day. Fosback's three letters would be released. Sport's career would be over. He might be tried for perjury. Angela didn't know what might happen to her for acting as his co-counsel, and for not turning him in. She hadn't had time to research the issues; she only had time to choose sides.

"You're worrying," Charles observed in the car.

"Well ...."

"Something eating at you. You two breaking up?"

"No. No, Sport and I are not ... *together* like that."

"Thought you were. He's a good man. Something else?"

"Yeah. Something else. I can't tell you, Charles,"

"What is it?"

Would it be wrong for her, as Charles's friend, to tell him how much his little dream was going to cost them? The ethical considerations seemed so abstract compared to the suffering Sport would soon undergo if Charles didn't change his mind soon.

She turned and opened her mouth to speak, but she

Thomas Keech

was stopped by the sight of Charles's lips, momentarily stretched and distorted with pain. She and Sport, wrapped up in their egos and their careers, had already hit him hard once; another blow might take him out.

"Nothing," Angela said. She had grown up thinking that her life was supposed to be under her own control. Letting events interfere with life plans was supposed to be a weakness.

"Nothing," she said again, surprised at herself. "Nothing."

She left Charles outside in Tynan's waiting room.

"I'm here," she began, "as representative of the plaintiffs in the crawlspace suit, to remind you not to release any personal information about any of them, to anyone."

Tynan leaned forward over his desk. "What is this about, Angela?"

"You might be getting a call ...."

"I *did* get a call." Tynan watched the color drain out of Angela's face. "From Fosback. About Mrs. Throckmorton. He just wants me to assure him that Mrs. Throckmorton is one of our Medical Assistance clients. I can't see how it could hur..."

As the realization hit Tynan, a broad smile flashed across his face, and he eased himself far back in his chair, enjoying himself tremendously. "I should have *known!* I always wondered how we paid her off so quickly. Sport called me at noon on the day after the crawlspace suit was filed, and he conceded that Mrs. Throckmorton was already paid off. Of course, we didn't even have to try to locate her casefile then." His eyes were suddenly cold. "And if we went to look for that file now, it wouldn't exist, would it?"

"I have no idea whether your department has lost her file or not."

Tynan ignored Angela's thrust. "There is no Mrs. Vir-

298

ginia Throckmorton. Fosback's found that out, and he's hanging it over Sport's head. Of course. Fosback wants that house that Charles owns. How much is the mayor offering for it?"

"I don't know what you're talking .... $185,000."

"It's a good deal. Sport should take it."

"It's not Sport's decision."

"Oh. Of course. Your client. Lawyer's ethics. What does Charles say about the deal?"

"We can't tell him."

"He's here with you now, isn't he? I can tell him." He buzzed Bobbie Jo and told her to ask Charles to step in.

Angela jumped up and held the doorknob tightly. The muscles in her arms were trembling.

"Don't! Don't! We can't take that house away from him. It would kill him. Sport and I already made that decision. We're not going to make Charles choose between his house and saving us. Don't you make him choose. Let him alone!"

Charles was pulling on the door from the other side. Angela finally let her side go. She faced him in the doorway.

"Don't go in. Don't talk to this man, Charles. He can't help you." Charles saw tears in her eyes.

"Come on in, sir," Tynan called from behind her back.

"Gonna talk to him," Charles brushed past Angela. There were no possible good outcomes that she could see. She walked out of the office and collapsed on the waiting room sofa, where Bobbi Jo brought her some tissues.

Charles closed the door behind him. "Lady is upset."

"Well, I think she's more worried about her colleague."

"Sport?"

"Yes. He might be in a little bit of trouble. Why don't you sit down?"

"I know what he did."

"You do? You know about the fictitious Mrs. Throckmorton, the forgery, the perjury, the fraud? The mayor is asking my help in investigating him."

"He helped a lot of people, like me."

"Yes, but ..."

"People *you* were lying on, pretending to be their friend."

Tynan's momentum was lost. "That's true. That's true," he said humbly. "I apologized to you in the hospital. I don't know if you heard me or not."

"Want to show you something." Charles stood up and pulled his shirt out of his pants, pulling it aside to show his surgical scar, a discolored seven-inch track winding its way across his midsection like a venomous millipede. "He saved my life. Want to touch that scar?"

"No, I can see it."

Charles leaned closer. "Touch it, brother."

"No, I don't have to. I can see."

Charles grabbed Tynan's hand and held it against the scar, pushing it in until he could feel Tynan's manicured fingernails against his flesh.

"He's a good man, Leonard. He saved a lot of other brothers like me. Now they're trying to rip him up over this legal chickenshit."

"I know," Tynan, leaning over the desk at an awkward angle, bowed his head. "I believe it."

"Then you know," Charles whispered harshly, "that you got to do something—if I see the color of this hand right, and if you are truly a brother to me."

"Oh, Mr. Fosback," Tynan's voice was clipped, but extraordinarily cheerful. "I began to get that file for you, but then I thought of something, and I checked it out with our lawyers. We can't give you Mrs. Throckmorton's casefile. We can't even confirm or deny that she is a client of ours. Under both federal and state law, I'm afraid, these welfare records are absolutely confidential."

Linda was absorbed in a tense phone conversation with her mother, and she completely ignored Keane breezing by. He wouldn't have stopped anyway. He was already annoyed by the multitude of signs and doors, and the gloomy gauntlet of stairways and lobbies that restricted movement inside the Legal Assistance Society's building. Keane intended to do a background story on the two lawyers who had so persistently tracked down the truth in the crawlspace matter. He was proud to have helped them smoke out some of the slimiest creatures in the bureaucratic basements.

But he also had another purpose that day. On the pretext of doing the background story, he wanted to share— "share" was a word he would never use in his column—experiences with the two people whom he had regarded as his comrades in this battle. He was going to ask them about their personal opinions, and about their different strategies at different times during the struggle. But what he would really be waiting for was their own questions. He wanted to be interviewed; he wanted someone to ask him about his private thoughts. He especially wanted to go through this process with Angela. He had had more than an offhand thought of asking her out again. He had never come closer to accepting the theory that even newspapermen need love.

Ever since Angela's first call from Bobbi Jo's phone outside of Tynan's office, Sport had been limply collapsed in a chair in Angela's office, drenched in sweat.

"Tynan knows everything," she sobbed, "and he's co-operating with Fosback. I'm really sorry, Sport. I did all I could."

The trembling started at that moment, and Angela's second call, suddenly saying that everything was all right, had weakened him further. Although his mind understood that he was on much safer ground now that Tynan would not release the welfare records, his body would not believe it, and he could not get up.

"Charles did it." She rushed up to him, throwing her briefcase on top of her desk.

"Oh, no." His body had been right. "He traded Aunt May's house to save me."

"No. That's the wonderful thing, Sport. He's still got the house. Tynan's on our side now."

"How did he do it?" Sport stood up and wobbled over towards her, embarrassed by his weakness.

"I don't know. I couldn't do it. Charles did it himself."

Sport leaned against her desk for support.

"Angela, you didn't have to do this—risk your own career too."

"Yes, I did." She turned to face him. "How could I do anything different?"

He reached out and placed a tremulous hand on her shoulder. He had never allowed himself to notice how pretty she was. He knew she flew away some weekends to see a boyfriend in Chicago. Sport knew he had never had a better friend, and he was afraid of ruining it. He took his arm down. But she then grabbed his hand. She stepped closer, her mouth moving closer to his. He did not believe what was happening.

Joe Keane suddenly barged into the room without so much as a knock.

"Glad to catch you two." Keane made his voice sound bored. But it was hard to cover up his disappointment that the woman he had hoped to make a little time with was kissing her colleague right in front of his eyes. Angela turned around and sat next to Sport on the desk, facing Keane, pretending to show an interest in him. But Sport was still shaking. Angela could not control her breathing or change the flushed color of her face. Her dark eyes were enlarged and languorously distracted.

Keane had never himself caused such a look to come into any woman's eyes. He now pretended to himself that he had always suspected that Angela was having an office liaison. He told himself that he was not hurt. But he didn't leave. Instead, he accepted their distracted, transparently false statements that they were ready to talk business, and he began a half-hour conversation about their lawsuit, and about Charles. As the minutes passed, Sport and Angela became more articulate and rational. They told him as much about their backgrounds, as much about their private thoughts and feelings as they dared, considering that he was a newspaperman. They defended Charles' stubbornness on the subject of 442 Jasper Street, trying to explain why money wasn't enough for him. When Keane left, Sport and Angela thought that they were all friends.

Keane began his column the next day:
> I have written in the past of a man named Charles Gage, and of the courage and persistence he carried around in his stomach until he had a hole in it so big the doctors had to sew it up. And I've written of his two tough lawyers, who dragged him off the operating table and into the federal courtroom just in time to save thousands of others from a similar fate.
>
> But today I'm going to write about another side of the same man. It's a story of mindless stubbornness and shameless greed. It's a story about someone who does not care

about the dreams, or the lives, or the livelihood of others.

Keane's column returned to this theme three times in the next several days. His campaign against Charles was relentless. Keane had appointed himself as the media savior of the Pettibone Waterside Towers project. Early the next week, he suggested in his column that the stubbornness of Charles Gage was only matched by the stubbornness of Crosley Pettibone. He wrote:

> If we wait for these two bullheaded men to agree on Fells Point, the financiers of Baltimore's last chance for downtown luxury development might slither out of here one night with no more conscience or regret than Bob Irsay showed after *his* heart-to-heart talks with the mayor.

Reminding everyone of he city's ignominious failure to keep the Colts in town was the ultimate insult, an insult that even Brendan Gotterdung had never dared utter. By printing this, Keane showed either that he was becoming dangerously reckless, or that he had finally learned to communicate with the mayor.

21 BETTER THAN REAL

"There you are," Fosback's voice from the back of the car was sharp. "315 West Ostend Street. Boarded up house. Look at that graffiti. Place has been empty for years."

"I want to repeat," Brad Stoufer, the investigator for the bar association, spoke as he looked out the side window at that derelict building, "that this is not a formal investigation. I can't put anything down in writing since there has been no formal complaint about Mr. Norris."

"Oh, there will be a complaint now," Fosback cackled.

Stoufer carefully checked the house number against the address listed on the Throckmorton affidavit. "Okay, let's get out."

"Why?"

Stoufer turned back to look at Fosback and Pettibone. "Your Honor, I'm not really supposed to be doing an investigation. I don't mind doing this informally, since you specifically asked for it. But you've got me here now, and your man has got to let me do things my own way."

"Leave him alone," Pettibone snapped at Fosback.

All three men got out of the chauffeured limousine. Stoufer examined the doorway to 315 West Ostend Street. The plywood was nailed shut, graffitied over and weathered gray at the edges by years of exposure. This block of row houses had flat fronts with no porches, and brick steps that went right down to the sidewalk. There had been a steel-pipe railing on the steps to 315, but someone had wrenched it half off and left it to dangle and rust. There was a dirty-looking man nursing a wine bottle on the steps next door. He stared closely at Stoufer, who quickly decided that he had done enough investigating.

"I guess its safe to say that Mrs. Virginia Throckmorton doesn't live here," he admitted.

"Gin-Gin?" The man with the wine bottle appeared to be speaking to Stoufer. Stoufer ignored him and turned to go.

"You guys lookin' for Gin-Gin Morton?"

Stoufer turned around. "Throckmorton. Virginia Throckmorton. She's supposed to live at 315."

"Yeah, Gin-Gin!" the man said, but he didn't say any more.

"Does she live here?"

The man put his head down and shook his head in a childish show of embarrassment. "She ain't never lived there. Live here."

"What?"

"Live here."

"But that's 313."

More shaking of the head. "We don't like that number 13—bad luck. We all says 15. See, Gin-Gin knock that 3 right off the do'."

"Are you saying that Virginia Throckmorton lives here?"

"Did."

"Did?"

"She lef'. Soon's she got that medical card and got her some pills for her sugar, she gone back to South Carolina."

"I should have told you," Doxie had no idea how much adrenaline would squeeze into Sport and Angela's bloodstreams with his next words, "that the bar association was pressured by the mayor into conducting a secret investigation of the existence of our client, Mrs. Throckmorton. It was supposed to be a secret, but I've been around long enough, and I know enough people, that not much is a secret from me."

Sport glanced over at Angela.

"They told me they were going out to Mrs. Throckmorton's house today. I should have mentioned it to you earlier. It's none of their business, unless a formal complaint is filed. I told them that."

"Did they talk to Mrs. Throckmorton?" It was Sport who first mustered the courage to say this.

"No."

It was an involuntary action. Sport's hand went out and grabbed Angela's. She looked over at him, but she didn't need to, for she could feel his fear. Doxie raised an eyebrow.

"She has apparently moved back to South Carolina, according to a neighbor. After she got her Medical Assistance card."

Both lawyers were quiet. They unclasped their hands. "Brad Stoufer, who for several years has been my co-chairman on the Democratic Lawyers Political Action Committee, called me as soon as he got out of the mayor's limousine. Apparently a Mr. Fosback, the mayor's aide, was made to walk home.

"As soon as I heard about this investigation, I called the Department of Public Welfare, to make sure that they wouldn't release any confidential records."

"Who did you talk to there, Doxie?"

"The Secretary, of course, Leonard Tynan."

"Jimmy, you did good," Charles peeked over his shoulder as the mayor's limousine turned the corner and sped away from West Ostend Street.

"Hurry up. Close that door. Leonard's got a man picking us up in five minutes in the alley."

"What about Gin-Gin? What if she come back?"

22 A NEPHEW'S GOODBYE

"You say he talks to his Aunt May?"

"Well, no, not exactly, Doxie, he ...."

"Because if he is psychotic, we may have a duty to arrange some type of guardianship over him."

"Over his property, you mean." Sport wouldn't waste words. "You're saying, because of the pressure on *us*, we should find a way to force Charles to sell the house."

Doxie's voice sank an octave lower. "Don't you ever accuse me, or this Society, of selling out its clients for its own convenience." He shifted in his chair. "It's hard. You don't feel all the pressure from where you are. Constant pressure from the conservatives to close down all Legal Services offices—but until now, we've always had all of the *local* politicians on our side whenever we were attacked by Washington. But Pettibone and Slidell, and Tynan, and the business community, and the unions, are all against us now. I don't know how long we can survive."

Doxie had broken his promise to himself by visiting the basement again. He looked around the vacant Chief Attorney's office, "the gym." The steam pipes running down the side wall had dripped permanent discolorations onto the floor. Another leak somewhere above the ceil-

309

ing had blackened a wide circle in the ceiling tiles. The windows hadn't been cleaned in over a year. The fluorescent lights were buzzing and flickering. There had been a complaint that morning about evidence of rats in someone's desk drawer.

"We may one day think of this time as the good old days of the Legal Assistance Society," Doxie added ruefully. "Looking around, that's hard to believe."

"But all that doesn't mean that we can say that Charles is crazy when we know ...." Angela started.

"So when you see," Doxie cut her off, "something so self-defeating as Charles's idiotic devotion to this house, and his determination to stay poor—because that's what it really is—and he's going to drag a lot of other poor people down with him, too—you start to wonder if the man really isn't crazy."

"What you mean is," Angela's stare was fierce, "you *hope* he's crazy."

"There is some concrete evidence of that fact. Isn't there, Sport?"

It didn't seem fair. "He did tell me," Sport admitted, "that he knows what Aunt May wants him to do. But believe me, Doxie, Charles is not crazy."

"Not him." Charles motioned with his head toward Ken Kiger, who was already in the mayor's office, sitting next to Pettibone, when Charles entered.

"Mr. Kiger represents the developers of the Mayor Crosley T. Pettibone Waterside Towers Luxury Condominium Development. They're the owners. I'm just the mayor. I don't have a penny in this project."

"Man threatens me with falling bricks, falling hammers, if I don't sell."

Charles explained no more. Pettibone leaned toward Kiger.

"Get out."

After Kiger had gone, Pettibone faced his visitor.

"Why are you doing this to me?"

"Nothing to do with you."

"What do you want?"

"Keep the house."

"What is so special about this house?"

Charles broke eye contact. "Nothing to do with you."

"See, I'm the mayor, and everything's got something to do with me."

"You ain't everything."

Pettibone was not used to this. He stared at Charles. His lips began to move rhythmically, but without sound. His features became distorted with the effort to keep the rhymes from coming out. Pettibone was determined to silence those rhymes, no matter what the cost. As he forced his lips closed, he could feel the rage rising in his limbs.

"Aaarrgghh!" A wave of anger pulsed through his body and snapped his head to one side. His arms flailed. He pounded on the table until the room echoed with the thud of fists on hollow wood. Pettibone roared at Charles. His upper body lurched jerkily out of his seat and onto the table, then slid back into the chair. His features were distorted, his skin was red, his cheeks were dripping tears. He started hiccuping.

Pettibone fixed his eyes on Charles from a distance of four inches. Charles didn't move. Charles had never had a child, but Pettibone reminded him of M.C. Charles was no longer frightened by babies.

"Aaaaarrrggh!" Pettibone roared again in Charles's face. Charles brushed the mayor's spittle off his shirt.

Pettibone felt something change inside him, a queasy shifting of juices and weights. His personality flowed and adjusted itself around the immovable object before him. His rage had failed him. It had turned him into a sweating and slobbering buffoon, but it had not frightened Charles. Pettibone saw this clearly now, and he squirmed.

He slid back off the table. He closed his mouth and froze his features. Still, his fingers twitched, tapping out on the table the last erratic pulses of his frenzy. He had no idea what he was going to do next.

"I apologize." Pettibone surprised himself.

"You," he jerked his head toward Charles, "you and your lawyer, you make fun of me behind my back, don't you?"

"No, sir."

"I don't know why I act like that."

Charles didn't hesitate. "Push people around."

The anger started to surge through Pettibone again. He did not try to fight it down this time, but he kept his mouth closed, and it passed through him like a shudder.

"Now they're starting to write in the newspaper about these rhymes. See, these little poems come to me. Always kill, kill, smash their heads. I've never told anybody about it before." Pettibone bowed his head.

"That's not right," Charles whispered. "Something wrong sir."

"I know! Can you help me?"

"A unit, they call it. Two bedrooms, one for me and one for Jimmy here, right in the place where the house is now."

Angela and Sport were stunned. Only Doxie, who had insisted on being present at every meeting with their most difficult client, smiled broadly.

"Is that it?"

"No rent or nothing for life."

"Any cash?"

"Ten thousand. And a job, lifetime—medical paid for."

Charles had turned down a similar offer before. It was

not clear what had changed. They had advised Charles not to meet with Pettibone alone.

"Well, it seems to me that congratulations are in order." Doxie broke the silence. "What you bargained for is worth many times what Peck and Peck offered you at first. You did very well for yourself, Mr. Gage."

"Thank you," Charles said.

"Thank you," Jimmy said.

But when they left, Charles slid out the door without meeting Sport or Angela's eyes.

"This is a good deal," Doxie expounded into the stubborn silence.

"He turned down that same deal last week."

"You two are still not happy! You held out for him against the most powerful political forces in the state, and you won. He got a great deal. And on top of that, the Legal Assistance Society is saved. Why are you two still looking so glum?"

"He refused this same offer last week."

"So? He thought it over."

Turning away from Doxie, Sport met Angela's eyes. He realized that she was thinking exactly the same thing.

The price of believing was to be sometimes made a fool of.

"I don't understand you young people. What is wrong with this settlement?"

"Doxie," Angela was unusually hesitant, "we don't want you to think that we're naive. But there was more to Charles, and 442 Jasper Street, and us, than just getting the best deal. At least we thought so. We fought harder than you know for this house, because we thought he really wanted it."

"Well, I guess he did. But he got a better offer."

"But we thought there was more to it."

"What's this 'more?' What are you talking about?"

313

"It's the way he loved that house more than money—we *thought* he loved it more than money—and the faith he had, seemed to have, in us, and ...."

"Don't waste your time, Angela. Doxie doesn't understand."

Sport appeared in Angela's office late that afternoon. It was understood that they would go out to dinner together.

"We were such dupes," he began. "All he wanted was more money all along."

"We don't know exactly what happened."

"I'm sorry I dragged you through all this."

"Sport, these have been the best weeks of my life." She had his full attention. "I tried to keep away from you before. I didn't want to be just another one of your hundreds of friends. Now I know why you have so many."

"You have a boyfriend."

She shook her head yes, then no.

"I think that's about done," she admitted.

"I didn't know."

"I can't talk about work with him. Too intense, he says. I'm off balance all the time I'm with him. Then I come back here, I'm off balance too."

"Why are you telling me this?"

"Because I don't want you to laugh at me for being naive. So, I'm asking you now. When you kissed me, did that just mean that you were feeling desperate?"

Charles had heard from Aunt May. A few days after he and Jimmy played their trick on Fosback on West Ostend Street, Charles had visited the house for the last time. Alone, he had carefully examined every wall, every doorway, every piece of molding, every trick of wood. He was searching for clues about her. But it did not seem that she was there anymore. He had looked everywhere, stared at the corners, imagined her view as she sat at the bedroom dressing table, but she was gone. And as much as he did not want her to go, he had known after a while that it was necessary.

She had touched him in her will, and she had taught him a lot through the house. He had seen all the pieces and detail and work and care that it took to do a life right, and he had learned that he didn't have to do it all alone. He had learned how very powerful was the basic honesty in his soul. But these were things he had already learned before his last visit there. He had walked through the house *expectantly* that bright, dusty, quiet Sunday afternoon. But it seemed to be merely a house. Part of the problem was that his friends, Sport and Angela, were no longer excited about the house itself any more. The house would always be special as the place where they all became friends, but he had never before realized that part of his own enthusiasm came from theirs.

"I think," he had spoken out loud, as if Aunt May were alive and touring her own house with him, "that I can go on without living here. I should do it. Thank you very much." He walked in a small circle around the bedroom.

He knew that what he said next made less sense now, because he could no longer feel her presence within the walls of the house. But in a way, it made more sense, and for the same reason.

"But what about you?" he asked.

The formal groundbreaking ceremony was scheduled for late in the afternoon. The city had been steamed so long under the summer sun that the debris in the gutters of Fells Point had turned fetid. In the alleys behind the bars, cases of empty beer cans piled against the walls emitted a sour odor. The aroma of melting asphalt and roofing tar mixed at street level with the enveloping odor of decay.

The ceremony was arranged a few blocks away from the bar strip, and out of sight of the destruction already made by Kiger's wrecking ball. Temporary wooden stands had been built by city workers the night before on a hard clay corner lot. All of the rubble and trash had been cleared off the site by city employees working under floodlights.

Angela parked her car on Broadway, the wide boulevard that stretched from Johns Hopkins Hospital to the waterfront. It was not too difficult to find a place to park at this hour. She pulled in to one of the slanted spaces in front of a row of bars. As she gingerly shut her car door, she heard the first deep rumble of an approaching thunderstorm. A sudden cool puff of air blew up the street from the harbor, scattering paper cups and other litter across the cobblestones.

Angela walked two blocks and stood at the end of a long line of parked limousines carrying the dignitaries for the ceremony. The cars and trucks of the press crews were scattered around the lot. No one got out of the long black cars. A few local residents were sitting on that part of the stand reserved for them; but a big crowd had not been expected, as this was primarily scheduled as a media event. The cameramen were scurrying around setting up their equipment on the lot.

Angela was looking for Charles. In the two weeks since he came in the office to announce the settlement, he had not visited or called. She didn't know if their friendship was over. She wanted to talk to him, or at least gauge the look on his face. She couldn't see him in the crowd, and she couldn't see through the dark glass of the limousines, so she waited. Stronger gusts of cool air flattened her clothes against her, but she didn't move.

The storm hit just as everyone started to get out of the limousines. For a moment, the officials, even Tynan and Slidell, glanced reflexively at Pettibone's car to see if the mayor would insist that they go on with the groundbreaking. But then the rain came in such thick wavering sheets that they dove back into the cars. The loud drumming of the rain was matched only by the sudden cracks of thunder. The passengers in the limousines looked out of the windows as if from the bottom of a transparent, lightning-struck river.

The street gutters soon filled and became roaring streams that washed half a summer's grime and decay past the clogged storm drains, down Broadway and into the harbor. The local people who had wandered over from the nearby shops and bars scrambled for cover early. Angela had waited a minute too long and was completely drenched, her hair flattened onto her head, her skirt, blouse and underwear soaked, her shoes full, her glasses streaming and useless. She leaned for support on the last limousine in line, unable to move or see, and scarcely able to breathe, bracing against the waterfall driving against her.

The back limousine door opened and a figure approached her.

"Get in!"

"I'm soaked."

Ken Kiger grabbed her by the arm and pushed her through the back door of the limousine. He pushed her onto the seat and closed the door after himself. She found herself squished between Kiger and Fundertow, the banker. Fundertow tried to be a gentleman and pretend he wasn't bothered by this dripping woman practically sitting in his lap. Kiger held her glasses as she tried to stop the water from streaming down into her eyes.

There was another man on the other side of Fundertow. The four of them were crammed into the third seat of the limo. There was a smaller, middle seat in which three men sat. Pettibone was on the left, his bodyguard was on the right, and Charles Gage was quietly sitting between them.

Angela may as well have been wearing a disguise. Charles was the only one in the car who recognized her. Their eyes met, but Charles just nodded and quickly turned around. There was something sly in his expression. She wanted to ask him what happened to Aunt May, but she wanted talk to him alone.

How much had his dream of Aunt May been worth? Angela had no doubt that Aunt May had been a wonderful woman, and that she had been fortunate, in the end, to have a nephew as eager to follow in her footsteps as Charles, even if it had taken him forty-five years to catch on. She had no doubt that there were a lot of great women like this in the city. And men. Not all of them so lucky as Aunt May.

Angela could not even press the water out of her hair without making worse the wet spot on the car seat that was spreading under the upholstered rear ends of Kiger and Fundertow. The car was rocked by the wind. Nothing could be seen out the windows. The drumming and whistling and rumbling of the storm made talking impossible. She concentrated her gaze on Charles, who looked straight ahead. She tried to figure if there was something sheepish in the tilt of the head of this newfound friend of the mayor.

Sport had stayed at the office for a meeting that was scheduled with Doxie. He said he didn't have the heart to come to the groundbreaking ceremony. But Angela hadn't given up on Charles. She needed to come. Someone had to follow this track to the end. She had followed it down to Fells Point, and now she was soaked to the skin, squeezed between two uncomfortable public figures, getting toward the end of that track, doing an investigation that was only necessary if it mattered that a nephew had been loved by an aunt.

As if a switch had been flicked in the sky, the rain suddenly slowed to a windy drizzle. Pettibone motioned for the entourage to get out of the cars. The air was thirty degrees cooler than it had been ten minutes before. The site was not prepared for rain, and all the dignitaries had to follow Pettibone's lead through the four inches of water and squishy clay to the temporary stands.

The TV camera for one of the local stations had gone on the blink because of the storm, and the technicians were scrambling to fix it. Pettibone stood at the podium, under an umbrella held by his bodyguard, and waited. Kiger and Fundertow, Slidell and Tynan, Angela and Charles, and twenty or so housing and community development officials and political hangers-on sat in the dripping rain.

Pettibone stood under the umbrella looking over his shoulder, waiting for the lights of the third camera to flash on. In the background, the gutters of Broadway could be heard roaring, while hundreds of flat-roofed city houses dumped freshets of water into the concrete alleys nearby. The rain picked up slightly, and the people in the stands huddled miserably. Pettibone looked at them and suddenly recalled how much enjoyment he used to get out of situations like this. He knew now that this had been petty.

"Let's go," he said quickly, easing his bodyguard away and leaning towards the microphone.

"Nobody will ever say," he began, "that it wasn't a lot of trouble getting to this point. I know I learned a lot along the way, and I bet that could be said of anybody involved with this project."

319

Pettibone pulled a legal pad from under his suitcoat and looked at it. "I have here the names of every last one of the hundreds of people who have helped to bring this project about." He pushed his glasses down on his nose and held the pad almost at arm's length, as if he were about to read it all. "Two hundred and seven people's names have been given to me, and I should give them all recognition now."

"... but I won't." He threw the pad away. The relieved crowd burst into laughter.

"Let's get on with it. It's raining. Ladies and gentlemen." He turned and accepted a shovel handed him. "We will now break ground for the greatest development project this city has seen in decades, the project that will revitalize this whole corner of the waterfront and serve as a catalyst for the future development of all of Southeast Baltimore.

"This project has taught me a lot. I've learned from all kinds of people. I've learned about competence and hard work. I've learned about courage and determination—but I've also learned about common sense, and humility, and when it's time to back down. I thank everyone for what I have learned. It has changed me.

"There are going to be some other changes. One of them I'll announce right now. I am taking my name off this project. I've made a solemn commitment on this issue. This is a great project, and it deserves the name of a great person. Ladies and gentlemen, I am proud to dig now the first spadeful of earth in the construction of Aunt May's Waterside Towers Luxury Condominium Development."

Charles looked over at her with just a little smile.

Angela nodded. She nodded again at him, and smiled. She tried to look casual, as if she had never doubted him. So her tears would have been embarrassing were they not camouflaged by the oceans of water that suddenly dropped out of the sky.

The lights went out as soon as she reached the table, so Eddie brought candles. Elena had expected to meet Slidell alone, but he was accompanied by Jason Blunt, the attorney that CORP had hired for its short-lived lawsuit.

"CORP is disbanded. We can't pay you any more."

"Fine, Sister. But Senator Slidell asked me to help."

"I'm sure whatever you do will help—him." She looked at Slidell for the first time since she sat down. He was soaking wet, his hair slicked down over the contours of his skull.

"There was a side deal worked out," Slidell began. "Housing for anyone who would otherwise be made homeless. Attorney Blunt has volunteered to work with the members of CORP to identify them."

"You'll need a thousand apartments."

"No. We'll need seventy-five."

"Why are you doing this now?"

"There's support for it now. People saw the study. It had an effect."

At the restaurant lights flickered on, then off, the candle between them suddenly seemed so small, then so important again.

"It's such a small, timid thing you're doing, Samuel. It doesn't make up for all that wrong."

"We have different opinions, Elena. I've never seen anything wrong with Waterside Towers. The only wrong I'm certain of is the wrong I did to you."

Flooded from the window wells outside, the tiny windows near the ceiling of the Acting Chief Attorney's office oozed steady streams of water that collected to a depth of half an inch on the casements before streaming down the walls in sheets. Sport tried to move the meeting elsewhere, but Doxie said, "No. No. This is exactly where I want this meeting held today."

"We all learn something from all of our cases," he began. Doxie was preaching again. But it had to be something more than that. He usually preferred preaching in the confessional atmosphere of his office on the third floor. "I know that we were right on the edge of extinction with this crawlspace suit, and I thought we were hanging over the edge with this Waterside Towers thing. We hung in there and protected our clients, and held to our principles. I'm proud of Sport, and I'm proud of Angela, and I'm proud of our client Charles Gage, and I'm proud of all of us.

"But I always knew that we were that good. What I learned this summer was something different. These cases have caused me to come down to the basement for the first time in years. I look around, and I see the burnt-out lights and the water leaks and the dead roaches ..."

"... and the rat shit," someone yelled.

"Yes, and the rat shit. I really had no idea of this. You did complain. But I've been so busy debating high principle and policy on the state and national level that maybe my head got a little too big. A little too big to listen. A little too big to notice the obvious.

"This place is a mess. You all have been complaining to me about it, but it never really hit home with me until these past few months, when all of you really got me involved in your cases, and in your lives, when I saw for myself what horrible conditions you have to work in.

"And I'm not here just to say I'm sorry. I'm here to announce that we have reorganized administrative management so that these things can be taken care of. We will have a new management commitment to creating a clean and dignified work place, one that we can be proud of. I promise!" Doxie shouted, to a truly enthusiastic chorus of cheers.

"And we have a new management person to help us!" Doxie walked over to the hallway door and waved someone in. "I want you all to meet our new Director of Maintenance, Kevin Mallory."

Epilogue

As the real-estate industry in Maryland slid into a recession, the projected profit figures for Waterside Towers suddenly shrank. T. Oswald Fundertow told the Board of Directors of the Bold Tip Development Company that it was Pettibone's fault. But they would not listen. As part of his severance package, he was given an excellent recommendation, and this helped him land a federal job as Assistant Secretary of the U.S. Department of Housing and Urban Development.

Joe Keane, feeling a new restlessness that he did not understand, quit the *Free American* and joined the staff of the *Baltimore State*. He made twice as much money there, but a nameless pressure nagged at him during the day and wouldn't let him sleep at night. He began to wonder what the point of it all was, and he thought sometimes about changing careers and becoming a lawyer.

Jody Hechtmuller stopped working nights, figuring that the legal problems of his office would work themselves out one way or the other. As his legal cases began to seem less and less crucial, he began to take more of an interest in the track.

Kneeling before Pettibone on the oriental carpet of the mayor's office, Fosback begged the mayor to allow him to keep his job. Pettibone reluctantly allowed him to stay, but from then on Fosback was assigned strictly to the City Solicitor's office, because he was deemed incapable of more subtle duties.

Jimmy was chastised by Charles for almost fouling up everything by acting without thinking. Determined to show that he grasped the main point of Charles's reprimand, Jimmy refused to sign his name to anything for the rest of his life.

Former Secretary Gotterdung, after a long period of unemployment, obtained a job at Peck, Peck and Peck, which changed its name to Peck, Peck, Gotterdung and Peck.

After several unsuccessful collection attempts, Attorney Stem wrote off the last $750 of Mallory's bill.

Bobbi Jo turned down Tynan's offer to take her with him to the Secretary's office; instead, she retired on schedule. Within a week, her husband had a heart attack and she was forced to take over the snack store. When he was ready to come back a few months later, she made him go find another job.

Governor Mallard finished his term with a two-month fact-finding cruise of the Bahamas.

M.C. was jolted in the next year by a shock incomparably greater than those suffered by any of the adults involved in these affairs. When his mother returned from the hospital and held up his new baby brother for him to look at, he was certain that she had accidentally brought home a tiny demon from hell.

As the last few weeks of the election campaign arrived, some observers noted a graver, more somber tone in Senator Slidell's speeches. He seemed subdued, and he was taken more seriously. People could sense that there was no hidden agenda, that this man was saying no more nor less than what he believed. Thus, as the campaign wore on, Slip was finally able to dispel the doubts that had caused his nickname to stick, and his most serious political liability disappeared all by itself.

Everything seemed simpler to him now. He now knew that he was running for governor for the simple reason that he believed he was the best candidate. One day it struck him that he *had* changed, and that he had changed because of Elena. But it wasn't the kind of change either of them had meant.

Elena worked hard and identified fifty-eight people who would be left homeless by the completion of Waterside Towers. She was supposed to pass the names along to Slidell.

When she typed the final list of names, she knew that she had saved each one of these people. But she did not feel elated. She did not return Slidell's calls.

"Elena?" He had caught her listening in as he left another message on the answering machine.

"Samuel?"

"I need the names. You said you were going to turn them in."

"I've got them."

"Well, are you going to turn them in?"

"Samuel, do you know what a tiny thing this is, fifty-eight people?"

"I miss you."

"Don't complicate things."

"Don't pretend they're simple. You've had those names for a while. You forced me to call you."

"I don't know who I am, Samuel."

"Come back."

"I don't know what's right."

"Come back," he said. "That is right."

Sport and Angela made love. The flooding violet dusk backlit the three long windows in the front bay and illuminated their trembling bodies. Later, ravenously curious, they tried to talk. The twilight slowly disappeared, and the streetlight filtered between the trees and telephone lines and the open slats of the venetian blinds, casting only the faintest obscure moving patterns on the bed at the back of the darkened room. Angela lay next to him, her features exotic in black and white.

They tried to talk, but their fingers would not stop smoothing each other's skin. Sport heard her words, but he was overpowered by her stark beauty in the wavering light. The insistent tip of her tongue reheated his feel for her flesh. The exquisite tension of feeling so close, yet being so different, could be released in only one way, and then only for a moment as they were driven together again in sweet shocks of momentary completeness.

He didn't know how long he had slept. He stood up and felt his way across the room toward the bay windows. He raised the blind at the center window and looked down into the street.

Cool, dry breezes had swooped down from Canada that morning, finally releasing Baltimore from the blanket of stale air that had smothered the city for weeks. Sport pressed himself against the screen to feel the crisp new air on his skin. The street lamp reflected the green glazed surfaces of the broad maple leaves undulating in the cool northern current. He listened to the leaves sighing in relief.

He wanted her to stay. Tomorrow, they would have to talk.